PRAISE FOR KIM LAW

"*Montana Cherries* is a heartwarming yet heart-wrenching story of the heroine's struggle to accept the truth about her mother's death—and life."
—*RT Book Reviews,* four stars

"An entertaining romance with a well-developed plot and believable characters. The chemistry between Vega and JP is explosive and will have you rooting for the couple's success. Readers will definitely look forward to more works by this author."
—*RT Book Reviews,* four stars ("Hot") on
Caught on Camera

"Kim Law pens a sexy, fast-paced romance."
—Lori Wilde, *New York Times* bestselling author, on
Caught on Camera

"A solid combination of sexy fun."
—Carly Phillips, *New York Times* bestselling author,
on *Ex on the Beach*

"*Sugar Springs* is a deeply emotional story about family ties and second chances. If you love heartwarming small towns, this is one place you'll definitely want to visit."
—Hope Ramsay, *USA Today* bestselling author

"Filled with engaging characters, *Sugar Springs* is the typical everyone-knows-everyone's-business small town. Law skillfully portrays heroine Lee Ann's doubts and fears, as well as hero Cody's struggle to be a better person than he believes he can be. And Lee Ann's young nieces are a delight."
—*RT Book Reviews,* four stars

soft

DEEP IN THE HEART

hearted

The Davenports

Caught on Camera

Caught in the Act

Holly Hills

"Marry Me, Cowboy" in *Cowboys for Christmas*

soft

DEEP IN THE HEART

hearted

Kim Law

Text copyright © 2018 by Kim Law
All rights reserved.

Published by Montlake Romance, Seattle

www.apub.com

Amazon, the Amazon logo, and Montlake Romance are trademarks of Amazon.com, Inc., or its affiliates.

ISBN-13: 9781503901346
ISBN-10: 1503901343

Cover design by Tammy Seidick

Printed in the United States of America

To Anne Marie Becker and June Love—
the other two of my "Three."
Thanks always for your friendship,
your love, and your never-ending support.

Chapter One

*"Love is precious, love is kind.
But love can kick you in the behind."*

—Blu Johnson, life lesson #27

It had been forty-two days since Waylon Peterson moved to Red Oak Falls, and Heather Lindsay still hadn't met the man. And she was quite proud of that fact.

She hadn't been to the Buffalo Nickel—where he was apparently a weeknight regular. She hadn't run into him at the ranch—even though she'd had to be out here several times in preparation for her friend Jill's wedding. And she hadn't so much as glanced around, hoping to catch sight of him while driving through town—even though the man was supposedly a dead ringer for Prince Harry. Which was *exactly* her type.

Nope. She'd been a bona fide Girl Scout when it came to avoiding the subject of the town's buzzing rumor mill. Just as she'd promised her other friend Trenton she would be. But she feared her time of compliance would soon be coming to an end.

"More brisket?"

A tray of prime grilled beef appeared under Heather's nose, and she closed her eyes and allowed herself one deep breath of the mouthwatering smell—and one tiny vision of helping herself to seconds. Then she popped open her eyes and shot their head foreman a droll look. "Really, Pete?" She pushed the platter away. "You know I have to be in a bridesmaid dress in seven weeks."

And *she* knew any extra calories would land squarely on her hips.

Pete waggled his brows and inched the platter closer. "Not even for a special day?" he taunted.

Heather narrowed her eyes at him. "No day is special enough for yet another yoga session." Some days she truly hated yoga. "*Neither* is your brisket. So, run along, evil man, and find another unsuspecting soul to fork calories into."

Pete chuckled and moved on. It was Labor Day, and though Pete had been manning the smoker since it had been fired up, the group of construction workers, friends, and family were actually at Cal and Jill's ranch. The couple had invited everyone over for a cookout, but more importantly, they'd invited the group to preview the extended-length trailer of the upcoming *Texas Dream Home* special.

Back in the spring, the popular home renovation show had chosen two companies from Red Oak Falls to compete against each other, and the entire town had immediately climbed on board. They'd cheered passionately, either rooting for Cal's team—a company previously known as We Nail It Contractors—or Heather, Jill, and Trenton's—Bluebonnet Construction. It had been a men vs. women showdown, and though arguments still occasionally erupted over whether the correct team had been declared the winner, the girls had graciously accepted defeat. Only, with their defeat, an opportunity had presented itself.

To be fair, the opportunity had been for Jill and Cal alone. Due to their contentious past, the two of them had sparked on-screen from day one, and the executive producer had jumped on their chemistry. He'd offered them their own show. However, there had been one small catch. The two companies would have to merge to make the new show work. The producer had wanted two hosts but only one company. Therefore, after wading through the hows and who-would-do-whats between all parties involved, Bluebonnet Construction and We Nail It Contractors had officially become known as Bluebonnets Nail It.

Heather almost laughed out loud at the thought. She still couldn't believe she'd agreed to the name. But at the same time, she *could* admit that it was catchy. And people had been eating it up. Business was booming.

"Who's up for cake?"

Heather audibly groaned as Blu Johnson appeared at the back door carrying her life-altering orange chiffon layer cake. Aunt Blu was foster mother to Heather, Jill, and Trenton—as well as to many other girls over the years—and her cake happened to be Heather's favorite dessert of all time. But favorite dessert or not, she hadn't been joking with Pete earlier. At five feet two, and with her late mother's curves, it wasn't easy keeping in shape.

"I'm in," Trenton piped up from the other side of the covered patio. She rose from the rocker where she'd been slouched. "I never miss cake."

Trenton never missed any food. And it *never* showed.

"Have a piece for me, will you?" Disgust dripped heavy from Heather's voice. Life could be utterly unfair when it came to body types and metabolism, but she wasn't about to give in now. If she could go six weeks without doing anything stupid to get the attention of the man who, according to every single female in town, was "the hottest male to ever grace the streets of Red Oak Falls," then she could avoid a slab of heaven on a plate.

As Trenton and the others made their way over to where Aunt Blu was now serving up healthy slices of the decadent dessert, Heather looked beyond the patio to the horse barn that had been built over the summer. As part of the new show, Cal planned to turn the ranch into a working cattle farm, and one vital piece of a working ranch was having a ranch manager who oversaw daily operations.

Enter Waylon Peterson. Otherwise known as Red Oak Falls' latest heartthrob . . . a.k.a. the man of many rumors. A.k.a. the last man she needed to fall for.

And if he really did look like Prince Harry? Then yeah. Like an anchor being chucked into the ocean, she'd fall. *Fast.* And land flat on her face. Because that's how it went for her. Three devastating heartbreaks behind her, and her radar still pinged only for the wrong guys.

She jerked her gaze off the barn, chastising herself for even letting the man enter her mind. He wasn't out there right now, anyway. He might live in the small apartment that had been built inside the barn, but he never stayed in Red Oak Falls over the weekends—and he apparently didn't loiter during holidays, either.

Must be nice, taking a job and being able to get away with such demands.

She frowned at the voice inside her head. It was none of her business what the man did with his weekends—or why he'd had it written into his contract that he would take every one of them off. Enough people speculated about that as it was. She didn't need to add to it.

"Start up the preview, Cal." The request came from one of the men who'd originally worked for Cal. "You've kept us waiting long enough."

A round of agreement followed.

"I suppose that is why we're all here today."

Cal moved to the custom-built fireplace with the mounted outdoor TV and held out a hand for Jill to join him, and as Cal's hand wrapped around her friend's, Heather's heart smiled.

"Jill and I want to thank you all for coming out today," Cal began. He talked for a minute about the pride they both felt at being asked to participate in the new show, as well as what it meant to have worked so hard with everyone in the original competition. He then invited each person there today to come back for the wedding.

"We'll be here," someone yelled out, "but only if there will be more of this cake."

Another voice seconded the suggestion, and laughter filtered through the crowd. Cal pointed a remote at the oversized television before he pulled Jill down beside him on the wicker sectional, and all talking ceased.

Everyone watched in silence as the voice-over set up the rivalry of the competition. Pictures of Cal and Pete, as well as Heather, Jill, and Trenton, were flashed on-screen and the group of onlookers cheered as each "player" was introduced. The two houses to be renovated were showcased next, followed by shots highlighting the beauty of the hill country. The sneak peek then shifted and became more about Cal and Jill. After showing a couple of heated glances the two had exchanged during filming—along with a handful of shared death glares—the trailer cut to a moment inside the house the girls had been renovating. It was the day they'd first been explaining to Jill the reality of her and Cal getting within twenty feet of each other . . . and how if they did, the two of them would likely go off like a rocket.

"*I don't want to be combustible!*" Jill shouted on-screen. She'd been standing in the middle of the bare-bones living room, shouting up at Trenton, who'd been perched in the rafters.

Heather smiled at the memory.

"*But our wants and our actions don't always make complete sense, do they?*" The response came from Trenton.

"*I will* not *be acting on any perceived* wants.*"

At Jill's on-screen declaration, Heather heard Cal murmur in real time, "Yet you did."

"And I'm glad I did." Jill's reply was so soft it was almost inaudible, and once again, Heather's heart squeezed for the love her friend had found. Jill and Cal were seriously perfect for each other.

"*Good,*" Trenton replied from the TV. "*Because I'd hate to have to kick his ass again.*"

Pete guffawed from where he stood beside his date, and Cal paused the video to scowl at his friend.

"She *never* kicked my ass," Cal asserted.

Trenton merely shot him a haughtily lifted brow. Because though she might not have kicked his *entire* ass, she'd totally gotten in several blows.

"You didn't," Cal mumbled. The comment referenced the point in time twelve years before when Cal had been the only one to return after his and Jill's Vegas elopement. No one had heard from Jill since they'd left—and then Cal wouldn't answer questions about her after he'd returned—so Heather and Trenton had taken it upon themselves to pay the man a little visit.

"That's okay, baby." Jill patted her fiancé's thigh. "No one thinks you're less of a man because a girl once had to set you straight."

The entire group chortled, and Cal good-naturedly flipped the lot of them off. He then restarted the video, and as clips from both renovations continued on-screen, Aunt Blu asked if a name had been decided for the new show.

"We got a decision today," Jill told her. "They're calling it *Building a Life*."

Aunt Blu tilted her head as if contemplating the words before giving a firm nod. The producers had decided that since the *Texas Dream Home* special would not only showcase the two renovations but also Jill and Cal's story of falling in love again, they wanted to capitalize on the popularity the romance would attract. Therefore, the new show wouldn't just be about home renovations. Simply put, it would follow Cal and Jill as they began to build all aspects of their new life.

There was the ranch and getting it up and running, the renos Jill had lined up for the first season, Cal's workshop—where he'd build custom pieces for each renovation—and then there would be the wedding. The first half of the season would lead up to Jill and Cal's nuptials, with the ranch's backyard being transformed into an outdoor oasis worthy of any Hollywood A-lister's ceremony. And who better to take on the task of that transformation . . . than Heather herself.

Heather gulped at the thought. She had no idea why she'd thought she could pull this off.

The video ended, reminding viewers to tune in starting in two weeks to fall in love with America's next favorite couple, and Heather rose as the group whooped with excitement. The enormity of the project weighed on her. She was no landscape architect. She had a green thumb, sure. Just as her parents once had. And yeah, she'd overseen the landscaping for their company's past projects. But before the two companies had combined, she, Jill, and Trenton had mostly been hired for smaller, more self-contained jobs. They'd been known as Queens of the She-Sheds, and as such, they'd created a niche business building unique backyard spaces for women—of which the landscaping jobs had been a *fraction* of the job at the ranch.

Those jobs had also not been *nearly* as high profile.

She slipped silently through the crowd, collecting used plates and empty soda cans, and doing her best not to let her rising panic show. She should have stuck to what she knew. Because the last thing she wanted was to screw this up.

With hands full, she turned for the house. She didn't break stride as she entered the massive kitchen. She tossed the trash in the garbage and hurried to the powder room, and once alone, locked herself inside. Then she thumped her head back against the door. Her breathing had turned shallow, so she closed her eyes and focused on calming techniques. As one-third owner of one-half of the newly formed company, she'd had options when it came to her role on the new show.

She could have sold her share—which she'd never really considered. She'd worked hard to build what had once been Bluebonnet Construction, and she was proud of that. And she didn't want to walk away from it.

She also could have stayed completely *out* of the picture, letting her portion become an investment only. That option would have left her free to seek other interests, and honestly, she'd given that one serious thought. Participating in the filming during the *Texas Dream Home* renovation had been enjoyable. Mostly because it had been a new experience. But unlike Jill, Heather never held any real desire to be in front of a camera. The problem, though, was that she didn't know where her desire *did* lie.

She'd certainly tried to map out a path for herself over the years. She had a college degree going unused, a couple of side jobs that had never panned out—and of course the exes who'd done more damage to her psyche than provide anything lasting and good. Yet through all of it, she'd never gotten a clear picture of what she truly wanted to do with her life.

A third option concerning the new show had been to maintain the status quo. She'd worked alongside Jill and Trenton for years, and she could have continued doing exactly that. In fact, she'd been quite happy doing that. They were good at the job, and working together had put her in daily contact with her best friends—whom she'd missed terribly during her years away from Red Oak Falls.

Only, maintaining the status quo no longer meant that everything would remain the same. Because the fact was, *nothing* would ever again be the same. Jill would be the star of a new television show, she'd be married . . .

And Heather had suddenly found herself unsettled.

She pushed off the bathroom door and moved to peer out the small window. The instant Cal and Jill had announced their intent to marry in the half-acre space, a design had formed in Heather's mind. A design she'd been a part of once before. So she'd thrown caution to the wind, and she'd taken door number four. She'd negotiated a new position for herself. One that very well might be over her head.

She'd prepared as best she could, though. She'd attended workshops over the summer, visited top-rated outdoor venues in person, and taken several online courses in landscape design. If that wasn't enough, then . . .

She dropped her forehead to the windowpane. Then she'd be no worse off than she was now.

Turning, she paced to the sink, now feeling more like a caged animal than someone who'd had to get away. She wasn't quite ready to return to the party yet, though. Not until she had her emotions under control. She didn't think about her parents as often these days. She didn't allow herself to. But taking on this project had brought them to the forefront. That was *their* backyard she would be building for Jill. *Their* plans for a wedding. They'd loved each other so much, so purely, that they'd planned to renew their vows on their fifteenth wedding anniversary. And they'd been letting Heather be a part of it.

But then they'd died. Just like that. One fire, one night, both dead.

And nothing in Heather's world had ever been the same.

She stared at her reflection. The blue of her eyes had come from her mother, and before that, from her mother's mother. Heather had known all four grandparents as a child, but within eight years, each of them had been gone. Two years after that, her parents had joined them.

Heather had been fourteen when it happened, and she'd been alone. And destroyed.

Aunt Blu had been great. Aunt Blu had been her *salvation*. Not to mention Jill and Trenton. The three of them had shown up at Bluebonnet Farms within the same week. They'd been Blu's first girls as a foster mom, and the bond between the four of them was—and remained—tight.

But she still missed her mom and dad.

And she still wanted what they'd had.

Being granted the kind of love they'd shared wasn't how it worked for her, though. She was attracted only to guys who ended up hurting her. She'd accepted that. But that didn't mean she couldn't do everything in her power to help make Jill's wedding spectacular.

She'd give this project her all, and whether landscape design turned out to be her thing or not, along with giving Jill a beautiful wedding, her work would honor the love her parents once shared.

~

He'd been living there for only a handful of weeks, but Waylon had yet to tire of the sight that greeted him Monday evening as he crested the rise in the long driveway of the Blue Hills Cattle Ranch. With the one-story log house sitting a quarter mile off the road, it made a tranquil picture nestled among the trees and rolling hills of the three-hundred-acre spread.

He sent up his usual "thanks" as he took in the view and headed down the hill. Cal could have easily turned him away when he'd shown up seeking a job. Waylon had never fooled himself about that. A ranch manager who wasn't 100 percent physically—and who requested every weekend off—wouldn't be first choice for everybody.

Nor would someone with Waylon's reputation.

He'd never lived in Red Oak Falls, but as a senior in high school, he'd become quite familiar with a handful of the residents. And granted, that lingering reputation *had* seemed to slow Cal's decision-making. But in the end, he'd looked Waylon up and down, as if deciding for himself if a person could change in seven years, then he'd given a nod and offered a hearty handshake. Waylon didn't know what Cal had seen that settled the decision for him, nor had he asked. He'd simply accepted the job with the same confidence it had been offered.

He drove toward the house now, unable to bypass it on the way to the barn, and caught sight of Cal's truck heading his way. Straddling the edge of the gravel road, Waylon waited for his boss to pass, but Cal slowed to a stop alongside him. The other truck's window rolled down, and Waylon could see Cal's grandmother sitting in the passenger seat.

"Didn't expect to see you until tomorrow," Cal noted.

Waylon had originally planned to tack an extra day onto the long weekend. "Plans changed," he replied. "No sense not coming back and getting to work."

"Well, don't start working tonight." Cal jerked a thumb back toward the house. "Join the party instead. I'm taking Granny home, but stop in and have a bite. There's plenty of food left over, and likely several people you've yet to meet."

Cal's grandmother leaned toward the window, her eyes turned to him, even though he knew they saw nothing. "Good to see you again, Sir Waylon."

He tipped the brim of his hat out of habit. "And it's good to see you, Ms. Irene. You're looking quite lovely tonight. Too bad you're leaving just as I'm getting home. I would've had to entice you into a dance or two."

Irene's smile was as bright as a woman's decades younger. "Such a flirt, you are."

"Only with those worth flirting with, Ms. Irene."

He turned his smile back to Cal as Irene straightened in her seat and gave his boss a conspiratorial wink. He'd met Cal's grandmother about a week after taking the job and had hit it off with the older woman immediately. Cal had brought her out and spent the day showing her around the ranch, talking nonstop as he painted pictures for her of the work going on to get the place functional, and Waylon had found himself making excuses to be around the older woman. She'd lost her sight years before, but she had a liveliness about her that pulled people in. Waylon had sensed from her that she was a woman who'd not only lived a full life, but one who'd also loved deeply. There was a calmness about her that he could use more of.

Before she'd left that day, she'd gripped his hands with both of hers and tilted her face toward his. Then she'd reached up and patted his chest with a delicate touch. She'd nodded, a look of certainty on her face, and told him he had a good heart.

The sentiment had struck hard, the words touching him as few had before.

He glanced toward the barn. "Been a long weekend. I might just head on home."

He was mentally drained as well—as he too often was from the ending of every weekend.

"Do what you need to do," Cal told him. "But you should at least grab a plate of food. No need letting good brisket go to waste."

Waylon chuckled humorlessly. There was no chance anyone at the house would actually let leftover brisket go to waste, but the idea of having hand-smoked beef for dinner instead of pulling together a sandwich in his microkitchen had merit. "Thanks. I might take you up on that." He could stop in long enough to say hello.

They spoke for a couple more minutes about the work planned for the week and the camera crews that would be invading the space in the coming days, then Cal pulled away and Waylon headed on up the narrow driveway. Waylon stopped at the house briefly and let Blu Johnson pile up a couple of plates for him. He greeted all in sight, climbed back into his truck, then pointed the nose of the vehicle toward the barn.

The structure had been completed before Waylon had arrived, and it housed seven horse stalls, a tack room, a feed room, an office, additional storage space, and the small one-bedroom apartment. The apartment was on the second floor, with a view overlooking both the ranch, as well as the interior of the barn.

As he pulled to a stop, his attention settled on the sky to the west. The sun had dropped below the horizon while he'd been at the house, but the remaining colors were the real show. The long streaks of light made him glad he'd ultimately settled into ranching as a career. It sure beat the years he'd spent in Vegas.

Stepping from the truck, he grabbed the food, needing both hands to balance it all, and kicked the door closed with the heel of his boot. He winced at the streak of pain that shot through his right thigh, but he didn't let the physical barrier slow him. He rarely did. Instead, he elbowed the barn's sliding doors open just enough to wedge himself through, his taste buds already salivating at the thought of the brisket, but made it barely ten feet inside before he stopped. Murmurs came from one of the back stalls, and a light was on in the tack room.

The hair on the back of his neck immediately rose before common sense took hold. The sounds were feminine in nature. Definitely nonthreatening. And if someone were there to do harm, they'd likely not announce it by turning on a light.

Releasing a breath, he forced his muscles to relax and eased closer, more curious now than concerned. He had his ears attuned to the sounds, but even fifteen feet away, he couldn't make out the words. He took two more steps. And then he stopped again.

It wasn't talking but singing coming from behind the stall door.

And the tune was agonizingly sad.

He stood frozen, listening, as the feel of his own heartbeat vibrated against his ribcage. The song drifted toward the rafters, seeming to hover above him, and he closed his eyes and listened. Soft words of both heartbreak and hope held him spellbound for another thirty seconds, before he couldn't take it any longer. He had to know who was in the stall.

And why she was singing to his gelding.

As if walking through a dense morning fog, he made it the remaining distance and peered through the welded bars that made up the top half of the stall . . . to discover a woman sitting atop an overturned bucket. She was positioned directly in front of Ollie—her back to Waylon—and in the small pool of light coming from the open tack room door, he could see that the horse stared down at her as intently as Waylon was now doing himself. She had both of them entranced.

The song ended, and he managed to refill his lungs. Then he watched as the woman reached up and stroked Ollie's muzzle. The horse hadn't taken note of him yet, but Waylon couldn't blame him. If he had a redheaded siren singing a song to him, he'd tune out the rest of the world, too.

The woman pressed her forehead to Ollie's, and Waylon found himself jealous of a horse.

And he still had no idea who she was.

Finally, he forced himself to break the spell she'd woven. He cleared his throat as subtly as he could manage, but the noise had her jumping to her feet. The bucket tumbled over and skittered toward him, and Ollie sidestepped, tossing his head back with a soft whinny. The woman stretched one hand out to calm Ollie, but didn't take her eyes off *him*.

"I'm . . ." she began. She lowered her eyes for a quick second before lifting them again, and suddenly she looked as skittish as his horse—but also a tad embarrassed. "Uh . . ."

"Heather." Waylon filled in. He had yet to meet her, but he'd recognized her the instant she'd turned around. Her name had been mentioned a few times over the last couple of weeks, and he knew what she looked like from a picture he'd seen at the house. "You're Jill's friend," he added, when she didn't so much as blink at her name.

Her throat worked as she swallowed.

"Right?" he asked. "The one doing the backyard?" Had he gotten it wrong?

And if he had, then *who* was she?

Heather finally nodded. Then she looked at Ollie.

She stared at the horse with a hard intensity, and Waylon suspected she was trying to get her embarrassment under control before speaking.

"Don't worry," he told her. He nodded toward the animal when she finally turned back. "I often sing to Ollie, too. The poor guy had his balls cut off one day, and suddenly he's a softy who wants to be cuddled and crooned to before bedding down every night."

That seemed to snap her out of it, and a hint of laughter made it to his ears.

Her smile was gorgeous.

"I'm Waylon, by the way. The—"

"Ranch manager," she filled in, and he gave her a smile of his own. It wouldn't beat hers, but he knew that women tended to like it.

"Right," he said. He glanced at her hand, which had lowered and was now feeding Ollie a chunk of apple. "So you're out here instead of up at the house because . . . you prefer feeding my gelding an apple over attending a party?"

Her dimples deepened. "Something like that."

She pulled another hunk of apple from a paper bag he hadn't noticed before and fed the treat to Ollie, and once again, Waylon found himself wishing he were the horse. Only, *with* his balls intact.

He also found himself far too interested in a woman he'd just met.

"I'm sure Ollie appreciates it." He couldn't take his eyes off hers. "The poor boy rarely gets the attention of such a beautiful woman, much less one who brings him apples *and* sings to him."

A touch of embarrassment returned to her features, twisting up the corners of her lips the cutest amount. But she also produced an exaggerated eye roll. "Well, that certainly didn't take long."

Confusion had him pulling back. "What didn't take long?"

"Your flirting." A spark flashed in her eyes. "I've heard all about it, you know? In fact"—she gave Ollie one final pat before grabbing the overturned bucket and heading Waylon's way—"I've heard *several* things about you, Mr. Peterson. And let me just go on the record right now and tell you"—she looked straight into his eyes as she stopped, her on one side of the stable door, and him on the other—"your charm won't work on me."

Had that been a challenge?

Because if it had been . . .

"Is that so?" He took a step back so she could join him outside the stall, and he let his eyes drift down over her jean-clad backside as she turned to refasten the latch. "Then I should give you fair warning. My record is quite stellar once I decide I want something."

She cut her eyes up at him. "Then I'd suggest you don't decide you want something."

He wanted to laugh at the quick words. At the easy flirting. But he had yet to decide if she really *was* flirting. In one instant, her eyes burned hot, and he read in them what was so often clear in the opposite sex's gaze. But in the next moment . . .

He couldn't pinpoint what it was, but something completely contrasting seemed to lurk in there as well. Something that had him taking another step back.

"Are you okay?" he asked casually. He adjusted his tone to match his question. "I mean . . . you *are* hiding out here in the barn when a party is going on up at the house."

The light from the other room barely reached where they now stood, and he was aware he could be totally off in his thinking. But at his question, he suddenly found himself being studied in the same manner that a science student might investigate her first animal dissection. Her eyes bored into his, leaving him feeling as exposed as the poor frog might feel if still alive, and he involuntarily clenched his fingers around the plates of food in his hands.

"I'm *fine*," she finally answered. Her gaze lowered to the scruff of beard running the length of his jawline. "And I'm *not* hiding out in here."

"Then what are you doing?"

She tossed the empty paper bag into a garbage can, and moved to the only other occupied stall in the building. "I'm feeding apples to your horses." She reached out to the larger of the two animals and rubbed the stallion on the nose. "And don't worry, I didn't overlook Beau, here. I gave the big guy a couple of treats as well."

Now he was jealous of Beau. "But did you sing for him?"

She glanced back, no doubt noting the added huskiness to his voice. But dang, there was some crazy electricity pinging between them, and he wasn't in full control of his reactions.

"I'm afraid I only give one performance a night."

She was short, the top of her head not coming anywhere near Beau's snout, and Waylon suddenly sensed sadness in her.

That's what he'd zeroed in on before. And that made him want to know even more.

"Too bad," he murmured. He took a couple of steps in her direction, unaware he'd moved until her gaze dropped to his bum leg.

He froze.

"So how do you know my horses?" He picked a new topic before she could ask about his limp. "I haven't seen you at the ranch before today, but clearly, the three of you have met."

She nodded and eased a step toward the main doors. "Dill introduced us."

Dill was the eighteen-year-old Waylon had hired to work part time. He came in on weekends, as well as Monday, Wednesday, and Friday mornings, while spending the rest of his time either in school or studying.

"I've stopped by on a couple of Saturdays," Heather explained. She didn't take her eyes from his, while her body language screamed "poised for flight." "Work on the backyard starts next week," she continued. "I needed to map out the space before ordering supplies."

"And what?" The barn now held an intoxicating aroma that was a mix of hay, horses . . . and oranges. "You can only map out the space on weekends?"

Her head cocked at his words, her eyes narrowing as if searching for the intent behind them, but he kept his features impassive. No way would he acknowledge the lunacy of his thoughts. Of course she hadn't come to the ranch only when she knew he wouldn't be there. They'd never even met. His schedule would have *nothing* to do with hers.

Yet the way she watched him . . .

"Are you asking if I only stop by when I . . . *suspect* you're not around?"

"Do you suspect I'm not around on weekends?"

A hint of dimples reappeared. "I might have heard a rumor or two along those lines."

The words had him grinning along with her. Yep. She knew his schedule. But what did that mean, exactly? "And what if I said the rumors weren't true?" He watched her carefully. "Would you want to know what I do with my weekends instead?"

His question seemed to surprise her, as her look once again shifted as if he were that same dissected frog.

After an endless few seconds, she angled her chin higher. "Would you actually tell me the truth if I did want to know?"

He had a feeling he'd tell her too many things. "If you asked nicely, I might."

But she didn't ask, nicely or otherwise. She simply continued to study him, as if unsure how to make up her mind about him. Or maybe unsure if she *wanted* to make up her mind.

He'd spent many evenings in town since moving there, and he'd had more than his share of women offering to *welcome* him to the area. It had been like that since he'd first started growing facial hair. And though he rarely encouraged the women to find someone else to share a meal with—mostly because he preferred the company of others to being alone—he had higher priorities these days than bedding every woman he met. Priorities that took him out of town every weekend.

He took another step in Heather's direction, and again, she matched his move.

They stood six feet apart, each facing the other, and he had the thought that if he could get her pointed toward the stairs to his apartment, he'd back her right up them.

"Do I make you nervous, Heather?"

"Of course you don't."

He took one more step toward her . . . and she took one more step back.

"Then why do you move every time I do?"

"Why are you moving at all?" she rebutted.

He grinned. "Would you believe me if I said I can't help myself?"

Unlike before, she didn't voice her answer. She simply shook her head. But she also seemed to be waiting for his next move. Not leaving. Not telling him to back off. She just waited. As if feeling the same pull of attraction that he was—and equally unable to resist.

He stayed in the same spot, though. Not making *any* moves. Because he didn't want to send her running, but also because he had no idea what to do to get her to stay.

After a moment, she ended the game for both of them. She glanced beyond him, to the tack room in the back. "Do you want me to turn off the light before I go?"

"What if I don't want you to go?"

Her gaze quickly jerked back to his, and he had the urge to shrug. To blow the moment off and pretend the words hadn't come from his mouth. But he *did* want her to stay. And it wasn't only that he didn't want to be alone again just yet.

"Join me for dinner?" He lifted the plates in his hands, and did his best to keep his tone light. "I understand the brisket is to die for."

A faint smile touched her lips. "The brisket is *definitely* to die for. But I've already eaten."

"Have you had dessert?"

His desperation for her attention astounded him, but when her gaze dropped to the plates, he could sense her yearning for whatever lay hidden beneath the foil.

"Stay," he urged. "By the weight of these plates, I have more than enough for two." He nodded toward the stairs that led to the apartment. "I could even offer you coffee or a glass of tea."

Heather didn't immediately reply. She let her gaze travel in the direction he'd indicated instead, moving up the narrow staircase before taking in the enclosed space with the single window overlooking the interior of the barn. His temporary quarters sat to the left at the top of the stairs, while the barn's open loft was accessed on the right. A small security light burned from a post opposite the apartment's only door, and Waylon watched as she took it all in. And though he was perfectly willing to share nothing more than dessert, he also knew that one hint from her and he'd offer more.

He'd beg for it if he thought it would get him anywhere.

"I . . . *ummm* . . ." She swallowed instead of finishing her sentence. Then she blew out a breath and returned her gaze to his. A tight smile appeared on her face. "No cake." She eyed the plates in his hands. *"Unfortunately."*

He glanced down in confusion. "Is it bad cake?"

"God, no." Her laugh arrowed straight to his groin. "Aunt Blu's orange chiffon cake is the stuff heaven is made of." She tossed another glance at his apartment, as if to casually check it out, but Waylon watched as her gaze lingered there. Then her front teeth bit down on her bottom lip. "But . . . *ummm*"—she swallowed again, and when she finally dragged her gaze back to his, her eyes had glazed over—"my hips."

He looked at her hips. "What about them?"

She jolted as he stared, and a look of horror registered on her face. "Ah geez." She dropped her head into her hands. "I so didn't mean to say that."

Waylon grinned. "You mean, you didn't intend for me to check out your hips?"

"No." She glared at him through her fingers. "I did not intend for you to *check out* my hips."

He checked them out again.

"Stop it." She flapped both hands at him.

"But I don't see anything wrong with them."

"There's nothing—" She bit off her words and narrowed her eyes at him. "I'm talking about the cake going straight *to* my hips. Unneeded calories, Mr. Peterson. Surely you've been around women enough to understand how that works? Especially on a short"—she looked down at herself and mumbled—"*curvy* woman."

Waylon's grin grew wider. "I certainly enjoy *looking* at hips." He eyed the body part in question once again, this time tilting his head as if to get a better view. "And especially on short, *curvy* women."

"Stop it," Heather spoke, barely moving her lips. She began backing toward the front of the barn, not stopping until she reached the doors. "And do *not* look at my hips again."

"No need to," he deadpanned. "They're already burned into my retinas."

She glared at him one last time before turning to locate the already-open doors, but just before she slipped through them, Waylon called out. "I'll save a piece of cake in case you change your mind."

She looked back.

"I'll also offer to help burn off those unneeded calories."

His voice deepened more than he'd intended, his suggestion abundantly clear, but she gave no reply. Instead, they stood facing each other once again, the shadows in the barn lengthening around them while Waylon silently begged her to change her mind. She intrigued him, she turned him the hell on, and she made him want to forget his troubles. At least for the night.

She apparently didn't feel the same, though, because in the next instant, Waylon found himself looking at nothing but the dark night. While one of the horses snorted behind him.

He turned to find both animals, heads hanging low over the yoked openings of their stalls, looking as poleaxed as he felt. "I know, boys." Waylon started for the stairs. He didn't bother with either the light or the open barn doors. "It was the highlight of my night, too."

Chapter Two

*"Don't be swayed by the wrong man
in the right cowboy hat."*

—Blu Johnson, life lesson #14

What in the heck had that been in the barn the other night?

Heather had been asking herself that for three days, and she still had no answer. But as she sat on the plush velvet couch in Red Oak Falls' most upscale bridal shop, she found herself once again returning to those handful of minutes after Waylon had caught her singing to his horse.

Had she seriously been flirting with him? *Why?* She knew better than to flirt with him!

And why did she find herself wanting to go back and flirt some more?

She fanned herself with the shop's brochure. Good Lord, she'd even considered going up those steps with him. And *not* for Aunt Blu's cake.

She thought about what he'd looked like. Prince Harry?

Hell, yeah. Though possibly even more built, and with dimples that could rival her own.

And then there was the cowboy hat. And honestly, who could resist a little flirting with Prince Harry in a cowboy hat? *With* dimples?

She fanned herself harder. She apparently couldn't.

But hot looks or not, Waylon Peterson was not someone she'd been interested in *before* Monday night, and he wasn't someone she was interested in *after*. And not only because she didn't want to be just another woman fawning over the hunky newcomer.

No. Her real reservations came from the nonflirting, non-woman-chasing rumors surrounding him. The ones that involved poker.

Whether he merely enjoyed swindling people out of their money for the heck of it—or if he was a full-blown gambling addict and did it to pay off his losses—it didn't matter to her. That type of person wasn't someone she'd ever be okay with. No matter what he looked like.

Only . . . then she'd met him.

And she'd wanted him.

She tugged at the neckline of her shirt. He'd offered to share his dessert, and she hadn't given the rumors one single thought. She'd simply looked up those stairs, and she pictured the bed she knew was up there. And she'd pictured *him* in that bed. With *her*.

Then she'd made him look at her hips.

Her face flamed at the memory. First of all, she didn't do things like that—go up to a guy's apartment just because he offered her "cake." She rarely even had such thoughts.

Not that she was immune to sex. She happened to love sex.

I'm surprised you can even remember sex.

She smirked at the smart-ass thought her subconscious seemed to think was funny. Her memory could use a refresher, certainly, but it wasn't as if she'd forgotten what it felt like to be with a man. To have one stretched out on top of her. And under her. And just generally wrapped around her.

She groaned under her breath. She really could do with that refresher.

She'd have to go without a personal reminder, though, whether it be from Waylon or from some other man. Because when it came right down to it, she wasn't a casual-sex type of girl. She simply couldn't figure out how to keep things light.

Nor can you choose a man who isn't a first-class loser.

She smirked again.

"What's with you lately?"

Heather quit fanning herself at Trenton's words and shot her foster sister a quick look. "What do you mean, what's with me?" Her words came out too fast. "Nothing's with me."

Trenton scowled. "Your cheeks are beet red."

"So? It's hot in here." Heather fanned herself even harder as if to prove her point and returned her attention to the raised pedestal sitting ten feet in front of them. They were in the back half of the boutique, waiting on Jill to appear in her first dress—and they had cameras hovering all around them.

"You've been spaced out since we sat down." Trenton's words came out as an accusation, and Heather fired a glare at her.

"No, I haven't."

"In fact, you've been that way all week." Trenton studied her as if peeling away a few layers to look deeper inside. "And if you haven't been spacey," she continued, her words now heavy with contemplation, "you've been biting someone's head off. What's going on with you? What did I miss?"

"You missed nothing. You're imagining things." Heather totally hadn't been biting anyone's head off. She'd just been a little *unsettled* since Monday night.

"Then what do you want to drink?"

Heather furrowed her brow at the unexpected question. "What are you talking about?"

"Penny asked you twice what you'd like to drink, and you didn't hear a word she said."

"Oh." Heather looked around for Penny, the owner of the boutique, and added noncommittally, "I must have been thinking about something else."

Trenton snorted. "You think?"

Heather ignored her. Instead, she found Penny maneuvering her way through the store, a nervous smile on the brunette's face, carrying a tray of fruity-looking drinks in slim tallboys. There was also a camera trailing her every move.

"Penny's nervous," Heather muttered to herself, and wished she could do something to help. Not everyone could handle the looming equipment that came with being filmed for a television show, and with the small space being packed with cameras, sound guys, and a varied number of other production personnel, Heather understood how out of her element the other woman must feel.

A ding sounded from the back room, indicating that someone had come in the front door just as Penny made it to Heather and Trenton's side.

"Thank you," Heather smiled graciously as she accepted the drink. She also did her best to catch the other woman's eye. She hoped to impart a bit of calmness with a quick look.

The show intended to capture the majority of the planning for Jill's wedding, and since Jill had wanted local businesses included as much as possible, Happy Veil's Bridal Boutique had signed a contract to be filmed. Which meant that not only did Penny and her staff have to get comfortable with the cameras in the space of one afternoon, but whatever alterations Jill's dress needed would also have to be done in record time.

Heather took a sip of what appeared to be a raspberry lemonade as Penny moved off and immediately let out a sputtering cough. The drink had vodka in it!

Trenton snickered at her side, and Heather mumbled, "Could have warned a person."

"Could have paid attention to begin with," Trenton quipped back.

"And you could—"

"Girls," Aunt Blu bit out under her breath as she joined them, a fake smile on her face. She'd been in the front of the store, looking through the jewelry and veil options, but now settled in between Heather and Trenton to wait for Jill. She carefully piled the veils she'd chosen onto the ottoman in front of them as she continued speaking through her smile. "Whatever has you two snapping at each other, you need to put a pin in it. This is Jill's day."

"Trenton started it," Heather muttered under her breath, but Aunt Blu turned to stare at *her* instead of Trenton. "What?" Heather questioned.

"What are you? Seven years old, or something?"

"No." Heather scowled. She took a gulp of her drink, and from behind Blu, Trenton's hand reached around and jabbed Heather in the ribs. "But she's still picking on me," Heather added.

"And there are still cameras watching us," Blu said behind the glass she now held. "Could you two please behave yourselves?"

Heather shot her foster sister a look, and then narrowed her eyes at Trenton's triumphant smile. But before either of them could continue acting like misbehaving children, a gasp came from Aunt Blu. They both turned to find Jill standing in the middle of the pedestal, and a more perfectly romantic gown there could never have been.

Heather rose to her feet, her mouth opening in surprise. "Oh, Jill," she whispered.

Jill's eyes met hers. "I know." She looked down at herself, a half smile curving her lips. "It's gorgeous."

"*You're* gorgeous."

"But it's not right for you," Trenton chimed in.

Heather frowned at her other foster sister before turning back to Jill. The gown was strapless, outlining Jill's toned shoulders to perfection, and the fitted, drop-waist bodice flowed seamlessly into continuous layers of organza ruffles. The whole thing made Jill look as if she were floating in a cloud.

"You don't think?" Jill looked at Trenton. She fidgeted with the first layer of ruffles, and the edges of her mouth pulled down slightly.

"Since when do you do ruffles?" Trenton explained.

"This is one of our most sought-after gowns," the attendant informed them. She moved in a half circle around Jill, fluffing out the six-foot train. "Women all over central Texas come to us for this dress."

Trenton glanced over at Heather before adding, "Which is another reason it's not for her." She set her drink on the side table and rose, her tone growing more certain as she continued. "You're not a clone, Jill. You're one of a kind."

Jill nodded—because she was. And even Heather had to agree with that.

"And you've never in your life been a ruffle girl," Trenton added wryly.

"But you *could* do ruffles if you wanted to," Heather inserted. They were in Texas, after all. Bigger was better. "Maybe this dress isn't the dress for you, but it's only the first one you've tried on. And this is *your* wedding, Jilly. Your special day. So you can do and be whoever you want for that day."

"I kind of just want to be me," Jill said, uncertainty filling her face. She looked down at the gown again, and fidgeted with the ruffles a bit more. She'd been both nervous and excited about doing this. Mostly because she'd had no real idea what style of gown she'd wanted. When she and Cal had run off to Vegas years before, they hadn't done the whole wedding dress and tux thing, but this time she'd wanted to do it right.

She turned her gaze to Blu, who had yet to comment. Blu remained the only one of the three of them who was seated, and she took her time before answering. "It's very lovely," she finally told Jill. "*You're* very lovely in it. And you definitely want to do white. It sets off your black hair."

"But the ruffles are too much," Jill said. "Right?"

Aunt Blu nodded, and Heather and Trenton lowered back to their seats. "Heather's our ruffle girl." Aunt Blu patted Heather's knee with fondness. "We'll leave the ruffles for when it's her turn."

Heather grunted under her breath. She doubted it would ever be her turn.

But she *would* look amazing in ruffles.

"Let's get you into dress number two," the attendant said.

The attendant led Jill back to the dressing room, and Heather took another gulp of her drink. As the cool liquid slid down her throat, she let her eyes roam over the dresses on display in the store. She could picture Jill in any number of them, but Trenton had a point. Jill wasn't exactly a ruffle girl, even if she had grown up in Texas. She was more straight and to the point. And now Heather felt guilty, because she'd helped pick out quite a few of the dresses Jill would be trying on, and they likely all had ruffles.

She blew out a breath. She'd been thinking more of what *she'd* like as she'd helped than what would best flatter Jill.

"I'm going to look around at the dresses again," she told the other two, but as soon as she stood, the bell in the back room sounded again, and she caught a glimpse of a man with dark-copper hair entering the store.

Her breath caught. Had Waylon come to the bridal shop?

Why would Waylon have come to the bridal shop?

But then the man stepped around a rack of dresses and turned toward her, and wide smiles broke out on both their faces.

"Len!" Heather squealed. She hurried to the huge man's side, subconsciously noting that of course this wasn't Waylon. Len's body frame was much larger than the man who'd been flirting with her in the barn. She threw herself into Len's arms.

Len had been one of the cameramen when they'd done *Texas Dream Home*, and given the amount of time he'd spent following Jill around, he'd become friends with all three of them.

"What in the world are you doing here?" Heather asked as he set her on her feet.

She patted his overgrown beard as if she'd missed it before stepping back so he could greet Trenton and Aunt Blu, who'd come up behind her.

"I heard that our Jilly was picking out a wedding dress today," Len said when he got a chance to answer Heather's question. He nodded hello to the closest cameraman as he moved farther into the room. "And given the help I assumed she had"—he shot down-the-nose looks at the three of them—"I knew she'd need a voice of reason tossed into the mix."

Trenton huffed. "I'm her voice of reason."

"Well, you're certainly the closest she's got." He patted Heather's shoulder as he spoke—as if to lessen the sting his words might leave—then he nodded respectfully at Blu. "And no offense, Miss Blu, but emotions can run high on a day like today. For everyone. I've seen it with all four of my sisters and all my sisters' wedding parties." He planted himself in the middle of the couch and crossed his burly arms over his chest. "So I decided that Jilly needed a man's opinion."

Heather and Trenton stared down at him in shock at the sudden change in plans—and seating arrangements—then cracked up when Penny stuck a girly drink in his hand.

"No laughing at the dude in the middle of the froufrou dresses," Len admonished. He then angled his pinky out and tossed his head back for a long pull on the lemonade.

Aunt Blu gave an unheard-of-from-her roll of her eyes and sat down beside Len. "Scoot it over, Big Red. Emotions, my ass. You're not the only voice of reason in this room today."

"Is that so?" He wiped the back of his hand over his mouth before jabbing a finger at the assortment of veils piled in front of them. "Any chance you happened to have anything to do with those?"

Aunt Blu huffed out her indignation. "Jill will be gorgeous in a veil."

"Jill is gorgeous with all that black hair shining," Len corrected her, and all three of them nodded in agreement. Jill's hair was fantastic.

But still, brides needed veils.

Penny and another of her employees hurried over as Blu and Len continued their good-natured arguing, placing matching club chairs on either side of the couch, and Heather and Trenton barely had time to settle into their seats before Jill reappeared in gown number two.

"No," Len said automatically, and there was another round of squealing and greetings.

"Len!" Jill pounced on the big man. Len didn't live too far away. Only up in Waco. But given the amount of work filling the company's calendar the last three months, a road trip to see their friend hadn't been feasible.

Once they'd all settled back down, Jill didn't even wait for a response from the rest of them. She simply agreed with Len. Though this dress was satin with ruching running the length of the gown, it also had ruffles. Its fitted silhouette outlined Jill's body exquisitely, but ruffles covered the single shoulder strap and seemed intent on attacking her slender neck.

She tried on the third gown, and the deep *V* plunged with ruffles.

Number four had a billowing train of cascading ruffles that Heather thought was absolutely to die for. She kept her enthusiasm to herself.

And when Jill came out in the next dress, a sleeveless beaded bodice stopping at the waist and falling into a full ball-gown skirt of ruffled chiffon, Len cursed none too gentlemanly and rose from the couch. "Who in the hell picked these out?" He shot Heather a dark, accusing look. "Not everyone needs to look like they're stepping out of a fairy tale. This one makes her look like she's being swallowed from the ground up."

He moved away from the couch as Heather attempted to argue that the timeless look of the chiffon would go well with an outdoor wedding, but Len pointed a finger at her.

"Don't move," he warned. He waved his finger around. "Any of you. It's my turn now."

The cameraman Len had greeted upon arrival followed the other man out of the room, camera rolling, while the sound guy, a lighting woman, and a producer hurried along behind them. Ten minutes later, all were back, and Len once again took center stage on the couch.

"Winner," he said, long before Jill made an appearance.

Heather crossed her arms over her chest as Len had done when he'd first sat down, and stuck out her chin. But then she lowered her arms when Jill emerged from the back room.

"*That,*" Len began, "is why I'm here."

Jill looked stunning. The dress was a V-necked chiffon with a crisscrossing bodice that stopped at the waist and flowed gently into a breezy skirt. It had the timelessness of the chiffon, the simple elegance that was Jill, and the beaded belt and shoulder straps added just the right amount of bling.

Penny and the attendant who'd been working with Jill hurried over with crystal bracelets and a matching headband, and another employee appeared and whipped Jill's straight black hair into a rolled updo that hugged the back of her neck.

A cream and pink bouquet found its way into her hand, someone whisked *all* the veils out of the room, and at the sight of her friend, tears suddenly seeped from Heather's eyes.

Jill's eyes were wet as well. As were Aunt Blu's and Trenton's. Even Big Red got a little misty.

No one had to say anything, while Jill simply smiled with her tears.

"Done," Jill finally spoke, and Len rose to take a bow.

Everyone in the room laughed at Len's antics, and as he moved to Jill's side and fawned over her a bit more, Heather found herself wandering through the rest of the store. She loved this boutique. She'd visited it the week Penny had opened its doors, and she was so happy that one of her friends would now get the chance to wear a beautiful creation from here.

She fingered the detail on the sleeve of a display dress and ignored the chatter of the handful of women who'd come in over the last few minutes. A soft ding sounded as she picked up a narrow tiara and held it above her head in front of a mirror. She cast a glance over to find a man and a little boy stepping through the front door. They moved to the counter that housed the costume jewelry, and she watched as the man helped his son pick out a present for his mother.

Joy filled the boy's face as his small fingers touched the rhinestones of each and every bracelet on display, and Heather found herself thinking about her own dad. He'd taken her shopping for her mother like that when she was a kid.

In fact, he'd taken her to all kinds of places, just him and her. She'd been close to her mother as well. They'd had many similar interests. But she'd been a total daddy's girl.

Dad and son moved to the register to pay for their purchase, and at the same time, Heather sensed someone at her side. She glanced over to find Len—who winked at her teasingly. His attention then settled on the man and his son, and he leaned in and whispered, "You'd look good with a little one like that."

Heather didn't reply. She couldn't because a lump had lodged in her throat.

Len straightened and returned his voice to normal volume. "Too bad you think I'm too old for you. Maybe I'd give you one. At the least, we could have made that date we had *far* more interesting."

She shot the man a droll look. "Don't even. You know I'd bore you in ten minutes flat."

They'd gone out one time while filming had been going on back in the spring, but it had been a friends-only evening. They'd set up a double date, using it to convince Jill to go out with a man who'd had his eye on *her*. A date that, Heather was proud to say, had been the catalyst for Cal finally making a move with Jill.

"I don't know," Len mused now. He flicked his blue gaze over Heather's body, and wicked naughtiness filled his eyes. "I think I might be able to make it ten *days* if given the shot."

The words made her blush. "Behave yourself. You know you just like to flirt."

"Oh, I do enjoy flirting. But I've also been going through a bit of a dry spell lately." He waggled his brows and stroked his ginger-colored beard. "And since I also know you have a thing for gingers . . ."

Before either of them could utter another word, a woman one rack over whipped around to stare at them. *"Ohmygod."* The woman's eyes went round. "If we're going to talk about redheaded men, we *have* to talk about Waylon Peterson." She looked around the store as if to take in all within earshot, and angled her chin higher so her voice would ring above the others. "Who's met him? Who's met Waylon Peterson?"

Len's brow lifted in question, and Heather shook her head. Then a hand shot up on the opposite side of the room.

"I've met him," the owner of the hand announced. "But not nearly as *intimately* as I'd like to . . . if you know what I mean."

The first woman fired back, "Oh honey, *everyone* knows what you mean."

"And *everyone* wants to have that same meeting," someone else chimed in.

Laughter bounced through the room, and Heather lowered her gaze and maneuvered to a display of bridesmaid dresses. She had no wish to be in the middle of the gossip, and even less desire to be thinking about the man at the center of the conversation.

"Who's making a move on him this week?" someone asked behind her. "Because you know you have to do it tonight if you want a chance at being this weekend's fling."

Heather flipped through the dresses as a chorus of "Mes" rang through the room, and barely held back a groan when Len reappeared at her side.

He leaned in close and whispered, "Have *you* met this Waylon?"

She didn't answer. Just kept flipping. But her cheeks outed her. They turned pink once again.

"Really?" Len sounded intrigued as he straightened. "And he's all that?"

"Oh, he's all that, all right." The mocking reply came from Trenton, who suddenly appeared on Heather's other side. Heather glanced over, but Trenton continued speaking only to Len. "I haven't met him personally, but I've seen him in passing enough times. I can see why the man's got everyone's motor running. What I can't figure out, though, is when *this one* met him." She cast her gaze toward Heather, the accusation clear.

"She met him Monday night," Aunt Blu's voice replied matter-of-factly, and Heather whirled to find her foster mother now standing behind her. Why was everyone crowding her?

And why were they talking about her as if she weren't there?

"He came by after you left," Aunt Blu explained. Trenton had left the cookout early, having had an exhausting weekend finishing up an overdue renovation. "He stopped by the house for a plate of food. Heather had gone for a walk earlier, but ten minutes after Waylon entered the barn, I saw Heather coming out."

Trenton stared at Heather.

"Wait." A nearby woman took a step toward them. "Are you saying that you were in the *barn* with him?"

Heather hadn't *said* anything.

The woman put both hands over her mouth, her eyes wide, as if having great respect for Heather's skills at capturing the man's attention, and the lady who'd started the whole conversation loudly proclaimed, "That's it. I'm finding him tonight. Then *I'll* be this weekend's date."

She wove her way through the displays of dresses, shouting out to someone who was apparently in one of the dressing rooms. She didn't make it out of earshot, though, before another voice rose from the crowd. "You'd better hope he wins at the tables this weekend, Kara. I hear he's more 'giving' when he wins."

Heather closed her eyes.

"And I hear the right woman can make him *give* all night long," Kara called back.

Kara cackled with laughter before disappearing behind a dressing room door, and Heather tried her best to refocus on the rack of bridesmaid dresses. Jill had chosen the colors for the wedding party several weeks earlier, so now that the wedding dress had been decided on, Heather and Trenton simply had to settle on a style.

But try as she might, she couldn't push Waylon from her mind. Was he seriously that big of a player?

"I'll also offer to help burn off those unneeded calories."

Yep. She'd say he was. He'd certainly been laying it on thick with her.

Rumors aside, she couldn't help but wonder if he really did head off with a different woman every weekend. Everyone liked to presume that he did, yet she'd not heard anyone come right out and say, "I slept with Waylon this weekend."

Mostly, though, she wanted to know because, for some reason, she'd had the urge to believe him when he'd implied it wasn't true.

And what if I said the rumors weren't true?

Would you want to know what I do with my weekends instead?

She hadn't answered him at the time, but she *had* wanted to know. And she found herself wanting to know even more now.

Jill reappeared from the back of the store, once again wearing the jeans and company-logoed pullover she'd arrived in, and Len headed in her direction. The camera and equipment guys were all packing to leave, the gaggle of women who'd been carrying on about Waylon had calmed down, and Aunt Blu's attention got snagged by a friend waving to her from outside the building.

And all too quickly, Heather found herself standing alone with Trenton. Who—Heather knew—would *not* let the fact that she'd met Waylon go undiscussed.

Anxiety twisted Heather's gut as she edged around another rack of dresses. She simultaneously avoided Trenton while zeroing in on the gowns in mint green. Mint green was the color Jill had chosen. It would go perfectly with a backyard wedding.

"Did you hear that he's buying a house?" A low voice spoke from a couple of displays over. "My cousin Cindy's best friend's sister is his real estate agent. She was supposed to keep it on the down-low, but she told her sister, and her sister told Cindy."

Heather glanced in the direction of the latest conversation. Were they still talking about Waylon?

"Why would he buy a house?" another voice asked. "Doesn't the apartment in the barn come with the job?"

Definitely Waylon.

"I have no idea," the first woman continued. "But I hear he's moving in soon."

The two women moved off, still talking, and Heather pushed the man from her mind once again. She pulled a full-length, off-the-shoulder dress from the rack and thrust it into Trenton's hands when her friend made yet another reappearance.

"You promised to tell me when you met him." Trenton kept her words low enough to carry just between the two of them.

"It was no big deal." Heather chose a tea-length style next. "And anyway, I've barely seen you this week."

"You've had breakfast with me every morning."

"Yeah, well . . ."

36

She had no real excuse, and she knew it. The three of them met every morning to go over work details for the coming day. And every day, she'd studiously avoided bringing up her run-in in the barn. Because she knew she'd get this reaction.

"So why did you go to the barn?" Trenton got right to the point.

"I didn't *go* to the barn," Heather corrected. "I *went* to the backyard. I have a big job starting next week, in case you've forgotten." She shoved another dress at her foster sister, having no clue what that one looked like. "I'm a tad bit nervous about it, so I wandered around the area, thinking about any last-minute changes I might want to make to the plans."

"And what? The plans are stored in the barn?"

"Stop it," Heather hissed out. "Quit being a jerk. I was in the backyard—*minding my own business*—and I heard what I thought were horse hooves. So I was worried the horses had gotten out."

She'd actually been quite concerned. She'd hurried back to the house for apples in case they were needed to lure the animals back inside, only . . . when she'd gotten to the barn, she'd found both horses locked up tight.

And no one around to have put them there.

"And anyway," she continued, shoving the odd experience from her mind, "I didn't expect *him* to show up at all. Cal had said earlier that he wouldn't be back until Tuesday."

Trenton eyed her as if looking for the lie in her words. "Whether you expected him or not, the fact remains that you met Waylon one night, and you've been out of sorts ever since."

Heather didn't look at her friend. "I am not out of sorts."

Trenton reached out then, one hand touching Heather's forearm, and Heather allowed herself to be turned. She faced her foster sister, but said "I'm fine" before Trenton could suggest otherwise.

"Are you really?" Trenton eyed her carefully. "Because you know how you can be."

Heather nudged out her chin. "It's been three years since I've *been* that way."

"And three years before that. And again before that."

Embarrassment stirred inside her. She couldn't help it that she fell so fast. It was in her blood.

"I've learned my lesson," she gritted out.

"Have you? Because I know he's your type." Trenton looped an arm through Heather's and leaned in even closer. "I know you're attracted to him even if you don't want to admit it," she said softly. "And I get that. I knew it would be that way the instant I got a good look at him. That's why I made you promise to stay *away* from him, Heather. Because you *can't* fall for him. And you know that."

She pulled her arm away and returned to the dresses. "He can't be all bad or Cal wouldn't have hired him."

Why was she defending the guy? She didn't even know him.

Trenton sighed. "I'm not saying he's all bad. But he does have some bad in him. He has to or there wouldn't be so many matching stories about him conning people out of money. So many questions about who and how many he spends his time with. And you know your tendency with guys like that."

Translation: *You have blinders on when it comes to men predisposed to screw you over.*

And yes, she knew that. She hated it, but she knew it. She was the worst judge of character in the history of mankind.

"Trust me." Her voice dipped to a rasp that shocked her with its unsteadiness, and she had to clear her throat before continuing. "I'm well aware that Waylon Peterson isn't the man for me, okay? Yes, I met him. Yes, he's good looking. Yes, he's totally my type. *Physically.*"

And yes, she'd wanted to strip naked and race him up the stairs.

Because seriously, it had been *three years* since she'd done that with a man.

"But I'm fine," she repeated. "I know better than to think warm fuzzies about a guy like that."

Trenton studied her with the type of look Heather hated most. The poor-Heather look. "I know you *know* better," she said carefully, "but I also know you have difficulty thinking any other way."

Heather shook her head, repeating "I'm fine" one more time, but as she said it, she began to wonder if she really was. About anything.

Men? Lack of men? Her life in general?

And if she *wasn't*, then what exactly was she supposed to do about it?

Chapter Three

"When backed into a corner, always maintain your calm."

—Blu Johnson, life lesson #65

"He's a natural on camera." The cameraman spoke to the producer as they both kept their eyes glued to the small screen set up in front of them. They were reviewing the last segment of the interview they'd just taped with Waylon.

"It's that laid-back Texas way he has about him," one of the female crew added in.

Waylon gave the woman a quick wink, and she returned it with a half-lidded I'm-yours-for-the-asking look. And damn, but she had a lot to offer. If Waylon were in the mood for asking.

They were set up just outside the barn as Friday inched its way into late afternoon, the producer having wanted one corner of the building in the backdrop while also capturing a portion of the sweeping views of the ranch, and Waylon had long since grown tired of the process. He'd signed up for it, though, and since the ranch was still a work in progress—meaning no animals needed his attention at that very moment—he wasn't sure what else he could do but smile, try not to be offended that they'd talked him into tipping his hat back a little too far on his head, and wait for it all to be over.

The cameraman shifted back behind the eyepiece, and the producer once again stepped to his side. "You mentioned wild hogs earlier," the producer said to Waylon.

"I did mention wild hogs. All ranches in central Texas have them."

"Tell us about the hogs. What do you do with them?"

Waylon cocked a grin at the question, and he couldn't help but notice a couple of the other female crew stop what they were doing and watch. He also caught sight of a brown SUV heading up the ranch's driveway.

"I kill them," he answered bluntly, and several shocked gasps filled the air.

"Why?" one of the women asked.

"Because if I don't kill the hogs, then they'll kill the steer."

"Ah." All heads nodded simultaneously. They'd clearly sent a Hollywood team to produce the show.

"And *how* do you kill them?" the woman with the I'm-all-yours look asked.

Waylon lifted his arms as if holding a rifle, and he mouthed the word "Boom." Then he gave another cocky grin, this time straight into the lens of the camera. "They're bloody suckers, too. Nasty creatures."

The women stood transfixed while the men appeared both disgusted and impressed.

Waylon was playing it up more than was necessary, but since the occasional camera in his face was to be a part of his job, he figured he might as well have fun with it. And wild hogs *were* a real issue in the Hill Country. "Watching for them is part of our daily routine," he continued. "We also regularly check fences, make sure the water stations aren't empty, doctor any animals that need it . . . and we kill hogs when we see them."

And by *we*, he meant *he*. At least for now.

"You make it sound like the Wild West," another woman said, and Waylon broke into a wide grin.

He tipped his hat at the woman. "What part of Texas isn't the Wild West, ma'am?"

The brown SUV rolled to a stop at the side of the barn, and Waylon forced himself to have no visible reaction. He'd been watching for that vehicle all week.

"What other areas of ranch management should we know about?" the producer asked. He scribbled notes as he talked. "What other jobs will you be handling in the coming days to help Cal get the place operational?"

"We'll be heading up to the auction in a couple of weeks, then bringing the stock home."

Heather got out of her car, but she didn't look his way as she passed through the open doors of the barn.

"Then . . ." he continued, mentally searching to recapture his train of thought. He turned back to the camera. "There will be branding, finishing the fence in a couple of pastures so we can move the cattle around as needed—"

Heather returned to her car.

"And . . ."

She opened the back of her vehicle and the top half of her disappeared inside. When she stood back up, each arm was curled upward, encircling what appeared to be heavy bundles of spindles balanced on each shoulder.

Waylon gulped. For a small thing, she sure was mighty.

"Mr. Peterson," someone said off to his right, and Waylon realized he'd quit talking and was not only watching Heather, but he'd turned in her direction as well.

As had several other men in the near vicinity.

He returned to the camera, wondering if he could call a halt to the interview right then and there, then tossed one last glance her way. And he found her eyes on him.

His fingers twitched.

"Mr. Peterson," the producer said again.

Heather disappeared back into the barn, and Waylon scowled at the man currently ruining his day. He'd been hoping to see Heather all week, and now she was within twenty-five feet of him, and this skinny-jean-wearing hipster wanted to talk to him about cows?

"Aren't we about finished?" Waylon asked.

One of the women snickered at his obvious need to hurry, while the one with the I'm-all-yours look pursed her lips sourly.

"Just a couple more questions," the producer answered.

Waylon forced himself to finish the interview without watching for Heather again, but once he was free to go, he strode toward the barn. Heather's car remained parked at the side, so he assumed she hadn't come back out. He headed for the second stall on the right, where others had been storing supplies throughout the week, and he found her there, head bent over a yellow piece of paper, pencil poised, checking items off a list.

"You here to sing for Ollie again?"

She didn't jump in surprise as he'd expected her to, and when she turned—in a manner he thought was a touch too casual—he narrowed his eyes on her. Had she been sticking around waiting on him?

"I'm too busy to sing today, Mr. Peterson."

Waylon's interest ratcheted into a new stratosphere. "Mr. Peterson, huh? You called me that the other night, too. I like it." He propped his shoulder against the side of the open stall door. "Has a bit of a naughty ring to it, don't you think?"

She shook her head at his blatant flirting and moved deeper into the stall. "You're a part of the show, I see," she said from behind a stack of boxes.

"I am. I signed the contract last week." He leaned his head to the right, but couldn't make her out between the lumber and the supplies. "Looks like you and I are going to be working together," he continued.

"I don't think so. I'm working on the wedding venue. I doubt any ranching will be needed for that."

"You never know." He took a step to his left, but still couldn't manage a direct line of sight. "Cal might decide to incorporate a couple of steer into the ceremony," he suggested. He shuffled over another foot. "I could be brought in to fence off a tiny pasture in the middle of your venue."

She poked her head out from behind the boxes, her gaze quickly relocating to his new position, and she shot him a cool stare. "Or maybe he'll want to bring in a horse who had his balls cut off."

Waylon blinked at the cheeky words, but she was gone again before laughter found its way up and out of him. "You've got a quick wit about you, don't you?"

"I've been known to be witty."

He grinned. He liked her.

He slipped quietly into the adjacent stall. "So what is it that's got you so busy today?"

He could see her now, but just the right half of her. She stood unmoving behind the boxes, the list she was supposedly working on tucked haphazardly in her back pocket, and at his question, she dropped her head and thumped her forehead against a box.

"I'm checking inventory," she replied. She closed her eyes as she spoke, and her words stretched thin. "Before we get started next week."

"Is that so?" He inched deeper into the space. Looked to him like she was doing absolutely nothing.

Maybe hanging out just to spend time with him?

The idea pleased him like no other, and he stopped moving once he stood directly across from her. He didn't say anything to alert her of his presence. He just waited.

"That it is." She licked her lips and tilted her head back to stare at the loft above her. Her top teeth nibbled on her lip. "Got a lot to do," she continued. "I don't mean to disturb you. Go on about your business."

He decided that his business was to stand right there until she realized that he was onto her. She'd definitely hung around to see him today—and she was now too chicken to own up to it.

Not speaking, so as not to give himself away, he just watched. She didn't do anything for a few seconds. Just nibbled on her lip some more, her gaze still fastened above her, until finally she stooped and dragged over a box about eighteen inches in height. She climbed on top of it, one hand on the stack of boxes still in front of her and the other outstretched as if to keep her balance, and she managed it all without making a sound. Once straightened to her full height, she carefully eased apart two boxes at eye level and peeked through. Then her mouth turned to a frown.

She leaned back and craned her neck to look toward the front of the barn, and Waylon clamped down on his laughter. She was looking for him.

Also, she was insanely cute.

When her shoulders sagged as if dejected that he'd left without saying anything else to her, he could hold out no longer. He rapped a knuckle against one of the bars between them, and that time, she *did* jump.

She rotated to face him, still perched a foot and a half off the ground, and her eyes flashed hot with annoyance.

"About finished checking off that list?" he asked.

"You—" She bit off her words and jutted her chin out.

"Me what?" He grinned.

She didn't finish her thought. She just climbed from the box and marched toward the open stall door.

He moved to join her, standing to the side as she came out, and was thrilled when she didn't immediately leave. Instead, she headed for

Ollie. She pulled a carrot from her front pocket, resolutely paying no attention to Waylon as she moved, while he trailed along behind her.

"Not talking to me now?" Waylon asked. Ollie had let out a few sniffs since Waylon had come in, but at Heather's approach, the sounds changed to low nickers.

"I'm just giving the horses a treat before I leave."

He studied the back of her head, her hair loose and the ends curling in, then trailed his gaze down over her stiff posture as she continued making her avoidance clear. So he decided to give her a taste of her own medicine. He didn't say another word as he headed for the feed room. The horses needed to be fed before he left, anyway. He might as well do it now. And when he returned, he saw that his move had paid off.

Heather remained in the barn, only she now looked at *him*. Something about the twist to her mouth as she watched him, though, had him slowing his steps on the way to Beau's stall.

"What?" he asked when she remained silent.

"I'm just thinking about something."

He opened the swing-out feeder door and tipped the bucket. "And what's that?"

"About the fact that you're buying a house."

His shoulders tensed at her words, causing him to spill half of Beau's feed at his feet. He sighed. "And where did you hear that?"

"While shopping for Jill's wedding dress."

"Is that so?" He downplayed the information as he grabbed a broom and swept up the mess. He supposed he should be surprised that he'd managed to keep the house a secret for as long as he had.

After rehanging the broom, he found Heather leaning against Ollie's stall. She'd bent one knee, her heel resting on the wood panel making up the lower half of the door behind her, and her eyes followed Waylon until he once again disappeared.

When he eventually resurfaced from the feed room, she continued to watch. Her silent scrutiny gave him the urge to turn the tables on her, again. Not that he'd done such a great job of it the first time. But he let her be for now. He liked knowing she was trying to figure him out.

He finished filling Beau's feeder in silence, and by the time he reached Ollie's, she'd apparently done enough thinking.

"Very little gets past people's notice around here, you know?" She gave him a smug look. "Especially for someone so new in town."

He dumped the bucket's contents into Ollie's feeder, and made sure he ended up shoulder-to-shoulder with Heather. Then he turned his head and locked his gaze on hers. "Yet some things obviously do."

"Like what?" She didn't look convinced.

"Like the fact that I signed the contract on the house over four weeks ago." He offered his own smug look. "Yet it's just *now* getting out."

A faint smile touched her lips and she dipped her head in concession. "Touché, Mr. Peterson."

His blood pumped harder. "There's that 'Mr. Peterson' again."

Her features didn't change as she eyed him. Nor did she acknowledge his comment. But something changed inside him as she watched him so carefully, and he found himself at a loss to explain it. He didn't simply want her naked anymore. He wanted to talk to her. To get to know her.

And though he *wouldn't* stop flirting—because seriously, if he *could* get her clothes off, he'd do it in a heartbeat—his priorities with this woman seemed to be shifting.

She pushed off the stall door, her designer-booted feet crunching the fine gravel as she moved to the other side of the aisle, and he let out the breath he'd been holding. He forced himself to release it slowly, though. He didn't want to sound as needy as Ollie. He also didn't want her thinking she'd gained the upper hand in whatever game it was they were playing.

She offered Beau his own carrot before reversing position and taking up the same stance she'd held at Ollie's stall, then she lifted her gaze to his apartment. Waylon could see the wheels turning in her head, and the truth was, if she were to look his way, she'd witness the same going on with him.

Why was he so fascinated by her? Why did he want her to be fascinated by him?

It had been a long time since anyone had looked closely enough to decipher the real man inside the packaging, and even then, it hadn't been enough. Nikki might have *seen* him, but she'd never truly understood him.

"So why buy a house?" Heather brought her gaze back to his. There hadn't been enough light to notice the other night, but her eyes were almost a translucent blue. Like the marble he'd once carried in his pocket every day for a year. "Doesn't the apartment come with the job?"

"The apartment does come with the job."

"Then why buy?"

He gave an easy shrug. "Why not?"

She glanced at the small living quarters once more. Beau nipped at the back of her head, and she lifted a hand without looking, another carrot between her fingers. "Seems the job would be easier if you stayed on-site," she pointed out. "Once the livestock is here, I'd think the days would start early. Maybe run late."

"You worrying about my sleeping habits or about my ability to get the job done?"

"I'm not *worrying* about anything." Her eyes flicked back to his. "I'm just curious."

He moved a couple of feet closer. "Maybe I'm curious about you, too."

She didn't take the bait, and shifted away. But as she peered back at him, he noticed that, unlike most of the women he'd spoken with since moving to Red Oak Falls, it seemed to be true curiosity—as opposed to gossip—that fed her questions.

"It's simple," he found himself answering her. "I want a house."

"But why?"

He opened his mouth to tell her. She'd find out soon enough, anyway.

He couldn't do it, though. He wasn't ready to share that part of himself yet. "Why were you singing to my horse the other night?" he asked instead, and at the change in subject, she reared back.

"What does my singing to Ollie have to do with your buying a house?"

"You tell me yours; I'll tell you mine."

A hint of a smile touched her lips, and Waylon felt something shift inside him once again. He really liked this girl. "I don't want to tell you mine," she murmured. They stood face to face, her flat against Beau's stall and Waylon wanting desperately to close the distance between them.

"If you won't tell me why you sang to my horse"—his voice took on a teasing quality—"then tell me why you hung around and waited for me today."

She didn't look away. "I didn't hang around and wait for you today. I was working."

"No, you weren't."

"I was, too. We start work on the backyard on Monday, and—"

Her words cut off when he reached around behind her. He didn't touch her, just captured the corner of the paper she'd tucked in her back pocket earlier. Tugging it free of her jeans, he smoothed out the creases—never taking his eyes from hers—then turned the paper so she could see the list she'd been working on.

"I got a glimpse of this earlier," he told her.

"So?" Her breath forced the word out as he held it up in front of her.

"So . . ." He reached behind her once more, and her chest lifted as she caught her breath. He inhaled the scent of oranges as his fingers closed over the pointed tip of the black pencil, and after he slid it from her pocket, he held it up for her as well. "This is my pencil."

He knew the throatiness of his voice gave him away. He was insanely turned on, merely from being this close to her. From breathing in the citrusy smell that had to be coming from her hair.

"I have a cupful of them on the desk in my office," he explained.

Her eyelashes fluttered at his declaration, and this time when she spoke, her words were as unsteady as his. "Are you implying you're the only one who could use that type of pencil?"

He dropped his gaze to her mouth. It would take no more than the dip of his head to put his lips to hers. "I'm saying"—he cleared his throat when the words barely squeezed out—"that *you* didn't use this pencil. That you'd already finished checking your list before you got here today, and that you grabbed *this* particular pencil off my desk to make it look like you were busy. And I know this"—he waved the pencil back and forth in front of her—"because the check marks on your list were made with ink."

~

Heather forgot to breathe.

Damn the man, he wasn't supposed to have noticed that.

She snatched the paper from him and shoved it back into her pocket, and when she saw laughter in his eyes, she bumped her forearms against his chest to shove him away.

"Scoot back," she grumbled. "And quit crowding me."

He scooted back. But he also laughed at her.

"And stop it." She glared. "How rude."

"Rude to point out that you were in here waiting for me or rude for laughing?"

She scowled even harder. What a jerk.

And what a moron she was for hanging around to begin with.

She took another step forward and shoved him in the chest again, forcing him to move a couple more feet back. "Just rude," she told him, and he laughed at her yet again.

"I might be rude, but I still want to know. You going to tell me why you were waiting for me, Heather?"

"I wasn't waiting for you." She bumped him again, and before she knew it, she'd backed him all the way across the aisle.

Ollie watched as if curious who'd make the next move, and Heather forced herself not to get all the way up into Waylon's face. Not to appear as if she wanted to pin him there in front of her. She stood a foot away, breathing hard—mostly in embarrassment—and crossed her arms over her chest.

"I don't know why all the women in town think you're all that, anyway," she complained. "You're nothing but a coarse, smelly—"

"Smelly?" He looked affronted.

"—jerk of a man," she continued, without breaking stride, "who thinks he's God's gift to women. And yes," she confirmed, "*smelly*. You smell like a horse." Mixed in with sunshine and the earth, she silently added. He smelled like a man should smell. She jabbed a finger in his face. "And *no* man is a gift to women."

The bastard laughed at her again. So she slapped a hand over his mouth.

"Stop it," she growled.

"Then tell me why you waited on me," he mumbled under her fingertips.

"I didn't wait on you!"

"Yes, you did."

"No, I didn't!" she yelled again. But she totally *had* waited on him. And that was not like her. Not the twenty-nine-year-old her. She'd seen him outside when she'd pulled up, intending only to drop off the last of the supplies, and she'd simply been unable to get back in her car and drive away. Not without talking to him first.

But why?

She yanked her hand away from his mouth when she realized she was still holding it there, and took a step back. What was she doing? She wiped her fingers on her jeans as if it would erase the feel of his lips. She didn't get worked up like this. She was the "calm one" as Jill and Trenton liked to point out. That's why she'd been the spokesperson for their business for all these years. People liked her. They responded well to her. And she *didn't* lose her cool.

But with this man . . .

She forced herself to calm down, and took another step away from him. This man—whom she didn't even know—might be trying to drive her insane, but she didn't have to voluntarily tag along for the ride. He stood watching her now, wearing a similar expression to that of the ball-less horse standing directly behind him, and though she was fairly certain her current demeanor did imply that she'd returned to calm . . . she *still* wanted to scream. At both of them.

Waylon for being so frustrating and Ollie for growing on her so fast that she thought it was cute that he and his owner wore the same expressions.

"For the record," Waylon said after the silence had stretched on several seconds too long, "I'm glad you waited. I wanted to see you again."

The humor disappeared from his eyes, and the gentle way he made the statement had her chest deflating. What was going on with them?

She shook her head. "There's no reason you should want to see me again." Just as there was no reason she should have hung around and waited for him. "You don't even *know* me."

"We could change that."

"I don't want to change it."

"Are you sure?"

His eyes were an odd shade of brown. Lighter than most brown eyes she'd ever seen, yet solid enough a color that she didn't think they could be called hazel.

She looked him over as she stood there, taking in his plaid button-down with the sleeves rolled up to the elbows and the worn jeans covering strong thighs and ending at dusty boots. He was 100 percent cowboy. He stood feet shoulder-width apart and rocked back on his heels, and he wore his hat pulled low on his head. The man exuded buckets of confidence by doing nothing more than simply standing. Yet at the same time, something about him said "uncertainty" to her.

She replayed their last few words, trying to figure out where the uncertainty might be coming from, and decided that *she* wasn't even certain of anything at the moment. Why she'd waited there for him. Why she was so drawn to him.

Whether she *wanted* to get to know him better or not.

She hated that he had the reputation he did.

"How old are you anyway?" When she finally spoke, he looked as startled by her question as she'd probably seemed when he'd asked why she'd sung to his horse.

"Why do you want to know?" he returned.

"Because I do." Because he was young. She just hadn't heard how young.

But if she knew for a fact that he was *too* young for her, then maybe she could stop this nonsense.

She thought about some of the things she *had* heard over the last few weeks. He'd apparently been in ranching only for the last couple of years, and immediately before that had lived in Vegas. He was originally from San Antonio. And in years past, he'd been inclined to orchestrate regional poker tournaments.

Those tournaments had drawn in several guys from Red Oak Falls, more than one of whom insisted that Waylon had been a little "too good" at cleaning them out of their money.

"Why do you want to know how old I am, Heather?"

His question pulled her out of her thoughts. "Can't a person just wonder these things?"

"Sure they can." His feet went into motion the second he finished speaking, and this time he backed *her* across the aisle. His long strides made it so she had to quickly scurry backward to keep from being stepped on, and once he had her pinned against Beau's stall—standing far closer to her than she'd been to him—he looked her straight in the eyes. "But often there's a reason for it. Are you trying to figure out if I'm old enough for you?" His voice was deep and seemed to vibrate through her body. "Because trust me, I am."

She didn't want to trust him.

And then it occurred to her what he'd just implied. She propped both hands on her hips and shot him an incredulous look. "Did you just call me old?"

"Not too old for me." He waggled his brows at her. "I like my women *mature*."

She huffed out a breath in disgust. "You don't even know how old I am."

"You'll be thirty in December."

That had her pausing. How did he know that?

How did he know *anything* about her?

"I've heard things about you, too," he said, as if she'd asked the question out loud.

"What have you heard?" Who would be talking about her? "And from who?"

"Just from Cal." Waylon's voice softened, his eyes following suit. "He mentioned how the three of you came to be friends," he said gently. "And during our conversation, it came up that you were six months younger than Jill." He shrugged, looking vaguely repentant. "Jill's birthday is in June. They got engaged three days after."

Did the man have an eidetic memory or something? "What else did he tell you?"

"Pretty much just your age."

His gaze flickered away, and she assumed he was holding something back. But whether Cal had shared her story or not, it was easy enough to find out. Her parents had burned to death in a barn fire that had been started by an electrical short. They'd died trying to save the horses—and likely each other—and Heather had been placed at Bluebonnet Farms shortly thereafter.

"And you just happened to remember my age out of the conversation?" She didn't push for what he wasn't telling her, because she didn't like talking about her parents' deaths.

"I just happened to remember your age," he repeated.

"Then how old is Trenton?"

She didn't know why she asked, other than to turn the conversation away from her. As if he instinctively understood her intent, he produced an instant sultry look. "Trenton is twenty-seven. But as I said, I like my women older."

"I'm not your woman."

"You're not yet."

She laughed under her breath at his audacity, and the tension of the previous moment snapped. "You have *got* to quit laying it on so thick," she mumbled. "You're as bad as Big Red."

"Who's Big Red?"

Crap. She hadn't meant to say that.

But also . . . was that a hint of jealousy that flickered over Waylon's face?

Interesting.

"No one that you need to worry about." She wasn't about to share anything about Len, because the last thing she needed was for Waylon to figure out that she had a thing for redheaded men. And if he ever happened to meet Len? Well, she was sure the other man would take great pleasure in working that into the conversation.

She let her gaze trail over Waylon's trim beard before inching back up to the dark copper peeking out beneath his hat. He really was a fine specimen of redheaded man.

"I feel like you're lying to me again," he accused. "Just like you lied about waiting for me in the barn. But that's okay." He lowered his chin and shot her an unwavering stare. "I'm excellent at figuring out secrets."

Heather laughed again. Because the man was not only hot as hell, but he had a ton of little-boy cuteness going for him as well. "Big Red is no secret," she assured him. "Trust me. He's nobody. He was a cameraman for *Texas Dream Home*, that's all. And a ridiculous flirt."

"Ah. So you like men who flirt?"

"I don't . . ." She blew out a breath. "Len is just a friend, okay? He's big and brash—"

"And smelly?" Waylon offered, and Heather burst out laughing.

"No. Len isn't smelly."

Waylon made a face. "I'm quite certain that I'm not, either."

She didn't give him the response she knew he sought. Instead, she simply shrugged her shoulders in a "whatever" kind of way, and Waylon narrowed his eyes.

"I'm not," he insisted.

"Whatever you say, *Mr. Peterson*." She fired off a grin that she knew highlighted her dimples the best, and though she was also aware she probably shouldn't taunt the man, the female inside of her patted herself on the back when his eyes heated to a combustible level.

"You're fun, Heather Lindsay. And I do like fun."

"I . . ."

He captured her hand in his, and instead of moving in closer as she'd expected, he tugged *her* closer to him. "I also like flirting." He glanced at her mouth. "Specifically, with *you*. I like *that* as much as I like it when you smile at me the way you just did."

Heather only blinked at him. Because she had no idea what to say to that. The man was excellent at turning the mood in the room.

He glanced at his watch, and regret filled his face. "But I *am* going to stop flirting with you for today. I'm afraid I've—"

"Already got a hot date?" Heather asked. It *was* Friday afternoon, after all. The beginning of the weekend.

His brown eyes studied her, and there was no apology in them at all. "The hottest."

Humiliation had her tugging at her hand, but he didn't let go. Instead, he reeled her in even closer, then he put his mouth to her ear. "But I'll see you again next week."

Goose bumps lit down her body.

"We'll pick up right where we're leaving off. Me getting to know you, you getting to know me." He leaned back and peered down at her. "Me flirting with you, you flirting with me."

"I'm not flirting with you."

"Yes, you are." His thumb slid over her knuckles. "And I like that, too. A lot."

His phone rang before he could taunt her any further, the sound breaking whatever sorcery he'd been casting. Without hesitation, he lifted his cell to check the display, and then his features morphed into something Heather had yet to see from him. Anger.

He released her, his eyes going instantly dark, and answered the call as he turned and took the stairs to his apartment three at a time.

After his door closed behind him, Heather remained where he'd left her, shocked at his abrupt departure. She also found herself concerned over who was on the other end of that call. Because that had *not* been the look of a man anxious to talk.

Chapter Four

"Never allow the seeds of fear to be planted so densely that nothing else has the space to grow."

—Blu Johnson, life lesson #47

Waylon stood on the porch that ran the length of the small stone house, key in hand, and fought to keep the pride that threatened to overwhelm him in check. Yes, this small home was now his. Yes, it had the potential to change his life for good—and he'd do absolutely everything in his power to ensure that it would do just that. And yes, he loved the eighty-year-old run-down cottage in a way he'd never thought possible.

But dang, he absolutely hated the fact he'd had to borrow money from his father to make it happen.

A car passed on the street behind him, slowing, no doubt, to get a good look at the newbie to the neighborhood, and he shrugged off the demons of his past and slid his key into the front door. His father was a good man. Waylon wouldn't dispute that. The man had proven himself over the last four years—and especially within the last six months—and he continued to insist he wanted to do more. And more would be terrific. Waylon's hope was that their relationship would only continue to improve.

At the same time, it was hard to put too much stock in someone who'd already chosen a different life over sharing one with Waylon once before. And his father had found it far too easy to do.

Waylon pushed open the wooden door, a creak accompanying the motion, and let the emptiness of the home fill him. The house had sat unlived in for several years, and though the foundation was stable and the bones were good, it *did* need a lot of work. Work he was more than willing to put in. But work that wouldn't happen overnight.

He entered the small foyer that widened into the living room, and immediately started opening windows to air out the place. Truth be told, he should probably handle quite a few of the renovations before moving in. But that simply wasn't going to happen. It was Wednesday afternoon now, and though no furniture would be delivered until that weekend, he would be staying in the place starting tonight. He had a bedroll in his truck, and he didn't need more than that. This was his home, and he'd live in it even if it were falling down around him.

His footsteps echoed as he moved from one room to the next, the hardwood under his feet in rough shape, but at least a portion of it salvageable. He caught himself reaching out to touch the walls as he passed through each of the doorways. The arched entries were one of the features he'd loved most about the house, as well as the stone that covered the exterior.

There were three bedrooms, none of which were terribly large, a small bathroom with the original pedestal sink and claw-foot tub, and a U-shaped eat-in kitchen that also had the original fixtures and cabinetry. And they were in *rough* shape. The cabinets had been painted a coral color at some point in the past, and the eat-in area had been papered in an enormous flower pattern with the occasional bird sprinkled throughout. It was atrocious.

But it was his.

He tugged at the corners of the wallpaper that had come loose in every room, and eyed the handful of fallen pieces long ago chewed on by mice. Before closing on the house, he'd had an inspection done of the electrical, which he'd been surprised to learn had been upgraded in the last couple of decades. It was in decent shape, as was the plumbing. The roof, though, was another matter. He stared at the largest of the yellowed water stains in the master bedroom, and made a mental note to begin looking for a roofer the following day.

Then it occurred to him that he *could* call the Bluebonnet crew and let them handle it. Or better yet, ask for Heather specifically. It would give him an excuse to have her around.

And he had recently discovered that she was more than capable of doing the job.

In the hope of getting a few additional glimpses of her, he'd borrowed the *Texas Dream Home* preview DVD from Cal. And glimpses he'd gotten. In fact, in the video, she'd come across as involved—and as *capable*—in the construction aspect of the business as both Jill and Trenton. Landscape design was definitely only the tip of the iceberg for this lady.

But even though he'd love a convenient reason to be near her, he'd have to come up with another way to make it happen. Because he wanted to fix up his house by himself.

He returned to the second-largest bedroom and stopped in the doorway, envisioning the final result. This would be the room he redid first. He'd strip the wallpaper, starting tonight, and have any holes patched and the room ready to paint by the weekend. He'd already picked out the paint and curtains, and the floors would wait until he could do the entire house.

The third bedroom would be offered to his father. Waylon moved to the embarrassingly small space and peered in, and though the grown-up in him hated the idea of having nothing more to offer the person who'd given him life, the child in him enjoyed it a bit too much. Latent anger wasn't good for the soul, he knew. It could eat at a person.

Or cause a person to be petty and take pleasure in offering tiny spaces to grown men.

At least he intended to make the offer. He didn't have to do that.

But then, he *had* taken the man's money. Wasn't it the least he could do?

He moved back outside and sat on the concrete steps centering the front of the house, then he pulled out his cell and retrieved his dad's number. It was late enough that work should be finished for the day.

"Waylon," his dad greeted him. Charlie Peterson was fifty-one, and would be a cowboy till the day he died.

"Hi, Dad. How are you?"

"Doing good. Just finished doctoring the last of the calves, and looking forward to a beer before turning in. Gonna be an early one tonight."

His dad had recently lost the job he'd held for the last several years, thanks to helping Waylon out with his physical therapy, but had picked up summer work in South Texas to tide him over. "The job still ending soon?"

"Got another week here."

"You still thinking of heading out this way?" Waylon hedged. They'd talked about that possibility when Waylon had first taken the job with Cal. Either as a temporary *or* permanent situation.

"If that's still okay with you . . ."

Waylon argued with himself for only a few seconds. It would be harder to continue working on their relationship if the other man was never around.

"I could use you at the ranch," Waylon finally offered. He'd talked about it with Cal. "Part time at this point, but we'll be bringing in several trailers of livestock soon. Branding will have to be done, immunizations, castrations."

"I'm your man for that."

"And you wouldn't have to worry about rent . . . if you didn't want to. You could stay with me. I've got an extra room." He stood and paced across the porch, hurrying to continue before his dad could reply. "I closed on it today, Dad." He faced the house, and the pride that had been swirling all afternoon took hold. "It's mine. And I couldn't have done it without you. Thank you for the loan."

"It's just money. Wasn't doing me any good sitting in the bank."

Still, Waylon knew had circumstances been reversed, he wouldn't necessarily have done the same. "That may be, but I'll pay you back." He did have more pressing expenses to see to first, though. "Just as soon as I can."

"There's no hurry. It made me happy to give it to you." There was a short pause as his dad cleared his throat. "And even though I did, that doesn't mean you have to . . ."

His dad's words faded into an uncomfortable silence, and Waylon knew he was referring to the offer of letting him live there. Waylon could picture his dad standing in the spartan bunkhouse where he currently worked, few personal belongings scattered around him and likely little expression on his face. There would be hope simmering in his eyes, though. It was a look Waylon had seen often in the last few months. And suddenly, the idea of having his dad live with him no longer felt like a "have to" situation so much as one decided upon of free will. An offer extended because that's what Waylon wanted to happen.

"I do have to, Dad." Waylon nodded, knowing exactly where he'd be if his father hadn't been there. "You lost your job because of me. You're currently broke because of me."

"None of that was your fault."

They had a difference of opinion on that one. "Nevertheless, *none* of it was something you had to do." He leaned against the post and dropped his head back to the peeling paint. "And I am grateful for it. All of it. Even if I haven't always made that very clear."

"I know you are. I've never thought otherwise. And if you're certain about the room . . ."

"I'm certain about the room."

"Then I accept."

His dad went quiet again, the silence not wholly uncomfortable, and Waylon waited. Knowing where the conversation would go next. It was the subject in the forefront of both their minds.

"You got a court date yet?" his dad finally asked.

Waylon swallowed. "Second week in November. Heard from my lawyer last week."

You've got to walk the line, his lawyer had insisted. *No screwing up. No slipups.*

No screwing up, Waylon had replied. *No slipups. You've got my word on that.*

If ever being good enough mattered, it was now.

And they will be proved wrong, Waylon had insisted. *They've got little more than the word of a couple of thugs.*

A couple of thugs whom you've spent a lot of time with.

His lawyer hadn't been wrong about that. He *had* spent a lot of time with them. Too much. And it worried the hell out of him.

"I'll be there in court with you," his dad told him now, and Waylon stared at the ceiling of the porch, suddenly wanting to smash the dated light fixture into next week.

He opened his mouth to tell his dad that he didn't have to bother. That he could handle it on his own. But those weren't the words that came out. Nor was that what he truly wanted.

"I'd like it if you were."

~

She shouldn't have signed up to do this.

They were only one week into the backyard project, and Heather had already decided she'd made a grave mistake. She was not cut out to design landscapes. At least not for something this grand in size.

"Hey, Heather."

She looked up from the sketches she'd been reviewing to find Troy Marcum knee-deep in the hole they'd been readying for the koi pond. "What do you need?" she asked.

"You sure this is the filtration system you want to use?"

She wasn't sure of anything at the moment. She rose and made her way over to him, careful not to get tangled in any of the power cords or miscellaneous equipment littering the area, then had to raise her voice to be heard over the Skilsaw that fired to life. "What's the problem with it?"

"I'm not sure it's powerful enough."

"But we're putting one on each end," she yelled back.

They were constructing an oversized pond that would cinch in the middle before opening back up on either side. It would also wind throughout other sections of the hardscaped areas as a small stream, as well as lead into a waterfall that tumbled over stacked boulders on the far end. The whole thing would be magnificent when finished. Assuming they could figure out how to do it right.

"But even with two," Troy replied, suddenly yelling into silence, "I don't think they'll be enough." He adjusted his volume. "Not for the water capacity this thing is going to hold."

A camera moved in closer, and Heather felt her posture stiffen. Why did they always like to catch the screwups on film?

"Let me get in there with you." She hopped into the deepest part of the hole, examining the specs on the attached sticker and doing her best to ignore the boom mic hanging over them. She silently prayed that she hadn't messed up yet again. She'd already had to send back a shipment of the wrong pavers, had forgotten to line up the guy to set the propane tank for the gas grill and fireplace, and had gone home at the end of each very long day wanting to do nothing but cry.

She *hadn't* cried, though. Not once. Because it took more than a few setbacks to bring a Bluebonnet to tears. She was tough, dammit, and tough girls didn't cry. But she'd also held the tears at bay for fear that her eyes would still be puffy the following day. No one needed to see that on camera.

The saw started up again as she pulled a sheet of paper from the back of her notepad. She ran her finger down the printed list of supplies and compared the filters on the list with what she'd ordered. And there it was.

"You're right." How had she managed to order the wrong one? "Are they both this size?"

Troy nodded, and she wanted to kick herself. She'd spent two weeks trailing one of the state's best pond guys to make sure she understood the needs and maintenance required for something of this size. *And* to ensure that she planned accordingly. Then she'd hired the guy as a consultant to help finalize her design, as well as go over her final list of supplies before she'd placed *any* orders. Yet somehow, she'd still messed up. How was that even possible?

"So what do you want me to do?" Troy asked.

She wanted him to turn back time for her so she could go back to just building she-sheds. Life had been much simpler when the biggest concern she, Jill, and Trenton had was that everyone in town thought they were only capable of building retreats for women.

Instead of saying any of that, she allowed herself to be helped out of the hole. "Check to see what you can do to help Sarah on the gazebo." Sarah was the one wielding the saw. After having once lived at Bluebonnet Farms herself, she'd been with the company for several years and had turned into one of their most valuable employees. When the two companies had combined over the summer, Sarah had upped her game and Jill had promoted her. "The day's almost over," Heather added, and silence once again filled the air. "Finish up with her, and I'll get a rush delivery on a replacement for next week."

"Works for me." Troy loped off toward Sarah, casting a glance at the two additional women Heather had working on the roof for the covered seating area, while Heather returned to her sketches.

In the middle of the pond would stand Jill's she-shed. It would be in the shape of a gazebo, with windows lining the top half of the walls and cedar lining the bottom, and it would initially house butterflies that would be released as Jill and Cal were pronounced man and wife. Surrounding the gazebo would be rich foliage that complemented the Texas landscape and stone walking paths that would lead to each of the three custom bridges. Cal was in charge of building the bridges, one of which would be where he and Jill exchanged vows, and the water surrounding it all would be filled with koi fish, water hyacinth, and water lilies.

With the hardscaped sections on either side of the pond and the natural shade from the existing trees, the area would be perfect for either entertaining or relaxing. And week-one issues notwithstanding, they were off to a decent start. They had the entire area for the pavers dug up, the gazebo half completed, and the electricity had been run.

The rattle of a trailer pulled her attention, and she looked up to see Waylon's truck rolling up the driveway. It pulled a massive gooseneck trailer, and Cal's truck—similarly equipped—followed Waylon's. Jill's blue pickup brought up the rear, and a camera crew had positioned itself at the barn, ready to record it all.

Seemed the cattle had arrived.

Heather hadn't caught sight of Waylon all week—other than a couple of glances when one or the other of them had been coming or going. He'd been as busy as she had. With the cameras now rolling, the pressure had ramped up for Waylon and Cal to get the ranch fully operational.

Setting her notepad to the side, Heather stood once again but remained where she was. She didn't want to be too obvious, but she did want a better look. Before the trucks made it as far as the barn, though, Sarah appeared at her side.

Heather glanced over. "Need a break?" She smiled knowingly with her question.

"I need to watch cowboys at work," Sarah muttered.

Heather chuckled softly and shot a quick peek at the camera positioned on the two of them. They both wore mic packs, and Heather didn't doubt for a second that if they stood there overtly ogling the men, the producers wouldn't hesitate to use the footage. So, though Sarah might voice her lecherous thoughts out loud, Heather intended to keep *hers* to herself. And as Waylon's truck came to a stop in front of the barn and the long-legged cowboy climbed from the front seat, she discovered that she had all sorts of lecherous thoughts.

Cal parked behind Waylon, and Dill came out of the barn with Beau and Apollo, saddled and ready to go. Apollo was Cal's horse. He'd been purchased and brought to the farm earlier in the week.

Dill handed the animals off to the two men before climbing into the cab of Waylon's truck, and in a blink, Waylon was up and sitting tall in the saddle.

"Damn," Sarah muttered.

Heather's mouth went dry. "Uh-huh."

She'd seen him on a horse a couple of times now, but there was something about seeing him *get* on the horse that turned her crank even more.

"He is one *very* good-looking man," Sarah observed.

Too good, Heather added silently. He made her think all kinds of naughty thoughts.

And dang but it irked her that he'd put no effort into seeking her out that week. For a man who'd promised his flirtatious ways weren't going to stop, they'd sure stopped in a fast hurry.

"I still can't get over how much he looks like Prince Harry." The words came from neither Heather nor Sarah, and Heather turned to find that the two women who'd been working on the seating area, Gina and Ashley, had decided to join them.

So much for not seeming too obvious.

"But Prince Harry in a cowboy hat," Ashley, the second woman, said, and Heather wanted to shout "See!" Because that's exactly what she'd thought. How was a woman supposed to resist that?

"I'd do Prince Harry in a cowboy hat," Gina murmured, and the way she followed the words by licking her lips had Heather cringing. But the sentiment was accurate.

"I'd do Prince Harry *out* of a cowboy hat," Ashley added, never taking her eyes from the man in question.

"And I'd do with some actual help back here," Troy shouted out to them.

Sarah waved her hand at the man without looking back. "Don't worry about us. We're just taking a quick break."

Troy mumbled something about women being way worse than men, but none of the women seemed to care. They were too fixated on Waylon, whose horse had reared up before he'd taken off. Cal followed a few paces behind them, and Heather watched as Waylon pulled his hat off and waved it for the cameras.

Damn, but she wanted to do Prince Harry both in *and* out of a cowboy hat.

She wanted to wear his hat *while* she did him.

And really, why couldn't she do that? Other women did things like that all the time. Sleeping with a guy didn't mean she had to fall in love with him.

"I seriously never knew I had a thing for gingers." Sarah chewed on the pad of her thumb as she continued to watch the men work. The entire group had relocated away from the barn, but a holding pen had been erected within sight of the house where the cattle would be unloaded. From what Heather understood, this would be only the first load of livestock brought to the ranch, but Cal intended to ramp up slowly.

They watched the activity at the top of the hill a few minutes longer before Heather reluctantly called a stop to their break. The day was fast getting away from them, and she needed to keep things on track. But as the others got back to work, she couldn't help but take one last peek back. And what she witnessed almost managed to do what all her screwups that week had *not*. Bring a tear to her eye.

Because Cal was simply the best . . . and her friend deserved every bit of that.

He'd finished herding the animals and turned his horse toward Jill, and when he reached her side, he held a hand down to help her up. She settled in behind him, her arms snug around his waist, and as if he couldn't pull in another breath without it, he turned and planted the sweetest kiss on Jill's cheek.

Heather sighed as she watched them ride off together. She knew they'd been playing to the cameras, but she also knew that what Jill and Cal felt for each other was real.

Being aware of that made Heather determined to put even more effort into their backyard, so after making a quick call to line up the new filters, she got back to work. She joined Sarah and Troy, and the three of them worked seamlessly for the remainder of the afternoon. When Troy mentioned that he had to leave a few minutes early to pick up his nephews, Heather cut all of them loose. Everyone had worked hard all week. She might as well show her appreciation by giving them an early start to their weekends.

As the last of their vehicles pulled away, she gathered the few tools still scattered about. She climbed onto the backhoe to ensure the parking brake was engaged, and as she turned to jump down, Waylon waited below her, his hand outstretched.

"Need some help?" he offered.

She eyed his long fingers. Her subconscious dared her to slip her hand in his—*just this one time . . . what could it possibly hurt?*—but she shook her head. "Thanks, but I'm good. I've been getting on and off these bad boys by myself for a while now."

She hopped down, landing within inches of him, and he flashed his pearly whites. "And, if I may say so, you look mighty fine doing it." He flicked a quick glance at the machinery before adding, "I'd be willing to bet you'd look even better *driving* it."

"You'd win *that* bet."

Waylon burst out laughing at her response, and she bent to grab an empty water bottle that had ended up by the back tire. When she stood, they moved away together.

"So, how's your week been?" Waylon asked.

"Busy. Productive." She eyed one of the production crew as they loaded their equipment into a van. "As well as feeling like I'm under a microscope."

Waylon followed her line of sight. "Tell me about it. I had no clue what I was really signing up for, but since Cal's been hanging with me most of the week, so have the cameras."

Comfortable silence fell as she grabbed a collapsible toolbox she'd missed before and Waylon rescued another wayward water bottle. She moved toward the reboxed filtration unit, but before she got to it, Waylon spoke from behind her. "I closed on my house."

She whipped around in surprise. "You did?"

"Wednesday." He nodded, and pride glowed back at her.

"Congratulations."

"Thanks. It's in rough shape, but I like it." He shrugged casually. "It fits me."

"Where is it?"

He named a street that was filled with older homes but in a solid, established neighborhood, and Heather almost asked why he'd chosen that particular neighborhood. Most of the people who lived there had done so for years, and though Heather didn't doubt the community would make him feel welcome, he didn't exactly fall into their age group. She decided it was too personal a question, though, so she kept it to herself. The whys and the what-do-you-want-out-of-life type of small talk could easily slip into too-deep territory. Best to keep things light.

She turned back to pick up the box, but Waylon beat her to it. He scooped it up, hoisting it in one arm, and peeking up at her as he rose. "You want to come home with me and check it out?"

This time it wasn't pride that glowed back at her.

She chuckled. "I don't think so, Mr. Peterson."

He growled under his breath at her use of his surname, and they ended up face-to-face again, her gazing up at him as if she'd never seen a cute guy before. "How about if I tell you that I'm considering hiring you for some work I need done around the place?"

"Then I'd tell you to give Jill a call. She handles our scheduling."

Waylon shook his head. "I don't want to give Jill a call. And I don't want Jill coming over to my house to check things out." He paused for a second before adding, "If I have anyone there, it'll be you."

Heather's breath caught at his deepened voice. His teasing had quickly shifted to something much more earnest. And something she refused to consider. He was far too dangerous to her peace of mind. "As you can see from where we stand," she said, forcing levity into her voice, "I would do you no good. I'm the outdoor person."

"That's not all you are."

At her questioning look, he explained. "I caught the preview of *Texas Dream Home*. I had no idea you had so many skills."

"Ah." She'd wondered if he'd seen it. He followed her as she moved around the perimeter of the pond. "Skills. Yep, I have them. I am a Bluebonnet, after all. If we can't do it"—she pumped her arms out at her sides, fists tucked in at her waist—"we keep trying until we can."

"Nice motto."

Heather peeked back at him. "It's not really a motto, just something I sometimes say."

She bounded down into the pond and made her way to the center island. Trenton and Jill had come by their construction skills a little easier than she, but at the same time, she'd always insisted on pulling her weight. It was her company, too, after all. Intrinsically, she may be better at designing both the insides and outsides of the properties, but that didn't mean she couldn't do just as much as everyone else when she had to. Only, now they had plenty of people working for them—men included—so she no longer had to.

She tucked the toolbox inside the gazebo, and as she came back out, she looked across to where Waylon waited for her. He hadn't replied to her last comment, and she found him studying her now, a healthy amount of curiosity on his face.

"I'm not that hard to figure out," she told him. It seemed safer, somehow, to talk with the gulf of the pond between them.

"Are you sure about that?"

"Positive."

"Then explain it to me."

She stared at him for a moment before answering. "It's simple," she finally said. "I'm a girl in a man's world. And I like it here."

"Ever wanted to be anything else?"

The question caught her off guard. Or more accurately, his precision caught her off guard.

"Haven't we all?" she answered flippantly, before heading for the second filter. But again, Waylon beat her to it.

"I can get it," she told him. "You're already carrying one of them."

"Sure you can." He didn't pick it up immediately. "Or you could let me do it."

"Why?" And then she saw the intent in his eyes. "Because you're the man?"

"That's as good a reason as any."

She blew out a breath. Men and their chivalry.

She kind of liked it.

"Fine." She spoke with a bored tone, not wanting to give away that she found the offer sweet, and motioned with her now-empty hands.

"Carry it. Have a good time. I'll just be back here being the weak female trailing along behind you."

The corners of his mouth twitched. "And I'll be the big strong man trying his best to show off."

He didn't need to try.

"They're going in my car," she told him. She kept any and all other thoughts to herself. "I ordered the wrong ones and have to send them back."

In a single move, Waylon had the other box up so he held one in each arm, and Heather caught her gaze lingering on the way his shoulder muscles bunched with the movement. He turned for her car, and as she followed along behind him, she let her eyes lower to his rear. Because why not? The view was right there for the taking, and the man totally had the goods.

Even with his limp, he moved with more swag than most guys she'd ever run into.

As she kept an eye on his buttocks, wondering what had really caused his limp—because again, there was much speculation about that—she caught one lone camera still out at the farm. And it was pointed at her. She wiggled her fingers in a wave, hoping to mess up any potential clip of her butt-gazing. But then she decided to ignore its existence altogether. The show was about Cal and Jill. Not her and Waylon's rear.

"So now that you've watched the preview," she said from behind him, eyes still following every shift of his glutes, "are you intrigued? Will you be at the viewing party next week?" The Buffalo Nickel was hosting a viewing party for all four episodes.

Waylon turned to face her, but kept walking backward. "You asking me to go as your date?"

"*No.*"

When he merely hiked one brow a little higher than the other, she almost laughed. Because the man never stopped.

She crossed her arms over her chest instead. "Definitely *not*."

"Definitely?"

"Not," she repeated, and this time when his smile appeared, the corners of his mouth inched higher, giving her dimples and all.

Then he lowered his gaze and swept a path over her body.

Dang, the man had skills. "Will you *please* stop flirting with me?"

He drove her crazy. And though she tried to follow her question with a glare of frustration, she failed epically. It came out more like an absurdly fierce smile. Try as she might, she couldn't stop the creepy smile from spreading into a real one as he stared back. He didn't say a word, but his look said everything.

"You're incorrigible," she told him, now half laughing, and more than half turned on. "I was just asking you a question. Making small talk. It's called *conversation*."

"Oh, I know what conversation is. And yes, I'll be there"—he let his gaze dip over her body once again—"hoping to . . . *converse* with you some more."

She rolled her eyes at him. Then, realizing they'd stopped walking at some point, she put her feet back in motion. Only, this time *she* took the lead.

He didn't trail for long, though, and they soon walked side by side as they made their way up the slight incline toward the barn. When they were within feet of the car, Waylon looked over. "For the record, I'm *still* not going to stop flirting with you. I like it more every day." He put the boxes in the back of her SUV. "I also like you more every day."

"That's a line if ever I've heard one." She pushed the button to close the rear door. "And I can say that with confidence because you haven't even *seen* me in days."

"Yet my 'like level' has still increased."

She shook her head at that. "You're so full of it. And *for the record*, my 'like level' has not. I refuse to let myself like someone who might be too young for me." She flashed him an accusing smirk. "I did notice that you skirted that question the other day, by the way."

Waylon cocked his head as he studied her. "Are you telling me that if I share my age, then you'll like me more?"

"I'm not saying . . ." She let her words trail off with a soft puff of air. Because this very much felt like a losing battle. "You're skirting the question again."

"Yes, I am. But that's okay because I'm cute." He smiled brilliantly at her, his dimples flashing deep, and for the first time in her life, she understood what it felt like to be on the receiving end of someone trying to use their dimples to charm. "Some would even say I'm irresistible," he added. And he gave her the smile again. "What do you think, Heather?"

She *thought* she wanted to kiss the outlandish smile right off the man's smug face. But she couldn't very well tell him *that*.

"Don't worry." He winked at her. "I think you're cute, too." He dropped his gaze by about two feet. "Even if you *do* wear a bit of dessert on your hips."

She gasped.

Then she shoved him.

The push forced him to dance a couple of feet backward in order not to land on his behind, but Heather didn't care. She wished he'd gone down flat on his ass.

"I can't believe you said that to me!" she sputtered out.

He captured her hand when she went for another shove, and that time it was *her* doing a dance to keep from losing her balance.

"And I can't believe you're so easy," he taunted as she stumbled toward him. "Seriously, you're fun."

"Fun?" The man said the strangest things. "Why? Because you like to tease me?"

He kept her hand in his. "No. Because you *like* being teased."

"I do not. And that doesn't even make sense, anyway." Using her free hand, she attempted to pry his fingers from hers, but she ended up with both of her hands trapped between both of his.

Not what she'd intended at all.

"Sure it does." He scooted in closer. "Teasing is a form of flirting. Which you enjoy." He separated their hands so that each of his now held one of hers. "And we've already established that *I* enjoy flirting with *you*."

She swallowed. They were standing out in the open, holding hands, and staring at each other in a way that only people who intended to do something about it should be staring at each other.

"I caught you singing to Ollie again the other day, by the way." His voice lowered to barely more than a whisper, and his breath was as warm as his hands. "I didn't let you know I was in the barn, but I stayed and listened. It was the same song you sang that first night."

Embarrassment had her dropping her gaze. She'd known she shouldn't have eaten lunch in the barn that day.

He finally released one of her hands, but only to touch a finger under her chin, and at the contact, she had to bite her lip to keep from moaning. What was it about this man? Did he bathe in pheromones?

"It's an incredibly attractive quality, you know. Being romantic."

She did not need to hear what he found attractive about her. "It's not romanticism," she denied. "I just like horses."

Her mother had sung to their horses.

"You ever ride anymore?"

Heather's breath caught at the way he'd phrased the question. Did she ride *anymore*?

Clearly, he did know how her parents had died.

The thought of him standing there looking down at her. Feeling sorry for her. Made her want to turn and run. She didn't want to think about her parents' deaths.

She didn't want *him* thinking about their deaths.

But they had died. And she'd not only lost both of her parents due to the fire, but the family horses as well. And every good thing she'd ever shared with either her father or her mother.

"Not in a long time," she finally forced out. It was either answer or risk his asking more.

Nerves skittered over the back of her neck as his hand tightened on hers.

"My mom and I would ride," she blurted out. Her breathing grew heavier. He hadn't asked *who* she'd ridden with, but she continued talking anyway. "Dad wasn't as into them as we were, but we still went out pretty often. Aunt Blu had a couple of horses when I moved in with her, too." Her words sped up as the fingers of Waylon's free hand slipped down her arm. "I took them out a few times." She no longer focused on him. "But mostly I preferred caring for them. Feeding them, watering them."

Singing to them.

She pressed for stoic as those first months played through her mind. Going from her house, her world, her horses . . . to someone else's world. Someone else's horses.

Someone else's mother.

"You're welcome to ride Ollie or Beau any time you want to." His tone gentled, and he recaptured her other hand. "In fact, I'd love to take you out right now if you're interested. Show you the ranch. Let you enjoy time with the horses." He winked. "Get you all alone."

She suspected he was trying to bring the mood back up with his last comment, but it didn't work. He'd made her think about her parents. That wasn't always easy to come back from.

"Go for a ride with me, Heather."

"I . . ." She hesitated because of how much she wanted to go. And not just to be with him. She longed to be on a horse again. It had been too long. And though she'd tried to forge ahead as a teen, to not let that one night define her, in the end, it had simply been easier *not* to ride horses. *Not* to pretend she wouldn't think about that night every time she sat in a saddle.

She opened her mouth to tell him "no," but the word wouldn't come.

So she shook her head instead. *No.* She wasn't ready for that.

He nodded, squeezed her hands one last time, and walked her to her car door. But as he opened the door for her, a whinny sounded from deep in the barn.

A slight smile touched Waylon's mouth. "You can't leave without telling them good-bye?"

He phrased it as a question, and her laughter came out sounding sad. "Why do I feel like you're trying to lure me inside?"

"Hey." He held his hands up. "It's not me. That was Ollie calling out to you."

"So it was." And so she didn't want to leave without telling the horses good-bye.

She closed her door and forced her parents back into the far reaches of her mind.

"Okay, but they're going to be mad at me. I don't have any treats for them."

"They'll get over it." Together they headed for the barn. "Plus, I think Ollie has a crush on you. He'll be happy just getting a smell of your hair."

Heather glanced over, and found Waylon wincing in embarrassment.

When she didn't look away, silently insisting he explain his words, he grudgingly admitted, "Your hair smells like oranges."

She grinned. She'd suspected that was what he meant.

Her pulse danced a little faster. Both at the knowledge he'd noticed such a detail as well as that he hadn't wanted her to know that he'd noticed. "Yes, it does," she confirmed. "It's my conditioner."

"Whatever it is, I smell it every time I get near you."

His words made her want him to get near her a little more often.

Pleasure flowed through her as they stepped through the open doors, and they were almost to Ollie's stall before she realized they weren't alone in the barn. Only, she wasn't quite certain who—or *what*—she'd heard.

She stopped walking and looked back. Waylon's office door stood open, but the room was empty, the wash area for the horses was dark, and no light came from under the small bathroom door. Also, nothing or no one was in any of the empty stalls.

And then she heard it again.

She pressed a hand to her mouth as the sound reached her ears for a third time and she recognized it for what it was. Pleasured groaning. Someone was making out in the barn.

Then Cal's deep voice carried out from the half bath. He wanted Jill's shirt off.

Heather squeezed her eyes closed tight. As if *that* would stop what was happening twenty feet away from her. Then she remembered that she wasn't alone.

She jerked her gaze to Waylon's, his frozen expression indicating that he'd figured the situation out as well, and when the sound of a zipper hit their ears, he clamped his fingers around her wrist and dragged her up the stairs to his apartment.

Chapter Five

"Be careful playing make-believe in real life."

—Blu Johnson, life lesson #82

"What are you doing?" Heather hissed out the second Waylon closed the door behind them.

"I'm getting us out of there!"

"But we could have just snuck out the way we came in." She pointed toward the front of the barn, and Waylon jerked his gaze around to see what she was talking about. Because his brain clearly hadn't quite caught up with his heart rate. And that's when he realized his mistake.

"Ah, crap," he muttered.

"What?"

But it was too late. She'd seen it, too. Since the apartment was on the second floor, when she'd jabbed a finger toward what would have been open *barn* doors—had they'd still been down below—she'd instead been pointing at his open *bedroom* door. With the unmade bed sitting just inside the small room.

Heather didn't say anything, but the sound of her breathing reached his ears.

"I . . . uh . . . haven't fully moved out yet." He attempted to explain. He'd been staying at the house since Wednesday, but hadn't bothered cleaning up here, yet. "I'm doing that tonight."

She didn't say anything, just continued to stare at his bed, and that didn't help matters at all. He liked her. A lot. He liked the way her eyes sparked when he said outrageous things to her, and how embarrassment could so easily paint her cheeks a pretty pink.

He liked that she was witty and flirtatious. That she sang sad songs to his horse. And that she wasn't afraid to say whatever was on her mind.

But he had *not* meant to coax her into his bed by literally dragging her to it.

Still. He did have her there. And he didn't think either of them wanted to go back downstairs while Cal and Jill remained in the barn.

He angled his head. "Last week's offer of dessert still stands."

She continued staring at his bed. "I didn't get the impression it was cake you were really looking to share."

He also liked that she didn't beat around the bush. "It still isn't."

She finally pulled her gaze from the rumpled sheets, and he held his breath as he waited. Because the expression in her eyes told him she was fifty-fifty on the matter. But then she blinked.

"Damn," he whispered.

"What?"

"You're going to say no."

She laughed nervously. Then she very purposefully put her back to the sight of his bed. "I'm going to say no." She blew out a breath. "But that might only be because we aren't the only ones in the barn."

He went dead silent for three complete seconds.

"Heather . . ."

"I know." She grimaced. "I'm sorry. I shouldn't have said that. I don't intend to come across as a tease. I swear. But sometimes things just blurt themselves out."

She began fidgeting with the deck of cards he'd left on the table, and he made the executive decision that if sex wasn't going to happen then distance was key. He moved to the small kitchen to put space between them and dug around in his fridge.

Finding a couple of soft drinks, he handed one over before popping the top on his, and dang if the sound of compressed air hissing out in the silent room didn't turn him on even more. Tilting his head back, he stared at the ceiling as he guzzled, but when a thump sounded from below—as if someone might have pinned another someone up against a certain bathroom door—he choked on his drink.

"We have to do something other than stand here and wait," he wheezed out, coughing between every other word. "Otherwise . . ." His gaze drifted back to the bed.

"Otherwise," Heather muttered, and he could still make out every breath she took.

Another thump came from below, and he made another executive decision.

"Ice cream." He said the words with steely resolve. "Ice cream helps everything." He moved back to the fridge, not waiting for her to comment, and grabbed the pint of banana split from the freezer before yanking open a drawer to search for a spoon. "And don't give me any crap about it going to your hips, either, because lady, your hips could rock my world."

He jerked his head up after realizing he'd said that out loud, then he whipped his gaze back to hers. And he watched as the blue of her eyes softened.

Damn her romantic streak. He could see it as clear as day.

And it spoke directly to his dick every time.

Additional door-rattling sounded from below, this time with a more urgent rhythm to it, and her gaze shifted back from soft and cuddly to panicked and stricken. Waylon ripped into the dessert and shoved a bite into his mouth. "Ice cream," he demanded. He passed over both container and spoon.

She followed suit, and they ate like that for a couple of minutes, both standing awkwardly in his kitchen-built-for-one, alternating the pint between them, to the beat of sex pounding out down below. And then suddenly, they heard voices.

Heather's gaze shot to the interior window. "Are they finished already?"

"Either that or they're taking it to another room."

And he would *kill* Cal if they were taking it to another room.

Heather groaned and stabbed the spoon into the remaining ice cream. "I can't look. If I see—" She shook her head as she bit off her words, her eyes giving him the kind of warning that could terrify small children. She freed the spoon and pointed it at the window. "You do it. You're the one who trapped us up here."

The last thing he wanted to do was look to see if Cal and Jill were finished. Because they very well *could* be taking it to another room. *Or* out in the open.

But he also didn't want to look because if they *were* finished, Heather would likely leave.

He couldn't very well hold her hostage, though. So he did as the woman asked and trudged to the window. After a wince and a quick glance, he could breathe a little easier. "The coast is clear."

She stared at him, her eyes a deeper blue than he'd seen before, then she slowly crossed the room to peer out beside him. And now she smelled like both oranges *and* bananas.

"Which means," he croaked out, "that we're now *alone* in the barn."

And she *had* said earlier that her "no" might have only been because they weren't the only ones in the barn.

Heather stared out the window for a moment longer, while Waylon held his breath and waited. He didn't really think she would change her mind, possibly take off her clothes. But no one would ever accuse him of not swinging for the fence.

Swinging didn't pay out today, though. She took a step away from the window.

"I should go."

He looked down when she spoke, noting that she stared at his chest instead of meeting his eyes, and he told himself to keep his mouth shut. To not beg the woman to reconsider. He didn't need more complications in his life.

But his mouth and his brain had apparently disconnected.

"Are you sure?" he asked, and her gaze lifted.

Then she looked at his bedroom.

"I'm sure." She finally brought her gaze back to his, and she sounded far more confident than she appeared. "I *would* like to, though. Don't get me wrong." Apology touched her features. "But I'm not like you, Waylon. I'm no good with casual."

The words stung more than they should. Casual was exactly how he'd allowed himself to be painted. It helped keep people at a distance.

It helped to keep from getting hurt.

He nodded. He wouldn't tell her otherwise. Casual was better.

He stayed where he was as she crossed the room, not trusting himself not to touch her if he followed, but he couldn't keep from saying her name before she could slip out the door.

Blue eyes met his.

"Will you think about it?" His words came out too soft. Too needy.

She licked her lips, and her gaze strayed yet again to the bedroom door. He could see her thoughts warring with each other, while at the same time he did his level best to make sure she saw nothing of his.

And then she surprised him by looking him straight in the eyes.

"I *will* think about it."

~

She *had* thought about it. Then she'd thought about it some more. And again, some more.

Then just to be certain, she'd mulled it one last time.

And now she drove around Red Oak Falls on a gorgeous Texas Saturday evening . . . wearing nothing but a trench coat and her scarlet-red five-inch heels.

What. Was. She. Doing?

You'll be doing Waylon *soon enough.*

"Shut up," she grumbled. But she also grinned at the thought. Because she *would* be doing Waylon soon enough. She may not have ever done anything like this, but that didn't have to mean she couldn't.

She flipped on the signal to take a left, continuing to make absolute certain not to break any driving laws so she wouldn't get pulled over, and headed down the street in front of Waylon's house. Normally he wasn't in town during the weekends, but at the café that morning, she'd overhead a couple of women talking about how they'd seen him at the grocery store late the night before. So after wolfing down her egg-white-and-veggie omelet, she'd *meandered* around town. And sure enough, his truck sat in his driveway.

When she'd checked again three hours later, the truck had still been there.

Granted, he could very well be holed up inside the house with some woman at that very moment. He might have been in there with her all day. But that was a risk she was about to take. Because the man had wanted her yesterday afternoon. In a way she hadn't seen from anyone in a very long time.

Three years to be exact.

She scowled as if the look would shut up the chiding voice inside her head, and without letting herself think about it anymore, she pulled to the curb in front of Waylon's cute little stone house. Whether it was the scariest thing she'd ever done or not, she *was* getting out of her car. She was here, she was practically naked, and she was going to do this.

Because grown women could have all the casual sex they wanted!

Carefully pulling the keys from the ignition so they didn't so much as rattle against each other, she eased out onto the sidewalk in the dark night, and with a gentle nudge, silently closed her car door. She then tiptoed toward his porch. She moved as if on a stealth mission, barely remembering to breathe as she went.

Why she was going about it this way, she didn't know. Maybe just in case she changed her mind at the last minute and wanted to escape without him seeing her?

Or possibly she simply wanted to ensure that no one else on the street realized Waylon was about to receive a visitor. And that the visitor was *her*.

Whatever the reason, she couldn't seem to shake the need to act like a prowler. Her pulse pounded at the base of her throat as she crept onto his porch. A light burned in the empty room to the left, but other than a couple of stacked boxes, a bulging duffel bag, and three gallons of paint, there was no sign of life inside the small home.

Nerves dried her mouth, and after forcing her saliva glands to work, she rubbed her palms down the front of her coat and lifted one hand. Three sharp knocks, and she thought her legs would wobble right out from under her.

What was she doing? She didn't even know *how* to seduce a man.

Waylon doesn't need seducing, you idiot. Just show him what isn't *beneath your trench coat, and your work here is done.*

She nodded. That should be true enough. But it didn't make her any less nervous.

The porch light gave a slight sizzle as it came to life, and Heather held her breath. The door then opened.

She frowned. No one was there.

What the—

Just as she was about to call out to Waylon, a perky voice came from below. "Hello."

Heather almost vomited on Waylon's front porch. Everything about her screamed to retreat. To run. To not look back.

She looked down instead.

And standing two feet in front of her, only coming up to her hips, had to be the cutest little redhead that Heather had ever seen. One pigtail was pulled back farther than the other, and what appeared to be pink paint was streaked across one cheek and into her hair.

And she had Waylon's eyes.

"Hello," Heather made herself say.

The girl's brow puckered as she took in Heather's coat. "Is it raining out there?"

"*Ummm . . .* it's *not* raining." Heather's hands trembled, and as if the nightmare couldn't get any worse, Waylon suddenly appeared behind the girl. He laid one hand on her shoulder, and his gaze *also* took in Heather's coat.

"Heather," he finally mumbled.

The child looked from Waylon to Heather. "Do you know my daddy?"

"I do." Heather tried to nod, but it came out a jerky, lopsided mess. What had she done?

Humiliation engulfed her.

"Her name is Miss Heather," Waylon told the girl. Then he looked back at Heather, and his gaze lowered to her heels. "And it appears as if she's brought me a present."

"A present?" Excitement rang from the girl, and Heather thought she might die on the spot.

The left side of Waylon's mouth quirked up. "A grown-up present," he told the little girl—though he didn't take his eyes off Heather. "One she'll have to wait and give to me later."

"*Oh.*" The news clearly came as a disappointment to the child.

"I'm so sorry," Heather pleaded. Her mouth dried out again, and before she could tell him that she'd just go, he took a step back and opened the door wider.

"Would you like to come in?"

The child's eyes turned bright once again, and her head nodded vigorously, while at the same time, Heather shook hers back and forth almost as rapidly.

"Oh, yes," the girl gushed. "Will you? You'll be our first company at our new house."

"Will you, Heather?" Waylon now seemed barely able to contain his laughter. *"Please."*

"I really should just—" Heather cut off the words at the dejected look on the child's face, and though a hard knot of dread lodged dead center in her chest, she swallowed her fear. "Sure. For just a minute."

In for a penny, in for a pound, she supposed. The damage had already been done.

The girl stepped back to stand by her dad, her spine straightening and her chin lifting as if properly accepting guests. "My name is Rose," she informed Heather. "And you have the most beautifulest shoes in the whole wide world. We're painting my new room. Would you like to come see it?"

Heather managed a polite "I'd love to" and in the next instant found herself trailing father and daughter down a short hall.

Waylon was a dad?

Waylon was a dad!

She had not seen that one coming.

She gulped as she crossed the threshold into what would soon be the pinkest room she'd ever laid eyes on.

"Don't you just love it?" Rose twirled in a circle, her hands lifting above her head with the move. "My daddy picked out the paint, but he's lettin' me help to paint it." She danced around the room on her tiptoes. "And we're gonna buy me a new bed just as soon as we finish."

"We'll buy the bed tomorrow," Waylon's deep voice corrected his daughter. "Tonight we're sleeping in the sleeping bags, remember?"

Rose gasped and whirled back to Heather. "That's right. We're pretend camping tonight. In Daddy's room. Did you want to pretend camp with us?"

"I . . ." Heather blinked several times. *Wow.* "I can't," she told the little girl, "but thank you for inviting me."

She finally allowed herself to look at Waylon again, and though she suspected his laughter still lurked just under the surface, what she found staring back at her were calm brown eyes. What in the heck kind of parallel universe had she stepped into?

"You're a dad," she said. Because nothing else would come out.

"I'm a dad."

"How?"

A hint of a smile reappeared. "Let me take your coat for you, and I'll explain how it works."

Her face heated.

"She said it wasn't raining, Daddy," Rose explained the situation to her father. "So I don't know why she has on a raincoat then."

"I don't know, either," Waylon murmured. "Awfully nice shoes, too. The two go well together." He held out his hand. "What do you say, Heather? Want to get out of that unnecessary coat?"

She was going to kill him.

"I'm good *keeping* my coat on." She narrowed her eyes at him. "And now that I've seen Rose's room, I really should go."

"No!" Rose stopped dancing, and her face fell. "You just got here. Don't you want to stay?"

"I don't want to interrupt your painting," Heather explained. She forced a smile she didn't feel and told herself that this was what she got for thinking she could handle casual sex.

"Maybe you could help us," Rose suggested. "Daddy has more paint brushes."

"I'm sure Miss Heather doesn't want to get paint on her pretty coat," Waylon explained to his daughter. "But she's more than welcome to stay and talk to us while *we* paint." He reached for the roller he'd obviously been using before Heather had shown up, and again, Rose nodded, her eyes shining.

"I think that's an *excellent* idea." Rose grabbed the smaller roller and smacked it into the matching roller pan.

"Careful," Waylon cautioned when pink paint sloshed over the sides.

"I'm sorry, Daddy." Rose's movements slowed, her brow furrowed in concentration, and Heather found herself mesmerized as she watched the little girl slide the roller pad along the ridges of the pan.

A painter's tarp covered the floor of the room, two walls had already been finished, and the remaining walls had been trimmed out at the ceiling and floor. Waylon worked on the third wall, the one adjacent to the door. In several spots of the unpainted areas, there was evidence of holes having been spackled and sanded.

"I can't get it off," Rose grumbled to herself as she continued to struggle with the roller, and instead of leaving like she knew she should, Heather found herself stepping farther into the room.

She squatted beside Rose. "Can I help?"

Waylon's gaze burned into the back of her head. She could feel it as surely as if she'd seen it. But she ignored the man as she gently gripped Rose's hand in hers. She helped the girl to unload some of the excess paint, and stayed where she was when Rose hoisted the roller with both hands and carefully moved to the fourth wall.

"Heather has painted walls before, too," Waylon told his daughter as they both worked. "But her job right now is to create a beautiful garden for her friend to get married in."

Rose gasped at the picture her father painted. "A garden?" Her small face lifted to Heather's. "Will it have fairies in it?"

"I'm not sure it'll have fairies, but there *will* be butterflies."

Rose's eyes widened. "I love butterflies."

"So do I. They're going to be a surprise for my friend."

"What's your friend's name?" Rose had given up on painting, and the roller now hung loosely at her side. Paint dripped, as much onto her jeans and shoes as on the tarp.

"Her name is Jill."

"*Jill,*" Rose dragged the name out. "That's *soooo* beautiful." She looked at her dad. "Don't you think that's a beautiful name, Daddy?"

Waylon nodded with grave seriousness. "Very beautiful. Almost as beautiful as Rose."

Dimples appeared on the younger Peterson, and Heather instantly fell in love. "My dad buys me flower roses sometimes," she informed Heather. "But he says they're not as pretty as me."

"I'm sure he's right. Because I've never seen a flower rose as pretty as you."

The dimples grew deeper, and Rose turned back to painting. "I wish I could see your friend get married. I bet her dress will be very pretty."

Rose's words were followed by a longing sigh, and Heather stood from her stooped position.

"It definitely will be." She made sure not to let her coat part along her thighs as she took a couple of steps away from the spray of paint droplets. "I helped her pick it out. It's white and flowy and makes her look like an angel," Heather shared. "And it has the prettiest sparkly belt I've ever seen."

Rose sighed once again. She continued painting the wall, and again, Heather felt Waylon's eyes on her. She really needed to get out of there. This wasn't the Waylon she thought she knew, and the longer she stuck around, the more he changed right in front of her.

She looked over to tell him that she was definitely leaving, but he'd gone back to painting. So she watched the duo work. Rose was making more of a mess than anything, yet she was giving it her all. Whereas

Waylon . . . Heather held in her own sigh. Waylon's arm extended up-ward with repetitive, strong strokes, and with every reach, she caught a wink of tanned flesh just above the waistband of his jeans. The denim bore a bit of pink itself, and his snug T-shirt accentuated the muscles in his shoulders and back with every move.

Dang. She'd really wanted that casual sex.

"Did you ever get married, Miss Heather?"

Heather jerked her gaze off Waylon and back to his daughter. "I sure haven't."

"Cause if you did, I bet your dress would be pretty, too."

"Oh, it would be," Heather told her. She filled her voice with wonder. "And that's because my dress would have *ruffles* on it. Row after row of pretty, fluffy ruffles. And they would float way out behind me"—she waved her hands out behind her—"and there would be so many of them that fairies would have to come to the wedding and carry the ends of my dress."

Rose giggled at the description, and Waylon caught her eye. "Ever come close?"

Heather stalled, caught off guard at the sudden memories that flooded her, and he followed up his question before she could form a reply.

"When?" he asked.

She licked her lips. How had he known?

She recinched the belt around her waist. "In college."

At least, the *first* time had been while she was in college.

Rose dropped the paint roller at her feet, and her eyes went as round as saucers. "You almost got married?" she asked in a hushed tone. "Did you have a ring?"

Heather nodded. "I did have a ring."

"I *love* rings." The little girl dug into the front pocket of her jeans and produced two toy rings. "Daddy got me this one," she announced as she held up the silver circle with a pink stone in the center of it. "And Papa got me this one." The other one was purple and the "stone" was a small daisy. "But I can't marry my daddy or my papa because they're my daddy and my papa," Rose explained. "I've got to wait until I find a boyfriend."

"There'll be plenty of time for that." Waylon moved to his daughter's side and picked up the discarded roller. "You have to be a kid first," he told Rose, and Rose rolled her eyes as if she were already way beyond her years.

"Daddy, you're so silly. I'm going to get a boyfriend when I go to the big school next year." She picked up Heather's hand and peered at her fingers. "Where's your ring? Is it beautiful?"

A lump threatened to stick in Heather's throat, but she pushed past it. Her exes didn't deserve her regret. "It *was* beautiful," she told Rose. "But I gave it away when we broke up."

A look of pure horror covered the child's face. "I'm *never* gonna give my rings away." She shot her dad a hard look. "You can't break up with me, Daddy. Ever. I want to keep my rings."

"And you will, Rosebud." Waylon blew his daughter a kiss, immediately turning her scowl to a smile, and Heather decided it was time to go.

"I'm going to get out of here." She motioned toward the door without looking in the direction she pointed. "You two will get more done if I go."

"You really don't have to." Waylon was quick to respond.

"I think I do." She gave no other explanation, afraid of what else she might say if she tried to explain. This man was supposed to be an easygoing, laid-back cowboy who flirted with everyone, probably slept with a fair number of them, and made a pastime of conning people out of their money. Yet he was currently barefoot, had pink splatters of paint both on his feet and in his hair . . . and he'd clearly bought a house for his young daughter.

Waylon wiped his hands on the back of his jeans. "Then I'll walk you out." He looked at Rose. "You stay here. I'll be right back."

"But, *Dad.*"

"Here," he repeated.

Heather held out her hand to the girl. "It was very nice to meet you, Miss Rose."

The girl gifted her with dimples again, and primly shook her hand. "And it was nice to meet you, Miss Heather."

Heather stepped from the room, not stopping until she reached the front door, and once there, turned to offer a quick good-bye. Only, Waylon captured the strap of her belt between two fingers. "Can I come see you after I take Rose back tomorrow?"

She shook her head. "I don't think so."

"Why not?" He tugged lightly on the belt. "You came by here. Dressed like this." His voice lowered. "I could even bring dessert."

She fought the whimper that tried to escape. This was *not* how the night was supposed to have gone. "I'm sorry," she whispered. Her insides quivered. "I shouldn't have . . ." Her voice started to shake as well. "I shouldn't be . . ."

"Hey." Waylon dropped her belt and snagged her fingers. She was embarrassed to her core. "Let me come by," he urged softly. His fingers were warm around hers, and his eyes grew serious. "Just to talk."

"There's no need to talk."

"Why not?"

Because she hadn't known he had a daughter!

She didn't say that, though. She didn't say anything, because she wasn't sure what any of this meant. How was she supposed to put the Waylon she'd shown up here to have sex with in the same space as *this* Waylon? It didn't compute.

"*Don't* come over," she finally made herself say. "If you still want to talk later, we'll do it next week."

His look of disappointment surprised her, but he nodded in agreement.

She turned away and shut down her racing thoughts, and moved toward her car as quickly as her heels would allow. She didn't quite manage the barrier of a car door, though, before Waylon's voice called out.

"Thank you for coming over tonight," he said, and Heather made the mistake of glancing back.

Rose had squeezed in beside her dad, her arm wrapped around his thigh. "Thank you for coming over tonight," she mimicked. Then both father and daughter lifted an arm and waved.

Heather returned the wave, unable to squeeze a single syllable past her throat, and slipped into the front seat. She didn't look over at them again as she started the engine, nor when she put the car in gear. And she very likely left a path of rubber lining the street as she squealed away.

Chapter Six

"Trust your friends. Even with the scary stuff."

—Blu Johnson, life lesson #19

"I tried to seduce him." Heather had called an emergency meeting at her house, sending out text messages well before the sun had come up Sunday morning, and though she'd allowed them to wait until dawn to show up, neither Jill nor Trenton had been pleased with the summons.

Her words, however, had them looking up from their coffee cups.

"You tried to seduce who?" Jill asked, while Trenton said, "Didn't I tell you to stay away from him?"

"I *tried* to stay away from him," Heather argued. But she hadn't. Not really. If she had, then her trench coat would never have come into play.

Jill still seemed confused—she'd barely gotten halfway into her first cup of coffee—but Heather watched as she sorted through her thoughts, and she could see when the pieces started to click.

Jill bolted upright in her chair. "Do you mean *Waylon*? You tried to seduce Waylon?"

"Of course she means Waylon. Where have you been?"

"She's been neck-deep in wedding details," Heather replied. "With cameras following her every move."

Jill pointed at Heather. "Yes. That. Cameras, wedding, renovations, ranch stuff. *Retakes.* Good grief, this having-your-own-show thing is exhausting."

"But you're still glad you did it?" Heather's concern for her friend momentarily overrode her own issues.

"Oh, goodness yes." Jill nodded. "I love it. But I'm sorry I've missed whatever has been going on with you." She looked from Trenton then back to Heather. "What *has* been going on with you?"

"Nothing has been going on," Heather answered. "Not really. Just Trenton worrying that I'd do something stupid since your fiancé's new employee looks exactly like my idea of a dream man in a cowboy hat."

Jill's eyes continued to clear. "*Crap.* Of course he's your type. Why didn't that occur to me?"

"And she apparently *did* do something stupid," Trenton added with a smirk. "Otherwise we'd all still be asleep right now."

"But I didn't," Heather corrected. "Well, I didn't go all the way stupid. I tried. But I . . . *it* didn't happen the way I'd planned." A child had thrown a wrench in her plans, and she still wasn't sure how she felt about that. "And anyway," she continued, "I'm blaming Jill for my actions."

Jill—who'd begun slumping over her coffee again—sat upright once more. "What did *I* do?"

"You did *Cal* in the barn."

Jill's mouth fell open at the announcement, and Trenton's smirk shifted from Heather to Jill. "You did Cal in the barn?"

"It's *our* barn," Jill defended.

"But you did him in the middle of the day," Heather exclaimed. She flapped her hands toward her friend. "And you weren't quiet about it at all."

"Well, I didn't know you were listening!" Jill fired back. "And anyway, *why* were you listening?"

"Because Waylon dragged me up to his apartment when we heard Cal unzip his jeans."

"Wait!" Trenton held up both hands, but Jill spoke before she could continue.

"*I* was the one who unzipped his jeans."

"Whatever." Heather blew out a breath. "I still didn't need to hear it."

"And I wish you hadn't."

"Hold on," Trenton tried again. She rose from the kitchen table. "Let me get this straight." She pointed at Jill. "You banged Cal in the barn."

"Yes."

"And you're correct," Trenton continued. "It's your barn. You can ride your fiancé every which way to Sunday in there if you want to."

Jill gave a knowing nod, and Trenton's trigger finger adjusted its aim for Heather.

"And *you* hung around and listened to it? *In* Waylon's apartment?"

"I couldn't help it."

"Right. Because he dragged you up there."

"He *did*." Heather rose along with Trenton. "We were heading to see the horses, and then we heard groaning . . . and then the zipper."

Jill dropped her head into her hands.

"And what? You were so overcome with lust that you turned on the man and attacked him while Jill and Cal were going at it downstairs?"

"No!" Heather crossed to the living room. She'd clearly gone about starting this conversation all wrong, but she hadn't known how else to do it other than just to blurt things out. She turned back to her friends. "Waylon's apartment isn't where I tried to seduce him. We only ate ice cream in there. While we waited on"—she nodded toward Jill—"*them*. And anyway, I wasn't there for very long because Cal was rather . . . fast."

Jill groaned into her hands. "He's not always that fast."

"Well, I would hope not," Heather replied. "Otherwise . . . *Jilly. Honey.*"

Jill's head jerked up. "He's no—"

"Stop," Trenton interrupted. "Cal's staying power isn't the issue here. It's that Heather tried to seduce Waylon."

"Right," Jill agreed. "I know that. I'm just saying that—"

"And if I'm reading her correctly right now"—Trenton spoke over their friend as she kept a shrewd eye cast on Heather—"then she's not yet convinced that she doesn't need to . . . *try* . . . again."

Jill's head swiveled to Heather.

"I'm not saying that," Heather argued. But she wasn't certain she *wasn't* saying it, either.

"Ah, dang it." Jill stood as well. "I see what you mean." She moved so she stood shoulder-to-shoulder with Trenton, and the two of them faced Heather as one.

"I think we need details," Trenton declared. "Because if you were only in his apartment until Cal got off—"

"I got off, too," Jill objected.

"—then *when*, exactly, did you try to seduce him?"

"And how?" Jill added.

"And why didn't it work?"

Both of them looked as curious as they did worried, and the humiliation of the previous evening returned. "I tried last night," Heather muttered. She still couldn't believe she'd gone over there like that. "He'd mentioned that he was moving into his new house this weekend, so I went over to . . . *see* him." She pointed without looking, arm outstretched, toward the coat that now hung by the front door. Then to the red heels sitting directly below it. "Wearing *those*."

Jill and Trenton took in the articles of clothing, and the small house grew unusually quiet. A songbird tweeted from outside as the sun continued to climb—while Heather's mortification level rose right along with it.

"And you wore *only* those?" Trenton finally asked.

Heather nodded, her humiliation complete. It was just like her. See a man, like a man. Stoop to a new low because of a man.

"Oh, sweetie." Jill rushed to her side, and within seconds the three of them were sitting together in the living room. Heather and Jill took the couch, while Trenton perched on a stool she'd pulled over from beside the fireplace. "Okay," Jill said. "Start from the beginning. We're here for you. We'll talk you through this."

"Better yet, we'll talk some sense into you," Trenton interjected. And Heather prayed that was true. Because she needed some sense talked into her. Or maybe knocked into her.

She took a deep breath and began. "The minutes in his apartment had been . . . *electrically charged*, you might say, and though nothing happened while I was there, it was clear that he wanted it to. That *I* wanted it to. The man is"—she puffed out a breath—"*hot.*"

"That's putting it mildly," Jill agreed. "But back up a bit. What's gone on between you two before this?"

"Like I said. Pretty much nothing. We've talked a few times," Heather confessed, glancing at Trenton with guilt. "We're both out at the ranch, so we've seen each other. And he's flirted."

"And I'm guessing that you've flirted right back?" Trenton accused, and Heather reluctantly nodded. Her friends knew her well.

"But I really don't mean to," she stressed. "It just seems to happen."

"Which is exactly why I told you to stay away from him." Trenton's tone softened to concern. "Heather. *Honey . . .*"

"I know," Heather whispered. "But I'm not falling for him. I swear to you. I only went over there for sex. I mean, why can't I have sex if I want to? Other women do it all the time. Casual sex, casual dating"—she shot Trenton a look—"fuck buddies they call up whenever they want to."

"Hey," Trenton protested. "It's not like I have them lined up just waiting for my call."

"Well, it's not like you have to do without, either." Heather turned her gaze back to Jill. "And you. Rolling around in the barn in the middle of the day."

"It was actually against the door."

"I *know!*" Heather shouted in frustration. She could still hear that door rattling in her head. "I was there, remember? It's a wonder the thing is still standing."

Jill cringed in mock apology.

"Your point is valid," Trenton said to Heather. "You're a grown woman. You *should* be able to have sex if you want to. And I'm all for women taking sexual liberties. Sleep with all the men you want. Big men, little men, white men, black men. Heck, I say try out a woman if that's your thing." She reached over and took Heather's hand. "But *our* point is that *none* of that is you."

"And that's okay." Jill laid her hand on top of theirs. "Not all women are cut out to handle that type of relationship."

"But I miss sex." Heather pleaded with her eyes, but even *she* knew that she was saying more than that she missed the physical act. She missed having a man care for her. Touch her.

She missed being in love.

She only wanted what her parents had had. Was that so much to ask?

"And anyway," she went on, "me showing up at his house in a trench coat and stripper heels wasn't even the worst part of it."

Jill sat back on the couch. "What could have possibly made it worse?" And then her mouth dropped open. "Please tell me he wasn't there with another woman."

"I'm surprised he was there at all," Trenton added. "Doesn't he normally leave town for the weekend?"

"That's the rumor. But I think I might have figured out where he's been going all these weeks. And no, he didn't have another woman at his house." Heather looked from one friend to the other, and she thought about Rose's pink bedroom and the two toy rings the girl dug out of her jeans. Then she thought about the Texas cowboy with pink paint splattered all over him. "He was there with his daughter."

Both women froze at Heather's words, and she could read the shock on their faces. They looked pretty much exactly how she'd felt when Rose had opened the door.

"He has a kid?" Trenton was the first to recover.

Heather nodded. "Cute thing, too. Looked to be four or five, red hair, dimples, loved my shoes."

All three of them stared at the shoes.

"Burn the shoes," Trenton demanded.

"And stay away from Waylon," Jill added.

"I know." She hated to admit it, but her friends were probably right. "But guys . . . you didn't see him with her. He's crazy about her. That has to be where he's been going all these weekends, right?"

"Then why not just bring her here?" Jill pointed out.

"To the barn apartment?" Heather questioned as if outraged. The cramped quarters were a nice benefit accompanying the job, she was sure. But the reality was, the place had been bare bones. And if she had a daughter, she wouldn't want her living in the rafters of a barn.

"Why hide her existence at all?" Trenton added. "Why not share with everyone that he's a father instead of allowing stories to be made up about him? Assuming they *are* made up, of course."

"I know that at least one story isn't," Jill confessed. "He definitely has cheated people out of money. I don't know how many or exactly how long ago, but Cal asked around before hiring him. That's why it never occurred to me that you'd be interested. Because—"

"I know," Heather interrupted. *Because she was a sucker for a con man.* She got it. "And that's exactly why I'd never get serious about him. But I just can't sort out the man everyone says he is and the man that I saw last night. It doesn't add up."

"Maybe you don't need to sort it out," Trenton suggested. "Because like you said, you'll never get serious about him."

"Right." She stood and moved to the fireplace. She wanted this thing with him to end right then and there. She'd made a mistake, she wouldn't do it again. And it shouldn't matter that what she'd heard and what she'd seen didn't correlate.

Yet nothing was ever that simple. At least not for her.

She turned back to her friends. "There's still that attraction thing," she admitted. "And trust me. It's *strong*."

Jill nodded, looking as troubled as Heather. "And there's your renewed need for sex."

"I have the solution." Trenton rose with her announcement, her voice climbing in excitement. She turned to Heather. "I'll hook you up with one of *my* friends."

"*Ewww.*" Heather recoiled. "No! I am not sleeping with a guy that you've slept with. *Plus* . . ."

But she bit the inside of her lip instead of expanding on the "plus." Because she didn't want to say it out loud.

"Plus," Trenton said for her, showing what Heather assumed to be only a portion of her disgust. "*Waylon* is the one you want."

"Just for sex," Heather argued.

"Which is now off the table," Trenton stated. She then shook her head when Heather didn't immediately concur. "There's no way you can do casual when a kid is involved, Heather. Don't kid yourself. If you don't nip this thing in the bud, then the next thing you know, you'll be baking for him."

"No, I won't."

"You always do," Jill pointed out. She rose once again to stand united with Trenton. "We watched it with Danny three years ago, and you told us yourself that's how you were with Chris and Dustin. That's how you always are."

"But I don't have to bake." Heather knew she was arguing for a cause she wasn't sure she wanted to take up. Hadn't she already written off sleeping with Waylon at least ten times since Rose had opened that door?

But at the same time, she also couldn't stop herself from still wanting the man. Because now that she *had* opened the door to the idea of having sex again, she *really* wanted sex again.

And if Waylon only got Rose on weekends. Which seemed to be the case . . .

"You'll start showing up to clean his house after that," Trenton mused out loud.

"Doing his laundry while there," Jill added.

"And hey, why not pick him up a little something every time you go shopping?"

"Stop it." Heather's voice raised. "I know." She clenched her fists at her sides. She knew what an idiot she was with men. And she knew the guys stood passively by and allowed her to do it. They broke her heart, they stole from her. And they took a piece of her soul when they left. "I know, okay?" She lowered her voice to a whisper. "I know what I'm like, so don't make fun of me. Because what if even one of those guys had been the one?" What if loving them had righted her world back to what it had been before her parents' deaths? "Would it have been so wrong to do all those things then?"

"Sweetie." Jill crossed the room and wrapped Heather in a hug. "We love how you are. You're the most softhearted, loving person we know. And you so deserve a guy who would return all your goodness right back to you. We're not making fun of you, and you know it. We're only telling you the things you made us promise to remind you of if you started to fall again."

"And especially if you're falling for someone who's questionable," Trenton added.

"But I'm not falling for him," Heather whimpered. "I know the kind of guy he is."

Only, she really wished he wasn't that kind of guy at all.

"And you know that neither of us can truly tell you what to do," Jill went on. She pulled back and looked at Heather. "But be careful, okay? None of us really know anything about him. Cal *does* like him, I'll give you that. He's a hard worker and he knows what he's doing. And that's what you want in a ranch manager. But sweetheart, we've all known plenty of 'good' people who aren't so good *for* us."

"Fine," Heather mumbled, feeling even more dejected than she had the night before. She crossed her arms over her chest. "I won't have sex, okay?"

Dammit.

"But I am going to have to talk to the guy again," she went on. "I showed up at the man's house in a trench coat for crying out loud. He's going to want to talk about that."

"Then talk to him," Trenton told her. "And tell him that you made a mistake. Tell him that you *don't* want sex."

Heather frowned. Because she definitely *did* want sex. But they had valid points.

Waylon was iffy in the morals department to begin with, and for that alone she should steer clear. Also, Waylon had a kid. Which only made him sexier. Therefore, her choice was clear.

She had to say no to Waylon.

～

Waylon barely got his truck stopped in front of the three-story San Antonio home before his back door was wrenched open.

"Grandma," Rose called out. Pure happiness lit her face. "I had the best weekend ever."

"Did you, now?"

Waylon watched in his rearview as Madelyn James unhooked his daughter from her car seat. The sour pinch to Madelyn's face didn't bode well for an easy drop-off.

"I did." Rose started searching for the toys she'd scattered during their hour-long drive. "We got a new house this time and then we painted my room—and it's the most beautifulest pink I've ever seen—and then we went to this huge, huge store and bought me a new bed."

After extending her arms to show how huge the furniture store had been, Rose crawled onto the floor, still gathering toys, and Madelyn turned to meet Waylon's gaze in the rearview. "A house?" Her eyes appeared almost black in the waning light.

Waylon said nothing. He didn't have to answer to this woman about anything.

"Yep," Rose answered from the floor. Her voice was muffled, likely due to her cramming her head up under his seat to look for her sheet of stickers. "You and Papa need to come see it, too," she continued. "It's old, but it's so, so pretty. Not big like yours, though. And it only has one floor. We don't have any steps 'cept the ones to the porch."

"I'm sure it's quite nice." Madelyn plucked the small suitcase off the back seat. "Is that why you're late getting home?"

Rose jerked up from the floorboard at Madelyn's harsh tone, and Waylon opened his door to put an end to the interrogation. He hated when Rose picked up on her grandmother's nastiness. "We're not late." He reached past Madelyn for Rose's seat, and Madelyn skirted back and away from him. "I told you when I picked her up that we wouldn't be back until bedtime."

"Which is *late*," Madelyn reiterated. "She has school tomorrow."

Waylon was well aware of Rose's preschool schedule. Her grandparents had refused to let him attend the first day with her only two weeks before.

"Daddy?" Rose looked from him to her grandmother, and her hesitant voice shattered his heart.

He puckered his lips and blew his daughter a quick kiss. "We're fine, Rosebud. Your grandma was just worried about you, I'm sure. She probably forgot that since I didn't get to pick you up until Saturday morning that I said we'd be back later than normal."

Madelyn made a grunting noise behind him. "It's not my fault her friend wanted a sleepover during *your* time."

But it is your fault you're a bitch.

Waylon kept that thought to himself, though, and helped his daughter gather the remainder of her things. Madelyn headed for the house, apparently satisfied that he truly was going to leave his daughter with them once again, and after Rose climbed into his free arm, he turned for the house to follow. He set the extra car seat beside the garage for Rose's papa to put in his truck, then squeezed his daughter tight as he climbed the steps to the porch. He hated Sunday nights. They were the worst. Some weeks he'd swear he left there with his chest split wide open.

"I'm going to miss you," Rose whispered in his ear.

Pressure built behind his eyes. "Not as much as I'll miss you," he whispered back. Their ritual drop-off whispering soothed his soul as much as it did hers. "But I'll Facetime you every night," he promised. "And I'll see you again in only five days."

She held up one hand, all five fingers splayed. "This many, right?"

"Right." Waylon kissed each of her fingers, wishing nothing would ever cause the uncertainty he could see in his daughter's eyes. "And next weekend I'm going to introduce you to some of my new friends."

Her small mouth turned into an instant grin. "Will we see Miss Heather again?"

Rose had talked about Heather nonstop since the night before. "I'm not sure if we'll see Miss Heather or not, but you might meet her friend. The one who's going to have butterflies at her wedding."

Rose's eyes sparkled. "That would be awesome."

They were at the top of the steps now, but he had yet to put his daughter down. This was getting harder to do.

"You'll see your other grandfather the next time I get you, too."

"Grampa?" The eagerness in her voice made his heart heavy.

"The one and only." His dad was one of his daughter's favorite people. "He's going to be living with us now. That other bedroom is for him. I just have to paint it and get it ready for him this week."

"That'll be fun." She laid her head on his shoulder. "I wish I could help, though."

Her excitement waned, and Waylon made a silent vow that he would get his daughter back. Whatever he had to do, *he* would be the one raising her.

"Is Grampa there now?" Rose asked. He could see matching sadness in her eyes as she peered up at him, her mouth twisted to the side. She didn't want him to go any more than he wanted to. However, Madelyn had returned, and she and her folded arms now stood waiting impatiently in the open doorway.

"He's not there yet"—Waylon ignored Rose's grandmother—"but I talked to him on the phone the other day. He has one more week of working at his job, and then he'll come here to see us." Waylon bounced her in his arms and forced a smile to his face. He couldn't let Rose know how badly this hurt him, or it would make it harder for her. "Do you think we should cook dinner for him his first night there?"

"I do." Rose nodded. "Can we fix him macaroni and cheese?"

"Absolutely. I bet he'd love that."

Marcus, Madelyn's husband, appeared in the doorway beside her, sharing a conspiratorial wink with Rose, and Waylon greeted the other man with a nod. It helped knowing that at least one of Rose's maternal grandparents could remember that these moments *weren't* about the grown-ups. That the root of their disagreements wasn't over who got to have their way.

It was just a shame that Madelyn was the mouthpiece for both of them.

"Hi, Papa." Rose crinkled her nose at her grandfather when he made a silly face at her. She loved both of her maternal grandparents, but as with Waylon's dad, she held extra fondness for Marcus. "Are you taking me to school tomorrow?"

"I sure am, kiddo. Did your dad wear you out good so you'll sleep like a log tonight?"

Rose snickered, and Waylon finally made himself put his daughter down. He never passed her off to either of her grandparents. That felt too much like giving his daughter away. So he set her down, and then he squatted in front of her as he was doing now.

"I love you, Rosebud," he whispered. His hunkered position burned a stake of fire through his bad leg. "And I'll think of you every single night."

"I love you, Daddy," she whispered back. She wrapped her arms around his neck. "And I'll draw you a picture every single day."

After hugging her close, Waylon leaned back and looked at the one person who loved him no matter what. And his guilt threatened to suffocate him. He'd failed her. He had to get her back.

"I'll see you soon," he promised. Then he did as he'd done for far too many weekends. He turned his back, and he walked away from his daughter.

Chapter Seven

"Sometimes 'No' really is the correct answer."

—Blu Johnson, life lesson #52

The smell of a blooming onion hit his senses first—it was one of the appetizers the Buffalo Nickel was known for—with the aroma of beer following at a close second. Waylon stepped inside the back door of the establishment, sidestepping a man headed down the hall to the restroom, then nodded at Callie, one of the servers he'd seen there several times before. He wasn't supposed to come in through the back, and he was hopeful Callie wouldn't rat him out. But he'd been running late and preferred to slip in unobtrusively. The viewing party was already in full swing, and from the sound of things, happy hour had been extended.

"Hey, good-looking. Was wondering if you were going to be here tonight."

Waylon looked down into the eyes of a woman who'd offered to show him her "special tattoo" the first night he'd met her.

"Wouldn't miss it," he told her. "Just had an errand that ran late."

Laughter cackled out from her. "I hope she was a good errand."

The woman patted him on the chest as she moved on past, and Waylon made himself step fully into the room. The place was packed.

The appointment with his lawyer had run late, so he'd already missed the first thirty minutes of the show, and as he scanned the crowd, even though plenty of chatter was happening all around, he noted that most everyone had their eyes on one of the many TVs.

Additionally, he noticed the cameras, which struck him as odd—having cameras there to record the crowd watching what had previously been recorded by cameras. But hey, who was he to complain? He would pull in an extra few thousand by agreeing to be part of *Building a Life*, and until he got his daughter back, every little bit counted.

And then his eyes landed on the woman he was searching for. The woman who'd apparently been avoiding him for the last seventy-two hours.

Heather sat with a couple of other women at a small table not far from the bar, and like the rest of the crowd, her gaze was directed toward a TV. But she did glance at the front door when it opened. A man and a woman came in, and Heather's attention returned to the show. Meanwhile, Waylon's gaze remained on Heather. Though work on the ranch's backyard project hadn't slowed over the last two days, Waylon hadn't caught a single glimpse of the auburn-haired beauty. And though it had taken everything he had not to seek her out, he'd known his patience would pay off. No way would she miss tonight.

Chances were good, though, that she counted on the crowd being too heavy for them to have any real kind of conversation, and she might be right. But he absolutely intended to try. Because the woman had shown up at his house wearing a trench coat—and he suspected little else had been on underneath. And he wasn't about to let that go.

Plus, she'd been nice to his kid. She could have turned tail and run the second Rose had answered the door, but instead she'd come in to see Rose's room. And she'd oohed and aahed over her toy rings.

The entire crowd gasped as one, sitting back in their seats as if in shock, and in the next instant their eyes went wide. So Waylon found a television. Whatever was going on . . .

111

His thoughts came to a screeching halt as he watched Jill Sadler on the screen, demolishing a kitchen with a sledgehammer. And she wasn't just poking at the walls, either.

Hell. No wonder Cal had fallen for the woman.

Waylon cut a glance at Heather and saw her smiling broadly. She watched the TV as if she might not have seen the footage before, yet she grinned with the kind of confidence that he recognized easily. Confidence that said she knew how the scene unfolded, and that the underdog had come out on top.

"I mean, I know how the contest ended and all," someone to the left of him said, "but I'll tell ya, I totally had my money on the girls the whole time."

"The girls *definitely* should have won," another person replied.

"Nah, Cal had it in the bag from the get-go."

As the conversations continued around him, Waylon watched as Cal appeared on-screen with Jill, taunting her as she took a break from swinging the sledgehammer, and he saw what the producers must have picked up on between those two. *Chemistry. Combustible.*

Whatever it was, they certainly had it. And Waylon wanted it.

He turned his attention back to Heather. He had an idea it would be like that with her.

The show cut to a commercial, and he began weaving his way through the crowd. He spoke with a handful of men and women he'd met before tonight, was introduced to several others, and generally felt good about being part of things. This was one of the things that had been missing from his life. The camaraderie in this town. It came across as genuine, and he found himself anxious to introduce his daughter to it. He'd been hesitant to share her existence at first. He'd wanted to make sure the job with Cal worked out, and then had decided to hold off on introducing her until after he'd closed on the house. The last thing he'd wanted was to be seen as an inadequate father, and bringing Rose out to the barn for his weekend visitations hadn't provided the optimum way to present himself. But he had a house now. He could officially start being a part of things.

Heather appeared on the screen, and he stopped in the middle of a throng of people to watch. She wasn't the focus of the scene, yet she was the only thing that captured his attention. It was the way she tilted her head when she was thinking. And how the tips of her hair always curled in as if they wanted to tickle her neck. He could look at her for days.

"Got to watch out for that one," a man beside him said, and Waylon looked over to find a guy half a head taller than himself, several inches wider, and with as much hair on his face as on his head.

"You mean Heather?" Waylon asked. He didn't know how he knew that's who the other man was talking about, but he instinctively tuned in to the fact.

"She'll drive you to drink, if you let her."

"How so?"

The man's mouth curved inside the copper-colored beard. "It's her damned dimples. They'll bring a man to his knees."

Waylon smiled, aware that his own dimples flashed, and watched the guy notice. "I've already had a drink or two thanks to that particular attribute of hers," Waylon confessed, and the big man laughed. "But I'm also not above giving her a taste of her own medicine."

A meaty palm thrust out toward him. "I think I'm going to like you. I'm Len."

~

Heather had laid eyes on Waylon thirty minutes earlier while he was standing on the other side of the bar, but he'd disappeared in the crowd soon after, and she hadn't seen a hint of him since. Nor did she know how or when he'd come into the bar. She'd been watching the door all night, and she'd lay money on the fact that he had *not* walked through the front door. Yet he was definitely in the building. Even if she hadn't seen him, she would have known. Her Waylon radar had been on full alert all evening, and the hair on the back of her neck had stood on end several minutes before she'd finally spotted him.

"Say no to Waylon," she murmured softly. It was the same mantra she'd been repeating to herself for three days now.

"Say no to Waylon."

Only, she knew that her defenses were down. Because no matter how many times she'd gone over it in her head, no matter how embarrassed she remained over how it had all gone down . . . she *still* wanted Waylon.

Sarah and Josie, who'd been sitting with her earlier, had been pulled away into other conversations, and not wanting to occupy a table where multiple people could sit, Heather moved to a vacated stool at the bar. Once there, she ordered a lemon drop martini and kept her gaze on the TV hanging on the opposite side of the bar. She also did her best to pretend that she *wasn't* waiting for Waylon. But she was totally waiting for Waylon.

Her decision to work off-site for the last couple of days had backfired, and now she was even more worked up than she would have been had she just faced him straight on Monday morning. She'd gone to the man's house to have sex. In a trench coat. And she couldn't hide from that fact.

Nor was there any chance he'd let her hide from it.

Yet now she not only had to face her humiliation, but she somehow had to convince Waylon that she'd changed her mind and no longer *wanted* to have the sex she'd shown up at his house to have. Because she *couldn't* have that sex. He had a daughter, and no matter what she told herself, if she slept with him, it would only be a matter of time before she started imagining playing house with him and Rose.

So no sex. And probably it would be best to have no flirting, too.

No Waylon at all.

Say no to Waylon.

Jimmy, the bartender, set her martini in front of her, and as Heather smiled her thanks, a male hand slid into her peripheral vision, two fingers extended to get Jimmy's attention.

Heather's shoulders tensed.

"I'll have a Jim Beam, neat."

She didn't have to look to know the owner of the hand—or the voice. She downed half her martini.

Then the hand inched forward . . . a forearm appeared and rested on the bar top . . . a brick-hard chest pressed firmly against her shoulder . . . and finally, Waylon leaned down and put his lips next to her ear.

"You've been avoiding me, Heather."

She took another gulp and stared at the TV. "I'm still avoiding you, Waylon."

"Any particular reason why?"

She ignored both him *and* his stupid question.

"Ah, come on," he said after several seconds of silence. "Don't be like that. It was a really great move."

He kept his voice low enough not to be overheard, and she appreciated the fact. She didn't need every person there to know that she'd gotten in line to board the Waylon train just like all the rest of the women in town. However, the problem with him talking that low was that in order to speak quietly and still be heard, he had to get right up in her space.

"In fact," he went on, his lips so close that his breath stirred the hair covering her ear, "it was the best move I've seen in a while."

Heat engulfed her, and she finally looked at him. The area where they were sitting was so crowded that he could barely squeeze his arm between her and the guy sitting next to her, and he was leaning in so close that along with his cologne, she got a hefty whiff of his minty toothpaste.

It was the same kind she used.

"You thought that move was great, did you?" From what she'd gathered, people made moves on him all the time. No way was hers the best he'd seen. "I call bullshit. What it was, was clichéd and tacky." She turned her attention back to the TV and muttered, "And one I clearly didn't plan well."

"Doesn't mean you can't try it again."

She choked out a laugh. "Not a chance, cowboy. I burned the coat."

Disappointment filled his voice. "That's a real shame."

It was also a real lie. It was a Burberry trench. No freaking way would she burn it, but she wasn't about to tell him that. Waylon's drink arrived, and Heather found herself sneaking another peek at him.

He'd donned another of his customary plaid button-downs for the evening—rolled up to the elbows, as usual—and had brought out what looked to be his "good" cowboy hat. It also appeared that he'd taken the trimmers to his beard. His entire look implied he'd spiffed himself up for going out for the evening, but what Heather wanted to know was whether he'd spiffed up because he'd been hoping to see her. Or whether this was just part of his regular maintenance routine.

Didn't matter, she reminded herself. Because she was saying no to Waylon.

He took a sip of his bourbon before staring forlornly into the amber liquid. "I really did like that coat."

A smile threatened at his dejected tone, but in the next second, she watched as he recovered quite nicely. He maneuvered more space for himself by leaning into the guy sitting next to her until the man was forced to choose between scooting over or sitting tilted at an angle, and after the guy shifted on his seat, Waylon propped both elbows on the bar. He then gave a nod to two women sitting across from him.

Both women giggled, and Waylon winked. And Heather wanted to elbow the man in the ribs. She couldn't believe he'd sit right there beside her while flirting with two other women!

He turned his attention to the TV she'd been watching, being so casual about it that if anyone were to glance his way, they'd assume he was focused on whatever was happening on the screen instead of on her. Which, in a better frame of mind, she would appreciate. She didn't need his attention on her. Nor did she want others thinking it was. Yet tonight, his avoidance irritated her. So she stared at the TV herself.

She ignored Trenton, who was making no bones about firing a what-the-hell-are-you-doing look her way from the other side of the room, and engrossed herself in the show. And when a commercial came on again, she held her breath. But she didn't have to hold it for long.

"Any chance you'll at least wear the shoes again?" Waylon asked. He still didn't look at her.

"The shoes burned faster than the coat."

That brought a smile to *his* mouth, and as he tilted up his tumbler, she caught his murmured, "Say the word and I'll buy out a shoe store for you." And though she tried to stop her laugh at his comment, she failed. It simply bubbled up and out, as if a pressure valve had been released.

With a hand to her mouth, she chuckled at the fact that she'd tried to seduce the man in the first place—only to find his daughter at the door instead of him. At the way she'd so childishly avoided him for days—only to then look forward to seeing him tonight. And at the "game" they were now both playing.

Only to want to play *another* kind of game entirely.

And then Waylon was looking down at her. And she was looking at him. And damn . . . but she still wanted him. But she still couldn't have him.

"Can we just forget it happened?" Her voice had turned breathy. *"Please?"*

He shook his head, his eyes warm on hers. "Not in a million years."

"Then can we at least not talk about it? I'm still waist-deep in mortification over here."

Though his hand moved as if intending to reach for hers, he stopped before touching her. Both of his elbows remained on the bar, but the fingers of one hand now dangled within reach of hers. "You have nothing to be embarrassed about," he said softly. He ducked his head when she lowered her gaze to the bar top. *"Nothing."* His eyes burned steady on hers. "Because it was fucking *hot*."

The guy on the other side of him glanced over, but Heather ignored him. "I'm sure you've seen better," she muttered dismissively. She really did just want to drop the subject. She might have been brave enough in the moment to show up at Waylon's the way she had, but after three days of tormenting herself over the stupidity of the act, as well as thinking about all the other women who'd likely come before her . . . Well, she truly did suspect he'd seen better. Likely from those who'd actually seduced a man before.

"And I'm sure I haven't." One of Waylon's fingers slid over the back of her hand, its calloused skin a sharp contrast to hers. "But I will agree to let it go if you'll answer two questions."

When she hesitated, their faces closer together than they had been before, he hiked his brow, and she could as good as hear him say that this was the best offer she was going to get. So she conceded. "Fine," she grumbled. She'd known he wouldn't just let it go. "You get two questions. Ask."

He held up one finger. "What was on underneath?"

"Absolutely nothing."

He blinked, not saying another word for an entire minute, and her inner femme fatale smiled in triumph. Some women would probably have whipped out sexy lingerie to wear for a trench-coat seduction, but not her. She'd gone there with one thing in mind, and she hadn't wanted to waste time with lace.

Plus, she'd tossed all her lingerie after she'd learned that Danny Shaver had been cheating on her three years before.

The noise of the crowd lowered, and she glanced back at the television to see that *Texas Dream Home* had resumed, and it was at the part where she, Jill, and Trenton had been interviewed about moving in with Aunt Blu. "You're actually missing a great show," she told Waylon.

"I'm DVRing it. I'll watch it later."

That surprised her. He was going to watch it later?

How sweet.

Or maybe not sweet, her subconscious pointed out. *He might simply be a reality TV junkie.*

True. He could be that. But she didn't think so. With little more than gut to go on, she suspected he would be watching it *because* of her. Which she found she liked a little too much.

Then she remembered that she was supposed to be saying no to Waylon.

"Two." He held up two fingers, and Heather held her breath as she waited for his next question. "Coat or no coat," he said, "do I get a second chance?"

"At what?" She played innocent.

His brow hiked again, and she forced herself to shake her head. Sadly.

"Can I ask why not?"

"That would be question number three, and I only agreed to two."

She waited for him to argue, but the man stayed true to his word. With a slight nod, he acknowledged her point and took another drink. She finished her martini, and as they both watched the television once again, she heard herself asking if *she* could have two questions.

"Anything I want," she clarified. "And you have to answer."

"What do I get for answering?" His eyes were on her again, and try as she might, it was hard to keep the noise of the surrounding crowd in her consciousness. Somehow, just being around Waylon made her feel as if they were alone.

This was bad, and she knew it. She liked him way too much.

"What do you want?" she asked.

He finished off his bourbon as he contemplated his answer, then he looked around the bar, taking in the space as if he hadn't seen it before. Heather scanned the room along with him. The building remained packed. Tables and chairs had been shifted around so they covered the small dance floor, every server employed at The Buffalo had been brought in for the evening and were either on the floor taking orders or at the bar picking up drinks or food, and every last TV was tuned to *Texas Dream Home*. But way in the back were the dartboards, and though that area had been occupied earlier in the evening, it was currently empty. There weren't any TVs back there.

Waylon faced Heather. "You play darts?"

"It's been a while, but"—she shrugged—"yeah." She'd once been very good at darts.

"Can we talk while we throw?"

She liked that he put it as a question. "And you'll answer whatever I ask?"

"Two questions."

"Won't take a lot of darts to get through two questions," she pointed out. She also knew that she had far more than two questions. She wanted to know about Rose. And him. How? When? Why did no one know about his daughter?

"Then give me one game," he said. "And we go from there."

She wasn't sure what he meant by "go from there," but it wasn't as if he was asking for that much. It was darts.

She eyed the television hanging above the bar. She had the show recording at her house as well, so she could definitely step away for a few minutes. And she *did* want to know about Rose. But then she saw that Trenton still had her eye on her. As did Jill. Jill had left Cal's side to sit in the booth with Trenton, and both were watching *her* instead of the TV. Heather stared back, knowing they had only her best interests at heart, but she also knew that she *was* going to walk to the back of the bar with Waylon. There were too many things she wanted to know, and she didn't want to find them out later through the rumor mill.

Knowing she had to do this, she gave her friends a tight smile, hoping to convey that she was fine. That this was *just* a conversation, and that she had *not* changed her mind. She would not be doing anything stupid. She would not be sleeping with Waylon.

Her smile only seemed to put more worry in their eyes. But then, Jill gave a small nod.

Heather rose before she could change her mind, and Waylon followed her. They made their way to the dartboards, not talking as they slipped through the crowd, and when they reached the back, Waylon flagged down the closest server.

He looked at Heather. "Another drink?"

"Please."

Waylon ordered, handed Heather a dart so they could both throw to see who would go first, then he held up one finger, indicating that she should ask her first question.

She threw a dart. It hit the board, but not impressively. "So Rose lives with her mother?"

"Actually, her grandparents. Her mother passed away a couple of years ago."

Heather's breath caught at the unexpected words. "Waylon, I'm so sorry," she whispered. Her chest ached at the thought. Poor Rose.

"Thanks."

"Rose . . ."

"She's fine," he said without her having to ask. His threw his dart, putting it inside the triple score in the wedge for four points, easily beating out hers. "She's a tough kid."

Heather knew from experience that she'd have to be.

She retrieved the two darts, then handed them over to him, and as she did, she noticed lines now etching the corners of his eyes. And though he seemed sad at the loss of Rose's mother—or maybe at the pain his daughter had to live with—he didn't appear overwhelmingly broken. Which made Heather wonder about the woman.

"Were you two together?" she asked.

"We tried to be a long time ago." He threw his first dart. "When Nikki first got pregnant."

There were so many questions that could come from those two sentences. "How did she—"

"My turn," he interrupted, and she paused at his words.

"What do you mean your turn?"

He threw another dart. Both earned a decent score. "My turn to ask questions. Your two are up."

"But I didn't agree to answer more questions."

He threw his third dart. "So you just want to play without speaking?"

Their drinks arrived, and while Waylon chatted with the server, Heather contemplated his question. They didn't have to play in silence. There were things they could talk about. The show that they weren't watching. Ranching. Construction.

The weather.

She downed a couple of swallows of her martini as he went after the darts, then admitted to herself what she'd known when she'd led him back there. They were going to go through far more than two questions.

"Fine." She waved a hand in the air as he returned. "Ask. But then I get two more."

"Of course." He handed her the darts. "Why do you call Blu 'Aunt Blu'?"

That's what he wanted to know? "I don't know." She took another drink, enjoying the tartness of the fresh lemon. "It was just easier, I think. Jill, Trenton, and I showed up, and we had to call her something. She wasn't our mother, and *Ms. Johnson* was too formal. But *Blu* was too informal. So"—she hit a bull's-eye—"she became Aunt Blu."

"And how long have you had a thing for redheaded men?"

Her entire body lurched as her arm came forward for the next toss, but instead of releasing the dart, she spun to face him. "What?"

He grinned. "I met Big Red earlier tonight."

She just stared at him.

"He said it's a thing with you," he went on. Then he scratched the whiskers on his cheek, simulating the sound of sandpaper, and pursed his lips. "So it's the hair, then? And not the Prince Harry thing? Because I have to tell you, for most women it's the Prince Harry thing."

Again, he grinned. And she downed her drink. She was going to kill Len.

"Big Red even said—"

"Stop," she finally interrupted him. "Just shut up. And say goodbye to your new *friend*, because I'm going to kill him."

Waylon laughed at her words. "Something tells me he'd enjoy your attempts."

She shook her head at the idea of the two of them talking about her. She'd seen Len come in earlier in the evening, but every time she'd glanced his way, he'd been busy chatting up one woman or another. She'd totally missed him talking to Waylon.

Turning back to the dartboard, she fired a missile, hoping to wow him with two bull's-eyes in a row, but it dinged off the metal ring and bounced back.

"I'm still waiting on your answer," Waylon pointed out, and though she was no longer looking at him, she could hear the smirk on his face.

She stared at the dart now lying at her feet, trying to figure out how to get out of the moment, and then decided "Why try?" She might as well give the man what he was looking for. So she turned back. And then she looked him over from boots to hat. "I've had a thing for redheaded men my whole life, okay? It's weird, I know. But it's my thing." It was one of the things she'd gotten from her mother. "So there. That knowledge make you happy?"

"You don't know the half of it."

She rolled her eyes at him—and ignored the heat sparking in his. *"Men,"* she grumbled. Then she kicked at the dart. "And I didn't even notice that you look like Prince Harry, by the way."

"Liar."

"I am not."

He stooped to retrieve the dart. "You are," he said as he stood. "And I know this because you suck at lying. Just like when you said you didn't wait for me in the barn. But you did."

"I didn't." She had trouble pulling in air.

"You also said that Big Red was nobody."

Oh, for crying out loud. "He's *not*," she insisted.

"Yet you went out with him once."

Waylon's eyes glinted as he spoke, humor dancing in his dark pupils, and she suddenly realized that they were standing chest to chest. She pushed him away from her. "Stop flirting with me. We're not doing that anymore."

He laughed. "Since when?"

"Since we agreed to forget what happened Saturday night."

His gleeful smile was back. "First of all, *nothing* actually happened Saturday night. If it had, I would remember that for sure. But if you're talking about you and your trench coat . . ." He threw three bull's-eyes in a row. "I already told you. I couldn't forget that in a million years. Not even if I wanted to."

She stared at the darts. Then at him. She was screwed in so many ways.

She motioned for the server to bring her another drink, and Waylon added a request for a plate of nachos, then she climbed onto a stool at a high-top and propped her arms on the table. "My turn. Why have you kept Rose a secret from everyone?"

He sat across from her. "Because it's no one's business until I decide to make it so."

"How many rumors floating around this town are true?"

"Not nearly all of them. Why don't I get a second chance?"

Because she shouldn't have given him a first.

She knew, though, that if time were rolled back, she'd likely do the same thing again. That was her MO, after all. Fall fast and fall hard.

Not that she was falling for Waylon.

"Because, like I told you last week," she answered, "I don't do casual."

"Then what was Saturday night?"

She wanted to be pithy. *Witty*, as he'd called her. But nothing clever came to mind.

Instead, she answered with the truth. "Saturday was a mistake."

His gaze didn't waver, but she could read nothing of his thoughts.

It was her turn, so she forged ahead, ignoring whatever might be going through his mind. Her voice lowered. "How many women in this bar have you slept with?"

Waylon cast his gaze around the room. "None."

He gave no other words and no explanations, and Heather wanted to believe him. *Terribly.* She wanted him to be the dad she'd seen Saturday night, and not the man living in Cal's barn.

But she didn't think she could count on that.

She turned to the crowd, unable to keep from sizing up the women and taking a guess at who he might have slept with, but at the realization that tonight's viewing party had ended—that many of the women he *may* have slept with had already left the bar—her stomach bottomed out. It was easy to say "none" when there were practically none to choose from.

On to the next rumor. "Where did you learn to cheat at poker?"

"Self-taught."

"Do you—"

He pressed a finger to her lips. It was no longer her turn. "Tell me about your parents."

Adrenaline pumped at his words, and she was suddenly ready for the game to be over. She could tell by the trepidation in Waylon's eyes, though, that he wasn't looking to hurt her. He lowered his hand, and Heather went through the pros and cons of continuing their game.

Before she could make up her mind, the server arrived, and by the time she and Waylon were alone again, she'd decided to stay. At least for the moment.

She licked her lips. "That wasn't a question."

"Okay." Waylon picked up a chip. "Then why don't you talk about your parents?"

"Who says I don't?" Hadn't she told him about riding horses with her mom just last week?

"Gut feeling," he answered. "Why don't you?"

"Because I just don't." Her voice went thin.

Waylon nodded as if absorbing her words, and put away a couple more chips. When he spoke again, she had to lean forward to hear him. "You still miss them?"

Her eyes felt too dry. "Terribly."

"I'm sorry."

"Thank you."

She took a drink, her head swimming a little as she tipped the glass back, and she moved on to her turn. She thought about what else she wanted to ask. There were so many things that she *could* ask. That she had a desire to know about. But she had a sense the evening wouldn't provide too many more chances. The game seemed to be wrapping up.

She reached over and helped herself to a bite of nachos, piling on plenty of beans and pico, and thought through the remaining rumors about him. One in particular seemed to be all over the place, and she nodded to herself. She had her next questions.

She looked up at him. "What caused your limp?"

"Broken femur."

She waited, expecting more, but he simply stared back at her. Finally, she graced him with a pointed look. "You've got to give me something other than that."

"You asking another question?"

"No. But I'm saying your answer isn't exactly enlightening." Broken femur had been the one part of the rumors that had remained consistent. Clearly, he'd already shared that fact with others.

"Ask your next question," Waylon said by way of reply, and Heather growled in frustration.

"Fine. But I'll be revisiting the limp one again next time."

Interest lit his eyes. "We get a next time?"

"It's not your turn to ask a question."

She ate another bite of his nachos. Did she want a next time?

She thought she might.

"Why don't you have custody?"

Trenton appeared the instant the words left Heather's mouth, and though Heather glanced up at her friend, she immediately turned back to Waylon. But the man had shut down. The genuineness that had filled his features only seconds before was gone, and in its place was the flirtatious charm she'd seen—and heard about—so many times.

"Ah." He stood from his chair. "The friend, come to rescue the damsel." He stuck out his hand. "Hi. I'm Waylon."

Instead of shaking his hand, Trenton dipped her chin and locked her gaze on his. "And I'm your worst nightmare. The damsel is finished here."

He dropped his arm back to his side. "I'd heard you were the tough one."

Heather snickered at the outraged look that crossed Trenton's face, then quickly straightened when Trenton's brown gaze snapped to hers.

"You've had too much to drink," Trenton announced. "And the party is over. I'm taking you home."

Heather looked at her drink, realizing she'd finished it yet again, and acknowledged that she likely was a wee bit tipsier than she'd realized. She hopped down and stuck out her hand. "Nice chatting with you . . . Mr. Peterson."

His eyes darkened at her formality, and Trenton pulled her away. The night was over.

Chapter Eight

"And sometimes you just need to say 'No'
until you're ready to say 'Yes.'"

—Blu Johnson, life lesson #53

The mid-September sun had been hot that morning, and though Waylon wouldn't want to be anywhere else or doing anything other than exactly what he was doing, he *was* ready for a break. One that included shade and a long guzzle of something cool. He and Dill rode side by side across the north pasture as they made their way back toward the barn.

They skirted a copse of hickory trees, turned east, and Waylon could pick out the barn in the distance. He caught Dill glancing at his watch, and Waylon nudged Beau into a trot.

"What's your first class today?" he asked. Dill was in his first year at Texas Tech.

"Programming." Dill's lanky legs wrapped around Apollo, and if Waylon hadn't known better, he'd think the kid was closer to fifteen than eighteen.

"Are you enjoying it?"

"I like riding a horse better."

Waylon chuckled. "Of course you do. But it's good to stay up on technology." A hot breeze washed over his face, and he wiped away a bead of sweat. "Much of the world relies on it nowadays."

"I know," Dill mumbled in a way that only teenagers seemed able to do. "And I promised my dad I'd give it a try, so I'm showing up every day. But I really just want to do this for a living, so I don't see the point of wasting the time or money on school." He looked around at their surroundings. "I like being outdoors. Knowing I'm contributing."

Waylon liked that part of ranching, too. Plus, it was man's work—running fence, protecting the land. It's what he'd grown up on, and what he intended to do for the rest of his life. But he had once wished he could at least *have* the opportunity for an education.

He glanced at the younger man as they passed the pasture where the cattle had been unloaded that first day. "College is good for you," he told Dill. "Broadens your horizons, teaches you to think."

Keeps you out of trouble, he added silently.

"I already know how to think."

"True. And working here will only give you more experience to draw from." He caught sight of a brown SUV parked near the barn. "But life isn't lived in a day. Or in a year." His gaze traveled to the house's backyard where he could see at least six people busy at work—none of them Heather. "So take the opportunities you're given, and enjoy them. Don't rush things."

Dill grew quiet, and though Waylon wondered if the boy was actually contemplating the words or brushing them off as inconsequential, he didn't look over to find out. Instead, he kept his eyes peeled for a particular auburn-haired woman who had finally given him more than two minutes of her time the night before.

She'd given him several, in fact. And greedy as he was, he wanted more.

Granted, it was the least optimal time for him to be pursuing a woman. He had too much going on in his personal life. Preparing for his custody hearing, doing everything he could to offset Rose's grand-parents' lies, meeting with his social worker to discuss how best to position himself to ensure he got his daughter back. And that didn't even touch on needing to make his house livable before bringing his daughter home full time.

Yet personal busyness or not, he *wanted* more minutes with Heather. He wanted to ask her more questions . . . and he wanted her to ask more of him.

He wanted to matter.

The thought threatened to drag him into a place he'd spent far too much of his life, and he subconsciously gripped the edges of the dark sucking hole and heaved himself out. Whether he was alone in life or not, he would not feel sorry for himself.

He did, however, allow the briefest thought that he'd love, just once, to find himself someone's priority instead of their afterthought.

"Did *you* go?" Dill asked, and Waylon looked over, mentally shak-ing the cobwebs from his mind.

"Did I go where?"

Dill stared at him as if Waylon had physically removed and then misplaced his own head. "To college. That's what we're talking about."

"*Oh.*" Waylon quickly remembered that he'd been trying to impart wisdom upon the kid. "No." He shook his head. "I was too busy get-ting into trouble to be bothered to fill out the entrance applications."

That and the fact it would have been a miracle to pull even a partial scholarship with the grades he'd accumulated.

"Then what do you know about it?"

Dill's question forced Waylon to think about the years leading up to his high school graduation. Mostly about the years between when his dad had left and when *he'd* done the same.

"I know that if I'd had the opportunity for an education, I'd have done a hell of a lot of things differently." At least, he wanted to believe he would have.

Dill stared at him for a moment, no words coming from either of them, and Waylon wondered if anything was getting through. Likely not. There weren't so many years separating the two of them that he didn't remember what it had been like to be eighteen.

"If nothing else," Waylon added, "focus on staying out of trouble. Trouble is no place to be, and it tends to follow you around a heck of a lot longer than *you* want to follow *it*."

Dill nodded as if he seriously meant it.

As they brought the horses into the paddock that connected to the barn, Waylon caught sight of dust trailing a gray four-door pickup. It was a truck he'd seen around town over the past few weeks, and therefore, one he knew the owner of. But what he didn't know was if that owner was there to see her friend . . . or if she'd made the trip special to talk to him. Because something told him she was coming for him.

Their brief introduction the night before had been laced with animosity, and given the protectiveness he'd sensed Trenton held for Heather, he couldn't say that Trenton showing up was at all surprising. Especially given the I'm-watching-you look she'd tossed over her shoulder before disappearing out the door.

He smiled at the memory. He thought he was going to like Trenton.

He also liked that kind of protectiveness.

"What's so funny?" Dill asked. They'd entered the barn and dismounted.

Waylon told the truth. "Just thinking about women."

Dill's face broke into a wide grin, the smile highlighting a lone pimple at the left corner of the kid's mouth. "You thinking about Heather?" he asked.

Heather had come up in conversations with Dill a time or two, and Waylon suspected a bit of a crush had developed in the boy.

"I wasn't," he answered. "But I am now."

He and Dill both turned to look out the open barn doors, where a single female could be seen from their position inside the barn. Her hair was pinned to the top of her head, with dark sunglasses perched just in front of the pile of curls, and Waylon couldn't help but wonder how she always looked so put together on worksites. He'd never seen another person be able to pull that off.

Then he was no longer staring at Heather, but at a long-haired blonde. And he acknowledged that *this* was what most outdoor workers looked like. At least the female ones.

Dusty work boots, worn jeans, and a dark T-shirt, which appeared to have come in second in a battle with a swirling dust cloud, made up Trenton's attire, while her hair was pulled back securely from her face. No curls and no overt femininity. Trenton wasn't a bad looking woman at all, though, no matter how simply she dressed.

Waylon spoke before Trenton could get her mouth open, gracing her with his best grin. "Just the woman I was hoping would visit me."

Dark eyes flashed a warning. "Don't start with me, Peterson."

Somehow, hearing his last name come from Heather's friend didn't do nearly the same thing for him as when the woman herself said it.

Waylon patted Beau on the rump and motioned for Dill to rub the horses down before heading off to school. Then he nodded toward the open space outside the barn. "Should we have this conversation out in the open?"

Trenton turned without another word and headed back the way she'd come. Once outside, Waylon couldn't stop himself from casting a longing glance toward the house's backyard. And what he found—now looking back at him—was Heather.

She wasn't watching Trenton. Or anything else. Only him.

He tipped his hat in acknowledgment, and smiled when she tipped her head in return.

"Rein it in, cowboy." Trenton stood at his side. "She's off-limits to you."

He didn't think that she was.

He forced himself to turn away from Heather, but motioned back toward her with his head. "Have you asked her that?"

Trenton narrowed her eyes. "Let me put it this way. She's emotionally *unavailable*."

"Or do you mean that I am?" Waylon stared at her, his gaze unwavering. It was a valid question, because he was pretty certain no one in town thought there was more to him than a good time and a better hand of poker. Except maybe Heather.

And granted, he'd done nothing to alter that opinion. At least, nothing yet. But he'd be introducing his daughter around soon. And she'd eventually be living there full time.

"Are you implying that you *are* emotionally available?" Trenton's words came out more slowly now, and with careful precision, and Waylon noted that she studied him as if not entirely dismissing the idea that there could be more to him than what everyone thought. He appreciated the attempt.

"I'm not implying anything," he answered. And if he were to imply something, it would be to the woman herself.

But honestly, Heather had him tied up in knots. He was crazy about her, but he didn't know what he wanted to do concerning her. He'd started out flirting, as was his norm. But even in the beginning there'd been more behind his words.

What she did was make him want to dream of a different life.

But could he ever hope she might dream the same concerning him?

He glanced her way one last time, and though she'd gone back to working on what he assumed would be the fire pit area, he didn't miss another quick glance tossed their way.

"You have a kid." Trenton's words pulled him back.

The statement surprised him, but only for a second. Of course Heather would have told her closest friends about Rose. If he still had Nikki around and the situation were reversed, he'd do the same. Nikki had been his best friend. She'd been his life for a large part of it.

"I do have a kid." His respect for Heather's friends inched up. They'd clearly known about his daughter for days, yet same as Heather, they hadn't spread the information around town. That mattered to him.

Trenton nodded as she continued to watch him, then glanced at Heather before saying, "She's got a seriously soft heart." All heat had left her voice, and only undisguised concern shone back at him. "Stay away from her," she said once more, her tone solid and unhesitant. But then she closed her eyes, and her throat moved with a swallow, and Waylon thought the action felt very much like nerves. When she reopened her eyes, though, there was no worry to be found. "And do *not* hurt her. Because if you do"—she tapped her finger to her chest—"you'll be answering to me."

She was back in her truck without giving him the opportunity to reply, and had her vehicle pulling away within seconds. So he turned back to Heather.

And as he watched a stray hunk of hair work its way loose and curl against her neck, he whispered the reply he would have given had Trenton stuck around. "I won't hurt her."

She might hurt him, though.

But even as he steeled himself for potential pain at the hands of the woman down the hill, he couldn't help but wonder who'd hurt *her* in the past.

～

Heather greeted Ollie with the expected apple at the gelding's stall, and after a couple of minutes of murmuring soft words to the horse, she patted him on the nose and told him she'd be right back.

"I have to say hello to the other two," she whispered. "You might be my favorite, but they need my attention, too."

She blew the horse a kiss as if he had any clue what the action meant, then crossed to the other side of the barn to dole out love on

Beau and Apollo. Cal had done well picking out his horse, and though she loved visiting with both stallions, she couldn't help but be more drawn to Ollie. Ollie reminded her of the horse she'd had as child.

The horse that had managed to *escape* the fire.

She rested her forehead against Apollo's cheek as memories tugged. Being around the animals was forcing a lot of thoughts about her parents. Not that she ever *forgot* them, but since a short time after they'd passed, she'd done an excellent job at keeping the heavier moments at bay. Now, however, with the backyard renovation, the horses—and Jill's wedding, most of all—she was finding it difficult to think of anything else.

Difficult not to relive that night.

She patted Apollo before walking away, then she pulled her crossbody lunch bag back to her front and went in search of a bucket. She'd made it a habit to stop in and greet the horses most days, but since the night Waylon had found her in Ollie's stall, rarely had she allowed herself to spend more than a few minutes alone with them. Today, though, she had an overwhelming urge to seek them out. She needed the comfort that horses could bring.

Of course, she'd also like to seek Waylon out. At least spend five minutes with him.

And she knew she shouldn't be thinking along those lines at all, but dang it, she hadn't even caught a glimpse of him in two days. Not since Trenton had warned him off.

Heather frowned as she thought about the morning after the viewing party. Before she'd even taken a seat at the café for their daily breakfast, Trenton and Jill had started in on her. They'd then spent a good twenty minutes harping about how long she'd talked to Waylon at the bar the night before. About how it had looked like "way more" than just clearing the air about the night in question. They'd had the idea that she could say "I made a mistake, I shouldn't have come to your house, and we're not going to be sleeping together" in less than a minute. And they'd clearly thought no game of darts should have been involved.

And yeah, she could have said all that in one minute. In fact, she probably had. But that wasn't all she'd *wanted* to say. And she'd explained that to her friends. The man had a kid. How could they seriously expect her not to ask about Rose?

Of course, she hadn't gotten the answers she'd hoped for due to Trenton interrupting. And Heather appreciated her friends looking out for her. She'd do the same for them. She *had* asked them to be her "guardians of men" in the past, after all. Or more accurately, her "guardians of herself *around* men." And they were doing an excellent job at it. But she did want answers to the three questions that had been repeating in her head for days.

Since Rose's mother was gone, why didn't Waylon have custody?

Did he not realize how special a father-daughter bond could be?

Did he not want that for himself?

She'd give anything to have just one more day with her dad. One hour, even. With both of her parents. She missed them both so much. But if Waylon didn't want that kind of relationship between himself and his daughter . . .

Well, that would certainly mar the Prince Harry hotness he had going on.

She opened the latch on Ollie's gate and carried the bucket in with her. "How about hanging with me for lunch today, big guy? That okay with you?"

She nuzzled the stripe running the length of Ollie's face, and the horse neighed softly. At the sound, the hurt that was permanently implanted inside her heart eased the tiniest amount. Being around horses was almost like being with her mother again. And it definitely made it easier to return to the time *before* her parents had died. Before she knew things she wished she'd never learned.

"I'll take you out for a ride soon," she whispered as she gripped Ollie's head in front of hers. She was almost ready to do it. "It'll be just like old times. Me, you . . . my mom."

A tear slipped from the corner of her eye, and she quickly swatted it away. Then she lowered herself to the overturned bucket. She kept up a running stream of conversation as she started on her lunch, and had only managed to finish a third of her veggie wrap when the hairs on the back of her neck lifted.

Glancing over, another bit of hurt seemed to ease from her heart. Because Waylon stood on the other side of the stall door, arm braced on the railing above his head, with what seemed like understanding staring back at her.

She wasn't exactly sure what he understood—nor what he'd overheard her saying to his horse—and she didn't ask. She was just glad to see him.

She swallowed the bite she'd been chewing. "We have to stop meeting like this."

"No. We don't."

She tried to make herself argue. Or at least feel like she should argue. Trenton and Jill would tell her she should. But instead, she lifted her sandwich. "Lunch time," she offered, though no explanation was needed. "Feel free to pull up a bucket."

Waylon's dimples flashed. "I thought you'd never ask."

He went for another bucket while Heather quickly guzzled half a bottle of water, and within a minute, Waylon returned. The heat of his body simmered next to hers as he settled in at her side, his legs stretching out in front of him, and she found her mouth suddenly too dry to force down another bite.

She picked at the spinach wrap, wondering what to say next. Were they going to flirt again? Or . . .

"I never answered your last question," Waylon said, and Heather looked over, surprised he'd take them right back there. But also thrilled.

"About why you don't have custody?"

He gave a single nod. "Do you still want to know?"

"I do."

She shouldn't. She really, really shouldn't. But she so very much did.

Lines carved the outside of Waylon's mouth and eyes, and he seemed to age ten years. "I'm working on getting custody." He picked up a piece of straw and fidgeted with it. "I have a hearing scheduled for the second week in November, and buying the house, taking this job . . . they weren't *only* things that I wanted to do. Both were intentional with the timing and the location. And are part of proving to the judge that I deserve to have my daughter back."

Back?

Heather swallowed. So he'd had her before?

"I would think a house and job are good." She tried to sound supportive, but her mind reeled with questions. "They show stability." Had he not had a job before? "Both of those things, along with living in Red Oak Falls, should provide a good environment for your daughter."

"Exactly."

Though she said what she felt were the right words, fear bloomed inside her. What could he have possibly done to make a judge decide to take a child from her father? Heather stared at him. She wasn't sure she wanted to know. "Do you think you'll win?" she asked.

"I have to win. She needs me." In the next breath, his cognac-colored eyes went hollow, the sight searing a gaping hole inside Heather. "But do I *think* I will?" He tossed down the piece of straw. "I have absolutely no idea."

Heather had the urge to reach over and touch him, if to do no more than put her hand to his. She wanted to offer comfort because she wasn't sure she'd ever seen a person who needed comfort more.

She *didn't* touch him, though. Because she wasn't sure they had that kind of friendship.

And then it occurred to her that he was sitting there opening his wounds and allowing her a peek inside him. Letting her see his fear of not getting his daughter back.

So she put her hand on his.

Waylon's palm closed over hers, his skin coarser, his touch solid. And he held her hand tight in his for a handful of seconds. Too soon, though, he offered a small smile and a quick nod, and slid his hand away from hers.

"My turn." He plucked her still-uneaten sandwich from her lap and helped himself to a bite. "Tell me about the song." He turned on his bucket to face her. "The one you sing to Ollie."

A soft breath escaped Heather. He had a knack for zeroing in on the important stuff. "It's one my mom used to sing to *our* horses," she answered without letting herself think about it. She stared at Ollie, then she surprised herself by adding, "She'd sing it when she was sad."

As a kid, Heather had never understood what could possibly make her mother so unhappy that she'd sit alone and sing to their horses. But after her parents had died . . .

She wet her lips. After they'd died, she'd often found herself doing the same thing.

Likely for some of the same reasons.

"You know *how* they died," she spoke softly.

"I do." Waylon leaned closer, resting his elbows on his knees. "And Heather, I'm so sorry for your loss. For losing them that way. That must have been horrible."

"It was horrible." She pressed her lips together. Horrible didn't begin to describe it. Then she blurted, "I was home when it happened. I heard my mother's screams."

"Heather . . ."

She kept her gaze glued to Ollie, the back of her nose burning with unshed tears. "They wouldn't let me get to her," she whispered.

She scrunched her shoulder and head together, pulling slightly away when Waylon lifted a hand to reach out to her. She didn't want to be comforted. Not yet. But for some reason, she *did* want to talk about that night. She'd shared the story before—to her counselors, to Jill and Trenton late one night about six months after they'd arrived at Bluebonnet Farms—but ever since, she'd steadfastly refused to broach the subject. Even in her own mind. Yet now . . . With Waylon . . .

The words tumbled out. "I was asleep when the fire started. Mom had gone out to save the horses, and . . . then *Dad* went in. But by the time I woke up . . . by the time I *realized* what was going on just two hundred feet from our back door, the fire department was already there. I ran out in my nightgown, tried to get to her. To them. But an officer held me back."

"I'm glad." Waylon's voice was heavy with emotion. "You didn't need to go in there."

She still didn't look at him. "Neither did she," she forced out, even though her throat threatened to close. "We had two horses, and I loved them both. But they weren't worth my mom's life. I guess she thought she had time to free them. But the fire spread faster than anyone would have thought."

"Hay burns fast."

"Yeah." She finally looked at him, and for a second she didn't see anything but the past. The flames. The screams. "But the fire didn't start where the hay was stored."

"Heather," he said again, and this time she did let him reach for her. He took her hand.

"I know," she said softly. She didn't return the pressure of his touch. "There was still hay in the stalls. The barn was made of wood. The air was dry," she whispered into the space between them. "And she did manage to save one of the horses." She gave him a tremulous smile. "*Mine.* He was wild with fear, but he escaped. I saw him come out." She closed her eyes as she pictured the horse her dad had bought the day she'd been born. "He didn't stop running."

"Did you ever get him back?" Waylon's voice barely registered.

"I never saw him again."

She forced herself to reopen her eyes, but she turned back to Ollie instead of looking at Waylon, and when the horse dipped his head as if to offer comfort, she leaned forward and touched hers to the animal's. Her heart was beating too fast.

"I'm so sorry," Waylon said again. "No one should have to go through that." He threaded his fingers between hers, and this time she did squeeze in return.

"Thank you," she whispered. She blew out a shaky breath.

A moment later she glanced over at Waylon, her head still resting against Ollie's, and realized she felt lighter than she had in years. She hadn't known she'd needed to talk about her parents, but it seemed the day to face old pain.

"I was so mad afterward," she admitted, and Waylon tilted his head as if not understanding.

"At your dad?"

"No." Heather sat up, startled. "Why would you think I was mad at my dad?"

Waylon shook his head. "I don't know. I'm sorry. Something about how you said that your dad went in to help. You paused at first, as if unsure if—"

"I just meant that *she* discovered the fire first," Heather stressed. "That my mother went into the barn first."

"Of course."

"I wasn't mad at my dad," she repeated.

She never wanted to be mad at her dad.

She shook her head in denial. "I loved my dad. I was mad at the *world*. My parents were my everything. We were so happy together. We had a great life."

Her throat went dry, and she lifted her gaze to look beyond Waylon to Beau's stall. She couldn't see the animal from where she sat, but she could hear him in there. Just as she could make out Apollo moving around. She loved horses. She had all her life. But until she'd agreed to do Jill's wedding, she'd struggled with a love-hate relationship with them.

"I've never seen two people more in love," she whispered. She brought her gaze back to Waylon's. "Maybe Jill and Cal. They have that thing. That spark. But my parents"—she swallowed—"they loved each other so much that I don't think they could handle the thought of living without the other. So they . . ."

She shrugged instead of voicing her last two words, leaving Waylon to fill in the space as he saw fit. Then she asked herself if *that's* what she'd been mad at all this time. That her parents had left her.

She let out a dry chuckle at the thought, ignoring Waylon's puzzled expression. Wouldn't her past counselors love to hear that? And it had only taken her sixteen years to figure it out.

Waylon opened his mouth, but she shook her head before he could speak.

"Don't," she pleaded. She was emotionally spent. "That's enough about my parents. You were right before. I rarely discuss them or their deaths, yet here I've sat and said more than I have in years. So, we're dropping that subject. In fact"—she shifted on her bucket, intending to sit, same as him, but there wasn't enough space for both of them—"given that I shared so much when you only asked about a song, I'm declaring your one question equal to two." She smiled, intentionally flashing her dimples. "So, it's now my turn."

He smiled in return—wowing her with his dimples as well. "Sounds fair to me."

Then in one smooth move, he had her turned, his legs widening to accommodate the two of them in the same space, and she ended up with her thighs tucked snugly between his.

Chapter Nine

"Listen to your soul. It'll tell you everything you ever need to know."

—Blu Johnson, life lesson #91

Heather stared down at their legs.

"What's your next question?" Waylon asked.

Her next question?

She forced herself not to drool. How about, how does one get their inner thigh muscles as hard as their outer ones? She couldn't begin to do enough exercises to pull that off.

Struggling to ignore the feel of the man's body, to think of anything *other* than that his thighs were pressed solidly around hers, she ended up focusing on nothing but breathing for the next several seconds. She didn't want Waylon to guess how disruptive his touch was to her thought processes, and she also didn't wish to stop this two-question thing they had going on. Though the last few minutes had delved way deeper than she'd have thought she'd be willing to venture, she found that she enjoyed the game. It seemed to be their thing.

She got herself back under control, and contemplated her next questions. Given the subjects they'd just explored, keeping the conversation light would be ideal. At the same time, there were still too many unknowns she needed answers to. So she crossed her fingers and jumped, and hoped Waylon wouldn't balk.

"How did you lose Rose?" she asked, and he immediately nodded toward his right leg.

"Months of physical therapy, plus an initial hospital stay." The skin over his cheekbones tightened. "So her grandparents took her."

"They *took* her?"

Before he could answer, she held up a hand. "Wait," she said. "That wasn't my next question."

He clasped her hands in his. "I'll give you that one." He glanced at their hands before continuing. "Yes, they took her. I was unconscious in the hospital for several days, and by the time I woke, they'd been called to take care of her. PT lasted for four months, most of it in-house, and I couldn't"—shame colored his eyes—"*care* for my own daughter."

Heather wanted to ask how he'd gotten hurt that badly in the first place, but she'd sensed a wall arriving with his shame. Now wasn't the time to ask for more there.

"You'll get her back," she said instead. No way they could keep her.

Waylon nodded. "I hope so."

She realized his thumbs were now drawing circles on both her palms, and she decided she liked the feel of his hands on hers.

"Next question," Waylon said, and Heather nodded.

"You told me Tuesday night that not all the rumors are true. What's one that isn't?"

He didn't hesitate. "How I spend my weekends."

"Meaning there's no gambling? No women?"

"There's only Rose."

She slid her thumbs along the backs of his pointer fingers. It made her happy to know she'd been right. "I suspected as much. It fits you much better."

His smile was slight, but Heather thought it was also genuine. As if he appreciated knowing she didn't see him as nothing more than a playboy with a gambling problem.

"I have visitation every weekend," he offered. "And until I had my house, it was easier to go to her. I wanted to show—to *prove*—that I'd do anything for my daughter."

"But why let everyone think you're something else?"

His smile turned teasing. "I'm pretty sure that makes about four questions for your one turn, but okay, I'll allow this one more. I let them think whatever they wanted because I couldn't stop them even if I'd tried."

Heather opened her mouth to ask why he felt that way, but he touched a finger to her lips.

"What was it like growing up without a mother?" he asked, and his softly spoken question pushed the air out of Heather. She had to take a couple of deep breaths before replying, because for once, she wasn't thinking about *her* heartache at growing up without a mother.

She was thinking about Rose's.

"It wasn't easy," she told him the truth. "A girl needs a woman around to learn girl things. To share broken hearts. A girl needs a mother because there are just some things no one can understand but another female. But I was lucky in that I *did* have my mom through a lot of my childhood. And even afterward, there was Blu. And Jill, and Trenton. It could have been a lot worse."

It hurt her to think about Rose growing up without a mothering influence, and she wondered what Rose's grandmother was like.

"What did you do after you moved out of Bluebonnet Farms?" Waylon asked.

Heather locked her gaze on his and once again answered honestly. "I made a lot of mistakes."

She knew he was waiting for additional details, but she wasn't ready to give them. She'd been engaged and had had her heart completely shattered twice. She'd gotten a college degree before discovering she didn't want to use it. And she'd eventually come home with her tail tucked between her legs, and *then* she'd almost fallen for the wrong guy yet again.

She wasn't exactly winning at life. She didn't want to go there today.

"My turn," she said instead of sharing details. When he nodded, as if understanding her need not to go there yet, she asked, "Who called you when we were here in the barn two weeks ago?"

Bemusement lined Waylon's brow, and Heather added, "When I was in here taking inventory."

Of course, they both knew she'd not actually been in the barn taking inventory. Her stubbornness refused to cave at the smirk now growing on his face, though.

"Inventory," he muttered around the smirk. *"Right."* He pointed back toward the stall that now held only half the supplies that had been stored there two weeks prior. "Where you were taking it . . . right over there."

"Exactly." Maybe *she* should start playing poker, because the poker face she currently had going on would fool anybody. "You got a call just before I left, and you turned and went up to the apartment."

The humor faded from his eyes. "Ah. Yes. That was my lawyer."

His abruptness surprised her, and she leaned in closer. "You don't like your lawyer?"

"I don't like the Jameses' lawyers," he corrected. "And I have to have *my* lawyer because they have *theirs.*"

"Because they took your daughter."

"And because they're trying to keep her." His jaw hardened. "While pushing *me* completely out of the picture."

Heather sucked in a quick breath. That was so unfair. He'd lost his daughter because he'd been incapacitated by an injury. And granted, she didn't yet know the details of how he'd obtained that injury, but he wasn't a bad guy. Anyone who spent a few minutes with him could see that. And no one should try to take a man's daughter from him unless he was a seriously bad guy.

In a blink, she hated the Jameses.

"Does Rose remember her mother?"

The anguish on Waylon's face threatened to crumple her. "I don't think so. And I can't decide if that makes me happy or sad. Sad because she'll never know her mother."

"And happy because she'll never know the pain of that kind of loss," Heather filled in. She understood that confusion completely.

Waylon squeezed her hands again, and she looked down to where their fingers lay entwined. One of his hands and one of hers rested on each of her knees, and nothing at all felt wrong about the intimacy of it.

"Do you really think coming to my house last Saturday night was a mistake?" Waylon's question brought her gaze back up. His voice had lowered, and as she sat there peering at him, he added, "Because I don't think it was. It might not have ended the way you'd intended—"

"I shouldn't have—"

"—but I was glad to see you at my door. Glad you met Rose."

This surprised her. "You're glad I met Rose?"

He'd previously stated that he didn't introduce Rose to anyone until he decided it was time to make it their business. Yet he was glad *she'd* met her?

He nodded, and Heather nodded with him. "I'm glad I met her, too." She bit her bottom lip. "She seems like a really terrific kid."

"She's the best."

She wanted to ask how Rose had lost her mother and if Rose's mother had been a good person. But it wasn't her turn yet.

Also . . . she wasn't sure she was ready to know the how of it all. It was hard enough to lose a parent. Was she really ready to hear how a small child had come to be without one of hers? Life could sometimes be so cruel.

"So then"—a twinkle began in Waylon's eyes—"you're saying it *wasn't* a mistake to come over?" The attempt to lighten the mood seemed a bit forced, but Heather went with it.

"I'm saying that I'm glad I met Rose. And since I had to come over to your house in order to *meet* her . . ." She let her sentence trail off, but found herself smiling along with Waylon. "What's your next question?" she prodded. She liked this game. "I'm giving you that last one as a freebie."

She mentally braced herself, expecting him to shift back to something tougher, but when he asked, "What's your favorite kind of flower?" her laughter filled the air.

Ollie blew out a breath as she chuckled, and she reached over and patted the animal, who remained close. She'd almost forgotten they were sitting in a stall with a horse. And she'd totally forgotten that she'd originally been in there eating lunch. She glanced at her watch. Whether she was enjoying the game or not, she had to get back to work soon.

"My favorite flower?" She repeated the question as she thought through her options. "I will say, that's not something I've thought too much about over the years. I love all kinds of flowers."

"You've got to have a favorite."

"Sure," she drew the word out as she continued to sort through the possibilities. She'd been given roses several times. Usually yellow because that was her favorite color. Bluebonnets, of course. She loved coneflowers, and she was definitely partial to sunflowers. She had a bed of sunflowers planted at her house. And she enjoyed all of them. But she wasn't sure any could be considered a fav—

She stopped thinking and abruptly sat up.

"I do have a favorite," she announced. "The partridge pea. They grow wild all summer and late into the fall. They were my mother's favorite," she added as she relaxed her spine and dropped her hands back to her thighs. She'd inadvertently pulled loose of Waylon when she'd jerked upright. "You see them all over the place, but Mom had the hardest time getting them to grow in our yard." She laughed softly at the forgotten memory. "I haven't thought about that in years."

"They're yellow," he said. "There was a patch of them on the ranch where my dad worked when I was born."

It didn't pass her notice that he'd just brought up his own past for the first time, and she thought about taking her questions there. She'd like to know about his childhood. About his parents.

But she followed his lead. "What's your favorite cookie?"

A bright smile beamed back at her. "Snickerdoodles."

He recaptured her hands and leaned in, his grin wicked, and Heather's laughter came out a bit strained. He was suddenly too close. And his lips were just a whisper away.

She glanced at his mouth, then she forced herself to drag her gaze upward. She couldn't kiss him. Even if she wanted to. This wasn't a kissing game. It was a get-to-know-you game.

"How did you break your leg?" The question came out throaty and needy. But it also had the effect of putting inches between them.

"My leg?" he repeated as he settled more firmly on his bucket. She instinctively knew he was stalling.

"The reason you walk with a limp," she clarified.

And then he lied to her. It was the first time since meeting him that she truly suspected he wasn't speaking the truth.

"Bar fight," he said with no inflection in his voice. "Flirted with the wrong guy's woman." He even followed up his lie with an out-of-place wink.

"Bullshit."

Waylon lifted his chin. "Bullshit?"

She nodded. "That's what I said. You keep calling me out when I'm 'fudging' the truth." She stared at him. "Such as waiting for you in the barn two weeks ago."

"You did wait for me in the barn."

"I did," she admitted. "Because I think I wanted to get to know you better."

He didn't say anything at that, but she took note of his awareness of the shift in conversation. She'd just admitted her actions were intentional. She'd just admitted this might not be solely a game to her.

Her friends would lock her up if she told them she'd said that.

"So I'm calling you out now," she continued. "Because I don't believe you broke your leg in a fight over a woman."

Waylon didn't immediately reply. Instead, he just continued looking at her. And Heather could see his internal struggle. He didn't want to lie again, but he also didn't want to tell the truth. Which made her want to know even more.

"You're right," he finally admitted. "I didn't get my leg broken in a fight over a woman."

She didn't move. "Are you going to tell me how you *did* get it broken?"

"Or maybe we could each refuse to answer one question?"

She shook her head, and his response was a look of resignation.

"Then how about I promise to answer that one at a later date?"

Heather considered his request. This made the second time he'd delayed discussing what had caused his limp, but she could understand a person needing space to prepare for certain subjects. *She* certainly did. So, she could give him that.

"Deal," she concurred. "But you owe me one." She then nodded his way. "Your turn."

"Which parent do you take after the most?"

Her smile caught her off guard. "My dad," she said softly. She opened her mouth to offer more, to tell him how the two of them not only looked alike, but they'd been so similar in personality, it had often seemed they shared a secret language. Yes, he'd loved her mother enough to run into a fire for her. But it had been he and Heather who could communicate with a look.

She didn't share any of that, though. Not yet. She just held the memories close. Because her dad was the touchiest subject of all for her.

She gave him a faint smile, hoping Waylon could see a bit of what she couldn't yet bring herself to share, and repeated, "I take after my dad."

His eyes softened as if he got it—and then he gave her whiplash with yet another subject change. "If one were to want to fix you an orange chiffon cake . . ."

Heather rolled her eyes. "You've got to let that go."

He grinned as he finished his question. ". . . would you actually *eat* it, or would you be too worried about your"—he lowered his gaze—*"hips?"*

Heather tried her best not to wonder what went through his mind when he looked at her hips. "Like you bake," she chided instead of answering, but the returning gleam in his eyes had her wondering if he actually *could* bake. Because that would be kind of hot.

The next thing she knew, she was picturing him standing in a kitchen, mixing bowl in hand, and an apron tied around his waist. Only, he wore nothing *but* an apron. Then the image shifted and he was presenting her with a perfectly prepared orange chiffon cake. And now *she* wore nothing but an apron.

She gulped. "Not until after Jill's wedding." She reached for her bottle of water. "But if you're such the cook, why eat at The Buffalo every night?"

"Is that your next question?"

She finished her water. "It is."

"Then will you believe me if I say I go to The Buffalo for the scenery?" He followed his question with another wink, and Heather scowled as she finally clued in on something. The man had a tell. How in the world was he even a remotely decent poker player if he couldn't lie without winking?

Before she could call him on it, he sighed.

"Fine. I'm just teasing." He motioned to the stairs. "You saw how small the kitchen is up there. I hated trying to cook in that tiny space. And to be honest"—he lifted one shoulder—"I prefer not to eat alone."

She didn't like eating alone, either. "It's lonely."

"It is. And I like people. I like being *around* people."

"Well then, that should work out fine for you." Her muttered words held a healthy amount of disgust. "Because people—*women*—apparently like you, too."

Waylon smiled broadly at that, and Heather suddenly thought of the women who'd been talking about him in the wedding dress shop two weeks ago. Of the others who supposedly sidled up to him at The Buffalo every night. They might have dined with him with regularity, but they apparently hadn't spent weekends with him. No matter how many might have claimed to.

He retook her hands, and he leaned toward her until she could make out the specks of gold mixed in with the brown of his eyes. "The real question"—his lowered voice created havoc on the surface of her skin—"is do *you* like me?"

"It isn't your turn for a question."

"Because I like *you*."

"Stop it."

He grinned. "Will you go out with me?"

She pulled back at that. He didn't release her, but she sat with her back rod-straight. "It's not your turn to ask the next question," she repeated. Her panic level rose. She should *not* be playing this game.

"When it is my turn, I'll still ask the same question."

She looked at Ollie as if he could save her, but Ollie had decided the two of them held no appeal and was munching on a mouthful of hay. Next, she considered ending things. That would be the smart move. Just get up and walk out. Because she didn't want Waylon to ask her out. She'd have to say no.

Say no to Waylon.

Her eyes snapped back to his. She'd forgotten she was supposed to be repeating that!

"We're just playing a game of questions," she reminded him. "This isn't anything more."

It couldn't be anything more, because if it were . . . if he truly did want to date her . . . then she'd want it, too. And then she'd do everything wrong. And she'd find herself in love without it being returned yet again.

Because this was Waylon. How was she supposed to *not* fall for him if she started dating him?

So she took the game along a route that would keep his faults foremost in her mind. "How long have you played poker?"

Waylon studied her as if guessing her intent, but she stared blankly back at him. She didn't go out with men who could hurt her, and a man with potential gambling issues—and a kid she would no doubt fall for as quickly as she would him—was a man too risky for her.

When he finally answered her question, his tone shifted, same as her intent. "I've been playing since my teens." The smile had disappeared from his face.

"And is that when you learned to cheat?" She swallowed. It wasn't her turn, but she didn't back down.

Nor did Waylon. "Will you go out with me?"

She shook her head before she could change her mind. Her throat had clogged, and words couldn't have made their way out if she'd wanted them to.

"Why *can't* this be more?" He had his thoughts on lockdown, but his gaze remained glued to hers, and it felt as if they were playing a game of chicken. Seeing who would look away first.

Neither of them caved.

"Because like I've already told you," she eked out, "I don't do—"

"Casual," Waylon finished for her. "Right. I'm aware of that." A muscle twitched in his jaw. "But what if—"

"Do you *still* cheat at poker?" Heather's words butted into his. Her heart was racing, and her natural sense of preservation was telling her to make him stop talking. *Now.* Same as it had been screaming for the past several minutes for her to get out of there.

That muscle in his jaw jerked once again. "I do not."

"Or do you just not get caught at it these days?"

She stared hard at him as she voiced the question. She needed to understand this one thing. If he would take other people's money . . . if he had no qualms about who his actions hurt, who was left behind with a broken heart . . .

"I've already answered the question once." Waylon's voice went flat. "Do you really want to waste your second one asking the same thing?"

"Fine." Her voice shook. "Then what did you do when you lived in Vegas?"

"I was a poker dealer."

A very real fear settled inside her. So much that it almost suffocated her. And then she wondered if he'd ever dealt cards for her father.

She shook the question from her mind. Of course he hadn't. Her father had been gone for sixteen years. Waylon wouldn't have been old enough to step foot on a casino floor sixteen years ago.

"Heather," Waylon said her name gently, and she realized she'd looked down at her lap.

She dragged her gaze back to his. "What?"

"I was a *kid* when that all went down, okay? A senior in high school." He spoke as if trying to calm her, when just a minute before he'd seemed upset as well. "And, yes. Those rumors are true. I'll admit that. I totally ripped some people off in the past, and some of them were from right here in Red Oak Falls. There's a reason those particular rumors have been swirling for weeks. Because I was *good* at what I did."

He hadn't taken his eyes off hers. "Counting cards, holding back cards, marking cards. You name the trick—I challenged myself to master it. I even brought Nikki in on my cons on occasion. We worked great as a team. But all of that is my past, Heather." He squeezed her hands, and it occurred to her that he still held them in his. "You need to understand that. It isn't something I'm proud of, but it *was* seven years ago. A lot has changed since I was that person."

She digested his words, wondering if she could believe them. Wondering if she would be stupid to even consider it.

"And in case you missed it," Waylon continued, his head dipping when she tried to look down once again, and a slight smile now touching his mouth. "I just told you how old I am." He added a wink. "Not that I really think it ever mattered."

He was right, it never really mattered. It had just been her attempt at an excuse.

A failed attempt.

"My turn," he announced, and the way his voice dipped suddenly made the air in the stall feel too thick. "What if I'm not asking for casual?"

She'd been struggling to breathe for a while now, and his question didn't help.

Was he really asking for more than that? And if so, would that change anything?

She pulled her hands free. "Can I answer a question with a question?"

"I suppose."

She nodded, the movement her attempt to encourage herself. She had to keep it real. "If not casual, then what exactly *are* you asking for?"

Waylon didn't answer at first, and the longer she waited, the more she wanted to withdraw the question. She tucked her hands under her thighs, her eyes remaining glued to his, and finally, he let out a ragged sigh.

"I don't know," he admitted. And he sounded completely lost. "I just"—he held both hands out, palms up—"don't know. But does that have to be answered right now? I want to go out with you. I *do* know that. I want to get to know you better. I want to spend more time with you."

He gripped the backs of her knees and tugged her closer, and she sucked in a quick breath.

"And I know that I wasn't joking before." His feet locked behind hers. "I like you, Heather. Possibly a lot. But I also understand your concerns. I get that. I haven't always been the most upstanding citizen, and that's hard for some people to take." He studied Ollie before returning his gaze to hers. "But the last thing I'd ever want to do is hurt you."

His words seemed so sincere, but she remained afraid. Because she'd heard those words before—or ones very similar. And she'd made the mistake of believing them.

"I'm not a bad person," Waylon told her.

"But are you a good one?"

"What does your heart say?"

Her heart *hurt*. That was the problem. She gave him a regret-filled smile. "That's the thing. I've been burned too many times in the past. The men I've known hurt me, Waylon. They broke my heart. And I let them do it because I can't see past my own desire for a relationship." It was humbling to admit that out loud. "I date a man, and then I fall. My blinders are thick. And to make matters worse, I have the world's worst judgment in men." Why stop with the humiliation, she thought? "So, no. I wouldn't trust my heart, even if I *wanted* to listen to it."

Waylon opened his mouth to say something else, but she stood and began gathering her things. She had to put a stop to this before she caved. Because she wanted to say yes.

She wanted to believe in him.

And she *wanted* to fall in love.

"I've got to get back to work," she told him. Then she implored him with her eyes. "Can't we just leave this what it is? Us hanging out. Us becoming friends?"

When he didn't immediately reply, she added, *"Please."*

He nodded without hesitation, and rose to stand with her. "Friends," he told her. Then he nodded again. "I like friends."

And though the words coming out of his mouth might not completely match the look in his eyes, Heather chose to believe them. They'd be friends. And that was all.

Chapter Ten

"Don't count on love from others."

—Waylon Peterson, seven years old

As was typical of Rose, she hadn't stopped moving since she'd climbed from her bed that morning. Waylon followed along behind her every few minutes, cleaning up whatever mess she'd left in her wake, while at the same time asking himself *why* he was letting it bother him so much. And it wasn't Rose's scattered toys that were the issue. It was the *reason* he was working so hard to pick up the toys.

"Is it time yet?" Rose asked while bouncing onto the scuffed toes of her pink cowboy boots.

Waylon checked the clock hanging over the recliner. "It's almost time."

"And then we're going to go meet all the new people, right?"

Pleasure expanded inside Waylon. His daughter was a lot like him. She loved meeting new people, and she loved feeling like she belonged in the middle of them. "And then we're going to go meet all the new people," he reaffirmed.

He picked up a doll that hadn't been on the living room floor only two minutes earlier, but before he could get it tucked away in Rose's bedroom, the doorbell rang.

"It's Grampa!" Rose shouted at the top of her lungs, and as had happened the previous weekend when Heather showed up, Rose was at the door, pulling it open before Waylon could remind her that he needed to be with her.

"Rosie," Waylon's dad said as soon as he laid eyes on his granddaughter.

Rose giggled with uninhibited glee. "It's not Rosie, Grampa. It's Rose!" She threw herself against his legs. "And I've missed you so, so much."

Charlie Peterson scooped up his only grandchild. "I've missed you, too, sweet thing."

Waylon watched with only a hint of bitterness as his dad hugged his daughter tight. His father loved Rose. That could never be disputed. Just as Rose was mad about her grandfather. The two of them hadn't seen each other since before Waylon had been put in the hospital, and along with his guilt at losing temporary custody of his daughter, Waylon hated the span of time she'd had to go without seeing his dad.

They'd actually only seen each other in person a handful of times in Rose's four years. A few instances when his dad had traveled either to Vegas or Texas to visit, and several others when Waylon and Rose had gone to him. But the two had talked via video phone since before Rose could speak. And in fact, his dad had been at the hospital the day Rose had come into the world.

Waylon knew that fact should matter even more than it did. His mother hadn't been there, and Rose had been almost three months old before *she'd* made it out from Tennessee.

But childhood hurts were hard things to overcome.

"We're going to meet all the new people today, Grampa. We'll have lunch in town, and then dessert, then we get to walk around the *whole* town and make new friends." Rose scurried out of her grandfather's arms. "I'm going to make ten new friends. Are you ready to go? Daddy said we could go just as soon as you got here."

Waylon reached for his daughter's hand. "How about we show Grampa the new house first?"

Rose's eyes lit up as she first looked up at Waylon and then to her grandfather. "Oh, yes," she said, her tone indicative of royalty having entered the building. "I must show you my room. I helped paint it and set up my new bed and toys, and it's"—she pressed both hands to her cheeks and sighed as if having never been happier—"the most gorgeous bedroom ever."

Rose shot off toward her room before either Waylon or his father could reply, and Waylon looked over at his dad and held out his hand. "Good to see you again."

"Good to be here." He gripped Waylon's hand, and as if they were suddenly back in the middle of his four-month stint of physical therapy, Waylon could think of little more than the fact that his father had been there when he'd first awoken at the hospital. And he'd stayed until he'd once again been able to live on his own.

He reached out and pulled the man in for a hug before talking himself out of it. And he ignored the heavy pounding of his heart. Without his dad, Waylon didn't know how he would have made it through that period of his life, and he certainly didn't think he'd be anywhere close to getting his daughter back.

"It really is good to see you," Waylon repeated. He drew back and took in his father. The man was weathered from so many years of working outdoors, but at only fifty-one, he remained a good-looking man. "And I'll go ahead and apologize now," Waylon added. "Because the bedroom I have for you here is little more than a cracker box."

"Any place with a pillow will do."

Charlie Peterson was a lifelong cowboy who'd grown up on ranches himself. And granted, he'd probably slept in places far worse than the pint-sized third bedroom in the small cottage house. But that didn't stop Waylon from once again wishing he had more to offer.

He took his dad through the single-story home, pointing out the upgrades and renovations planned for down the road, as well as what he'd already managed to accomplish in the last week and a half. Then the two of them spent several minutes in the "Palace of Miss Rose." Finally, they made it to door number three.

His dad's bedroom had a fresh coat of paint, this one more neutral— a pale brown rather than Rose's pink—but even with the new twin bed and mattress set, the freshly painted four-drawer chest, and the antique lamp and side table Waylon had picked up at a yard sale the day before, it remained a poor excuse for a room.

"It looks terrific," his dad announced, and remorse for last week's pettiness punched Waylon in the gut. The man was trying. They both were.

And really, the remaining hard feelings were mostly a long-held grudge, anyway. Waylon had been seven when his dad walked away. Seven when he'd learned it was possible for a parent not to love you as much as you loved them.

He should have gotten over that by now.

An hour later, as Waylon and his dad followed up their meal with coffee at an outdoor table in the middle of town, Rose was already up to seven new friends. Most were adult women who'd fallen for his daughter the second she'd flashed them her dimples, but there were a couple of kids in the mix as well. Rose had never been what anyone would call a wallflower, and her gregariousness was shining now more than ever. She currently rattled nonstop to a dark-haired girl who was not much older than Rose herself, while the girl's mother stood at the girl's side, smiling politely.

Waylon had never met either mother or daughter, and had been grateful to see the wedding ring circling the woman's finger. Several females who'd stopped by earlier, some of whom he'd had dinner with at The Buffalo in prior weeks, had seemed more interested in the fact that he had a child than in the child herself.

"I have a new room," Rose informed the little girl. "And it has bunked beds, so Daddy says I get to have sleepovers." Rose grinned at the other girl, who'd shared that her name was Izzy. "Do you want to come for a sleepover tonight?"

"I . . ." Izzy's mother jerked her gaze from child to child at the out-of-the-blue request from a virtual stranger, and Waylon immediately reached out a hand to slow his daughter's enthusiasm.

"Not this weekend," he told Rose gently. "Grampa just got into town. We're spending time with him this weekend."

The space between Rose's eyebrows puckered. "But I thought he was going to live with us."

"That's correct. He is going to live with us." Waylon looked over the girls' heads to Izzy's mother, offering an apologetic smile at the awkward moment. "But you haven't seen him in a long time."

And I have to take you back to the Jameses' tomorrow night.

Waylon didn't voice his last thought, not anxious to share that Rose's grandparents had custody instead of him, but he could see his daughter's remaining uncertainty about why her new friend couldn't come over.

Before he could form a new argument, Izzy's mother squatted beside the girls. "Your dad is right. You entertain your grandfather this weekend"—the woman pointed across the road to a small park—"but if your dad doesn't mind, I'd be glad to take you and Izzy to play on the swing sets for a while." She looked at Waylon. "You'd be able to see her from here, and I promise to keep an eye on her."

Waylon glanced in the direction the woman pointed. Rose had seen the park when they'd first arrived, and he'd already promised to take her over.

"Can I, Daddy? Please. I promise to listen to Ms. . . ." She paused and looked up at the other woman. "What's your name?"

"Mrs. Davies," the woman said. She reached across the table and shook Waylon's hand before doing the same with his dad. "My first name is Maggie. I'm one of the first-grade teachers here in the county, and my husband is head of the city council."

"Nice to meet you, Maggie. And yes"—he turned to Rose—"you can go play with Izzy. Grampa and I will be over after we finish our coffee."

"Yippee!" Rose and Izzy both shouted, and they headed off with Izzy's mother, but instead of resuming the conversation with his dad, Waylon watched as the older version of himself sat up a little straighter.

Waylon turned, hoping to see what had caught his dad's attention, and found himself eye to eye with Heather. His first thought was that he'd asked her out the day before. And she'd said no.

And that had bothered him far more than he liked.

Then he realized that Heather wasn't who his dad was looking at. It was the woman standing at her side. And if Waylon was reading Blu Johnson's return look correctly, she may just be as intrigued by his dad as Charlie was of her.

Waylon turned back to the table. "Dad—"

But his dad was up and out of his seat, one hand outstretched.

"Charlie Peterson," he announced as Blu came forward and slipped her fingers into his.

Heather glanced quickly at Waylon, surprise in her eyes.

"Blu Johnson." Blu kept her hand in Charlie's for a beat too long. "And you must be Waylon's dad."

Charlie laughed heartily, because there was absolutely no denying the family resemblance. Then he pulled up another chair so the two women could join them and motioned for the server to bring additional coffees. Blu made herself at home, talking as she settled in, explaining who she was and that she owned an all-girls foster home, but Heather hung back. Her gaze traveled to his father for an extended moment before swinging back to Waylon's.

"Where's Rose?" she finally spoke as she lowered into the faded, green plastic chair.

"Who is Rose?" Blu echoed. She wore an expression that was a mixture of politeness, general interest, and genuine intrigue.

"She's my daughter." Waylon watched as the older woman's face registered shock.

A hand went to her chest. "I didn't realize . . ."

She trailed off as she turned to Heather.

"I met her last weekend," Heather shared without making direct eye contact, and though Waylon knew she had to be thinking about just *how* she'd met his daughter, he was impressed to see no hint of pink touching her cheeks.

"She's with me only on weekends for now." Waylon pulled Blu's attention back from Heather. He also used the moment to point out his daughter and her new friend on the other side of the street. "But I'm hopeful that'll soon change."

Blu glanced at Heather again, as if Heather held answers Waylon hadn't been willing to share, but instead of continuing down the path of his single parenthood, Heather adeptly turned the subject to his dad. The four of them talked for several minutes, his dad relaying stories about his years working as both a ranch hand and a ranch manager, even bringing the focus around to the spread where Waylon had spent the first seven years of his life. Rose's great-grandparents' ranch.

"Waylon was born on that piece of land," Waylon's dad proclaimed. He braced his elbows on the table and leaned in as if telling a secret. "We didn't even make it out of the drive before his head appeared. When my boy decides he's ready to do something, there ain't nothing standing in his way."

"Is that right?"

Waylon thought of his and Heather's first conversation, when he'd told her that when he set his mind to something, he tended to get it.

She shifted her gaze to his, as if thinking the same thing.

Blu and his father talked for several more minutes, about nothing in particular, but then Blu braced her own elbows on the table and leaned in, same as his dad. "So how long are you in town for, Mr. Peterson?"

Waylon choked on his coffee at the sound of the not-so-subtle flirting, and tried his best not to compare how Blu had just called his father Mr. Peterson in the same way that Heather called *him* that. He looked at Heather to see if she'd picked up on what was going on right beside them, and found her eyes now on Blu. And tiny wrinkles creasing her forehead.

Yep. She'd picked up on it.

"Call me Charlie," his dad replied, his voice lowering an octave, and Waylon watched in horror as Blu tried it out.

"Charlie." She said the word softly. As if seeing how it felt on her tongue. "Are you here just for the weekend, Charlie?"

Waylon kicked Heather under the table with the toe of his boot, and as his dad explained that he was there for "a good long time," Waylon nodded toward the ice cream stand over by the park.

"Dessert?" His voice was tight with hurry.

"I don't—"

She'd been about to comment on the fact that she didn't need the extra calories, he had *no* doubt, but when Blu giggled at whatever his father said next, Heather's chair was shoved back even faster than his own. He refrained from taking her hand as they hurried across the street, but he did make certain to remain close. It had been barely twenty-four hours since he'd last talked to her, and whether they were just friends or not, it felt as if it had been a month.

He glanced back as they stepped onto the sidewalk, and saw that the other two hadn't even realized they were now alone. Or maybe they'd yet to figure out they hadn't been alone in the first place.

When Heather's gaze followed his, he said, "We seem to have a thing for sharing ice cream whenever two people are . . . you know."

Her gaze shot back to his. "Is that what—"

She fired another look at the table they'd vacated.

"But Aunt Blu doesn't do that," she murmured. She continued to watch. "In the sixteen years I've known her, I've never once seen Blu's head turn for another person."

Waylon had heard the same about the woman. Before tragedy struck, Blu Johnson had once had her own family. A husband, three daughters. All taken out together in a single car accident. A few years later, she'd opened her door to girls who *had* no home, and from what he understood, Blu's commitment since then had been only to her girls.

Not that she was making a new commitment now, Waylon mused.

He looked back across the road. But her head certainly had been turned.

Whatever was happening over there, though, it was none of Waylon's business. He knew that. But absurdly, the notion of his dad coming to town and suddenly being more interested in Blu than, say . . . in *him* . . . lodged a knot in his throat.

He and Heather turned to the ice cream window as one, both in their own thoughts and both silently agreeing to ignore whatever it was going on behind them, and Waylon noted that she didn't even protest when he ordered two waffle cones, each with two scoops.

Chapter Eleven

"Don't be afraid to ask for what you want."

—Blu Johnson, life lesson #86

Heather still couldn't believe Aunt Blu had been flirting with Waylon's dad earlier that day.

Heck, she'd been equally floored just to find out Waylon's dad was in town.

One glance, and there'd been no doubt, though. The man didn't have the close-cropped beard like Waylon, and the copper had begun to fade, making its way toward white, but he'd definitely been Prince Harry, Sr. A spitting image of the younger Peterson.

Therefore, Heather couldn't exactly blame Blu for being entranced. But still. It had been twenty years since she'd lost her family. Why start dating now?

She'd have to bring Jill and Trenton in on this turn of events. The three of them would be getting together at Aunt Blu's the following day due to a new foster girl arriving. They liked to go over and help the girls acclimate. So she'd share the news then. Additionally, maybe by then she could figure out what *she* thought about the idea. She wasn't sure whether she should be happy about this new development or not.

She glanced at Cal and Jill's ranch house as she drove past. There was no sign of either of them at home, but there was a production van sitting in the driveway. No production people, though. She craned her neck to get a better view, but the house seemed locked up tight. Rarely did filming happen on a Saturday, but with the van there, something must be going on.

She kept driving, the silence of the land leaving her feeling more alone than usual, but she didn't let herself falter from her mission. She'd made a decision earlier today. A big one.

After accepting ice cream from Waylon, they'd hung out at the park with Rose and her new friend. And though there hadn't been a lot of conversation between her and Waylon—as if he'd still been a little sore over her turning him down the day before—she had learned that he planned to bring Charlie and Rose out for a horse ride the following day. And at the mention of "her favorite horses," Rose had run over, and her enthusiasm had been contagious. Heather had listened to the girl telling anyone within earshot all about the last time she'd been on a horse, and the more Heather had listened, the more her own desire had grown.

She missed riding. And she *wanted* to ride.

So, she'd decided to take Waylon up on his offer.

She parked at the barn, and as she stepped from the vehicle, she looked toward the backyard. They'd begun on the fire pit that week, and the boulders for the waterfall had been positioned into place, and all in all, things were coming together.

Actually, all in all, things were looking rather terrific. And that was *her* doing.

There'd been no additional setbacks, they were progressing on schedule and remained on target to complete on time, and at breakfast the morning before, Jill and Trenton had not only gushed about how great it was coming together, but they'd pointed out that her confidence in the project seemed to be soaring, as well.

Heather kept her pride in check, though. She wouldn't go so far as to say "soaring." They were still weeks from finishing. Anything could still go wrong.

But she did walk a little straighter these days.

She wasn't half-bad at this. After getting past her initial nerves, the ability to toss out answers or to improvise at the first inkling of a hurdle had come easily. As well as simply seeing the big picture and understanding what elements to add to the design to improve upon it.

Nonetheless, along with her fledgling sense of success, she'd begun to worry over a larger issue. That being, what would come after this job wrapped up. She'd written her position into the show with this project in mind, but the reality was that she hadn't looked too far down the road.

And now that she was looking?

Well, she didn't see a huge call for major landscape design in Red Oak Falls.

Maybe if *Building a Life* eventually got larger?

She turned for the barn. The show might expand down the road. She could possibly talk the producers into seeking out the occasional project that centered more around a backyard than the house reno. That could be fun. But being a regular part of things only to handle general landscaping for weekly renovations wasn't what she wanted.

Entering the barn, she paused a few feet in, her ears picking up on something odd, before it occurred to her that the oddness was the relative silence. Two of the horses weren't in the barn. Moving deeper inside, she confirmed that the remaining horse was Ollie, and wondered if Jill and Cal were shooting on the others somewhere. That would explain the production van.

Or heck, possibly the van was simply parked for the weekend and Jill and Cal had gone out for a romantic ride around the property. They could be on the ranch at that very moment, christening the land, same as they'd done the barn.

She made a face at the thought.

Note to self. Steer clear of any sightings of horses.

She could definitely do that.

Going into the tack room, she grabbed a saddle and headed back to Ollie's stall. She wouldn't make a big deal of this, it was just a horse ride on a beautiful Saturday afternoon. One which would allow her space to think through options for what came next. But halfway to Ollie, her feet stalled. Because it was *not* just a horse ride on a beautiful Saturday afternoon. And she couldn't fool herself into believing it was.

It was *her*. Getting on a horse. And willingly ushering old memories in.

Although she didn't necessarily want to let the past return, she also knew she couldn't avoid it if she mounted a horse.

Ollie poked his head over the door and neighed at her.

"I'll be there in a minute, boy." Heather offered a shaky smile. "Just as soon as I catch my breath again."

A vision of her mother appeared suddenly. Her mother standing in their greenhouse, her dark hair knotted on the top of her head and a trowel poking out of her back pocket. She'd been explaining to Heather the process for creating the hybrid tree sitting on her workbench. The tree had been a surprise for her father's birthday—Heather had been six at the time—and her dad had gushed upon receiving it.

The tree had also burned in the fire. It had been planted just to the left of the barn.

Heather forced out a breath and tucked the memory into a *new* box. One she might *want* to revisit someday. This one was a good memory. Maybe she'd soon pull others out like it and add them to the box as well.

After dragging in one more breath and letting it out slowly, she made her way to Ollie's side. She readied the horse, her focus only on the moment at hand, and used a mounting stool to swing onto his back. And then she was riding again.

She turned for the doors. It would be a *beautiful* horse ride today. On a *glorious* Saturday afternoon.

Sunlight was the first thing to register as she and Ollie stepped from the darker interior, and Heather lifted her face to soak it in. Peace settled inside her, while at the same time, her heart continued to thunder. The quiet of the land now provided comfort. She couldn't explain it, but she knew her mother was with her. In fact, she'd almost swear it had been her mother's idea to come out to the ranch to begin with. Rose might have been the instigator, but Ellen Lindsay had been the voice in Heather's ear.

It had been like that a lot lately. Though she'd long been a daddy's girl, her mother was the one either one step ahead of her or just behind her lately. Always there, always beckoning—and sometimes pushing. Her mother was why Heather was doing Jill's backyard, after all. Why she was finally allowing herself to remember more than the bad.

"I miss you, Mom," she said to the clouds, then she squeezed her thighs and set Ollie into a trot.

They moved across the open land, every hundred feet kicking it up another notch, and as the wind caught in her hair, Heather began to laugh with a joy she hadn't felt in years. She'd missed this. Missed enjoying the beauty of the land. Being with horses.

"I miss you, too, Acer." Acer had been her horse. The one who'd escaped the fire. As a teen, she'd imagined he'd found a magical place after he'd disappeared, one where he could run and roam free.

But deep down, she'd always assumed it had been something quite the opposite.

There'd been no sightings of an injured horse in the area, but then, she also wasn't sure Aunt Blu would have let that information pass on to her if there had been. Not at that time. She'd had too rough a first year. So, when she heard a soft whiny behind her now—one that sounded exactly as Acer's had—she didn't turn. Because for some reason, it made sense that her horse would be with her today as well. Even if only in her mind.

But when she heard what sounded like a brief stampede, she did look back. And she almost lost her grip when the noise spooked Ollie.

"Woah!" She tried to calm the horse as he shot forward, but there was no stopping him. Just as there were no other horses anywhere around.

She looked from side to side as Ollie pounded over the land, searching for the source of the noise, but she saw nothing except a soft breeze whispering across the dried brush.

"Mom?" she asked shakily. And then a lone gallop sounded in the distance. It was probably either Beau or Apollo, but a tear slipped from the corner of her eye just the same. As if it really had been her mother reaching out to her.

Ollie continued to run. His panic subsided, but as his enjoyment of the moment took over, Heather leaned into the movement and let him have the lead. She had no specific place to go, and no hurry to get there. So Ollie—and her mother—could take her wherever they deemed best.

And where they sent her was to the spring she'd heard was on the property.

She pulled back on the reins as the small pool of water came into sight, and she breathed in the smell of freshwater. The spring was connected to one of the many streams winding through the town. It was surrounded by tall oaks and pines and mostly shaded at that time of day, the sun having long since passed over. That's why she didn't notice the lone horse off to the side at first. But then she realized it was Beau.

She pointed Ollie in the other horse's direction, while searching the area for either Jill or Cal. Or a camera crew. And as she dismounted, her concern billowed into fear. She pulled out her cell phone.

Only, the water moved before she could punch Jill's number . . . and then Waylon burst up from beneath.

And he had no clothes on.

Heather's eyes bugged while Waylon froze, his hands in the middle of raking his hair back.

"What are you," she began, but couldn't seem to get either her mouth or her eyes to function properly. She kept looking at him.

At all of him.

Or at all of him that was currently out of the water. Because thankfully, that was only from the waist up.

But still . . . waist up was staggeringly awe-inspiring.

She blinked and tried again. "Why . . ."

But her lips ended up moving silently once more, as if she were a fish out of water.

"How . . ." Her voice trickled to a whisper that time. Then finally her brain engaged, and she whirled, turning her back to Waylon.

She stared in the direction she'd come, her mouth dry and her eyes forgetting to blink, and when the sound of swishing water came from behind her, it was as if she'd been prodded with a live wire.

"Why are you naked?" she shrieked. "Why are you *here*?"

"I had to kill a hog." His voice was as calm as hers was shrill. "And I decided to wash the blood off me before going home."

Kill a hog?

And how was he going to *get* home? His truck wasn't even there.

She almost looked back, confused and simply . . . *flabbergasted* by the whole thing, but she caught herself in time. It registered that the water had quit moving, so that meant Waylon was likely now standing on the bank. In all his glory. Then her gaze landed on his wet clothing, spread out to dry, on a rock not far from her feet. His boots and hat sat innocently beside them.

"Oh, dear Jesus," she muttered. She grabbed the clothes and tossed them over her head. She had to say no to Waylon.

Keeping her eyes staring forward, one question rang loudly through her mind. How on earth was she going to say no to Waylon when he was standing naked right behind her?

Or maybe he wouldn't suggest anything she would have to say no to?

A whimper slipped from her throat as the sound of rustling clothes started, and she squeezed her eyes shut.

She should have called Trenton after having had lunch with him in the barn the day before.

She should have gone *over* to Trenton's after having ice cream with him earlier today.

Or called an emergency meeting! She nodded to herself. That's what she should have done. Because she knew what she was like. And she'd known things were heading into murky territory with him. Hadn't she wanted to say yes when he'd asked her out?

He picked up his jeans.

What she really should have done was admit to Jill and Trenton during one of their daily breakfasts that everything was *not* fine. That she'd been thinking thoughts.

And she absolutely should not be standing there within feet of a half-naked Waylon Peterson, who was now likely pulling his wet jeans up over his long, muscular thighs . . . while eyeing *her* as he did it!

"Two questions," she muttered, and didn't realize she'd said the words out loud until Waylon spoke behind her.

"What did you say?"

She opened her eyes and stared at the sky. "I said two questions. Let's play two-questions."

"Okay." A belt buckle rattled behind her. "Whose turn is it?"

"I have no idea, but I'm going first. Why didn't you tell me your dad was coming to town?"

"Because you didn't ask?"

She frowned at the answer. She'd expected something a little deeper than that.

And she hadn't yet asked because she'd been more focused on Rose.

"So what are you saying? That we're not going to share things unless the other specifically asks?"

The sounds behind her stopped. "Do you want to share things with me, Heather?"

She shook her head. "Never mind." That hadn't been her point, either.

Her point had been that when she and Aunt Blu had come upon Waylon and his dad, it had hurt her feelings to realize that Waylon hadn't mentioned his dad's visit. Even though they'd talked just the day before.

"Forget I said anything," she added. "That wasn't my next question."

"Then what is your question?"

She could tell he'd moved closer.

And his clothes were rustling again.

"What's he doing here?" she blurted out. She didn't really have a question. She just didn't want to think about how close Waylon might be standing to her.

"He's going to be helping me out at the ranch. He's going to live with me. What are you doing riding Ollie?"

She looked at the horse. "Trying to figure out what I want to do with my life."

Once again, all movements ceased. "And what *do* you want to do with your life?"

She shook her head and whispered, "I have no idea."

Nor had she meant to bring that up.

"Do you not like what you're doing now?"

She didn't point out that he'd just asked a third question. Nor did she immediately answer. Instead, she focused on the clouds above her that looked like two hands clasped together, and she pictured her mom and dad as they'd been on their wedding day. A 10x14 of that photo hung on the wall in her living room.

"I have no idea." She gave the same answer, and she also did her best not to wonder if Waylon was going to reach out and touch her. If he might kiss her. "And that's bothered me for a while."

Then she just let herself talk.

"My parents instinctively knew everything about their lives," she explained. "Dad taught horticulture at the college, and Mom was a florist with a knack for making anything grow. They'd both known from an early age that they would somehow be involved with plants. They even met at a nursery." A laugh slipped from her, but there was sadness in the sound. "They both reached for the same prickly pear."

It had been love at first sight for her parents, and dang it, but that had made her believe that kind of love was real for everyone.

"I went to college on their insurance money," she continued when Waylon remained silent. "I got a degree in early education, and I took a job teaching kindergarten."

"I could see you teaching kindergarten."

His voice came from directly behind her now, and she found herself more anxious than worried. Her panic over finding him naked had subsided.

"Me too," she agreed. "Teaching kids felt ideal. But wow, I hated it."

She closed her eyes again, only this time in order to see the past.

"I love kids," she shared. "I'd love to raise a family and have summers off with them. But the funny thing is, I absolutely abhorred teaching. They weren't my children, and there were too many rules and paperwork. I just wanted to see the smile on a child's face when she learned her ABCs. Or when he wrote his name for the first time.

"So I came back home." She should stop talking. She was getting too personal. But like before, her mouth didn't want to function correctly. "And we started Bluebonnet Construction. And I liked it. But honestly, I never really liked the *construction* part of the job. I liked making things pretty, though, and now I get to make Jill's wedding pretty."

She could feel the heat of Waylon's body.

"But I don't know what I want to do after it's finished."

She finally stopped talking and opened her eyes. And then she waited.

"Heather." Waylon's voice had a tight, dangerous quality when he spoke.

She didn't answer.

"Look at me."

She shook her head. She couldn't look at him. She couldn't turn around. She should have gotten back on Ollie and ridden away the second she'd seen him in the water.

Only, she did turn. And she did look.

And though he was now fully dressed, she could see every last desire that she held being reflected right back at her.

He wanted her.

He needed her.

"Can I have one more question?" he asked.

She nodded. She wanted to hear his question.

"Do you know what you want right now?"

She told herself not to answer. That there was still time to walk away. Still time to hold her heart in check.

But at least part of that was a lie.

"I want you," she answered with confidence. She reached up and opened the top three buttons of her shirt. "And I want this."

Waylon's eyes burned hot. "You're sure?"

She finished with the buttons and shrugged out of her shirt. And then she stood in front of him, her white demi-bra on display and her breasts begging for his touch. "I've never been more certain of anything. But it's been a long time, Waylon, since I was even *kissed* by a man."

He reached for her, his calloused hands landing at her waist instead of the few inches higher that she'd hoped. "How long has it been?"

His voice was as rough as his hands, and intoxication threatened to submerge her.

"Three years."

He nodded. "Then I promise to be gentle."

In the next breath, he leaned in. His hands stayed at her waist, his thumbs digging slightly into the flesh of her stomach, and the only other part of him that touched her was his mouth. But with barely a brush of his lips, he pulled a moan out of her.

She leaned forward when he didn't press for more, this time her seeking him out. And when he resettled his mouth over hers, his lips were full and warm and soft. And they made her heart beat too fast. Then they began to move against hers. *Slowly.* And she almost cried out at the agony of it. The man was like a drug she couldn't get enough of.

The kiss continued as it had started, slow and mesmerizing, and it lasted for an eternity. Waylon would barely touch her, then pull back. Then retouch. Then nibble.

He tasted of water and sunshine and need, and Heather thought she might die at his feet if he didn't hurry up and take more. She was standing there with no shirt on, dammit. Take her! But then it occurred to her that *she* could do the asking. *She* could take charge of the moment.

So she did.

"Waylon." Her lips moved against his.

"What?" The whiskers lining his upper lip tickled, and she licked her top lip as she savored the taste of him.

"Not *that* gentle."

He smiled against her mouth, and her hands reached for his belt buckle.

"It might have been a while," she assured him, "but trust me. I'm suddenly all caught up."

In the next breath, Waylon's hands were everywhere. His mouth returned to hers and his fingers dragged her bra straps over her shoulders, and then her breasts poured into his hands. They groaned together as he cupped her, his fingers squeezing as if she were the best thing he could ever have in his hands, and then Heather remembered where *her* hands were. She got busy on the buckle, undoing it as he trailed his mouth to her ear. The button of his jeans followed. Next, he tugged at her hair while scraping his teeth down over her neck, and when he dipped his head and sucked a nipple into his mouth, she yanked at the still-wet denim.

"Faster," she panted. She appreciated foreplay as much as the next woman, but five minutes earlier, she'd seen this man naked. And she wanted him naked again. "I need flesh," she growled out. "I need *you*."

Her bra hit the ground, her jeans reached her ankles. "And I need *you*," he replied.

He palmed her rear and pulled her up, flush with his body, and she got her first solid feel of what lay beneath.

"Ah, geez," she whispered. She dangled in the air, and she almost came right then. "Hurry," she pleaded. Her body vibrated in his arms.

Another whimper escaped when he dragged her higher, his damp clothing catching and pulling against her now-sensitive skin, and caught a nipple between his teeth. And as her body bowed tight, her need for him reached a fever pitch.

In the next instant, she was back on the ground and his clothes were being ripped from his body. Heather caught her breath as she watched. The man in motion was a sight to behold. Muscles stretched and flexed, parts were exposed—with one standing impressively at attention—and only after his jeans caught at his boots did she remember that she had to free her legs as well. She kicked out of her boots, panties following jeans, and then she was back in Waylon's arms.

Ten seconds after that . . . Waylon was in *her*.

~

Waylon hadn't even recovered his breathing when it occurred to him what they'd done. He looked over at Heather, who now lay flat on her back on the shirt he'd spread on the ground for her, and traced his eyes down over her curves. She was gorgeous. She was all he'd imagined she would be.

But he could not believe what he'd forgotten.

As if sensing his review of her, Heather turned, her eyes languid with lingering desire and a soft smile curving her lips. But she apparently read the worry in him, and she shoved up.

"I swear to all that's holy, Waylon Peterson. If you're going to lie there and tell me this was a mistake. That you regret it"—she pointed a finger at him—"while we're both still sweating and out of breath . . . then *I'm* going to turn Trenton loose on you."

He captured her finger. "It definitely was no mistake." And he had no idea how she could imagine he might think that it was.

"Then you just regret it?"

"Hell, no, I don't regret it." He pushed up to sit beside her and reached for his jeans, and when she scrambled for her own clothes, he stopped her with a hand.

He shook his head when she glared at him, and he could see her uncertainty tucked behind her bravado. The look caused a spot deep inside of him to ache. She'd said she'd been hurt before. More than once. And it destroyed him to think she worried about that with him.

"I regret nothing," he stressed softly. He pulled his wallet from the back pocket of his jeans and tugged out the condom tucked securely behind his emergency one-hundred-dollar bill. "But we did forget something."

The air seeped out of her. "That's all this is about?"

"All it's about?" He literally gaped at the woman. "Sweetheart, an unexpected pregnancy isn't a small thing to me. I would never wish Rose away, but I've already done the accidental thing once, and I'd prefer not to repeat it."

"But I'm not going to get pregnant."

He curled his fingers around the prophylactic. "And how do you know that?"

She grabbed her shirt, and slid her arms into it. Sans bra. "Because I'm as regular as clockwork."

"You can't know—"

She stopped him with a hand in the air. "Trust me, I do. I've had seventeen years of this. Like. Clockwork." She looked at her watch. "It's Saturday now. The twenty-third. Come Tuesday, probably at around two in the afternoon"—she looked back at him—"I'll have your proof."

"But—"

"No buts," she interrupted him again. "The bigger question should be mine." She looked at the hand holding the condom, and concern tightened her jaw. "I mean"—she chewed on the inside of her cheek—"there *is* the question of diseases."

"You mean me?"

"Well, I don't mean me," she snapped at him. "I just told you that I haven't been with a man in three years."

"Well, if I can trust you about a lack of pregnancy, then believe me, you can rest assured that I don't have a disease." He shook his head. "I don't sleep around, Heather. Not like people want to believe."

"Yet you *are* carrying a condom."

He wanted to laugh at the absurdity of the conversation. Carrying a condom in his wallet had been a rite of passage as a teen, and he supposed he'd never grown out of it.

He handed over the packet. "Check the expiration date."

The corners of Heather's mouth turned down as she snatched the condom from his hand. She held it up and squinted at the faded date. And then Waylon did laugh at the incredulity that filled her face.

"It's over two years old," she said.

"Yeah. And I purchased it well before that." He took back the packet and shoved it in his jeans. "You're not the only one it's been a long time for."

"But . . ." She frowned at him. "How?"

"How?" He barked out a laugh and stood to gather the rest of their clothing. "I just don't. Being a single dad doesn't leave a lot of time for such things."

She followed him up, stepping into her panties as he handed them over. "But you only have Rose on the weekends."

Waylon stopped, one arm in the sleeve of his shirt, before letting the material drop back to the ground. He reached for her hands, then he allowed her to see the sincerity inside him. "It was just me and Rose for a long time. A lot longer than the years Nikki has been dead. And yes, I do only have Rose on the weekends. For now. But nothing is a higher priority than getting my daughter back."

A voice in the back of his head suggested that Heather could be a priority as well. If she was willing to make *him* one.

"So we're good." He nodded encouragingly. "As soon as we see what Tuesday brings. And if it'll make you feel better, I can provide proof concerning me. After the last time I was with someone, I got tested. Because yeah, before Rose?" He twisted his mouth to the side. "I *did* sleep around. Too much." He'd once done a lot of things he hadn't been proud of. And though he wished he could say that all the moments for which he felt shame had come before Rose, that also wasn't his reality. "I'm not that man anymore, Heather. And you can trust me when I tell you that a sexually transmitted disease is the last concern you should have with me."

She studied him as if testing the weight of his words. Then she disentangled their hands and picked up her jeans.

"Then, I guess we're good." She stepped into the denim, and with one quick move, the lusciousness of her lower body was covered. She then plucked her bra from his outstretched hand and shoved it into the back pocket of her jeans. "We'll talk on Tuesday."

Chapter Twelve

"Naked experiences can sometimes be the best—
whether physical or emotional. Enjoy them fully and for
what they are . . . but don't forget to put your clothes back
on when finished."

—Blu Johnson, life lesson #70

"I slept with him."

Jill and Trenton, who'd both started up the steps to Aunt Blu's front porch, froze at Heather's words. Then both of them were staring at her.

"You slept with him?" Trenton questioned, and Heather nodded.

"But I didn't mean to."

"You didn't—" Trenton bit off her words, and her hands turned to fists. "I swear, I'm going to kill him."

She started back toward her truck, and Heather had to run after her to catch up. "No, you're not! He didn't do anything wrong."

Her younger foster sister glared down at her, fury on her face. Trenton wasn't especially tall, but at five feet two, Heather looked *up* to most people. "You don't think him sleeping with you when you didn't want to was wrong?" Trenton asked.

"But I *did* want to."

Trenton took a step back, confusion now mixing with the anger. "Yet you didn't *mean* to?"

Heather groaned. She messed this conversation up, same as she had the last time. "I don't mean *that*. He didn't do anything wrong. I was an active participant. I just meant that sex hadn't been on my mind before it happened."

Which was a bold-faced lie. But she *could* say that it hadn't been her *intent* when she'd gotten on the horse.

"Do you want to start all over with your story?" A muscle twitched in Trenton's jaw, as if she was consciously working to loosen it. One thing that could immediately set Trenton off was if she thought a woman had been victimized.

"Can I ask something first?" Jill slipped the question in, and they both turned to look at her. Jill remained where she'd been on the steps.

"What?" Trenton said, and Jill looked over at Heather.

"How was it?"

"Jill!"

"What?" Jill turned to Trenton. "You know we have to ask. Look at her." She flung an arm out toward Heather. "She might have screwed up how she started this story, but she's standing there with need written all over her, Trenton. She needs *us*. She *needs* to talk about it. Hell, she's going to chew her bottom lip off if she doesn't get to spill her guts. So we can point out all the reasons she shouldn't be doing it afterward, but right now, what's done is done. And she needs to share what she did."

Heather hadn't really thought too much about that part of it. She'd been more fixated on admitting to her friends what she *had* done. But she absolutely needed to talk about it. Because it had been *good*.

Fast, but still good.

"Fine," Trenton grumbled. "How was it?"

Heather let herself smile for the first time since climbing back onto Ollie the day before. "Where should I begin?" She knew the color of her cheeks gave away everything. "With the fact that what instigated it was seeing him naked?"

Jill eyed her carefully.

"Or should I begin with the fact that he was naked . . . in *water*?"

Even Trenton paused at that.

"Naked?" Jill gulped.

"And what was *that* like?" Trenton added, and the three of them laughed together for what seemed like the first time in weeks. It was good being able to just be "girls" with her friends.

"What was that like?" Heather repeated. She set the square cookie tin she'd brought with her on the steps then waved both hands in front of her face as if fanning herself. "Honey, I should have been charged a cover for what I got to see. I mean"—she pictured the man as he'd first come up out of the water—"that man is *ripped*."

He'd also had a handful of small scars along one side of his ribs, as well as a small round one on his left hip. All of which she *hadn't* asked about.

"What was he doing in water?" Trenton clearly needed more details to paint the picture.

"And what water?"

Heather grinned at Jill's question. "Water that's on *your* property," she answered, and without anyone suggesting it, all three of them moved to the steps and sat side by side. They crouched in closer so if anyone opened the door behind them, they could talk without being overheard.

"There's a spring out on the south pasture," Heather explained. "You know, where the stream connects up with the ranch?"

Jill nodded, and Heather continued. "And I had no clue that Waylon was even on the property."

"What were you doing out there?" Trenton asked.

"I wanted to ride a horse."

Both women took her hand at the soft admission.

"It's been a long time," Heather went on. "And just being around them so much again"—she shrugged—"I don't know. It's kind of bringing everything back up. My parents' deaths. Riding with Mom."

"I'm sorry." Jill patted Heather's hand.

"Don't be sorry. I think it's time. I mean, there were horses out here when we lived with Aunt Blu. It's not like I haven't been on one since. But I sometimes think I shut down too much back then." She looked from friend to friend, letting herself picture the house she'd lived in for the first fourteen years of her life. She hadn't seen that house since the night of the fire. "My parents were dead. One horse died with them. *My* horse disappeared into nothing. And I had to figure out a new life for myself."

She paused as she thought about the fact that she was still figuring out a new life.

"I'm just saying," she continued, "that for some reason, I feel my mom reaching out to me lately. In a way I never have before."

"What about your dad?" Trenton asked, worry clear in her eyes. "I know you've said you were always a daddy's girl, but even back then, what little you talked about things, you never talked about him."

Heather studied her friend. Was that true?

"I *was* a daddy's girl," she insisted. "I hung on his every word, and I have so many early memories of tagging along with him, either at the house or around town. Even sitting at his desk as he taught classes. And that's not to take anything away from my mom. We had our things, too. Plenty of them," she defended, even though no one said otherwise.

"You loved them both," Jill acknowledged. "We know that. We're not suggesting differently. But Trenton is right. You've never talked much about your dad, and we've always wondered why."

Heather leaned against the step behind her. "You've talked about me like that?"

They both nodded, but Trenton was the one to answer. "Of course we have. Because we love you. And we worry about you."

"You don't have to worry about me. I'm fine."

They patted her hands.

"But we can if we want to." Jill's words broke the tense moment, and Trenton nudged her chin toward Heather. "So back to Waylon and his naked body."

Heather chuckled, the noise free and light. "I swear, Tree, I think you need to get laid as badly as I did."

Trenton snorted. "Oh, there's no doubt about that. It's not been three years for me, but even at three months, a girl gets an itch."

They all laughed together, then Jill and Trenton joined Heather by taking up her same position of elbows on the step behind them, and as one, they lifted their faces to the blue of the sky. The day was beautiful, with just the right amount of wind dancing along the air. Heather was going to miss moments like this. They'd already started to be fewer and farther between, what with Jill's engagement and the constant flutter of activity surrounding the new television show, but as a group, the three of them subconsciously seemed to be trying to hold on as long as they could.

Without saying anything, Heather held one hand out in front of her. Trenton laid hers over Heather's, and then Jill finished the stack.

Heather looked from foster sister to foster sister. "Friends forever?"

"And ever and ever," Trenton added.

As one, they dipped their hands as a football team might do in a huddle and declared, *"Friends forever."*

It was a move from their early years, when it had been only the three of them at Bluebonnet Farms. They'd formed a club called The Three, and though each of them had spent years apart after they'd turned eighteen, each trying her best to do her own thing, they'd all come back to Red Oak Falls—and to Aunt Blu—within a week of each other.

Jill and Trenton turned her way as she recounted her time with Waylon, and once she finished, Jill asked, "Is this a one-time thing?" Her tone was grave.

Given how she'd simply climbed on Ollie and left within minutes of finishing, Heather wasn't sure if Waylon would want it to be anything more.

"I know it should be."

It would certainly keep the risk to her heart at a minimum.

Waylon came across as a good guy. She'd lied when she'd told him she wouldn't listen to her heart. Her heart had already spoken, and it said good guy. But he also had a history of cheating people. Of gambling being a big part of his life. And heart or not, that didn't bode well for her.

She nodded, her heart cracking with each up-and-down of her chin. "It was a one-time thing."

All three of them sat with expressions of loss, then Trenton said, "Will you promise to tell us what happens next?"

"No matter what it is?"

Heather nodded once more, understanding why they doubted her. She could give them that promise, though. Because there wouldn't be the kind of next they were talking about. "I expect to talk to him Tuesday. We *uhmmm*"—she squeezed her eyes closed, not wanting to say the words out loud—"forgot to use protection."

Her friends didn't say a word. They didn't move or make a sound of any kind.

So Heather eventually reopened her eyes and peeked at them. "It's fine," she assured them, despite their matching looks of incredulity. "I'm supposed to start my period on Tuesday."

"And you're regular," Jill stated, as if needing to hear it herself. "You always have been, right?"

"Practically to the hour." Which meant, she'd know exactly when she *could* get pregnant. If the moment ever arose that she wanted to.

She caught the way Trenton was looking at her now, and knew her foster sister wasn't only thinking about unplanned pregnancies. There was more reason than one to use a condom.

"It's fine," Heather assured again. But she didn't go into the reasons she wasn't worried about diseases. Because she'd believed Waylon when he'd told her he hadn't been with anyone in a long time. And she wanted to hold that one to herself.

"Then update us after you talk to him," Trenton finally spoke, and Heather nodded in agreement.

"I will. Definitely."

They rose to go in, but Heather remembered the other two things she was supposed to tell them. "There *are* just a couple more things . . ."

"Good Lord." Trenton hung her head as the three of them once again stopped on the steps. "Please tell us you didn't already run off and marry the guy."

Heather smirked. "No. I didn't already run off and marry the guy."

"Are you going to?" Jill looked as worried as Trenton.

"*No.* And I don't even want to." Mostly.

Jill nodded, the move slow and deliberate, her look saying that she wasn't quite convinced of Heather's words. "Then what is it?"

Heather lifted the silver tin she'd brought with her. "I made him cookies."

"*Heather.*" Trenton gave a look.

"I *know*," Heather stressed the word. "I slept with the guy one time, and I went home and baked for him. It was stupid. But look"— she waved the tin under Trenton's nose—"I didn't give them to him. I didn't even let myself come up with an excuse to seek him out in *order* to give them to him."

And she'd wanted to. Badly.

Trenton took the cookies from Heather. "At least that's something," she mumbled. She pried at the lid. "What kind did you make?"

Heather crinkled her nose as she answered. "Snickerdoodles."

"Why do you say it like that?" Jill peeked into the now-open box and reached in for one. "What's wrong with snickerdoodles?"

Heather didn't look at either of them as she answered. "Snickerdoodles are his favorite."

"Of course they are." Trenton dropped her cookie back into the tin. "Well, at least you didn't take them to him."

"True." Jill took a bite of *her* cookie. "And the other thing you need to admit to?"

That's when Heather flicked a quick glance at the still-closed door, making sure Aunt Blu hadn't come out to see what was taking them so long.

"You know that Waylon's dad is in town." She lowered her voice to a whisper. She'd assumed everyone knew that Waylon's dad was in town by that point.

They both nodded. "And?"

"And he looks like an older version of Waylon," Heather explained. She swallowed as she stared at Blu's front door. "And *apparently*, I'm not the only person around here who likes redheaded men."

When both her friends only continued looking at her in bewilderment, Heather indicated the front door, and they turned as if expecting to find the explanation there.

"Just spit it out," Jill finally said. "We have no clue what you're talking about."

"What I'm talking about is that if Aunt Blu were still of a certain age . . . then it might be *her* in need of 'protection' right now."

It took a couple more seconds, but what she was saying finally registered.

"No." Trenton shook her head. "You're wrong. Aunt Blu doesn't date."

"I know she doesn't. And I have no idea if this will turn into anything more than just a conversation on the street." Heather grabbed one of the cookies from the tin and took a bite of it. "But you guys didn't see her yesterday. *Or* him. I don't even know exactly what that was going on out there, but it was definitely flirting." She stared at the other two. "And giggling."

Trenton frowned. Then she looked at the front door. "I'll talk to her."

"I'll do it with you," Jill added.

Heather wasn't positive they needed to get involved. At least not yet. Nothing had *really* happened with Waylon's dad, and anyway, Aunt Blu had a right to speak in any way and with any*one* she wanted.

But there was also no way Heather was going to miss out on the conversation.

They headed inside, determination running through each of them, only they stopped as they reached the hallway that led into the den. They could hear a creak of movement on the second floor, as if the new girl had arrived already and was spending time getting herself settled. But Aunt Blu was also having a moment. She sat in her favorite recliner just inside the room, with photo albums stacked on her lap. The top one lay open, and as Blu traced a single finger over one of the pictures staring up at her, Heather instinctively understood that her foster mother was looking at her late husband.

She swallowed. She'd never seen Aunt Blu look so lost.

"Let's hold off on talking to her," Jill suggested. "It might not just be Heather who's reached a tipping point in her life."

Chapter Thirteen

"Add fertilizer to your life, and see where it can grow."

—Blu Johnson, life lesson #21

Waylon took Highway 71 out to Log Cabin Road, then made a right and headed east. He hadn't been out that way before, but he'd been told that Bluebonnet Farms was only five more miles down the road. Heather lived on Bluebonnet Farms. Not in the main home with Blu, but in the smaller cottage that had been the original home on the property. She didn't know he was heading her way right now, and for all he knew, she might not even be there. But she wasn't at the viewing party at The Buffalo. And he hadn't seen her since early that morning at the ranch.

Yet it was Tuesday. It was time for them to talk.

He glanced at the wrapped package lying beside him as he slowed, then steered to the other side of the road. As he passed the slower-moving hay truck, he threw up his hand in greeting. Then he thought about the possible outcomes of the evening.

One, no pregnancy. Just as Heather had predicted.

Just as he wanted.

They could continue as they were—only he wasn't exactly sure what they "were"—and he'd have no additional long-term worries or commitments. That was the optimal scenario. The one that made sense.

Or two. A pregnancy. Rose could have a sibling.

He pressed on the gas, inching the speed up too high for the narrow road, and almost missed the turn that took him to the farm. Slowing rapidly, he made a wide sweep to the right, his back tires sliding in the gravel, before straightening the vehicle and seeking out the home where Heather lived.

He hadn't given thought to Rose having a sibling in years. It didn't seem to be in the cards for them, and it wouldn't be ideal if it happened now. Yet he'd caught himself thinking about it over the last couple of days. Playing out how things might change if Heather *were* pregnant.

Would she want him to be in her life?

He shook his head at his foolish thoughts. They'd had sex once, and within minutes of finishing, she'd climbed onto Ollie and ridden away.

I'll see you on Tuesday.

She'd said the words, and as they'd foretold, he hadn't heard from her since. Not that *he'd* tried to see her, either. Other than watching her from his office window that morning.

He'd had paperwork to catch up on before he and his dad spent the rest of the week branding, and though he'd told himself he wouldn't glance out the open window even once—that he wouldn't so much as seek a glance of her—when laughter had drifted up from the backyard, he'd lifted his head from the papers scattered around him and sat there for fifteen full minutes doing nothing but watching her.

He'd thought about their brief question and answer session when she'd caught him at the spring Saturday afternoon. She might not know *what* she wanted to do with the rest of her life, but she was excellent at what she was doing now. He could see the passion in her as she worked. She'd said that her parents had always just known how their lives would play out, and Waylon had the feeling that whatever it was her parents had had, she'd inherited.

He passed the main house, then saw Heather's down a small slope. And as he took in the many flowers and greenery surrounding it, he smiled.

Yeah, she had what her parents had, all right. A total green thumb.

As he pulled to a stop thirty feet from her, he also saw that her green thumb was currently hard at work. Though the sunset was fast approaching, she was on all fours in the landscaped area spanning the left side of her small porch, frayed shorts covering her cute rear and a bright blue tank riding just above the shorts. He also caught earbud wires running from her ears. Therefore, it didn't surprise him that she hadn't turned as he pulled up.

Cutting the engine, he pocketed the keys and stepped from the truck, and as if sensing she was no longer alone, Heather glanced over her shoulder. She didn't move from her outstretched position at first. She hadn't caught sight of him.

But the instant she did, her entire body jerked.

Three seconds of pandemonium followed. Heather simultaneously turned in his direction and tried to push to her feet. She lost her balance. She teetered.

And then she fell flat on her rear in the middle of a leafy bush.

Scowling up at him, trowel in one hand and a tiny purple flower in the other, she yanked out her earbuds and growled. "What are you doing here, Waylon?"

"Hello to you, too." He'd intended to offer her a hand up, but a natural sense of preservation held him back. He'd never seen her in such a foul mood. "You weren't at the viewing party," he explained. He watched as she scrambled to her feet. "And it's Tuesday."

"I'm aware of what day it is." Moving both the trowel and flower into one hand, she used her teeth to yank off the glove of her other. "And I wasn't in the mood for a crowd tonight."

He'd been disappointed to discover she wasn't at the bar. He'd enjoyed mingling with everyone the week before, and had been looking forward to doing it again tonight. As well as seeing Heather, of course. But there'd been no way he could stay there and wonder what her absence meant.

Was she not there because she *was* pregnant?

Because she *wasn't*?

"You knew I'd want to talk," he pointed out, and she rolled her eyes as if bored.

"Of course I knew you'd want to talk." She tossed the trowel to the ground. "And I'd planned to call you tonight."

Surprise hit him. "I didn't know you had my number."

"Yeah," she grumbled. "I'm resourceful like that." She inspected the bush she'd landed in, stooping to assess the damage, while at the same time returning the flower to the half-empty flat. "I got your number from your dad today." She spoke as she worked. "He came down to check out the job we're doing out there."

She'd talked to his dad? His dad hadn't mentioned it. "So you and Charlie hung out?"

She eyed him over her shoulder.

"What did you think of him?" Other than the few minutes before Waylon had suggested they leave his dad and Blu to their own devices on Saturday, he hadn't thought Heather had been around him.

She gave up on the shrub and pushed back to her feet. "What I think is that if he hurts my foster mother, he'd better hope the three of us never find him."

Waylon loved her protective streak.

But he also found himself defending his dad. "He's not a bad guy."

"I never said he was. But from what I can tell, he's not the settling type, either."

Sounded as if she'd pegged his father right. Waylon didn't know a lot about the man's love life, he just knew that Charlie Peterson did as he pleased. He'd never remarried, he'd taken several jobs throughout the years, seemingly wherever the urge struck, and Waylon had only ever seen him with a handful of women. And none had registered as anything lasting.

"I'd say that's fairly accurate." He studied her, thinking about her look of shock when she'd first realized that Blu and his dad had been flirting. "But let me ask you this . . . would you actually be okay with Blu hooking up with anyone?"

Disgust marred her face. *"Seriously?"* She cringed. "Just stop. Don't say 'hooking up' when referring to Aunt Blu. *Ever.* That's just so . . . *wrong.*"

"Yet she is a grown woman."

"And she's been doing just fine for twenty years without 'hooking up'." She held her hand up to stop any more discussion of the subject, her expression remaining as irritated as when he'd first arrived, so Waylon decided to push another button.

"How about bad moods, then?" At her confusion, he added, "Does Blu have bad moods? Is she where you learned to do them so well?"

"Oh, for crying out—" She bit off her words and scowled. "It's cramps, Waylon. You've heard of them, right? And bloating."

Her eyes suddenly blinked too rapidly to be natural, and he thought she might cry.

He wasn't sure how to fix it.

"I feel like crap, okay?" She spoke more evenly, but she still wore the look of a woman with one foot already dangling off the edge. "I always do the first twenty-four hours, so I'm sorry about the mood. But this is why I didn't go to the party. Because all I want to do is growl at people and"—she literally growled—*"chocolate.* Good Lord, I want chocolate." She peered over his shoulder to where he'd parked. "You don't happen to have any stashed away in your truck, do you? Because I'd do about anything for some chocolate right now."

Waylon ignored her backhanded offer of "anything" and sorted through their reality. She wasn't pregnant. Which he'd already guessed from her current mood. But strangely, her words settled uncomfortably inside him.

"So you're not . . ." His gaze dropped to her stomach, and Heather barked out a laugh.

"No, Waylon. I'm *not*." She stared down at herself. "Like I told you. Clockwork."

He nodded. "That's good."

Wasn't it?

Yes. It was good. He gave another nod. His life was too crazy. Kids and marriage weren't on his radar.

"Yes." Heather eyed him suspiciously. "It is good."

"But you *do* want kids someday?"

Her brow furrowed. "What?"

"Never mind." Why had he asked that? She'd already admitted she did. It's why she'd originally taken a job as a kindergarten teacher.

He turned for his truck, ignoring her when footsteps followed behind him.

"Where are you going?" She hurried to keep up. "Are you just going to leave now?"

He opened his truck door and reached in. "You don't want me to leave?"

He had *not* been going to leave. No way. He was finally seeing her again, and he intended to stay until she forced him out.

But he did like knowing that she didn't want him to go.

"I don't know," she denied. "It just seemed . . ." Her words slowed as he turned back, and when he held out a wrapped, flat box she finished with, "kind of odd."

She lifted her gaze, and he gave her a closed-mouth smile.

"You brought me a present?"

He forced it into her hands without answering, and she immediately tugged at the yellow paper. He'd seen the wrapping paper in the drugstore the day before, and it had reminded him of her. Very sun-shiny. Today notwithstanding.

With only two strips removed, Heather looked up again. And damn, but this time there *were* tears in her eyes.

"You *did* have chocolate." She stared down at the box he'd picked up after taking Rose home. "Why would you bring me chocolates?"

"Cramps, bloating . . . *cravings*." He twisted his mouth and waited for her response.

And her response was to rip the remainder of the paper from the box.

Waylon held back his laughter, but the lightness of the moment and the gusto with which she tore into the box were comical. Apparently unneeded calories were *not* a concern at that moment.

After picking out one of the heart-shaped, dark-chocolate pieces, she lifted it to her mouth and shoved it in. A groan rolled out of her. "What kind of guy are you to know that?"

Relief washed through Waylon. The Heather he'd come to know was back. "I'm a dad who lived with Rose's mom for a long time. Even *before* the dad part came into play."

"Yeah?" She chewed on the chocolate, moaning in sync with the movement of her jaw. "Tell me about that," she mumbled as she plucked out another piece. "About Rose's mom."

Waylon thought fondly of Nikki. As he always did. She'd had her negatives, but he wouldn't trade having had her in his life for anything. "We were best friends since birth," he said simply. "We lived our whole lives together."

Heather paused before selecting a third piece, recognition lighting her eyes. "Your dad said you were born on her grandfather's ranch."

"Right. Dad worked there at that point. Nikki was born two days after me—though in a hospital—and we lived there for another seven years on her grandparents' ranch. The friendship that started in those early years, though"—he almost choked up as he thought about how he'd been unable to help his friend in the last months of her life—"it remained solid until the end."

Even *with* all their mistakes.

"That's really special," Heather said softly. She'd slowed her intake and now watched him more carefully.

"*She* was special," he admitted. "We did everything together."

"You must have loved her a lot."

He wished it could've been as easy as Heather made it sound. "Nikki's the only person I've ever truly loved. But if you're thinking we were 'in love' . . ." He shook his head. Nikki hadn't wanted that. No matter how much he had. "No."

Heather moved to the swing hanging from a tree in her front yard, and when she motioned for him to join her, he did. Then he shared more about Rose's mother.

"Nikki was a shining star," he told her. He wasn't sure how else to explain it. "She loved *living*. She loved experiencing things. After we graduated high school, she couldn't wait to get out of town. She wanted faster, better, bigger. She wanted *more*. She'd dreamed of moving to Vegas for years, so I went with her."

"At eighteen?"

He plucked out a piece of the chocolate. "We were legal adults, so yeah." He didn't point out that he'd have been living on his own even if he hadn't moved to Vegas. "At eighteen."

"And you said you dealt cards?"

"I did. I had to pick up odd jobs for the first couple of years. I couldn't get hired in a casino for a while. But Nikki immediately became a showgirl." He smiled at the memory of her coming home telling him they'd offered her the job. That had been the reason she'd wanted Vegas in the first place. She'd been athletic her entire life, and she'd always longed to play sports. Volleyball, softball, track. She'd even have tried out for football if anyone had let her.

Her parents had insisted she take dance, though. And only dance. They'd put her in classes before she'd started elementary school, but as soon as she'd gotten the chance, she'd "shown them." She'd moved to Vegas . . . and she'd danced. Just as they'd always wanted her to do.

Of course, she'd also gotten involved in some bad situations. If she thought it, she tried it.

And Nikki had been open to plenty of ideas.

Waylon told Heather about all of it. He had no reason not to. "And though, as a child, Nikki had always done as her parents insisted," he continued, "she'd resented their actions from day one. There was always animosity there."

"Between Nikki and her parents?"

"Right." He didn't point out that they'd blamed him for that animosity. He'd always been around, so he'd been the scapegoat. Because it couldn't possibly be the fault of the Jameses.

He wrapped an arm around Heather's shoulders as he continued talking, the orange scent he'd forever associate with her drifting up, and she leaned into his chest. "Neither of us were angels, that's for sure. Either before Vegas or after. We hung with the wrong crowds, we got into trouble here and there. And once we were on our own, we lived together to save on costs. That made us even closer."

Heather only played with the chocolates now, moving them around in the box. "So that's when you two . . ."

"It eventually turned to that, yes." He and Nikki hadn't slept together at first. Nor had they planned to. "We both went out with others regularly. Nothing but hookups, mostly. But if we weren't with someone else, then sometimes . . ." He ended with a shrug. It may never have been a great love between them, but being with Nikki had often felt right.

"And you said the pregnancy hadn't been planned?"

He let out a lone chuckle. "Definitely not planned. She'd been a full-on addict at that point."

Heather's shock was evident. "Drugs?"

He nodded. "That's how she died. Accidental overdose. She did stop using during the pregnancy, though." He'd insisted. "But *only* for the length of the pregnancy."

Of course, her temporary abstinence had been a lot better than the alternative she'd first suggested. Thank goodness he still had Rose.

"What happened after she got pregnant?" Heather turned toward him, and his arm dropped from around her shoulders. She took his hand. "You didn't marry her?"

"I asked her." And he'd honestly wanted to. He'd wanted her to be the one.

It hurt that she'd never fully understood him. He hadn't needed the partying, the wildness. He'd gotten into it because he'd felt "lost." It had been his way of being seen. But inside, that had never been him. He'd have been truly happy settling down with Nikki. The two of them and Rose.

"So, she didn't *want* to marry you?"

He looked down at the woman who held his hand in hers. "She didn't want to marry anyone. She wanted to perform, to party." He wished all that he wasn't saying about Nikki could somehow come through. "She loved the Vegas lifestyle. I did talk her into moving off the strip after Rose was born, though. To try a 'family' thing."

He'd done and offered every possible thing he could think of, but nothing had been enough. He and Rose hadn't been what Nikki wanted.

"She did love Rose, though." He didn't want Heather to think differently. "And she wasn't a *bad* mom. Drugs just have a way of getting *in* the way. But after a year of 'playing house,' as she put it, she couldn't do it anymore. She'd already gone back to dancing months before, and she was beginning to resent me for keeping her from the life she desired. So, she moved out. Rose and I took care of each other from that point on, but Nikki still saw her on occasion. Only, she was never . . ."

He let his words trail off, uncertain how to explain it. Nikki had loved their daughter, but she'd simply never been able to be the mother Rose needed.

"That's okay." Heather cupped his cheek, her voice softening. "I get it. Not everyone is cut out to be a parent. I've met a lot of girls over the years, most of them while they were staying with Aunt Blu. And no matter how little it makes sense to some of us, there are simply some people in this world that seem to be missing"—she wore a perplexed expression—"a parenting gene, I suppose."

It did seem like she got it. "Your parents were good ones?"

"Yes. They were." Her smile was faint. "I was one of the lucky ones."

Waylon found it ironic that she'd lost both parents in a fire at a young age, yet she considered herself one of the lucky ones.

He covered the hand on his cheek. "You'd make a good parent, too."

"I'd like to think so."

"Ever thought about it?" He pulled her fingers to his lips. "Trying to get pregnant for real?"

She stared at him, straight on and unblinking. "With whom, exactly?" Her tone matched her blank expression. "One of my exes? Or maybe from a sperm bank and do it on my own?"

He was pretty sure he'd just stepped onto a land mine. "So your exes were not Prince Charmings?"

"That's putting it mildly."

"Want to talk about it?" He'd like to talk about it. He'd been curious since she'd first brought them up.

She glanced around instead of answering, her eyes widening as if just realizing it had grown dark, then she checked her watch. "Maybe another time. I have *Texas Dream Home* recording, and I'd rather watch that right now than think about my past." She nodded toward the house. "Want to watch it with me?"

"Absolutely." There was little he wanted more.

He rose, keeping her hand in his and pulling her up behind him, and together, they moved to the house. Before they could step inside, however, she stopped and put her back to the door.

"You aren't scared of ghosts, are you?"

At her question, he peered over her head and took in the cherry-red door that led into her home. "You're not saying that you have a ghost in there?"

Her grin reached her eyes. "I am *not* saying that." She tucked a hand behind her and pushed the door open. "But I do suspect you're about to see one on TV."

～

They'd ended up not only watching that week's episode of *Texas Dream Home*, but also *Sleepless in Seattle*. They'd pulled up his streaming account on her TV, and he'd offered to let her choose. So she'd gone old school. And romantic.

Surprisingly, Waylon had admitted to having seen the movie before. Then he'd quoted several lines as they'd watched, impersonating each actor. He'd had her rolling with laughter a number of times, adding a level of fun to the evening that she hadn't expected. Waylon was a fun date. If dating was what they were doing.

She hid a yawn behind her hand, and cringed when she caught him watching.

"Sorry," she offered. "I don't mean to be a wet blanket, but I'm going to have to call it a night."

"No need to apologize." He closed the photo album he'd been perusing. It was one from when her parents had still been alive. "I'm just glad you haven't spent the last few hours biting my head off like when I first arrived."

She smirked at his lame attempt at humor, then found herself smiling along with him. This had been a nice night.

"Take the rest of the cookies," she offered as they both stood up from the couch. He'd found the remainder of the snickerdoodles from her Sunday morning bake-off, and though she'd refused to admit the truth, he'd correctly guessed that she'd been thinking of him when she'd made them.

"Given that you've sat here and almost polished off that whole box of chocolates yourself"—he shot his own smirk—"I think I *will* take the cookies. If only to save you from not fitting into your bridesmaid dress."

"Ha, ha." She gave him a flat look. "You're a riot and a hoot."

He reached for her hand. "I also look quite dapper in a suit." He looked down at her, and the humor faded from his eyes. "Just a tidbit of info," he told her, "in case you were considering taking a date to the wedding."

No reply came. They hadn't talked about what they'd done out at the ranch the Saturday before, and though they'd sat side by side for the last several hours—and had touched more than once—there'd been no implication this was anything more than a "checkup" to ensure she hadn't gotten pregnant.

Yet he wanted to be her date to Jill's wedding?

Instead of responding, she led the way to her door. Only, once there, she didn't know what to do. Or *say*. So she just stood there.

"I really do like your place." Waylon scanned the room as if he hadn't been sitting in it all evening, and she risked a glance to find him looking at anything but her.

"Thanks. Jill, Trenton, and I renovated it." She could hear the breathlessness in her voice. "It was the first house we did."

"Is that so?"

He looked around for a moment longer, his Adam's apple bobbing as he swallowed and his movements seeming as uncomfortable as she felt, before he finally brought his gaze back to hers. And when he did, Heather saw for the first time what she hadn't realized she'd been looking for all evening. He wanted to kiss her.

"I knew you were good at your job," he continued. He threaded two fingers between hers. "Maybe I'll still ask you to help out at my place."

"And maybe I'll think about helping out." She wasn't ready for him to go yet. She glanced at his mouth. But she also didn't think it wise to let him stay.

So she opened the door.

"You sure you're not scared of ghosts now?" As they'd watched that week's episode, Waylon had not bought into the idea of the past owner still "living" in the house Cal's team had renovated. Heather had no doubts of the woman's existence, though. She hadn't seen Mrs. Wainwright for herself, but Jill had sworn the woman had been over there.

Just as she'd sworn Mrs. Wainwright had gotten her own happily ever after.

"Maybe I *am* scared." Waylon's eyes glowed with anticipation. "Walk me to my truck?"

She nodded. "I think I might need to."

They moved silently through the night, the moon having risen to cast a soft glow over the land, and she thought of the flowers she'd been planting when Waylon had shown up. She'd taken the afternoon off to come home and set them out, knowing Waylon would be looking for her before the day's end. And though her grumpiness when he'd arrived hadn't been faked, it also hadn't been due entirely to her monthly cycle. At least, not in the way he'd believed. There had certainly *been* cramps. There always were. But her mood had also been affected by the fact that she'd gotten her period to begin with—even though she'd known she would.

Because the idea of having Waylon's baby . . .

She shoved the thought away. It had been ridiculous to go there.

"I'm kind of impressed," she broke the silence as they approached his truck. "We had a whole night of conversation, and we didn't once have to resort to a game of two-questions."

Waylon put his back to the truck door. "Don't knock two-questions." He pulled her in front of him and propped his forearms on her shoulders. "It's a great icebreaker."

"Yeah? Is that your normal pickup line?"

"My tried and true."

He winked then, and she smiled at his wink.

She put her hands to the side of his waist, hooking her fingers through his belt loops, but then she caught a glimpse of something . . . *odd* . . . sitting on the front seat of his truck. She leaned to the side, trying to make it out—while Waylon's arms lowered and clasped around the small of her back.

Then her mouth dropped open when she recognized what it was.

"Is that another present?" This one clearly wasn't a box of chocolates. It was a small gift bag with tissue paper sticking out the top. "Why do you—"

She stopped speaking at the grimace that tightened Waylon's mouth.

"Who's it for?" She pulled back, but his hands stayed firm around her.

"Nobody." He spoke through a stiff jaw.

Doubt crept in. "What is it, then? You got another woman you need to check on?"

"No other woman, and you know that. I told you how long it's been for me."

He had told her. And she'd believed him.

She still believed him.

Yet something was clearly going on with him. She tried to look around him again, but his arm tensed, stopping her movement, and this time when she lifted her face to his, she detected an entirely different emotion.

Was that embarrassment?

She eyed his shoulder, imagining she could see through it to the front seat of his truck. What was she missing here?

"What's in the bag, Waylon?"

"Can't you just forget you saw that?"

"I don't think I can." She sunk her teeth into her bottom lip as she thought through the moment, and she fought the urge not to let this bother her. But the more he tried *not* to show her what was in the bag, the more she wanted to know what it was. "Can I ask another question then?"

One thing had plaguing her for the last few days, and it reared its head again in that moment.

"Sure." He remained looking uncomfortable.

She didn't take her eyes off his. "I know it's been a while for you, but before that . . . before *me*, just how many women were there?" She had to force herself to sound normal. "And I mean *serious* relationships. You mentioned that you'd once slept with a lot of women. So how many of 'a lot' were something real?"

She knew she sounded jealous, and she had no right to be. They weren't dating. This wasn't a thing. Saturday afternoon had just been a moment. And one that probably shouldn't be repeated.

But she couldn't help but want to kn—

"I've had none," Waylon said, and her jaw went slack.

None? How was that even possible?

"But I'd have liked for there to be."

At his soft admission, she heard the vulnerability. He really did want something serious? Nerves began to tingle inside her. "You'd have to date to make that happen, though, wouldn't you?"

"Something like that."

And he hadn't dated anyone in years.

She began to wonder if that lack of dating was due purely to his being a single father, or was there more to it? The tension remained in him, both in the arms that held her and in the angle of his jaw, but suddenly he peered down at her.

"Want to date me, Heather?"

Her breath caught at the question. She sidestepped by nodding toward his front seat. "What's in the bag?"

He shook his head. "It's nothing."

"I don't believe you."

"It's not anything you want to see."

Determination stared back at her when she made no response, and finally he sighed. And he closed his eyes.

"Please don't . . ." He quit talking and shook his head, then he settled her back a couple of feet and opened his truck door.

After retrieving the small gift, he handed it over, a blank expression now covering his face, and she immediately ripped the tissue paper from the bag. It was too dark to make out what lay inside, so she reached in and pulled out something soft.

Then she stared down at the tiny bib with the words "Mommy loves me" written on the front. And her mind went blank.

"Go out with me, Heather."

Goose bumps lit down her body. "I . . ."

"Just say yes." His tone wasn't soft, but she heard the need in his words. Then he touched a finger beneath her chin and brought her gaze to his. "You know you want to, and you know I'm going to keep asking."

"But why?" She gripped the bib in both hands.

"Why do I want to date you?" He looked as uncertain as she. "Other than that it just feels right? That it feels like what we *should* be doing?"

"But dating always ends so badly for me."

He closed his hands around hers. "I promise I'm not bad for you."

She'd told him about her exes while they'd watched *Sleepless in Seattle*. The college boyfriend who'd broken their engagement *after* he and her roommate had gotten married—and had used *her* wedding savings to fund his and his new bride's honeymoon. The fiancé who came after that, who'd disappeared the day of their engagement party—along with the money he'd embezzled from his company the previous six months.

That one had not only made the news, but had resulted in her being interrogated, as if she'd had something to do with it.

And then there had been Danny Shaver, right here from Red Oak Falls. Danny hadn't attempted to take anyone's money or marry her friends. Nor had he been a flat-out criminal. He'd merely had an issue with sex. They'd dated for nine months, and all the while he'd been sleeping with at least ten other women, both local and living in the cities where his job took him. Yet he'd sworn to her from early on that she was his one true love.

She hadn't gotten engaged to Danny, at least. She had that going for her.

But that had been her only advantage. Everyone had given her the poor-Heather look, accompanied by reminders that they'd warned her about him all along. It had been the same look she'd gotten the previous two times. Along with the when-will-she-learn whispers.

She clearly wouldn't learn, and that was the problem. No matter how careful she might think she was being, she always chose a guy who had a moral or two that had taken a sabbatical.

And then she fell for him, hook, line, and sinker.

"I want to get to know you, Heather," Waylon said now, apparently giving up on waiting for a reply. "That's what it boils down to." He dipped his head to look at her. "I like you. I think you like me. I enjoy being with you . . ."

He paused, eyeing her, and she added petulantly, "I enjoy being with you."

He flashed his dimples. "And I want to *be* with you more. That's all I'm asking. Let's see if this is anything. Can't that be enough for now?"

She so wanted to believe in Waylon.

"Maybe," she finally answered. Then Chris, Dustin, and Danny flashed through her mind again. "But I don't want to go public."

Incredulity creased Waylon's brow. "What are you suggesting? That I just be a booty call?"

"No." She shook her head. "That's not what I'm saying at all. It's just"—she stared at him, wishing she could make him understand—"*yes.* Okay? Let's go out. Let's date. I *want* to date you. But all I'm asking is that we keep it to ourselves for just a little while. You've got to understand. When dating fails for me, it fails spectacularly. And I *so* hate the looks I get when that happens." She ground out the last part. She hated to feel so stupid.

Just because she wanted love.

"Okay," Waylon said without her having to explain further. He squeezed her fingers. "Not public. For now."

"Thank you."

He gave a small smile that matched her own. "But we're starting tomorrow. Be ready at six o'clock. I'll pick you up."

Her eyes went wide. "Six? I'll barely have time to shower after I get in from work."

And she had no idea what she would wear. Did she even have date clothes?

"Then shower quickly," Waylon told her. He leaned in then, and before she recognized his intent, his mouth was on hers.

He kissed her there in front of her home, his hands still holding hers and his mouth torching her with its touch. And Heather tried her best not to let herself start to fall. But she knew it was a lost cause. The man had not only brought her an I-got-my-period box of chocolates . . . but he'd brought her an I'm-pregnant gift as well. So yeah, it was too late to put the brakes on now. She'd already dived headfirst off the cliff.

He ended the kiss, pulling back and flashing a silent promise in his dark eyes, then he drove away in his truck.

Heather stood alone in her front yard, and she looked down at the bib still clutched in her grip. But instead of continuing to think about Waylon, she let her mind go to her parents. Her mother had been absolutely crazy for her dad. One hundred percent over the moon in love with the man since the moment they'd first met.

And her dad had loved her mother just as ferociously.

At the same time . . . her dad had *not* been perfect.

Did that mean their love hadn't been perfect as well?

She lifted the bib and studied the tiny stitching that made up the lettering. And she thought of the box of chocolates. Maybe perfection wasn't what she was supposed to be looking for after all. Maybe all she needed was perfect for *her*.

Chapter Fourteen

*"The girth of your hips isn't as important
as the smile on your face."*

—Blu Johnson, life lesson #33

They'd gone out four times now. *Before* that afternoon's horseback ride.
Every night except the two when Waylon had had Rose, and then on
Tuesday night, when they'd attended the viewing party separately.
Waylon had even stopped by her house on his way home from return-
ing Rose Sunday night. Just to give her a kiss.

A very long kiss.

Heather sighed to herself. The man was doing it right.

The first date had been dinner at his house. Charlie had disappeared for the evening, and food had been waiting when they'd arrived.
Waylon had brought in an eggplant parmesan from a local Italian res-
taurant, a salad, and a bottle of red wine—and though she'd still been
borderline grumpy from cramps, the mixture of wine, good food, and
better company had easily turned things around.

The next night they'd driven to San Marcos to take in a movie.
Though Jill's wedding was fast barreling toward her, Heather had once
again tossed her worries over eating too many extra calories. A movie date required buttered popcorn, as far as she could tell. And with

Waylon either feeding it to her or trying to sneak licks of the butter from her fingers, she hadn't been about to pass it up.

Dates three and four had been at her house and his, respectively. Three had been him bringing her a new shrub to replace the one she'd landed in the first night he'd shown up. He'd also picked up hyacinth bulbs, along with a truck bed full of mulch, and together they'd worked in her yard until well after dark. Four had been at his house the night before, where both she and Charlie had helped rip up the existing flooring that was too damaged to keep.

The night didn't sound romantic, but it had been Heather's idea, and they'd all had a terrific time. Plus, it had given her an opportunity to get to know Charlie better. As far as she was aware, there'd been no additional communication between him and Aunt Blu, but she'd been thinking about it all the same. Blu got lonely. Heather understood that. And everyone deserved to find love if they wanted it. The problem in Heather's mind was that she didn't know if Charlie Peterson wanted it.

He did strike her as a good guy, and he was actually a lot like Waylon. They both had fun personalities, and their senses of humor could be hilarious.

Also, they both seemed lonely.

Another perk of the three of them spending the evening together was that it had allowed her to pick up on a subtle "dance" between father and son. As if neither wanted to be the one to show his hand first. Only, she had yet to figure out what hands they each were holding.

She dug her heels into Ollie's sides as she rode, pushing the horse to go faster, and as she leaned in closer, she momentarily closed her eyes. Hooves pounded underneath her, and she imagined her mother's comforting touch reaching down from above.

After several minutes at a fast pace, she eased up and sat straighter in the seat, and as she and horse both began to catch their breaths, Waylon and Beau trotted up next to them.

"I get the feeling you'd be just as happy today if I weren't here," Waylon teased, and Heather grinned over at him. She enjoyed his company, that was for sure, but he wasn't far off at the moment. She'd gone without riding for too long.

"You brought the food," she pointed out. "I would have been hungrier if you weren't here."

His laugh rumbled through her belly. "And you downed that sandwich as if the size of your hips had never been in question."

She made a face at him. "The size of my hips is always in question."

"The only questionable thing I see is when I'll get the opportunity to see them again." He winked with the audacious words, and Heather pulled Ollie to a stop.

"Your winking outs you every time, you know?"

He bellowed another laugh. "Are you saying you don't believe that I want to see your hips?"

They were back within sight of the barn, but Heather had no desire to hurry an end to their time together. She'd cut work a little short that day due to the producers wanting to bring some bigwigs out to see the work being done, and as soon as Waylon had been able to get away, they'd set out exploring the ranch. "I'm saying," she told him, "that I flat out offered to show you my hips back at the spring earlier. And if I'm remembering correctly, *you* changed the subject."

She danced Ollie around him and Beau, circling man and beast, and enjoyed watching him as he turned his head along with her movements and watched *her*.

"I did change the subject," he admitted.

"Care to explain why?" She kept circling.

Though it had been clear during their first few dates that extracurricular activities would have been somewhat *messy*, Heather had informed him the night before that *that* was no longer the case. There had been plenty of kissing each time they'd gotten together—including today—and a hefty amount of petting and just making out in general.

Yet she'd come right out and offered sex not an hour before, even letting him know she had condoms on her person. And he'd passed.

He grabbed Ollie's bridle to halt her movements, and eased Beau up beside her. He sat facing one direction and she the other, and he leaned in to nibble at her neck.

"I absolutely want to see your hips again." His husky voice fired tingles over her body. "And your breasts," he continued. His lips nipped at her ear. "And I really, *really* want to slide deep inside you again."

She shivered at the words.

"But"—he continued, his hot breath still at her ear, his whiskers tickling her just below—"I'm not going to do that tonight, either."

She scowled. "Why not?"

She'd never had so much trouble getting a man to take her clothes off.

"Because we rushed it before," he said matter-of-factly. He began circling her as she and Ollie had done to him. "And I don't want you thinking this is just about sex."

"I don't think that."

He grabbed her bridle and leaned in once more, but this time instead of going for her neck, he put his face inches from hers. "This is me wooing you, Heather Lindsay." Sincerity shone back at her. "This is me romancing you."

Her heart flipped. "I'm the one who's supposed to be the romantic here."

"Yeah, well"—he kissed the tip of her nose—"you don't own the license to romance." He tilted his head, and this time kissed her tenderly on the mouth. And when he pulled back, it wasn't only desire she saw, but raw honesty. "I don't want you *just* having fun with me." His voice cracked with emotion. "I want you falling *hard* for me."

"Waylon . . ." She wasn't sure what to say to that. Was he falling just as hard for her?

He kissed the tip of her nose again before turning his horse for the barn, and Heather was left either to go with him or stay there looking after him. So she instructed Ollie to follow. And as she and Waylon entered the paddock together, she caught Jill watching from the covered patio of the house.

"We're no longer alone." Waylon spoke under his breath. "I just hope Trenton isn't waiting in the barn with a gun."

Heather grinned. She knew that Trenton would *like* to be waiting in the barn with a gun.

"Are they okay with this?" Waylon asked. He watched her as they rode. "With us dating?"

"How do you know I told them?"

His smirk was telling.

"Fine. I told them. And they're not exactly happy about it, okay?" She thought about the three-way phone conversation they'd had after Waylon had driven away last Tuesday night. "They always have my back, though. They support me. Whatever I need to do."

They also picked her up when she fell.

"They're good friends," Waylon offered.

"There are none better."

They led the animals into the barn, and after finishing the rubdown tasks and putting out feed, Waylon walked her to her car. The sun had fully set, but the landscape lights that had already been installed in the backyard had been left on. Heather considered running down to turn everything off. Instead, she just stood there and took it all in. Waylon did the same.

In the dark, and with no furniture, the area was still mostly shadows and shapes, but she knew what the final picture would look like. It became clearer every day.

She'd tweaked her original designs. Nothing major, but she'd added in extra curves with some of the wooden structures and changed up a handful of textures. She'd also made the last-minute decision to install a rustic zigzag fence running along two sides. It would blend beautifully with the barn and surroundings, while adding a nice punch as a backdrop for the wedding.

"It's going to be quite impressive," Waylon spoke at her side. "Certainly tops anything I've ever seen."

"Thanks." She snuggled into him when he dropped an arm around her shoulders. "I'm pretty proud of it myself."

"As you should be."

He turned her to him, his other arm closing around her, and she lifted her face to his. "I had a good time tonight."

Waylon's hands caressed her back. "I have a good time with you every night."

They kissed, and she let her fingers trail over his torso. The man had lit a fire inside her that she didn't want to tamp down. She slid her palm lower, not stopping until she covered his erection, and groaned when he pulsed under her hand.

"*Waylon.*"

"I know" was his reply, but he didn't take things any farther. Nor did he pull back. His mouth just kept driving her to the brink.

Her hands moved to the patch of scars she'd noticed the day they'd made love, and she thought about his limp. In five dates, there'd been no mention of either of those things. Which she found odd. For two people who'd started out their relationship doing so much talking, they'd gone strangely quiet for the last week and a half.

"What happened here?" she whispered. She slid the pad of her thumb over the puckered scar four inches above his waist. "I noticed these before. When we were . . . *naked.*"

One side of his mouth hitched up. "I'm surprised you noticed anything when we were . . . *naked.* Things happened somewhat"—he fake-grimaced—"*fast.*"

She laughed at the memory. "It definitely *was* speedy. Not that I'm complaining," she hurriedly added at his crumpled expression. "I'm sure it wasn't as fast as Jill and Cal were that day in the barn."

Waylon gripped her chin and brought her mouth to his, his hard touch a promise. "Just to be safe," he growled out as he pulled back, "I'll make sure the next time is a lot longer."

"Just make the next time soon." She once again slid her hand lower. *"Please."*

"Heather." He captured her hand, but he didn't pull it away. "Romancing," he reminded. "Wooing you, remember?"

She smiled and captured her lip. She really did like the idea of that. "I remember."

"Then let me do this." His mouth brushed hers once again. "But yes"—he ground her hand into his erection—*"soon.* I promise."

She thought she might have nodded agreement as he separated them, but agreement was the last thing she wanted to give.

Waylon clasped both her hands in his then, and he looked down at her with solid intent. "I pick up Rose tomorrow," he told her, "and she, Dad, and I have plans for the circus tomorrow night." He kissed her knuckles. "But I want *you* to go out with me Saturday night. You, me, and Rose." His gaze burned steady on hers. "Let's go to the park. They're showing *Snow White* as this month's movie, and Rose is looking forward to seeing it."

Heather's breath caught at the idea of it. She'd love to experience a movie in the park with them. She'd love to be a part of his time with Rose.

But nerves had her stalling. There were just so many unanswered questions.

"People would see," she said instead of bringing up any of those questions. "They'd know we're on a date."

"Yes. They would." He pressed a kiss to each palm. "But would that really be so bad?"

She swallowed as she fought through her nerves. If this thing between them was ever going to go anywhere, she eventually had to take a leap of faith. Things had to turn out right for her at some point, didn't they?

But was it with *Waylon* with whom they'd turn out right?

The sound of hooves passed in the distance, and Heather dropped her forehead to Waylon's chest. Was her mom telling her that she could trust in him?

"Did you hear that?" she whispered.

"Hear what?"

She turned her head and pressed her cheek over his heart. "Never mind." It was easier not to attempt to explain it. "And no, the park with you and Rose would *not* be so bad. It wouldn't be bad at all."

~

She might have insisted she meet them at the park instead of letting him pick her up, but Waylon finally had Heather exactly where he wanted her. She sat with her back a little too straight and doing her best to put too much distance between them, but he had her on a blanket while his daughter played nearby with three new friends and he stretched out at her side. And if that didn't look like two people out on a date, then he didn't know what did.

He picked up the pink rose he'd previously plucked from the bouquet his daughter had insisted they buy for her—a bouquet containing one rose of every color available—and reached up to tap its petals on the underside of Heather's nose.

She gave him the same long-suffering sigh she'd handed out the last time he'd done that.

He grinned. "You're not eating your food."

Her plate sat in front of her, still half-loaded with all of Rose's favorites. Rose had helped him pull everything together for the picnic;

therefore it was a tad carb heavy. He'd noted over the past weeks that Heather tended to steer clear of carbs more often than not, so he'd also made sure to bring along plenty of fruit. And she'd eaten mostly fruit.

"I'm full," she told him.

"You're worrying about your hips," he replied in the same monotone.

She graced him with her sigh once more, and again he smiled. This was fun.

"Hey, Heather." Marci Hammery, a woman Waylon had seen around town, neared their blanket. "Waylon."

"Hey, Marci," they replied together.

She addressed Heather. "Did I see a mention of the calendars at the end of this week's episode?"

Waylon watched as the women talked.

"You did. It was in the preview for next week. They filmed a segment on them, and we're hoping it'll bring in additional money for the school." Heather's face brightened. "I've been told they'll be mentioning your photography business as well."

"Really?" Marci's hand went to her throat. She glanced over at Waylon and smiled, as if to include him in the conversation. "That's fantastic. Both for the school"—she laughed lightly—"and for me."

"Let's hope it increases business all the way around."

The two talked for several more minutes, and though Waylon couldn't have made it any clearer that he was there with Heather, while she was otherwise occupied, two other women passed close by their blanket and gave him "the look." Only "the look" had recently changed from hey-baby-take-me-to-bed-and-then-do-it-again-a-second-time to hey-single-dad-are-you-looking-for-a-wife. The new look could be as disconcerting as the old. Especially when he was on a date with another woman.

After Marci left, Heather picked at her broccoli salad and explained that Bluebonnet Construction had done a calendar earlier in the year as a fund-raiser for a local elementary school. The school's playground equipment had gotten destroyed in a storm, and there'd been no budget to replace it.

"It ended up being a lot of fun," Heather told him. "We featured some of the more unique she-sheds we've built over the years, and both the school and other she-shed owners have already reached out to ask if we'll be doing it again next year."

"Quite philanthropic," he said.

"We've contributed in other ways over the years, too. We always enjoy it. It's a little different now that the companies have combined and we have to swing most things past the producers, but I'm hoping we can do additional projects like that." She picked up a strawberry and brought it to her mouth. "And don't think I didn't see those two women," she murmured before sinking her teeth into the fruit.

He tried his best to hide his smile. "What women?"

"You know exactly what women. As I'm also sure you're aware how their message has now changed."

"I don't have a clue what you're talking about." He pasted on his best innocent expression. "What message is this you speak of?"

She rolled her eyes. "Don't even. You're not stupid, and neither am I."

"But I do believe you're jealous."

"What do I have to be jealous about?"

He'd give her credit. She almost sold the look. But he still saw the green of jealousy ringing her glorious eyes. He grabbed a handful of the quilt they sat on and tugged, knocking her off balance and into him. "Not a damned thing," he said with a heated growl.

"Waylon . . ." She pushed off him. She'd been trying to avoid him touching her in public all afternoon.

"*Heather,*" he mimicked. He popped a grape in her mouth. "You're out here having a picnic with me and Rose, and I'm spread out before you like I'm your dessert. You think everyone hasn't figured it out yet?"

"What I *think* is that you could be a bit more subtle." She tried to be serious, but she couldn't hide the fact that she liked his attention.

He tugged on the quilt again, a little easier this time, and inched her closer. Then he leaned up and loudly whispered, "I don't want to be subtle. I want the world to know you're my girlfriend."

Happiness mixed in with her long-suffering sigh. "Is that what I am?"

"Is that what you want to be?"

She nodded, giving up on the pretense of being annoyed with him, and to keep from pulling her down on the blanket with him, he shoved another grape into her mouth. Then he grabbed her plate and settled it on her lap. "Eat up, woman. You're going to hurt my little girl's feelings. She helped make her favorite macaroni and cheese, just for you."

Heather's gaze shot to Rose, who was currently running in circles to show off the fairy wings Heather had brought for her, then she scooped up a large bite of the pasta. The fork disappeared between her lips, and Waylon found himself unable to take his eyes off her mouth. She chewed rather sensuously.

She went for another bite, and right before wrapping her lips around her fork a second time, she mumbled, "I might as well give up on watching my hips."

Waylon felt movement below the belt. "Not a problem. I watch your hips enough for both of us."

That had her looking down at him again. Then she took another bite. And another. And each time the tines of the fork slipped between her lips, her chewing got a tiny bit sexier.

Waylon finally pulled his eyes from her mouth—it was either that or risk embarrassing both of them—but he couldn't help the occasional glance in her direction. Finally, he decided to find something other than her mouth to think about. "So, have you given any thought to taking a date to the wedding?"

She paused with the fork in the air.

"It is only two weeks away," he added.

After a slow chew and then an even more mesmerizing swallow, she licked the remains of cheese from her lips. "You're quite demanding as a boyfriend, aren't you?"

He loved the sound of that. "I'm about to be even more demanding."

He could tell from her half smile that she understood his meaning. He might have spent the last eleven days doing his level best at romancing this woman, but even *he* had his limits.

She carefully set her plate beside her. "Don't say things you don't mean, Mr. Peterson."

"Oh, I guarantee you I mean them."

He dragged the flowers over and positioned them in front of his jeans. It had been only two days since they'd taken the horses out, but yesterday alone, one or the other of them had found an excuse to be in the barn together no less than five times. A couple of the instances, someone else had already been in there, so they'd made up a topic of conversation. But the other times . . .

He groaned under his breath as he thought about those other times. Just before he'd had to leave to go pick up Rose, he'd almost suggested they pull a Cal and Jill and do it up against the bathroom door.

He wanted their next time together to be more special than a quickie, though. He wanted to do everything he could to let her know she was special to him.

"I sit here minding my own business," she said, plucking at the petals of the pink rose now lying forlornly by itself, "yet I find myself terribly curious to know exactly what it is you're thinking." She picked up the juice packet Rose had insisted she drink, and sucked on the straw.

"And I find myself highly regretting the smooth moves I've been working so diligently to display over the last two weeks."

She smiled at him then. A real, beautiful, sincere smile that possessed no pretense or double-entendre. And he saw that his patience was being heavily rewarded. "Don't ever regret romancing a woman," she told him, her tone soft and tender. "It's the best part of falling for someone."

Oh, damn. He was going to need a larger bouquet of roses.

"If I *were* to ask you to be my date for the wedding"—she dipped her lashes as if about to request something far more enticing than a night out in the middle of a crowd—"would you do something for me?"

He immediately nodded. "Name it, and it's done."

"Would you tell me more about your childhood?"

He mentally faltered at her request. They'd spent the better part of five evenings together now, and plenty of additional hours in and around those nights either talking at the ranch or on the phone after his dad had retired to his room. Yet throughout that time, neither had brought up their childhoods. And it wasn't as if Waylon had been hiding from the discussion. It just wasn't a subject he made a habit of talking about.

With Heather, though, he found that he wanted to tell her. She had the desire to know more about him, and that made him ecstatic. Because that could only be a positive when it came to their relationship.

Her request also gave him hope that she might soon be willing to talk about her own past. About her parents' deaths. And he was pretty sure she *needed* to talk about that.

"Are you asking me to be your date?" He spoke in a way that left no doubt that he would take the conversation as another step forward, and she immediately nodded.

"I'm asking."

Adrenaline coursed through him. "Then I'm telling." He swooped up and planted a loud, amorous kiss on her parted lips, then dropped back to the ground with a smile. "What do you want to know?"

Bright spots of pink landed on her cheeks. "You are a *bad boy*, Mr. Peterson."

God, he could fall in love with this woman. "Like all the rumors you've heard?"

"Possibly *worse* than the rumors I've heard."

She shot him a mock perturbed look, and he rolled to his back with a laugh. He'd warned her. His record was quite stellar once he decided he wanted something.

"So, you've never mentioned your mother." She finally steered the conversation to his childhood, and he stared up at her. "I assume she was around?" she asked.

"Was and still is. In a roundabout way." He propped himself back up on his elbow and plucked a chicken strip from her plate. "Her name is Joan, she's fifty, an accountant in an insurance company, and she followed my stepfather to Nashville nine years ago so he could chase his dream of being a country music star."

The info seemed to shock Heather, and she slowly put down her juice. "Wait a minute. Nine years ago?" Her brow crinkled. "So then, you've lived in Nashville?"

"No. I moved in with Nikki's parents the last two years of high school."

Heather's brows shot up. "You lived with Nikki during high school?"

"I did." He grinned. "That was the only time—until Vegas—that she openly defied her parents. She told them they could either let me live there until I graduated, or she would move to Nashville with *me*."

"She was ballsy."

He chuckled and pushed on up to a sitting position. "You don't know the half of it." He reached for a soda. "And yes, before you ask about the other part of what I told you, Mom's husband is a wannabe country music star, and from what I can tell, he's pretty much in the same place now as he was nine years ago. With Mom still supporting him."

"Well, doesn't he sound like a winner?"

He acknowledged her remark with a tip of his hat. "My thoughts exactly."

"So, do you see her often?"

"I've seen her twice in the last four years. Three months after Rose was born, when she and Boyd came to Vegas. She'd used all her vacation time going to gigs with Boyd, or they would have made it out sooner. And then Rose and I went to Nashville two years later. We're due for a trip soon."

Heather blinked. "And that's it?"

"That's it. I talk to her every couple of weeks, though. We stay in touch." He'd never understood why his mother's lack of attention didn't bother him more. She'd done her part after his dad had left, he supposed. She was a good enough mother, she just had other interests now.

"So then . . . your dad."

Waylon worked to maintain his relaxed posture, and picked at the chicken finger he had yet to finish. "What about him?"

His dad was harder to talk about, no matter that he was living with him now.

Or possibly, the fact that the two of them *were* living together made it even more difficult. Because everything was going well. He should have nothing at all to complain about. Only, every nuance about their arrangement felt just a hair off-kilter. As if the two weeks they'd lived under the same roof had consisted more of "pretending" to be improving their relationship rather than actually doing anything to truly grow it.

"When did they divorce?" Heather watched him in the same hesitant way that she asked the question.

"When I was seven."

"When you moved from Nikki's grandparents' ranch?" She was sharp. He'd known she'd pick up on that.

He intended to confirm her question orally, but only managed a nod.

"And what happened after that?"

The way she continued tiptoeing with her questions told him that she'd picked up on the underlying tension between them. He shrugged, knowing his condensed version wouldn't suffice. "Dad and Mom divorced, Dad found another job, and Dad didn't take me with him."

She held up a hand. "Slow down. Why change jobs?"

"Who knows? Greener pastures, I guess."

Lack of understanding pinched her features. "But why not stay where he'd been working? Did a divorce have to change his job?"

"Who *knows*, Heather," he repeated, because he truly didn't know. He'd never asked.

"Okay." She backed off. "I'll let it go. But what did you mean by he *didn't take you with him*?"

"Just what I said." He forced himself to maintain eye contact. "He didn't take me with him."

As he said the words, it occurred to him that Nikki was the only person with whom he'd ever shared the story of his parents. And Heather had every right to know. So he tamped down his defensiveness, and he started at the beginning.

"Mom was an okay parent," he shared. "Nothing special, nothing bad. But she also probably would have been happy never having a kid. I was an accident, and I'm pretty sure that's the only reason they married in the first place."

"You and Rose were both 'accidents'?"

"We were." He hated thinking of his daughter that way, but the fact was, she hadn't been planned. "The difference is that Rose *has* a parent who knows his life wouldn't be as good without her in it."

The pain in Heather's eyes matched that in his soul. "Rose is a very lucky girl," she said softly, and she reached out a hand to take his.

"I like to think so."

Of course, he'd also lost custody of his daughter. Which meant that *he* very well might not be so great for her.

At the same time, he was also now trying to take her from two people who could provide far more for her than he'd ever be able to. And two people he knew she was happy with. That knowledge often kept him awake at nights, and what he typically wound back to was a single question. Was he fighting for custody for Rose's benefit, or was he doing it for himself?

Was *he* the best thing for his daughter?

"Waylon?" Heather's gentle voice brought him back from thoughts of his impending custody battle.

"Sorry." He cleared his throat. "Anyway, back to my story." Back to thinking about how he would do better for his daughter than his dad had done for him. "There was nothing 'wrong' with Mom. She provided a good home, and I never wanted for the basics. And my stepdad didn't beat me nor get up in my business, so that was a plus. But even as a kid, I often felt like I played second fiddle." He paused before admitting, "Nor was I a priority for my *dad*." And this part, he'd never even said to Nikki. "No matter how much I tried to be."

He looked for Rose then, needing *not* to be looking at Heather, and watched as she played with several girls. Rose would never be left feeling as if she wasn't the most important thing in his life. Whether he had custody of her or not.

"I begged him to take me with him," he continued after a minute. He suddenly wanted to get the story out, and he wanted Heather to understand him. "And I mean, *begged*," he added. A seven-year-old boy could cry. He knew.

He rubbed his hand over his once-broken leg.

"But he said no. Said I needed to stay with Mom."

Heather had grown quiet, and though he still didn't look at her, she kept her hand wrapped tightly around his. "I'm sorry," she said now. "That must have been difficult."

"Yeah." He nodded. He didn't tell her that he'd also overheard his mother offering to let his father take him. After Waylon had spent an entire afternoon trying to hide his tears.

His dad hadn't wanted him, though. More important things to do, Waylon supposed.

He shared with Heather that from that point on, he'd started acting out. Doing little things to get attention, until the little things eventually evolved into big things.

"I'm not trying to blame others," he went on. "At least, not completely. I'm just saying that there's a lot of anger that courses through a person when their entire world gets upended." He placed his other hand over hers. "As I'm sure you're well aware."

They both fell silent before Heather said, "Have you talked to your dad about all of that?"

Waylon jerked his gaze to hers. "No. I haven't." Surprise colored his words. "And I don't intend to."

"Why not?"

"Why would I?"

"I don't know. Maybe it wasn't quite the way you remember it?" she offered. "Maybe you need closure to move past it?"

"It was exactly the way I remember it, and I have moved past it. I'd moved past it by the next summer." And he wasn't about to tell his dad that he needed to "talk about his feelings." "I spent summers helping out on whatever ranch Dad was working at, and I spent school years with my mom."

He'd also spent summers honing poker skills from the ranch hands working with his dad.

"So you've always had a relationship with your father, then?"

Waylon eyed her. "Sure."

"It was just strained?"

Strained. He almost laughed at the simplicity of the word. But it was certainly accurate.

"Exactly. But it's better now." He was ready to wrap up the conversation. "Since Rose was born, it's been better. Both of us seemed to change without having to work at it. And then last spring"—he thought about waking up in the hospital and his father being there—"I wouldn't be where I am now without his help. He helped me through my injury. Through the PT." He needed to tell her about his injury. About why he'd gotten injured in the first place. "And he loaned me the money for the down payment on my house."

Heather watched him carefully. "The house you need in order to get Rose back?"

"Yes." He found his daughter in the crowd once again, then he thought about having that conversation with his dad. The one Heather had suggested. If he did, though, his question to his father wouldn't be why he'd taken another job after the divorce. Ranchers often moved around. Waylon knew that.

What he'd want to know was why he *wouldn't* take Waylon with him when he had left.

And if his dad had any clue just how badly that had hurt.

"The house I need in order to get Rose back," he repeated Heather's words, his voice drifting into the family-filled night surrounding them, and he admitted to himself that what he really wanted to hear from his dad was that he'd messed up. That he *should* have taken him. That he regretted how things had turned out.

But that conversation hadn't happened over the last twenty years, and Waylon had no reason to believe it ever would.

Chapter Fifteen

*"It's a fact of life that people will lie. Sometimes to serve
their own interests, sometimes simply because they're algae
dirtying up the bottom of a pond. And some will surprise
you with their honesty. It's up to you to decipher the truth."*

—Blu Johnson, life lesson #68

Heather sat on the front seat of Waylon's truck, *not* glancing at the man beside her, and doing her best not to let the scene at the Jameses' replay in her mind. And she'd been that way for the last thirty minutes.

While Waylon seemed to be processing the events by making small talk.

"Thank you for going with me."

She glanced over for only a second. "Thank you for asking."

At least, she'd meant those words *before* they'd arrived at Rose's grandparents'. Since climbing back into the truck to come home, though, she wasn't sure if she was more grateful to have gone—and witnessed what Waylon was up against—was more horrified that she'd started a relationship with the man sitting beside her to begin with, or if she was simply terrified at the idea that the reality lay somewhere in between.

She looked out her window, still not ready to bring up the moments after Waylon had pulled up in front of what had to be a million-dollar home.

"Rose asked me to tell you she'd draw you more pictures this week."

Heather looked down at the paper in her lap. When Waylon had picked her up that afternoon, Rose had presented her with the picture of the three of them watching a movie at the park the night before. She'd also informed Heather how very much she'd missed her today.

Heather blew out a shaky breath. She could totally fall for that girl if she weren't careful. In fact, she likely already had. The movie last night had been one of those special kinds of experiences that she wouldn't mind repeating. The movie had started while she and Waylon had been talking, and Rose had sprinted back to their blanket. Only, instead of sitting by her dad, she'd settled in on Heather's lap. Where she'd stayed until she'd fallen asleep.

Heather had carried her to the truck while Waylon followed with their belongings, and it had taken a huge effort not to climb into the cab of the truck and go home with them.

Waylon had looked at her as if he'd been considering suggesting the same.

"That's part of our ritual." He glanced at her now, and clarified, "When we whisper on the porch. We say the same thing every week. I'm going to call her every night, and she's going to draw me a picture every day. But tonight, she said she's going to draw you one every day, too."

"Oh, geez," Heather muttered. She pressed a fist to her chest. She'd definitely fallen.

"My girl is special," Waylon said, his voice now more musing than telling, and when Heather glanced his way once more, she saw the worry he must carry with him all the time.

"I can't imagine the judge won't rule in your favor." She didn't know where her conviction had come from. That would have been her thought last night. *Before* speaking with Madelyn James.

But now?

Waylon's chuckle fell flat. "I can't imagine Marcus and Madelyn won't pull out everything they have to keep that very thing from happening." He gulped. "And you witnessed all you needed to under-stand how they plan to pull that off."

"Please tell me what she said was lies." Her words were pure plea. As Waylon had been talking to Rose on the porch, Rose's grandmother had been filling Heather's ears with vile thoughts.

Waylon does drugs—and has for years.

Waylon has a habit of leaving his daughter home alone. For hours at a time.

Waylon has a wide range of gambling issues, not the least of which is an absolute addiction to the game.

And Waylon was put in the hospital for conning the wrong person in a poker game.

Heather shook her head, wishing the words away, and Waylon pulled the truck over to the side of the road. He killed the engine and turned to her, and the two feet separating them suddenly felt more like fifty.

"Almost all of them were lies," he said.

"Almost?" She didn't even want to guess which was true.

Once again, he seemed to age before her eyes. "First of all, I'm sorry she cornered you that way. I should have guessed she'd pull some-thing like that, but sometimes, even *she* surprises me."

Waylon had overheard the taunts as he'd returned to the truck. Madelyn had been spewing it all out again, as if someone had hit repeat and she couldn't stop talking. Upon realizing what she was up to, an all-out shouting match had ensued. Rose's grandfather had hurried Rose into the house, Rose crying her eyes out, while Waylon had shut Madelyn down.

He'd then tried to get inside the house to comfort his daughter, but the Jameses wouldn't allow it.

"Almost," he said again. The sides of his face pulled down. "And for the record, I'd already planned to tell you everything I'm about to share with you now. I'd intended to do it tonight. Even *before* Madelyn started in on you. That's why I wanted you to come with me to take Rose back. Dad is gone to visit with some friends for a couple of days, and I'd decided I needed to share everything before we go any further." His eyes begged for understanding. "I was selfish, though. For not telling you before now. But it's only because I wanted to enjoy a bit more time together before I risked losing you for good."

Fear blossomed at his words. She didn't want to lose Waylon, either. "Which part is true?" she asked.

"The hospital."

Her thoughts tripped over themselves. Madelyn had said he'd been put in the hospital for conning someone in a poker game. Yet hadn't he told her that he didn't do that anymore? That he hadn't since high school?

"You lied to me," she accused.

"I lied to you. And I apologize for that."

Thankfully, he didn't try to reach out and touch her. Because she would have pulled back.

"And no," he continued, "I don't have an excuse for lying other than shame at admitting my actions. But I do have a reason for doing what I did."

Heather wasn't sure she wanted to hear it, but he had her trapped in his truck. She looked out the window. They hadn't even made it back to Red Oak Falls.

"You did it because you have an addiction to gambling?" She spoke without looking at him.

"No, Heather." There was certainty in his words. "I do *not* have an addiction to gambling. I don't have any addictions, and I never have. Not to gambling, not to screwing people over, not to drugs."

She didn't mean to, but she glanced back at him. She didn't speak, though.

"The rest of what she said was lies," he repeated his earlier claim. "I did *experiment* with drugs in the past. Years ago. And there were parties when we first moved to Vegas. Sometimes I would join in and sometimes I wouldn't. But the rest of it"—he shook his head—"not even close."

"You've never left Rose home alone?"

Pain carved deep lines in his face. "Nikki did that," he admitted. "The Jameses have money, as you could see, and they aren't above using it however it will benefit them best. They found someone Nikki used to party with, who plans to testify to that lie. She'll say it was me who was supposed to be home with Rose that day. Not Nikki. And certainly not that Nikki had gone off partying herself, and had blacked out and completely forgotten our child."

Revulsion swept through Heather. "How can they do that?"

"They can do anything their money will allow." He laid his hand on the seat between them, palm up, but Heather only stared at it. She couldn't take his hand. Not yet.

"Is someone going to testify about drugs, too?"

He nodded. "A guy I went to high school with. We got into some trouble together early on, played poker a time too many. I haven't talked to him since I moved away."

"Then how are you going to fight them?" Her voice shook. "How are you going to get Rose back?"

"That's where the hospital stay comes in." He pulled his hand back and clenched it in his lap. "They'd already tried to get custody of Rose once. After Nikki died. I guess they thought they could win by fighting fair at that point, simply by going on their name. Because they're 'somebody' in San Antonio. But the case was heard in Vegas, and the judge sided with me. Rose was best off with her dad."

"Of course she is."

His mouth twitched with her vehemence, almost curving into a smile.

"But then they tried again." No hint of a smile remained. "After I moved back to Texas. I was working on a farm close to Odessa, and I got another subpoena. They were filing for custody again, and this time they were doing it in their hometown. And they'd hired the best attorneys money can buy."

"And they'd found people to lie for them," she guessed.

"Yes. Though I didn't realize that at the time." He stared over her shoulder, looking out the window but likely seeing little. Darkness was fast approaching, and they were sitting on the side of a mostly deserted road. "I got wound up worrying about shelling out more for legal fees. I don't have a lot of money, and I never have. But Rose and I do okay. Only, the first round of lawyers depleted me. And now I had to do it again?"

He brought his gaze to hers.

"*And* I had to compete on their playing level?"

"So you started cheating at poker?" She didn't understand how he could get away with something like that for very long.

"First of all, I started *playing* poker again. I'd quit when I began working in the casinos. It had become a bad hobby, and one I no longer wanted to be a part of. I still had legit skills playing the game, though. So, I started entering tournaments. Took home good money. Occasionally there would be a weekend game someone pulled together—and I usually took home *their* money." His mouth twisted to the side. "There was this one guy who lost a lot to me one night. And I mean a lot. He wasn't happy about it, but I was desperate. No way was I about to give him a chance to win it back. But then I got news that the Jameses had someone to testify that I do drugs. As in, actively doing them today. That I can't be trusted around my own kid."

"But a drug test—"

"Couldn't prove I hadn't done anything prior to the thirty days before the test was administered."

She stared at him. "And you said this is a guy from your past?"

He nodded, his expression solemn. "Whom I didn't end on the best of terms with. He'd hooked up with Nikki one night, didn't treat her the way I thought he should have . . . so I cleaned him out the next time we got together. He'd been saving for a much-needed car, and I walked away with all of it."

"Oh, Waylon."

"Yeah," he muttered. "Karma and all. So anyway, I panicked. I set something up, just like I used to do. Just that one time. And I walked away with a hell of lot of money." He thumped a closed fist on his thigh. "I'm still shocked at how it all came off. That money would have given me the cushion I needed. But they caught on to my scheme, and they wanted their money back—as anyone would. And they made that very clear, in a very physical way."

His slid his palm over his side.

"They didn't just beat me to within an inch of my life. They sliced into me, too. It's a wonder I'm alive."

Tears trickled over her cheeks, and she reached for his hands. "I'm so glad you are alive."

He gave her a half smile. "I am, too. But I lost my daughter because of my stupidity. And that's all on me. It'll forever be on me. It was four days before I woke up, and by the time I did, Rose was hundreds of miles away and my dad was sitting vigil at my side."

"Your dad loves you," she whispered. "I see it every time I talk to him. He may not have done things right when you were a kid, but he does love you."

Waylon nodded again. "I know. He wiped out his savings for me—not only for the down payment on the house, but for a chunk of my legal fees—*and* he lost a job he'd had for several years to stick around and bring me back to life. So yeah, I know he loves me. And I love him."

Heather wasn't sure she'd ever heard such a lack of enthusiasm in a ringing endorsement. Poor Waylon. His seven-year-old heart still beat with pain.

"You're prepared for your upcoming court date?" she asked. Fear for both Waylon and Rose had her contemplating the investments she'd made with the remainder of her parents' insurance money. It had to be worth quite a bit by now. She hadn't touched it in years.

She could offer it to Waylon. Maybe that would help.

Then it occurred to her what she was doing. This wasn't her battle, and Waylon and Rose weren't *her* responsibilities. No matter how much she might want to help. She hadn't even been officially dating the guy for two weeks, yet here she was thinking about cleaning out her bank accounts for him.

Would she never learn? She couldn't simply jump in the deep end and insist people love her.

So she kept her mouth shut. Because she *was* learning. Because whether she had the desire to help due solely to Waylon being a good guy, or whether it was because she *did* want this to turn into more, she had to help herself first.

"I'm as prepared as I'll ever be," Waylon answered, his words returning her to the present. "We can disprove everything they intend to bring up. It'll just be a matter of who the judge believes. Money"—he lifted a shoulder—"or me."

"My bet's on you." She scooted across the seat, and when she got close enough, she lifted his arms and put them around her. "Thank you for sharing this with me."

"You believe me?"

She could see the doubt in his eyes. "I believe you."

And she'd believed *in* him even before she'd gotten the details. Even if she was afraid to.

"I also believe in us," she told him. "And since I do"—she decided on the spot that she'd had enough romancing—"and since your *father* isn't home tonight, I want you to take me home. I'm going to pack an overnight bag." She gave him a tender smile. "And then I'm coming over to your place."

Surprise touched his eyes, and almost as quickly, the heightened tension of the last few moments lifted. "Thank you." Sincerity burned heavy through his words. "I won't let you down."

Chapter Sixteen

"If at first you don't succeed . . . regroup,
and then hit it out of the park."

—Blu Johnson, life lesson #5

Waylon paced from the window on the left side of his front room to the window on the right side, each pass ending with a view of his front porch. And there was still no sign of Heather.

She'd changed her mind. She wasn't going to show up.

It had been far longer than the time needed to pack a bag and drive the short distance to his house, so Waylon determined she'd decided he wasn't worth it. She didn't need the trouble. He'd known telling her everything would scare her off.

He turned his back to the front of the house, needing something other than Heather to focus on, and then he had it. In the event she *did* show up, he should set the mood. No sense just standing around waiting on her like a dog in heat. He'd light candles.

He rummaged around in a box in the kitchen he'd yet to unpack. It contained random plastic containers and a few oversized utensils he hadn't found a place for yet, and he finally came up with two unused eight-inch tapered candles—one white and one yellow—and a pink candle in a glass jar that was burned almost all the way down. Rose liked it when he burned candles. Especially the smelly ones.

Locating a lighter in the same box, he'd just produced a flame when a faint knock sounded at his door. It struck him that the knock wasn't the same determined rap she'd given the first time she'd shown up at his house, and understanding dawned that she was nervous for the upcoming evening. That knowledge set him even more on edge.

He hurried to the front of the house, pink candle now burning in the jar in his hand, but he made himself pause before swinging the door open. He pulled in a calming breath. And then he opened the door wide.

And the candle almost dropped to the floor.

Heather's nerves showed in her smile. "Hello, Mr. Peterson."

Damn.

"Hello," Waylon managed to croak out. He took in her trench coat.

She glanced down, her hands fidgeting with the material on the lapels. "This seemed . . ." She looked back up, and she must have seen something in him that calmed her. Because her smile evened out. *"Appropriate."*

"Definitely appropriate."

It took her shifting her eyes as if trying to look around him for him to remember to step to the side and let her in, and as she eased past, he remained in the same spot, still holding the flickering candle.

"I thought you burned the coat," he said, and she looked over her shoulder at him.

"No way would I burn this coat. Me and this particular article of clothing go way back."

Jealousy licked at him. "Has it played into a lot of seduction scenes?"

"Only one failed attempt."

She was still looking at him, and Waylon finally let himself take in the full effect. And when his gaze reached her feet, his blood pressure soared. "Cowboy boots?"

Her grin slipped into temptress mode. "It seemed more logical."

He swallowed. "How do you figure?"

"Because in just a few minutes . . . *Mr. Peterson* . . . I'm also going to be wearing your cowboy *hat*. It seemed I should have on boots to match."

Waylon didn't blink. "I think I'm going to owe you one."

"What do you mean?"

He finally remembered that he remained standing in the open door, so he slammed it closed and blew out the candle. "Because I promised that the next time I got you naked, it would last longer than the first time." He trailed his gaze over her once more. "But I'm no longer sure that's going to be the case."

She laughed, the sound light and fun, and the happiness on her face emboldened him. "We do have all night," she pointed out.

He set the candle on the floor. "And I intend to use it."

~

The nervous energy she'd shown up with vanished as Waylon advanced on her, and she lifted her chin with determination. "The hat," she said, and he stopped.

He wasn't wearing a hat at the moment, but he quickly retrieved one. He ducked his head to peek at her as he placed it on her head, and the devil that danced in his eyes assured her she'd chosen right in tonight's attire. The trench coat had definitely been the way to go.

"Anything else the lady wants?" he asked, and she giggled lightly at his words.

"Only what the man can give me."

He put his hands on her then, lightly skimming his palms from her shoulders to her hands, and as his fingers slid over hers, a low groan rumbled inside him.

"What's on underneath?" He nudged his chin toward her, and she shook her head.

"You'll have to unwrap me to find out."

"I do like unwrapping pretty packages."

His grin grew wicked when his fingers tugged at the belt of the coat, and she held her breath as the two sides of the fabric slid slowly apart. It opened just enough to give a top-to-bottom glimpse of what lay beneath, and as Waylon took her in, she congratulated herself on another decision well made.

Lace boy-cut panties covered her lower parts, while up top, she wore nothing but a long gold chain that hung deep between her breasts.

"Yep." Waylon licked his lips. "This one's going to be fast."

He hadn't touched her, yet Heather's entire body ached with need. "Put your hands on me, Waylon." She nodded, unwilling to continue to wait any longer. "I'm taking charge here, and I say it's time for your hands to be on my body."

His eyes met hers. And then he reached for the front of the coat.

She breathed in short pants as he inched the sides of the trench open, her body being exposed bit by bit, and as the cooler air of the room kissed her skin, her nipples puckered tight.

"Beautiful," he murmured. And finally, he cupped a breast in his hand.

"Waylon." She gasped at his touch. "More. *Please.*"

But he had other intentions. His thumb slid slowly over the turgid point, before reversing direction and doing it again. By the third pass, the lace of her panties was drenched.

"Change in plans," he muttered as he continued to hold her with one hand and take her in with his eyes. He scraped the fingers of his other hand over the front of her panties. "You're *not* the one in charge today. I am. And I've decided to take this slow after all." He squeezed her breast and dipped his mouth to what his hand held. "But I'm still going to do it all again later."

His lips touched her, and her chest arched forward. Her hands lifted, gripping him as his tongue laved over her most-sensitive point, and when his fingers applied pressure through the lace, her legs began to tremble.

"I thought we might do this in a bed," she whispered. She was quickly losing the ability to stand.

"I thought we might, too." He tunneled his fingers under the lace. "But I've changed my mind on that as well."

"Waylon." They both moaned as his fingers connected with flesh. "I need—"

He backed her into the wall and pinned her with a thigh, then he raked her coat over her shoulders and trapped her arms at her sides. "I need, too," he ground out. His eyes burned with heat. "And I'm about to take."

His mouth and fingers went on a journey, leaving her capable of nothing but dropping her head to the wall and enjoying his actions, and within minutes he had her wound to the point of explosion. He didn't slow, though. He touched her everywhere, and though she was one press of his thumb away from heaven, the man had yet to lose a single article of clothing.

As she inched closer to release, he finally gave a bit more. He ripped his shirt over his head, cupped her butt in his hands, and lifted her off the ground. She immediately wrapped her legs around his hips, but her arms remained trapped. The wiry hairs dotting his chest scratched over her breasts, the thin links of the chain she wore wove between them, now heated from their actions, and the rough texture of his jeans ground erotically into her crotch.

"Waylon." She whispered his name because she couldn't think of anything else to say, and as her body spiraled higher, her thighs clamped tighter.

Her back bowed when she crested, an animalistic sound ripping from her as pleasure exploded, and her arms strained against her constraints. But Waylon never slowed. His mouth suckled as she called out, his actions extending her orgasm until the sounds became little more than a whimper, and when she went limp, he was there to catch her.

She opened her eyes as reality returned, realizing she remained against the wall and was being fully supported by Waylon, and only then did she become conscious of his erection still throbbing against her.

"Good?" he asked. His jaw was as tense as the rest of him.

"Great," she murmured.

He gave a quick nod, stooped with her in his arms to retrieve his fallen hat, then he plopped it back on her head and went in search of his bed.

Chapter Seventeen

"It's not all romance and rainbows. It's also reality."

—Blu Johnson, life lesson #59

Waylon groaned as his orgasm rolled through him. His hips clenched involuntarily, and he gave another hard push, and with Heather's breasts jiggling in front of him, his groan turned to a roar. Once depleted, he dropped, landing on Heather's chest harder than he'd intended, while his own heaved for oxygen. The dampness of her skin didn't go unnoticed, and he pressed a kiss to the curve of her breast. He'd done good in a few minutes' time. Not wanting to crush her, he forced himself to move, sliding his arms along her body until he found the strength to lift himself up.

"We make this a habit, and you're going to get me fired." He wasn't seriously complaining, but over the last eight days, the woman had turned into a sex fiend.

They were in his office in the middle of a Monday, she had on his hat once again—only this time she wore *only* his hat—and she had one of the black pencils from his desk tucked behind her ear.

He eyed her ear . . . or there *had* been a pencil there. He trailed his gaze to where the freshly sharpened writing utensil had rolled. He'd teased her when they'd knocked the cup of them over earlier, about how he'd previously caught her pretending to take inventory while actually waiting around to see him, and the next thing he'd known, she'd turned the thin piece of wood into a form of foreplay. She'd teased it over his body, using a combination of it, her mouth, and her hands, until he'd pushed her hands away, stripped her of every last shred of clothing, and taken her up against his office wall.

Realizing they were making too much noise, he'd moved them to his desk, but something told him that anyone who'd happened to have entered the barn during the last ten minutes had likely hurried right back out again.

"At least we lasted longer than Cal and Jill," she proclaimed, and the mischief in her smile told Waylon what he'd already suspected.

"I knew it." He pushed off the desk and tugged up his jeans. "That's why you insisted you couldn't wait until tonight."

"I *couldn't* wait until tonight."

He looked back at her as he disposed of the condom, ready to argue the point, but promptly lost his train of thought. She'd lifted to her hands, her arms braced behind her and her naked breasts swaying in his direction.

Her mouth puckered into a pout. "I wanted you *so bad*, Mr. Peterson. And I had to have you right now."

He waggled a finger at her. "You're evil, Ms. Lindsay."

"Maybe a little bit. But you like it."

Hell yeah, he liked it.

He grabbed her by the knees and pulled her forward until she straddled him, then he plundered her mouth. She still wore nothing but his cowboy hat, and though he didn't intend to unzip his jeans again, he decided to show her that two could play her game.

He dropped to his knees and locked her thighs over his shoulders, and then he spread her wide with his fingers. He made love to her with his mouth then, and he didn't stop until this time it was *she* who screamed out with her release.

Once she finished, Waylon sat back on his haunches, out of breath yet again, and Heather thunked her head to his desk. His hat tumbled to the floor, and she began to laugh. And as far as Waylon was concerned, there was nothing more wonderful than a warm, luscious woman spread naked before him, laughing with wild abandon.

He almost told her he loved her right then and there.

"I suppose I deserved that." She finally got herself under control enough to speak, and when she lifted her head to peer at him, still sitting between her knees, he silently begged that she would love him back.

She pushed back to her elbows. "How many people do you suppose heard that?"

"I suspect more than heard me."

He failed to put lightness in his tone, and Heather picked up on his shift in mood. The laughter faded from her eyes, and though she rose to a sitting position, he stayed on his knees.

"What's wrong?" she asked.

"Nothing is *wrong*. I'm just wondering if I can ask you something."

She nodded immediately. "Of course. Anything. What do you want to know?"

Waylon slid his hands along the back of her calves, his actions more that of hanging on than one of comfort. And he shared what was on his mind. "You're so happy and full of life. You're vibrant and beautiful, and you light up any space you occupy. And I have no doubt that anyone who meets you is better because of it. But I know that inside, you still hurt. That you ache over your losses. I've told you about my past. About my hurts." He silently pleaded as he looked back at her. He'd hinted for this conversation over the last couple of weeks, but he'd never come right out and asked. "You never talk about yours, though. Will you talk to me about it now?"

She didn't say anything at first, but Waylon held his ground. He needed her to be able to share this with him. If not . . . could she ever really love him enough?

"I do still carry hurts," she finally said, and Waylon let out a relieved breath. "Because it was my father's fault that my mother died."

~

Heather looked beyond Waylon, her eyes on the doorknob she'd locked when they'd first come in, and she ignored the fact that she was sitting on his desk without a stitch of clothing on. She also didn't let it faze her that Waylon remained crouched between her knees. She'd just said out loud the one thing she'd never uttered in her life.

Her father was the reason her mother had died.

Granted, her father had died in the same fire. And that loss was as great to Heather as losing her mother.

But Gene Lindsay had been a man who'd had only two speeds. All or nothing. He'd loved Heather's mother with his all. He'd given to his students, to his daughter, his all. But he'd also handed over his all to his gambling addiction. He'd had a problem, and though he'd hidden it well, Heather had overheard one key conversation that had pieced it together for her.

"I heard him on the phone the night of the fire," she told Waylon. "Pleading with someone. Begging for 'just one more week.' I'd been at a friend's house, and it was already dark by the time I walked home. His conversation reached me before I made it to the house, and I realized he'd stepped out onto the porch to take the call. The tone in his voice terrified me. I wasn't trying to eavesdrop, but I also didn't want him to know I was there, so I hid in the bushes. But after the call ended, and before I could make it appear as if I'd just gotten home, Mom came outside with him."

Waylon's hands slid down to her ankles.

"They argued," she said softly. She let herself picture that night. "I'd heard them argue before, but not often. And never like this. There was utter panic in my mother's voice."

"*What're they going to do this time?*" Heather repeated her mom's words. "*The last time you ended up in the hospital.*"

She looked at Waylon. "I didn't know what they were talking about, but Dad *had* been in the hospital the year before. He'd claimed to have had a car wreck, and he was beat up pretty badly. Only, our car was fine."

Waylon grimaced.

"He assured her that everything would be okay. That he'd take care of it."

She laughed with no humor.

"He left the house, and I eventually 'came home,' and the next thing I know, I'm waking from a dead sleep to the sound of screams, both human and equine." She let her eyes go unfocused. "I ran outside, only the entire barn was engulfed already. It was discovered later that Mom had gotten trapped under a beam. I don't know if Dad died trying to help her escape or if he'd just stayed in there with her out of guilt. Or maybe love. Either way, he died along with her, and I was left on my own."

Waylon rose to his feet. "How do you know he hadn't gone into the barn first? Or that they didn't go in together? You said before that your mom went—"

He stopped talking when she looked at him again.

"After I finally quit trying to run into the barn, I slumped against my dad's car. It was parked near the barn that night. Which was unusual, on its own. But the even stranger thing was that the hood of the car was hot. At two o'clock in the morning. He'd clearly just gotten home."

"And you noticed this yourself? In your distraught state?"

She gave him a sad smile. "I've tried hundreds of times to convince myself that wasn't the case, so don't even go there. It was hot. I noticed it. And even if I hadn't, I overheard one of the police officers pointing it out to the fire captain. Dad had been out for hours. Probably trying to win back the money he owed."

Waylon sucked in a breath. "Gambling?"

"That's what it seems."

"No wonder my past habits worry you so." He gripped her hands. "Heather, I'm so sorry. I wish I could change that for you. I wish I could be . . . *perfect.*"

She didn't respond. She didn't know how.

When she continued to just sit there, he picked her shirt up from the floor. "What did he play?" he asked gently.

She allowed him to tug the material down over her head. "Horses, I think. Which is ironic, isn't it? Mom loved to ride, but Dad just liked to watch them run." She put on her bra before Waylon could direct her arms into her shirtsleeves. "And likely, it was only horses because that's what was easily accessible. He went to Selma on a regular basis. He and Mom always claimed he was teaching a class down there, but there were also the handful of times a year he and his college buddies would fly out to Vegas. Boys' weekend." She cut her eyes up at him. "I never actually met any of his friends, so I have no idea if he went on his own or with others. But those trips became the thing that brought Mom and I closer. I always thought of it as girls' weekends since Dad was off doing his thing, but looking back, I think it was just Mom's way of coping. She'd make the days special for us. We'd go riding, get our nails done, work together in the greenhouse all day. Anything really, just so we weren't sitting in the house waiting for Dad to come home. She was likely stressed to her breaking point, worrying whether he'd return having won money or if he'd owe more instead, so I'm sure anything we did helped take her mind off it."

She hopped off the desk, wishing there was a bathroom in the office but unwilling to walk bare-bottomed out into the barn to get to one. So she stepped into her panties.

"I didn't put the phone call from that night together with the fire at first," she told him as she searched for her jeans. She found them under the desk. "I was too shell-shocked from everything else. But Aunt Blu set me up with a counselor, and while waiting for one of my sessions to start, I overheard another patient standing out in the hall. He was talking on his phone. *Just give me another week. I'll get you your money.*"

She stepped into her jeans and tugged on her ankle boots.

"It was like dominoes falling into place," she went on. "Dad's trips to Selma—where I knew there was horse racing. And I know this because Mom and Dad took me there once. I was only seven or eight, but I was taken aback at how much Dad got into the races. I did think it was funny, though. I'd never seen him that animated over anything but my mom. Add in his Vegas trips, their occasional whispered arguments that more often than not seemed to center around money or her pleading for him to quit"—she lifted her shoulders—"*something*. I couldn't figure out at the time what that something was, she'd just plead for him to quit. But I did once hear her call Dad an addict. Dad denied it."

Waylon looked pained. "I am not an addict," he reminded her. "I swear to you."

"Okay."

"Heather." He cupped her cheek. "You can believe me. I don't have issues. This spring was one time, and I won't do it again. I promise you. If I have to take a second job to fight for Rose, I will. If Dad needs to take a second job with me, he's assured me that he will. But I won't mess up again. Never at the cost of my daughter."

"Okay." Heather nodded. She wished he'd stop. She didn't want to talk about that. "I believe you."

But she didn't know if she really did. She just knew that she *wanted* to believe him.

Waylon sighed, his frustration at her response evident. But he went back to her story. "How did the fire start? Do you remember?"

"The fire captain said faulty wiring."

"But you don't believe him?"

She shook her head. The idea that the death of her family had been due to her dad had never set well with her, but even that night, in the middle of all the madness, she'd known something was off. The entire evening had been too wrong.

"The barn had been built only three years before," she explained. "And it wasn't a do-it-yourself project. Dad must have won a lot that summer because suddenly we got a barn. So no, I don't think it was faulty wiring. At least not the unintentional kind. Also, there was the van parked in front of our house that night."

Waylon reared back. "A van?"

She nodded. "Right out on the road. I saw it before I went to bed. I couldn't tell who was in it, but there were at least two people. I kept an eye on it for an hour, peeking out my window, but it never moved. Nor did whoever sat inside ever seem to look away from our house."

He gaped at her. "Did you tell this to anyone? To the police?"

"No."

"Heather . . . why not? They might have been able to find who'd done it."

"But I still wouldn't have had my parents back, would I?" She felt hollow. "And what if my fear turned out to be right? What if my dad *was* the cause of it? I didn't want the whole town knowing he'd killed the woman he claimed to love."

Her voice caught on the last word, and she looked down at her hands. She pressed her lips together, trying to hold in her tears.

"You know he loved her." Waylon wrapped her in his arms. "You've told me so."

"But it couldn't have been like I always thought." She spoke into his shirt, her voice muffled. "How could their love be so perfect when his gambling was what made her sad? Why she'd sit alone and sing to our horses?" She shook her head back and forth, her face rubbing against his chest. "And if he didn't love her as much as he'd always said he did, does that mean he didn't love me as much, either?"

"Oh, baby." Waylon tilted her face up. "I never met the man, but I'm *positive* he loved you. I don't know how anyone could know you and not love you."

Heather only looked at him, trying to decipher what he'd just said. Was he *only* talking about her dad loving her? Or was there more behind his words?

She stepped from his embrace, needing distance to think, and she unlocked his office door. Waylon followed her out, but when she got to the main doors, she stopped. They stood open, and she could see Jill's backyard spread out down below. She, Jill, and Trenton would film a final scene there the following day, but her crew had finished the work on it that morning. And it was exactly as she'd intended.

She leaned against Waylon when he stopped at her side, her gaze trailing over the spaces filled with so many plants her mother had once loved. "For their fifteenth wedding anniversary, they'd planned to redo their vows. Mom wanted to hold the ceremony in our backyard, and I was helping her design it. It was another thing we were doing together. She never got to see the finished product, so I'm giving it to her now. She would have loved what I've done here."

Chapter Eighteen

"Real friends are forever, no matter
where their paths may lead."

—Blu Johnson, life lesson #71

"And, that's a wrap!"

Heather hugged her best friends, unable to hold back her smile. She'd done it. Jill and Cal's backyard was stunning. The wedding would be held in four days, the forecast was for perfection, and final wedding décor would be put into place Saturday morning before the wedding.

"You did good," Jill told her. "Not that I ever had any doubt."

"I did good," Heather agreed.

An intern removed the mic packs from the three of them and headed for her next assignment, but Heather, Jill, and Trenton hung back. This was the last scene they would film, just the three of them, and they weren't ready to let it go.

Aunt Blu also stood off to the side. When she'd arrived, Jill had explained that she'd asked her to come, and Heather had understood that Jill was also seeing this moment as a culmination of sorts. Blu had quietly watched the scene unfolding before her, her gaze on the three of them and her own emotions on full display with the satisfaction she wore on her face, but Heather had also caught her glancing toward the barn a time or two.

Charlie was at the barn. And he'd also sent a handful of looks *their* way.

There'd been no additional mention of Blu and Charlie being together over the last few weeks, and because of that, neither she, Jill, nor Trenton had brought up the subject with Aunt Blu. But the longer Blu had watched them laughing together that morning, the more Heather had sensed her loneliness.

Maybe this moment wasn't just a culmination for *them*.

When the last camera had been packed up and taken away, and no microphones were listening in, Jill waved Aunt Blu over. "Can we all sit in my new she-shed for a minute?"

With only days before the wedding, Heather suspected this might be their last quiet moment alone. The four of them made their way to the eight-sided structure, and one by one, each entered the small building. But no one sat.

"I have something for all of us." Jill clasped her hands together in front of her. "A friendship gift, I suppose. It's not a lot, but so much is changing . . . has already changed"—unheard-of tears suddenly filled her eyes, and Heather lifted a hand, as if to reach out—"so I wanted to commemorate 'us' in some way."

"You make it sound like we aren't going to be us anymore," Trenton objected.

"You'll always be bonded," Aunt Blu stated knowingly, and no one dared dispute her. "You'll always be an 'us'."

"We will be," Jill agreed. "We've gone through too much together for that not to be the case. And all of it started with you, Aunt Blu." She pulled their foster mother in for a hard hug, and Heather watched as Blu's arms squeezed tightly around Jill. "*We* wouldn't exist without *you*," Jill whispered, "and I know that matters to you the same as it does to us. That's why I wanted you here today as well. Because *you* are a part of *us*."

Jill retrieved four small gift bags that had been tucked into one of the storage benches, and after passing one to Trenton and another to

Heather, she settled on the bench with the last two in her lap. Heather, Aunt Blu, and Trenton each lowered to a seat as well.

"We're changing," Jill stated without further hesitation. She forced a smile, but Heather could also see her nerves inching higher. "I see it the minute I open my eyes every day. We're not the same as we were before all this started. And that hurts a little. But at the same time, I can't wait to see how we all evolve."

Heather didn't say anything for a moment. She only concentrated on the feel of her heart beating. If she spoke too soon, she'd end up all teary like Jill, and she already suspected that whatever lay in the bags was going to do that anyway.

But she also couldn't deny Jill's words. They *were* changing. In so many ways.

"Possibly we've already changed even more than you know." She pushed the words out, and the others turned to her.

"How so?" Trenton asked.

Heather kept her bag clasped tightly between her fingers, and she averted her gaze to take in the pond and the hardscaped areas outside. Her breathing picked up. She'd been thinking about this even more since talking with Waylon the day before. Telling him about her parents, about the knowledge she'd sat on for years, had finally made her see other things she'd been avoiding. Like allowing herself to explore what she really loved to do.

She *was* like her parents. Far more than she'd ever given herself credit for. And it was time to admit that out loud.

"I've loved doing this," she began. She brought her gaze back to her friends. "More than I ever thought I would. And I'm so glad that you, Jill, have finally landed in your true calling."

Jill had wanted to be an actress her whole life, and now she had both TV *and* construction. The best of both worlds.

"But I'm not sure what *I'm* going to do next."

All three of them looked perplexed. "If you love this," Trenton began, "then why not do this?"

"How many projects of this size do you see happening around here?"

"Maybe more than you think once the new show takes off."

"Possibly." But that could be years down the road.

"But you need it to be yours," Jill guessed without Heather having to attempt to explain any further, and with those few words, Heather finally understood what she'd been unable to figure out on her own. She needed her future to be hers. She wanted a "hers" and not just an "ours."

"I love 'us,'" she told them. She took each of their hands one by one, leaving hers in Aunt Blu's when she finished. "You all know I do, just as I know you love us, too. But yeah, I think I need something that's truly mine. I don't want to *just* be on standby for large projects for Jill and Cal, and I don't want to get sucked into smaller, more routine jobs, either. I like creating. I like bringing beauty to life."

"So, then what are you going to do?" Trenton asked. "Start your own company?"

Heather sat back in surprise. For some reason, the concept of starting her own company had never occurred to her. She'd been too mired in how everything else was "wrong."

"Not that either of you would be doing projects just for *me and Cal*, by the way." Jill took in both of them. "We're all three still very much a part of this company. And you can always be as much a part of the show as you want."

"I know we are," Heather agreed. "And I know I can. But like you said, we're changing."

She leaned into Aunt Blu when her foster mother wrapped an arm around her shoulders.

"And it's never going to be quite the same again." Aunt Blu said out loud what the rest of them were thinking, and the small space grew quiet with individual thoughts.

Before long, Trenton cleared her throat, the sound coming across more as a subtle break in the moment than any needed act, and without having to hear actual words, Heather understood. Her younger foster sister had been having "changing" thoughts of her own.

"I've been thinking," Trenton said, and Heather found herself holding on to Blu. "The calendars that we did back in the spring . . ."

"What about them?" Jill asked when Trenton paused.

"I liked doing that. I like helping people."

"We could easily incorporate a fund-raiser into the show," Jill suggested. "We'd just need to present a plan first. Maybe have a couple of ideas to toss out?"

"I want to incorporate a *foundation* into the show," Trenton informed them. She glanced at Aunt Blu, and Aunt Blu returned an encouraging nod. "Bluebonnet Foundation," Trenton went on. "And I don't want it centered around the show, but I *would* like to have it tied to it. I want to start the foundation off by working to provide transitional homes for young women when they have to leave foster care. Not a large house to be shared by many, but more like tiny homes, each built for one."

The tears started in Heather. "Oh, Trenton," she whispered. "That's a beautiful idea."

"From me, especially, right?" Trenton teased, but Heather knew the wall was all an act. Trenton may be hard, but she was as capable of deep emotion as the next person. "Aunt Blu and I have already talked about it," Trenton continued, reaching over to put her hand on Blu's knee. "And she's willing to donate part of her land to provide space for the housing."

Now all of them were crying.

They'd each had such a hard time when they'd first left. That's why they'd been hiring girls who went through the system with Aunt Blu since they'd started their own company. To give the girls a place to belong, even if they had nothing else in their lives.

Heather's chest ached to think about how they'd impacted so many other lives. How many more would be impacted because of them.

"Have you looked into starting up a foundation yet?" Jill asked.

"Only the high-level stuff. I plan to get serious about it soon, though. I'd love to break ground on the first home by January, if not before." She exchanged another glance with Blu. "I'd planned to wait until after Jill's honeymoon to bring this up, since things have been so crazy lately, but now seemed like the right time."

"I'm glad you told us." Heather leaned over and wrapped Trenton in a hug. She loved her foster sisters more than life itself.

"And I'm glad I chose *now* to present us all with our gifts." Jill swiped at her eyes and held up one of her bags. "Because this week is *only* going to get crazier." She kept the fourth bag tucked at her side and nodded at Heather and Trenton. "Open up."

The three of them—Jill included—reached inside the gift bags at the same time, not bothering to remove the tissue paper, and pulled out identical ring boxes. They were no larger than an inch-and-a-half square, and Heather gave Jill a puzzled look. "You got us jewelry?"

In the construction field, none of them had ever worn much jewelry, though Heather tried to more often than the others.

"They're thumb rings. I couldn't think of how to say what I wanted to any better."

Jill watched as Heather and Trenton each pried open the lids, then she let out a shaky breath as they lifted the thin bands from their cushions.

"Bluebonnets," Heather murmured, as she took in the details of her ring. It was made up of three connecting bluebonnets, the entire thing in gold, and each flower laid out on its side in a never-ending circle. "It's beautiful."

"There's an inscription." Trenton had her ring turned to the side and was squinting to make out the words.

"The Three," Jill said before either of them could read it. She slipped her own ring over her thumb. "Mine says, THE THREE—THE HARD ONE."

Heather bit her lip as she read. "Mine is THE THREE—THE SOFT ONE."

Trenton began to chuckle. "And mine says THE THREE—THE ONE WORTH THE EFFORT."

"Jill," Heather whispered through the fingers she'd put to her mouth. "They're perfect."

Trenton nodded, unable to say anything. And then they were crying again, and though things were definitely changing, Heather knew they would always be The Three.

And that they'd always have Aunt Blu.

Jill held out the final bag. "I got you something, too."

Heather held her breath as she waited to see what Jill had picked out for Aunt Blu, but instead of digging into the small gift bag, Aunt Blu cleared her own throat. "And I've got to admit that I've been changing, too."

Heather exchanged looks with her foster sisters. As if they'd all known this was coming.

But she wasn't so sure they were all ready to accept it.

"You want to go out with Charlie," Heather said before Aunt Blu had to find her words, and at the declaration, Blu's head slowly began to nod.

"I think that I do," she stated softly. "We've been talking a little."

Her cheeks heated with the comment, and Heather had to wonder how "little" it had been. She chanced a glance at Jill and Trenton, and noted Trenton's head tilted as if she were working through the same thought.

"Text messages, mostly," Aunt Blu continued. She fidgeted with the ribbon on the bag. "And I know it's crazy after all this time. Gerry's been gone twenty years, and I'm an old woman, and all."

Jill reached over and rested a hand over Blu's. "Any age can find love, Aunt Blu."

"And you're not even old," Heather added. Blu was only in her midfifties.

"Still . . . Charlie *is* younger than me. He's only fifty-one. He's also—"

"And you think this could be love?"

At the interruption, all of them looked at Trenton. Her words hadn't been hard, as they too-often were when it came to discussions of love and forever, but neither had they been tender. They were just words.

"I think I've had no desire to get dressed up for a man since I lost my family," Aunt Blu explained carefully. The deaths of Gerry and her girls had sent Blu into a depression that had taken years for her to climb out of, and it was a climb she'd managed only by opening Bluebonnet Farms in her family's memory. "But as for love"—she shook her head—"that's not even on my radar."

"Then why now?" Trenton questioned. "What's so special about Charlie Peterson?"

"I don't know that there's anything *special* about him," Aunt Blu said. "I don't know him much at all. That's what dating will figure out. But he does make me smile, Trenton. He makes me laugh and feel young again, and he makes me want to see what it *can* be."

"It's just about sex, then?"

Heather shot Jill a panicked look. Trenton seemed to have forgotten the moment was about Aunt Blu. In fact, Heather wondered if she'd even forgotten the man in question was Waylon's dad. She seemed to be far more stressed than she should be over the idea of their foster mother going out on a date.

Aunt Blu reached up and cupped Trenton's chin, offering a soft smile and a look shared just between the two of them, then she patted Trenton's cheek and whispered, "I promise that I'll be careful. You don't have to worry about me."

"I didn't say I was worried."

Though few people probably knew it, Trenton was closer to Aunt Blu than anyone who'd stayed at Bluebonnet Farms. Even Heather and Jill. And that's because Trenton and her mother once lived temporarily with Blu and Gerry. Years before Trenton's mother took off. So, there had already been a kinship between the two, even before Trenton had shown up alone at her door.

"Then if you're not worried," Aunt Blu continued, "is it okay if I am? Just a little?" She offered a wobbly smile to all three of them. "I'm not worried about *who* Charlie is. He's not perfect, and I know that already. He regrets"—she glanced at Heather—"missing out on so much of his son's life. And I'd imagine he's done a few other things he isn't exactly proud of. He's been a single man for a lot of years, and he's taken a lot of single-man privileges." She tried another smile, but that one didn't take. "But I've been single for a long time, too. And though the guilt is strong"—her voice dropped to a whisper—"I *do* want to do this. Gerry would be okay with me doing this. In fact, he's probably mad that it's taken me so long. But I'd like to have your blessings, too."

"You don't need our blessings, Aunt Blu." It was Jill who answered.

Heather remained silent for another moment because her mind had been whirling on the obviousness of Blu's words. She and Charlie hadn't been talking just "a little." They'd talked enough that Waylon had come up in conversation. Along with Charlie's regrets.

It made Heather wonder if Charlie ever planned to speak to his son on that subject.

"Just how long *have* you two been talking?" she finally asked.

Again, Aunt Blu's cheeks flushed hot. "Since the day we met."

They'd been texting—or *whatever*—for almost four weeks, and none of them had had a clue.

"I've been busy," Aunt Blu continued. "Too busy to do anything more than talk. Kelsie's been at the house for the last three weeks, and she needed my attention. But also, I had to think about this. I couldn't just say yes the first time he asked."

So he'd been trying to get her to go out with him for a while?

Heather couldn't help but think "like father like son." "If he wants you, he's not going to stop," she told Aunt Blu, and Blu laughed softly.

"I've already decided the same thing."

"And you really do like him?"

Blu cupped Heather's chin this time, and she pressed a kiss on her forehead. "I like the giddiness that he causes." She took in all of them, and Heather could see that though there was excitement in her eyes, there was also hesitancy. And fear. "I like the giddiness and the excitement of seeing what comes next, but I'm not going to lie and say I don't have reservations. I'm scared the holy hell out of my mind, if you really want to know. But *you're* all busy changing. Maybe it's time for *me* to change a little myself."

The honesty of the words seemed to seal the deal for all of them.

Jill spoke first. "Don't worry, the fear will go away."

"And the giddiness might just grow." Heather grinned as she teased.

"And though I offer my grudging support . . ." Trenton's words lacked earnestness, but they could all see she was faking it. She winked at Aunt Blu. "I also reserve the right to kick the man's ass if he ever even thinks of hurting you."

Aunt Blu tilted her head down and looked over her glasses. "Dear. You won't be kicking alone if that man hurts me."

"Yeah." Heather sat up straighter. "You'll also have me there, too."

"And me," Jill added.

Aunt Blu grinned like the vibrant young woman her late husband must have once seen when he'd first fallen in love with her. "And *I'll* be leading the pack."

Jill reached over then, and dipped her hand into the gift bag they'd all forgotten about, and retrieved a small broach nestled on top of a soft cushion of black velvet. She presented it to Aunt Blu as if it were the most precious object she'd ever held in her hands, and they all took a moment to admire the piece of jewelry. The broach held three sprigs of bluebonnets, identical to the ones on their rings, and when Jill flipped it over, Blu read the inscription out loud.

"The Brave One—The Mother."

~

The plastic of the bucket under Heather's rear felt a little less hard than normal, and as she looked up into Ollie's eye, she nodded her head. "My butt is fleshier," she told the animal. "And that's all your owner's fault."

The horse neighed, and Heather imagined Ollie telling her that he had no sympathy, because his owner had chopped off *his* balls.

"You're right." She nodded. "You win. You got dealt the worst hand in this one."

She dug another carrot out of the bag she'd brought with her and leaned back to slump against the wall of the stall. It was Friday afternoon, the day before her best friend's wedding, and the only place Heather had wanted to be was sitting in a hay-filled stall with a horse.

"You should feel pretty special, though." She took a bite of a carrot, herself. "I gave up going with him to pick up Rose because I missed you so much."

With the backyard work completed on Monday, she hadn't been out at the ranch nearly as often this week. There had been a handful of renovations with delayed timelines, and with Jill and Cal heading out for their honeymoon the following day, Heather had pitched in to help get everything caught up. It had been a long week, but it had given her a lot of time to think.

And though she'd been thinking, she still didn't know what came next. She had some money stashed away. The investments left over from her parents' life insurance money. She *could* start her own business if she wanted to. But the thing was, she didn't know if she wanted to. It was scary to think about. She'd be on her own if she did that. Unlike when she, Trenton, and Jill had started Bluebonnet Construction.

Sink or fail, it would be on her. And what if she failed?

She tilted her head farther back. But what if she succeeded?

Closing her eyes, she wished she would hear the sound of hooves, but nothing came. Her mother wasn't going to tell her what she needed to do, it seemed. But maybe her father would.

She made a face. Would she even listen to her father if he tried to get a message to her?

He'd been the reason her entire world had gotten ripped out from under her. She'd loved him so much, but until she'd talked about it with Waylon, she'd never let herself admit how angry she was at her dad. Even after all this time. He should have been better. He had her mom, he had *her*. He'd had all he'd needed. Why did he have to do something so stupid and screw it all up?

Who did that?

Why did people do that?

Ollie nudged at her hand, and she opened her eyes and fed him another carrot. "I love him, Ollie." Her heart ached with her fear. "I'm in love with your owner, and I'm terrified of it. It could work out . . . and years down the road he could do it again. Screw up again."

She listened for the sound of horse hooves again, and when none came, she whispered, "I don't think I could stand by my man like she did. I'm not that strong of a person."

She let her eyes drift closed once more. "Or he could break my heart before it ever gets that far. Like everyone else has."

But they hadn't, she realized. Not the way Waylon would.

She sat up at the understanding. "They didn't break my heart, Ollie. They broke my dream. I wanted the relationship more than I'd wanted those specific men. I think my ego may have even been hurt more than my heart."

She stood and began to pace. This was big for her.

"All this time, I've been thinking they crushed me." She looked back at Ollie and shook her head. "There were signs," she told him. "With each of them. I ignored the signs at the time, but there were signs that they weren't right for me. That's why they didn't break me. Because deep down, I never let them in that far."

She slowed her footsteps as the next thought hit. She'd never shared her dad with them. But she had with Waylon.

"There are signs with him, too," she told the horse. "You know there are. And I've been staring them straight on this whole time. So what do I do?"

She traced the gold ring circling her thumb.

"What do I do," she repeated, this time in a whisper. "He's lied to me already. About his past. He's taken from others. Who's to say he won't do it again?"

Was she burying her head in the sand once more?

Ollie bit at her hand, and she dug out an apple. "You know you have to share with the others," she told the horse. She caressed the hair covering his snout. "I have one more for you, but then I have to go see them, too. Give them treats, too."

The horse nickered, and she shook her head.

"I know," she told him. "I also have to make a decision. And I think you're right. I need to learn to trust my judgment."

She dropped her forehead to his.

"And my judgment says that Waylon is the one," she whispered. "I so want him to be the one."

A noise sounded at the front of the barn, and embarrassment hit. Charlie hadn't gone with Waylon to pick up Rose. Instead, he'd stayed at the ranch to repair fence line.

He must already be done.

She hurried from the stall, working up how to explain his overhearing her declaration that his son was the one, but she drew up short at the sight of a man in a suit. He'd made it to the steps that led to the apartment, and when he realized she stood in front of him, he stopped.

A welcoming smile lit his face, and he reached out his right hand.

"Ms. Lindsay." His tone was one of respect. "I'm glad I found you."

She shook his hand. "I'm sorry, do I know you?"

"No." He waved his hands in front of himself, his smile remaining in place. "We've never met, but I've heard of you. In fact, I'm here because I came looking for you."

She tried to tell herself that she should be concerned. This was a man she'd never met, and as far as she knew, she was pretty much alone on the ranch. And she was definitely alone in the barn.

But the judgment thing she'd just been talking to Ollie about insisted he was legit. Whoever he was.

"Let me start all over," he said. He reached into his coat pocket and pulled out a business card. "My name is Phillip Hollander. I own a landscape architecture firm based out of Atlanta." He handed over the card. "Hollander Associates. We're a small firm, but we're winning large contracts. Waterfronts, public parks, urban design, corporate. We do it all, and we're growing at a fast rate. I have connections all over the world, and a recent dinner saw your name coming up."

She stared, dumbfounded. "*My* name?" she questioned. "Heather Lindsay? Of Red Oak Falls, Texas?"

He chuckled at her confusion. "Heather Lindsay." He nodded. "Of Red Oak Falls, Texas." Then he motioned back the way he'd come. "That's your work out there, isn't it? Where the wedding will take place tomorrow?"

What kind of rabbit hole had she fallen down? "It is."

"Then you're the lady I want to talk to. I came by a couple of weeks ago. The executive producer of *Building a Life* is an old friend, and he invited me out to take a look at the project. You see, I don't want to be just any landscape architecture firm. I want to be the best. When I hear of a star in the field, I like to see their work personally. Talk to them myself." He nodded toward the backyard. "And if that's what you can do with three months' training on your own, I can't wait to see how you'll grow."

He stuck out a hand once more.

"I'm here to offer you a job, Ms. Lindsay. Working for me, and growing from the ground up. And I'm willing to offer you a very comfortable salary to do it."

Chapter Nineteen

"You gotta know when to fold 'em."

—"The Gambler," as quoted by a
ranch hand in Wyoming, circa 2005

The wedding had been beautiful. Even as a man, Waylon could recognize that. Jill and Cal had glowed with happiness, their love undeniable, and the venue couldn't have been more spectacular. Additionally, Waylon couldn't be prouder of Heather.

Only, he'd *love* to lay eyes on the woman again.

The wedding party had been transported via limousine to the reception hall rented in town, and Waylon and Rose, having not been in the wedding itself, had been left to get to The Carriage House Hotel on their own. They'd been there for thirty minutes now, and he'd yet to see Heather.

"Daddy?" Rose tugged on his pant leg.

"Yes, Rosebud?"

She smiled brightly, as she did most times when he called her by her nickname. "I want to dance with Grampa, but he keeps dancing with Ms. Blu."

Waylon sought out the man in question. Music had begun playing shortly after they'd arrived, and sure enough, his dad had his hands wrapped all the way around Blu Johnson. Not that he was surprised to see it. Heather had told him about their conversation with Blu earlier in the week, and when Waylon had asked about it, his dad had shared that lately the texts had morphed into "sexts." Which was not something Waylon had *ever* wanted to hear. And now that the foster girl Blu had taken in had been placed with a family member, Charlie Peterson planned to take the *T* off sext.

Waylon dug his thumb and forefinger into his eyes.

"Dad?" Rose tugged on his pant leg again.

"I'm sorry, Rose, but you're going to have to . . ." *Wait in line*, he thought, as he watched his dad's hand slide lower down Blu's back. If he told Rose that, though, she'd go over and line up behind her grandfather. "Be *patient*," he said instead. "Grampa will dance with you. I'm sure."

It just might be a while.

Waylon picked Rose up and began to dance with her himself, as he kept an eye out for his date. He'd not actually gotten to take his date *to* the wedding. Nor bring her to the reception. And in fact, he hadn't even gotten the opportunity to speak to her since she'd crawled from his bed the morning before. But she was still his date. And if things went according to plan, she'd be a lot more before the end of the night.

"You look very beautiful in your dress, Rosebud." He kissed the top of her head as he searched the crowd.

"I know that, Daddy." She gave him her bored voice. "You told me that earlier."

He squeezed her tight. "And I'll probably tell you again before the night is over."

He pulled back and winked at her, and she giggled like her mother used to.

Sadness over the way Nikki had wasted her life suddenly rushed him, and he wondered how much Rose knew about her mom. He'd told her very little himself. With Rose being so young when Nikki passed, he'd never figured out just what to share and what not to, so he'd basically given her a picture of her mother, and that was about it.

But he should have done better. Nikki had been a light in this world. She might have had problems, but the good parts of her were all in the little girl now in his arms.

"I love you, Rosebud." He kissed her on the nose.

"And I love you, Daddy." She leaned forward and kissed him on the nose, same as him.

He continued to sway with his daughter in his arms, and after catching sight of Cal and Jill returning to the ballroom, hope grew that Heather wouldn't be far behind. It took a couple more minutes, but suddenly, there she was, so beautiful in pale green. The color was perfect for her.

"I'm going to tell Heather how pretty she is, Daddy."

Waylon had stopped moving when he'd seen her, and he and Rose now both stared.

"Are you going to tell her, too?" Rose asked.

He knew he should look at his daughter when speaking to her, but he couldn't make himself take his eyes off the woman he loved. "I sure am. And I might even tell her twice."

Rose giggled again, then scrambled out of his arms, but before he could head off toward Heather, he spotted another beautiful woman close by.

Rose had stopped a few feet away and turned back when she'd realized he hadn't followed. "You go on." He motioned toward Heather. "I'll be over in just a minute."

She pursed her lips. "But where are *you* going?"

He stooped so he was at Rose's height, and pointed out Irene Reynolds, who sat at the next table over. "Do you see that beautiful woman sitting right there?"

"The one with the white hair?"

"Yes," he answered. "The one with the white hair." He saw Ms. Irene's lips lift into a smile.

"I do see her, Daddy. And she's pretty, too. I love her blue dress."

He kissed Rose on the cheek. "You go see if Heather wants to dance with you, and I'm going to ask this lovely lady over here to dance with me, okay?"

Rose glanced at Irene once more before nodding. "Okay."

She bounded off, and by the time Waylon reached Irene's side, her smile was bright.

"I've been eavesdropping on you, Sir Waylon."

"I hope you didn't hear anything too bad."

"Only that you plan to dance with two different women tonight." She *tsked* teasingly. "I always knew you were a flirt."

He threw back his head with laughter, and then he reached his hand down to hers. "May I have this dance, beautiful lady? But I do need to hurry. I wouldn't want to get caught."

She giggled, and let him lead her a couple of feet away. They'd been dancing for only a few seconds, doing little more than picking up their heels as they swayed, when Irene lay her hand on his chest.

"I always knew you had a good heart." She patted the white shirt under his suit jacket. "I should have also known you're a daddy."

He smiled as he watched Rose, who was now dancing with his dad. "And how would you have known I'm a daddy?"

"The gentleness inside you." She kept her palm flat on his chest, but now rested her cheek beside it. "The father of a little girl has a softness about him."

He looked down at the top of her head. "Don't you be going around telling people I'm soft, Ms. Irene. No cowboy needs to be known for that."

She chuckled, the sound muffled against him. "Okay, then. It'll be our little secret."

"Oh, secrets with my secret lady."

Her smile grew wider, and they both fell silent. Then Waylon's gaze landed on Heather once again, and he saw her watching him. She had the kind of look in her eyes that he'd love to see every day for the rest of his life.

"You must have just seen your lady," Irene murmured. "Should I run and hide?"

He laughed and held the woman a little tighter. "I'll bet you were a riot in your day. Am I right?"

"That would be correct."

"Tell me how you knew I'd just seen her. "

She tapped his chest with her finger. "It beats strong for her."

He grinned. "Not soft?"

"Not for this one, no."

He had to agree. He let his eyes smile at Heather, hoping she could see his love, and he agreed with Irene. "Never for this one."

The song ended a few minutes later, and he escorted Irene back to her seat.

"Thank you for the dance, young man," she said before he could give the same thanks to her. She patted his hand. "Now go ask your lady."

He paused, still half-bent over the table. "Ask her . . . *what*?"

She couldn't possibly know what he intended to ask Heather tonight. Could she?

"Love is special, Sir Waylon." She held her hand over his. "Love can get you through anything. Don't wait. Go ask her now."

Waylon wasn't going to ask her at that very minute, but he did leave Irene and head straight for Heather. And when he reached her, he took her in his arms.

He kissed her, not caring who might be watching, and silently prayed she didn't get upset over the kiss. And when he finally pulled back, the satisfied sigh that slipped out of her told him he was going to be just fine.

"I missed you," he told her.

"And you just found me." She wrapped her arms around his neck and stood on tiptoe. "Miss me like that much more," she whispered, "and I might show you where the coat closet is."

Her words had him grinning from ear to ear as he danced her in a wide swath around the floor, but a couple of minutes later, he wanted to bring things down a notch. Make them more intimate. So he took one hand in his and brought it between their bodies, and he held her palm over his heart. He kept her tucked in against him as they danced, in a way that should let her know he planned to keep her there for quite a while.

A few minutes later, he brushed a kiss over her forehead. "Now that you've made your appearance in your special dress, I can tell you that I have a surprise waiting for you at my house tonight."

Her breath tickled his neck. "Was I *going* to your house tonight?"

"You absolutely are."

Her head turned, and he knew she was looking for Rose, so he twirled her out from him before bringing her quickly back.

"Rose *loves* sleepovers," he reminded her as he resettled her against him. He returned his palm to the small of her back and pressed her close. "And so does her daddy."

Her lips curved languidly, and she leaned her cheek against his chest. "You'd think with all the sex we've been having lately, we'd be getting tired of this."

"I don't plan on ever getting tired of this."

She peeked up at his words, and he let his features grow serious as their eyes connected. He wanted her to understand where he planned to take them tonight, but he also intended to build the anticipation awhile longer.

"Don't you want to know what your surprise is?"

She nodded, her eyes still on his.

He could feel her need, so he leaned over and put his mouth to her ear. "Orange chiffon cake," he whispered, and she instantly stopped dancing.

"Please tell me you aren't making that up. Did you get Aunt Blu to—" She glanced around as she spoke, and Waylon watched as her gaze landed on Blu. The older woman was once again in his dad's arms, and Heather's entire body seemed to soften at the sight. "She did it," Heather whispered. She turned back to him. "They're on a date."

"It certainly looks that way."

He followed her eyes back across the room and watched the other couple for a moment longer, and as had happened the day the two of them first met, Waylon experienced a tug of jealousy at the thought of his dad now spending more time with Blu than he did with him. Not that Waylon had any demands on the man's time.

It would sure be nice, though, if the time they *did* spend together didn't still carry the weight of two ships passing in the night.

Tonight wasn't the time or place to be worrying about a relationship that had likely already reached its pinnacle, though. Tonight was about Heather. And him.

He turned her back to him. "Blu didn't make the cake."

She eyed him contemplatively. "You don't really expect me to believe that *you* made Aunt Blu's orange chiffon cake?"

"I told you I would." He kissed the tip of her nose and restarted them dancing. "And in case you're wondering if it was made especially for you"—he twirled her under his arm—"we *literally* put your name on it."

She lifted her hand back to his. "My name?"

"In pink."

Her smile was one of the top five things he loved about her, but when her lips curved with naughty intent, it jumped straight to number one. "So you're saying that Rose helped you make this cake?" Her throaty voice matched her smile.

"I am saying that." Waylon brought her fingers to his mouth. "But I do *not* plan on letting her be around when you eat it."

He felt her shudder in his arms.

"Is that because you plan to feed it to me yourself?" Her gaze was fastened on his mouth. "Or because you intend to work the calories off me while I *lick* the fork clean?"

He groaned under his breath. "You're killing me, here."

She wrapped both arms around his neck and whispered, "Just wait until you get me home, Mr. Peterson."

He lowered his mouth to her neck, another groan slipping out, but at the same moment his lips landed on her warm skin, he sensed a subtle shift in her mood. She'd turned her head and was looking toward the door leading into the back hallway, so Waylon followed her line of sight, trying to find what had bothered her.

"What is it?" he asked. No one out of the ordinary had come into the room. Some of the show personnel who hadn't been there before walked in, but given there'd been cameras all over the place throughout the day, he didn't think that would be the issue.

"Heather?"

She dragged her gaze to his, her look stark.

"What is it?" he repeated.

"I met a man yesterday afternoon."

That stopped him. He quit dancing, and sought out a quieter spot in the room.

"Not *that* kind of man," she said as he practically dragged her across the floor.

He didn't speak until they had a modicum of privacy, then he forced himself to unclench his jaw. "Okay. Then what kind of man did you meet?"

Worry tightened the skin around her eyes, and she said, "The type that offered me a job."

He waited, knowing there had to be more to it. A job offer was typically a good thing.

"A job I think I'd really love," she added. But again, her worry remained, and he continued to be at a loss.

"That's good, isn't it?" he asked. "If it's something you'd love. You've been trying to decide what comes next."

"But this job is in Atlanta."

"It's what?"

She nodded, her concern remaining. "I was trying not to think about it tonight. I didn't want to bring it up until I'd had time to sort through my thoughts about it, but then I saw the show's executive producer come in, and . . . well, he's the one who told this guy about me . . . and suddenly I couldn't help but think about it."

Waylon stared at her. "Were you even going to talk to me about it? I mean, *before* you decided to leave?"

"Of course I was. But like I said, I haven't even had time to think about it myself. Right after he made the offer, Trenton and I had to meet up with Jill, and there's been one thing after another since then, and I've just . . ." She stopped talking and frowned. "Why are you looking at me like that?"

"Heather. You know I can't just move to Atlanta. Not right now. Not with things the way they are with Rose."

"And I don't even know if I want to take it or not," she argued.

"But you're thinking about it?"

"Yes, I'm thinking about it. Don't I have to? It's with an up-and-coming landscape architecture firm, and he came here looking for *me*. Do you know how special that is? I don't even have a degree in that field, yet they want me. And the projects he showed me that they'd done . . . They were just *wow*, Waylon. *Truly* amazing." Excitement glowed from her. "And I'll tell you, there was nothing normal and routine about any of them."

He continued to stare. "But Atlanta?" He forced the question out. Everything about him was trying to shut down. "Do you even want to live in a big city? Have that kind of lifestyle?"

"I don't know. I've never thought about it before."

He dragged a hand down over his face. He couldn't believe this was happening right now. Right when he was about to—

Someone yelled over by the door, and he and Heather turned.

Waylon dropped a protective hand to Heather's arm as the man shouted out again, and he looked for Rose. Whoever this guy was, he didn't sound as if he were there to party.

When the voice rose up once more, the music shut off and everyone looked toward the door. Waylon found Rose standing with his dad, and a second before his gaze shifted to land on the culprit, a memory surfaced.

"There he is," the guy yelled. "I've been looking for you."

Waylon felt his world being swept from under his feet. His gaze landed on the man's face, and he saw red-hot anger being directed at him.

"Yeah, that's right," the guy said. "You." He pointed at Waylon, and all heads turned to him. "I found ya, now. Thought you could get away, huh?" The man moved toward Waylon, the guests parting as if they were the Red Sea. "Looks like you're some kind of fancy movie star now. You cheat to get that, too?"

Too many things hit Waylon at once.

The guy's name was Patrick.

Heather had gone stiff at his side.

And how would he even know Waylon had a part on the show?

Fear for how this guy's showing up could impact every aspect of his life burned through Waylon, and as Patrick made it across the room, a police officer appeared at the same time.

The cop's name was Billy. He was a guest at the wedding.

"Everything okay here?" Billy asked. He looked at Waylon. The two of them had met right after Waylon arrived in town, and they'd eaten dinner together several times.

Waylon opened his mouth to reply, but Patrick beat him to it.

"No, everything's not okay here." Patrick jabbed a finger in Waylon's chest. "This man stole six thousand dollars from me, and I came to get it back."

All remaining conversation in the ballroom ceased.

Patrick suddenly lunged forward, kneeing Waylon in the right thigh, and gasps echoed through the room. Waylon almost went down. He reached out as he collapsed, catching himself on the back of a chair just in time, while Billy restrained Patrick by locking the man's elbows behind his back.

Cal headed toward them.

"What's going on here, Waylon?" Billy kept his voice low, but Patrick continued lashing out.

"You pay me my money, you asshole, or I'm going to finish what the last guy started."

More gasps hit Waylon's ears, and he forced himself to ignore the searing pain in his thigh. He had to think. And the main thing that came to mind was that this guy wasn't going to stop.

Waylon found his dad in the crowd, and saw the fear on his daughter's face.

"Dad?" he called out. "Take Rose and go home?"

His dad nodded, and Blu stepped to Charlie's side. She reached one hand out for Charlie's arm and rested the other on Rose's shoulder, and Waylon nodded as if the two of them had spoken. "Take Ms. Blu, too." He worked to keep his tone gentle, and he looked at Rose. "Let Grampa and Ms. Blu take you home, okay?"

Rose shifted her gaze to Patrick, but Waylon moved to stand between the two, not wanting Rose to be a part of this in any fashion. Cal reached his side and stood shoulder to shoulder with Waylon.

Fear remained on his daughter's face, and Waylon nodded encouragingly. "Show Ms. Blu the cake we made, okay? Let her see if it's as good as the ones she makes."

"You made a cake today, Rose?" Blu asked, bringing a level of calm to the situation that Waylon had yet to accomplish.

"We did," Rose slowly answered. She looked from Waylon to Blu. "It's orange cake. But it doesn't have your name on it. We wrote Heather's name on it."

Blu held her hand out to Rose while also turning her away from the commotion. "Then maybe we can taste a piece that doesn't have Heather's name on it. Does that sound okay?"

Rose glanced back one last time. "That's okay. I suppose. There's lots of pieces like that."

She suddenly let go of Blu's hand and ran to Waylon, and threw herself against his legs. She hit in the same spot Patrick had just kicked, and Waylon groaned, but he held his daughter tight.

"I love you, Daddy. And I'm going to stay up until you get home."

The reminder of a time when he hadn't come home hit him. Along with the fact that Rose had been moved halfway across the state at that point, and it had been weeks before he'd even been able to talk to her on the phone. "You stay up, Rosebud. Absolutely. And I'll be home. I promise. I'll be home very soon. But don't you eat all the cake, okay?"

She finally giggled. It was stilted, but it was a giggle. "I won't, silly. It's a big cake."

Rose ran back to Blu and Charlie, and Waylon decided to ignore Heather for a few minutes longer. He couldn't face her until he got this mess moved out of the room. But even once he did get it out, he didn't know what he was supposed to do. The custody hearing was in four weeks, and he had no doubt the Jameses would try to use this against him if they caught wind of it. Was he going to have to come up with the money somehow just to keep Patrick from causing more trouble?

Not that he owed this asshole one dime of that.

"I want my six thousand dollars," Patrick said, his elbows still pinned behind his back.

"And I can only draw out a few hundred from the ATM tonight." Waylon tried to think fast. He hated that this had ruined the reception. "It's a weekend," he pointed out. "If you want more, you're going to have to wait until Monday to get it."

"I can wait."

"I'll bet you can," Waylon muttered.

Pissed off, but unsure what other choice he had at the moment, Waylon looked at Billy. "Can you take him outside? I'll be right out."

"Sure thing, Waylon."

Then finally, it was time to face Heather. He took a deep breath and sought her out. But it took only one glance, and he knew. He was losing her.

"Heather—"

She held up a hand. "I don't want to hear it." Her lips barely moved when she spoke. "No more excusing away your actions. No more"—she shook her head, the move tight and her eyes expressionless—"no more lying, Waylon. No more *nothing*."

She finished without an ounce of warmth, and Waylon wanted to slam his fist into a wall. "Just let me go take care of this." He tried his best to remain calm, all the while knowing that the whole damned room was watching. "Ten minutes," he pleaded. "Give me ten minutes, and we'll talk."

But she'd started shaking her head again before he'd finished. "Really, there's no need. I've made my decision already."

Disappointment nauseated him. They were no longer talking about *them*. Or about the man who'd just interrupted the reception. She was going to take the job. She was going to walk away without so much as a conversation.

"Don't do this, Heather." The crowd was forgotten. "Not because of what you just witnessed. I told you about this guy before. I didn't steal anything from him. What I won, I won fair and square."

Her posture remained stiff. "And I told you this is a great opportunity for me. It's one I can't pass up."

He locked his jaw, and he pleaded with himself not to say anything more. Not to be that guy.

But this was Heather. He had to give it one last try.

"You know me, *and* you know my heart." He reached out to put her hand to his chest, but released her when she immediately pulled back. "And you know that I love you," he finished softly. His eyes burned steadily into hers, ignoring everything inside him that called him a fool. He'd never told a woman he loved her before, and this was how it happened.

He stood unmoving, praying she wouldn't turn away. Praying he had to mean more to her than that.

That *they* meant more.

But she proved him wrong with barely a moment's hesitation. She didn't say another word as she turned, and he watched until the door nearest to her swung closed silently behind her. It was over.

He'd lost.

Chapter Twenty

"There are some elemental truths in life.
People have needs, people need others,
and people need to move on from the past."

—Blu Johnson, life lesson #42

Heather parked her SUV on the road in the exact spot where the van had sat the night of the fire. She hadn't been back on this street since that evening, yet as she'd spent the last week sorting through the items she planned to take with her to Atlanta, she kept pulling out the albums Waylon had looked through the first night he'd been at her house.

And as she looked through them herself . . . she kept wanting to come back to her childhood home.

Her cell dinged a text, and she saw that it was from Trenton.

Sorry. Running late. We'll be there in 5!

Heather hadn't seen either friend all week and was excited to be spending time with them before she left the following day. Jill had only returned from her honeymoon that morning, and Trenton had been buried in work throughout Jill's absence. Heather could have been there alongside Trenton, but after being horrified during the events the week before, she'd played hermit and hadn't left her place all week.

Well, she'd left long enough to walk up to Aunt Blu's house. However, after making it up the hill only to realize that Charlie Peterson was there, she hadn't ventured out again. Nor had she knocked on the door to find out just what Charlie had been doing inside the house.

She opened her car door now and stepped out, then she leaned down, resting her elbows on the hood of the car. The hood was hot, which made her think of her dad, and she dropped her head and let it hang. Her dad had had issues. Logically, she got that. She'd known other people with addictions throughout their lives. In fact, Cal's uncle had only recently gotten out of an extended-stay rehab center for his own addiction. His was to liquor, though. And maybe that made it make more sense to her somehow? She could see it, touch it, taste it, so there was understanding for how it could take over a person's life?

She blew out a breath and lifted her head to take in the two-story brick house sitting two hundred feet off the road. She wasn't sure about anything lately. All she knew was that her mom and dad were supposed to have had a perfect relationship. The perfect love. But if *they* couldn't even manage to pull it off, then how in the world was she supposed to? Because clearly, she couldn't.

Putting her hands flat on the car's hood, arms spread slightly, she lifted up as if about to do push-ups. She held the position for a moment, then gave a small nod and pushed the rest of the way off the car.

She was getting on that plane tomorrow. Decision made. This was the right move for her.

The plane ticket had been purchased during the last week, a temporary housing solution arranged, and her bags had been packed. But the contract to be employed by Hollander Associates still lay unsigned on her dining room table, because just as with every other aspect of her life, she'd questioned her decision since making it.

But as she'd told Waylon, this was a terrific opportunity. The amount of knowledge she'd glean from those she'd be working with would be phenomenal and the experience unmatched. And living in Atlanta should be fun. She'd never had a real urge to live outside of Texas, much less in one of the more congested cities in the country. But as Phillip had explained, not nearly every job would be in or around Atlanta. They were a nationwide company, soon to be opening a branch in the UK.

But you'll still have to be working in a larger city if you want to take on the substantial projects.

She frowned. She knew that. And she was okay with that. Taking this job didn't mean she couldn't return to Texas when she wanted to. Jill would have babies eventually, and Heather would want to come back and visit.

What if you also want to come back and live here?

She feared that day *would* come, actually. Because she was going to miss her friends like crazy. Just as she was going to miss Waylon. But she refused to live every day wondering if he would someday turn into her father—or if he might already be.

She'd heard nothing from him that week. Not that she'd expected to. But it had been hard to go cold turkey. At least, that's the excuse she kept giving herself, that her issues with missing him had more to do with what she'd gotten used to over the last few weeks than that she truly missed *him*, the person.

But she *did* miss him, and she knew it. As well as Rose. And the horses.

As close as she and Waylon had grown over the last few weeks, she hated the idea of moving away without so much as a good-bye. Without telling Rose good-bye. But she also knew that's how it had to happen. The things the guy at the wedding had said . . . they'd made her wonder if more of what the Jameses had told her could also be true.

Because Waylon had sworn to her that he'd only run the one con that spring, yet this guy had a completely different story.

So she wouldn't seek Waylon out before heading to the airport. She might send Rose a postcard from Atlanta after she got settled, though. Apologize for not seeing her before she left.

Jill's pickup rolled up behind Heather's, and the two women Heather was closest to in the world stepped out. She unconsciously rubbed her finger over the band encircling her thumb as her eyes took in their matching ones. Even if she was a thousand miles away in Atlanta, they were still sisters. They would always have one another's backs.

"I called the owners earlier in the week," Trenton shared.

When she'd made the decision to come, Heather had called Trenton to see if they'd go with her. "Given that we're here, I'm hoping they said it was okay."

Trenton slipped an arm through hers. "They said they'd welcome us all."

The owners of the house greeted them at the door, the wife smiling with unsure welcome, as if she was half-worried Heather might break down upon seeing her old bedroom and half-worried Heather might suggest she never leave. Heather had news for them, though. She didn't come to see her old bedroom, nor the place they'd once eaten their meals. Nor any other room in the house. She'd come only to look out back. Where the barn had once stood.

Seeming puzzled by Heather's lack of interest on the inside, the woman led them to the back door. And as the feeling of rightness swept through her, Heather pulled her shoulders back and stepped into the yard.

Definitely no barn. The backyard wasn't as nice as her mother had once kept it, either, but it was lovely in its own right. The nursery was gone, and in its place was a kids' jungle gym. The row of peonies—some of the plants having come from Heather's grandmother—remained, dividing the backyard from the "pasture" where the barn had been. And seeing the plants still thriving now gave Heather hope. Plants survive. Even under the direst of circumstances. People could, too.

The homeowners returned to the house, giving them privacy, and Heather reached for her friends. Together, they walked across the lawn and stepped to the other side of the hedges. No barn, as she'd already noted. But the patch of ground was covered with partridge peas, her mother's favorite flower. And Heather instinctively knew she was supposed to come there today.

"I finally talked about my dad," she told Jill and Trenton. She glanced at each of them. "I talked to Waylon about him."

Then she filled them in on what she'd been unwilling to accept in her heart before. By the time she'd finished the story, they'd all lowered themselves to the ground to sit, taking in the field of yellow wildflowers with the wide blue sky behind it.

"It's beautiful here," Heather whispered. And she knew her mom would have made a beautiful bride as she'd renewed her vows.

They remained sitting for several minutes, Heather knowing that when she walked away this time, she truly *wouldn't* be coming back. So she was in no hurry to go.

Trenton tilted her head onto Heather's shoulder, prompting Jill to do the same on the other side, and after a couple of minutes Jill said, "You do know he was going to ask you to marry him?"

Heather did not want to go there. "Who was?"

They both lifted their heads and scowled at her, so she scowled back.

"And anyway," Heather groused. "How would you possibly know that?" She'd been pretty sure of it herself. He'd been acting like he had a secret all week, dropping little hints as if he couldn't contain them all inside him.

She'd convinced herself otherwise since then, though. Decided she'd imagined it all. And even if she hadn't, at least she'd been saved from making the mistake of saying yes for the third time.

Jill dropped her head back to Heather's shoulder. "Because he asked for our blessings."

"He . . ." Heather pulled away. "He what?"

She looked at Trenton for confirmation, and Trenton nodded. "The idiot man sold me on himself, too."

Her heart started pounding. "You gave him your blessing to marry me?"

Trenton nodded again. "I did."

"Both of you?" Heather turned an accusing glare on Jill.

"He's a good guy, Heather. He's proven himself."

"But you don't know what he's done. The guy who showed up at the wedding—"

"Got carted off in handcuffs," Jill finished, and Heather was hit with shock.

"He did?" But why? Waylon was the one who'd taken money from him.

"You left too soon," Trenton told her. "You should have stuck around and given Waylon a chance. He loves you."

She couldn't believe they were saying this to her. She shot to her feet. "You're supposed to have my back." Her voice hitched. "To support me."

"We do support you." Trenton stood with her. "And we'll visit you in Atlanta if you really do decide to go. But we also tell each other when another is wrong."

Jill rose as well. "And you're wrong."

"About Waylon *and* about taking this job." Trenton forced Heather to meet her eyes. "If Atlanta is the type of job you want, then start a company right here. Quit being scared to put faith in yourself."

Heather's throat grew tight. "Like Red Oak Falls could support a business like that."

"Texas could. Why limit yourself? Then you get good enough—"

"And big enough by continuing to take on larger projects on the show . . ." Jill joined in.

"And you'll be fielding calls nationwide in no time." Trenton's features softened. "And you'll have done it *all* yourself."

Heather stared back at them, fear like a black, jagged edge around her vision. She'd never realized how scared she was of so many things. Was she too chicken to reach for what she really wanted?

"Do you love him?" Jill asked, and Heather startled at the change in subject.

"That doesn't matter," she said.

"Of course it matters," Trenton pushed her. "Do you love him or not?"

"I've loved men before," Heather argued, and both of them laughed.

"No way you've ever loved anyone the way you do Waylon," Jill guessed. "We've watched you, sweetie. We backed off from this thing between you two a while ago because we saw what was happening."

"And we wanted that to happen," Trenton admitted.

Heather gawked at her. "But you don't even believe in love."

"I don't believe in it for *me*," Trenton corrected. "But look at Jilly. She's found it. Twice with the same man. And it's real. This could be real for you, too. So we're just saying, don't throw it away because you're too afraid he'll leave you someday."

"Or because you're afraid he'll eventually do something to make *you* leave *him*," Jill added.

But I've already left him.

Heather didn't say the words out loud. She couldn't make herself speak. Because she knew that Waylon would never consider taking her back. She'd turned her back on him after he'd said he loved her. She'd walked away without a word.

And she'd done it in front of Jill's *entire* wedding party.

The three of them grew quiet, and Heather took one last look at the wildflowers growing where the barn had once stood. Though there was upheaval roaring inside her, there was also a newfound peace. She nodded, holding back the tears that threatened to fall. It was time to go. And in more ways than one.

She turned for the house then, her two best friends walking at her sides, and she'd made it only a few feet when she heard horses pass behind her.

Jill stopped. "Did you hear that?"

Her question surprised Heather, and she looked over at Trenton to see if she'd heard it as well. Only Ollie had heard it with her before. Trenton had already turned back toward the open field and was stretching her neck out as if to see. "I don't understand," she murmured. "There aren't any horses back here."

Comfort settled over Heather's shoulders. "It's my mom," she told them. "She's been talking to me lately. I think she's telling me it's time to forgive my dad and get on with my life."

Neither of them questioned her on speaking with her mom, but Jill did ask, "And what's she telling you that your life *is*?"

Heather wanted to be the fearless person they thought she could be. She really did. But inside, she knew that wasn't her. She was made to take the easy route, she supposed. Not to put her neck on the chopping block.

She linked her arms with her friends'. "She's telling me that my life is in Atlanta."

~

Waylon stepped from his lawyer's office two weeks before his court date, and though he wouldn't feel 100 percent until he had Rose home with him for good, he felt better about his case than he ever had. Patrick's showing up at the wedding had actually ended up playing in Waylon's favor. After Billy had hauled the man away for public intoxication and assaulting a citizen, Patrick had begun to squeal. He still wanted Waylon to give him his $6,000 back, of course. But that had been about pride. What he'd shared about the Jameses, though . . .

Well, the Jameses had finally messed up.

They'd uncovered Patrick a couple of months before, and had been keeping him on "retainer" until they felt he could be of the most use. And apparently, the most use meant having him throw around lies and accusations while the cameras were rolling. Waylon and his attorney had been able to piece together that the Jameses had planned to subpoena production for the tapes, to be used during the hearing. From their point of view, video of Patrick spewing lies would have been catching Waylon red-handed, and for good measure, they'd also instructed Patrick to start a fight. Meaning, get Waylon to throw the first punch. They'd forgotten, however, that although Waylon had plenty of vices in the past, fighting had never been one of them.

He looked over at his dad, who walked tall beside him. As the man had promised, he was standing by Waylon's side throughout this whole process. He'd insisted on coming today, and though Waylon could have easily handled the appointment by himself, he *had* appreciated the support. Just knowing he had someone in his corner as he'd worked through final plans with his lawyer had made the day a little easier.

They continued down the busy sidewalk in downtown San Antonio, Waylon seeking out his truck parked near the back of the next lot, and he didn't notice when his dad stopped walking. Discovering himself alone, Waylon turned back to find the other Peterson standing in the middle of a city of steel and pavement, with far too many cars whipping past, looking about as out of place as Waylon had ever seen him.

Yet as he stood there, his dad also seemed to be *comfortable* in a way Waylon had never seen, either. Or maybe it was just the first time Waylon had been able to actually see his father that way.

"Everything okay, Dad?"

Charlie nodded. Then Waylon noticed his hands trembling.

"Dad?" Waylon rushed back, but before he could reach his dad's side, his dad held up his hands to ward Waylon off.

"I'm good," his dad said. "Just thinking." His thoughts seemed miles away. "And regretting."

The heavily weighted words cemented Waylon's feet where he stood, and the two men remained in the middle of the foot traffic, facing off, four feet apart. "What exactly is it that you're regretting?"

Fifty-one-year-old eyes that matched his stared back solemnly, and Waylon clenched his jaws together in frustration. Surely they weren't going to have that conversation now? In the middle of the sidewalk?

He wasn't even sure he *wanted* to have that conversation. Hadn't they been doing okay without it?

But a part of him *did* want to have it. And that same part wanted to do it right here and right now. Because he was tired of feeling like he was in limbo. Tired of faking it so he didn't have to face reality. His dad shouldn't have left the way he did. He shouldn't have continued for years without acknowledging that fact.

And the part of Waylon that wanted to have this conversation also selfishly wanted his father to hurt because of his actions.

His dad took off his hat and clasped it in his hands, obviously ready to clear the air, and a muscle in Waylon's jaw twitched.

"I'm regretting many things," his dad started, eyeing Waylon as if keeping tabs on a feral cat. "First off, I watched you in there today. Fighting for your daughter. And I know how that fight will continue when it's before a judge. I've also watched how you are *with* her." He scrubbed his fingers over his cheek and stretched out his jaw. "I was always the more traditional type. Thought a kid needed to be raised by his mother. I thought getting out of the way was the right thing to do."

"It wasn't." Waylon could only manage two clipped words.

His dad nodded. "Maybe not. And I can see that Rose is definitely better off for having you in her corner. But your mother and I couldn't make it, son. We tried."

"Excuses." A bead of sweat rolled between Waylon's shoulders. This didn't feel like a real conversation. Not the one he wanted.

"It's not excuses." His dad picked his monologue back up, but he no longer looked directly at Waylon. "The thing is, we never should have gotten married in the first place. We fought all the time, and that was no good for anybody. Hell, I stayed out in the pastures more than I ever stayed in the house. What good was I doing by sticking around?"

"I stayed out there with you."

When his dad's words cut off and he looked back over at Waylon, Waylon continued.

"Do you not remember that? How, if I wasn't in school, I rode right there beside you until after dark? I also headed out with you before sunrise. I was your damned shadow, Dad. Because I looked up to you. Because I *loved* you"—his voice cracked, but now that he'd started, he was unwilling to stop. "And you never *once* returned that love."

Pain filled his dad's eyes. "That's not true. I loved you. It broke me not to have you with me."

"Yeah? Then why not take me when you left?" Waylon ground out. "Like I begged you to do." His dad started to shake his head, but Waylon pushed on. "Don't you *dare* say that it was because Mom needed me there with her. I *heard* her tell you I could go."

"That doesn't mean that she didn't need you."

"And saying all these words now doesn't mean you ever believed them, either." Disgust coursed through him. Why have a conversation if you weren't really going to have one in the first place? He was done with this crap. "Be real for once in your life, Dad. We've been living together for six weeks now, pretending things are fine and that we're getting 'better.'" He air-quoted the word. "But neither of us believes it. Hell, neither of us has even made one honest attempt at *making* anything better. We just skate along the surface, hoping the ice doesn't crack. And now you think you can fix all these years of pain by feeding me a line of crap?"

He nearly spit at his father's feet.

"Prattling on with useless words does *not* mean you're clearing the air," he told his dad. "We have issues, and I'm tired of ignoring them. Deal with it, or get the hell out of my house."

The ultimatum suddenly set Waylon free, and as he took a step back, gasping for air as his tirade came to an end, his dad's eyes bulged with fear. Feet shuffled along beside them, someone bumped into his dad. But Waylon didn't look away from the man who had all his same features. These were things that should have been said years ago.

"I don't want to leave," his dad begged. "*Please*, son. I'm sorry. I'm not good at this, okay? I never have been. It's one of the reasons I couldn't make things work with your mom. But I'll work on it. I'll do whatever you want me to do to fix it."

"Because you don't want to lose Rose?"

Waylon wanted Rose to have a relationship with her grandfather. She loved him very much. But if she had to, she could have that relationship with his dad living in another house.

"No." His dad's voice carried more assuredness than it had before. "I do love Rose, yes. But it's not *her* I want to stay for. It's you, Waylon. I want to do right by *you*. I swear I never meant to hurt you before, and I do understand that I did." His dad's chest rose with the breath he pulled in. "And truth be told, I'll probably find a way to do it again. But tell me, and I'll make it better. Tell me, and I'll do my best to be the dad to you that *you* are with your daughter. Because I never understood that a man could be that kind of dad before today." The steam ran out of him. "I never understood, Waylon. And that's the *biggest* regret in my life. That I wasn't that kind of dad to *you*."

Waylon stared back at the man he'd spent too many years resenting, and as if forgiveness had been sitting there waiting for him to take it, he suddenly felt as if he'd been handed the most precious gift of all. He'd just needed to hear the words. To see that he wasn't the only one in the relationship who'd been hurting for the past twenty years.

The last shred of resentment lifted, and at the same time, his remaining worry over whether he was truly doing the right thing for his daughter floated away with it. He *was* the right thing for Rose. He finally had no doubts. And his dad living in Red Oak Falls was the right thing for *them*.

He nodded as his thoughts tumbled into an order that made sense, and when he looked around as if coming out of a long slumber, he caught more than one pair of eyes cut toward them. And he almost laughed right there in the middle of downtown San Antonio. When he and his father finally decided to clear the air, they certainly did it right.

But at least they'd done it. Heather would be happy to—

He stopped the thought before he could finish it. Heather wouldn't anything. Heather was gone. She'd walked away from him without so much as a word or a chance for explanation. No matter what kind of professional opportunity she'd been presented, he'd deserved better than that. *They'd* deserved better.

At the same time, he wasn't a barbarian. He understood the need to chase a dream, to take an opportunity when it presented itself. And because he did understand, he also hoped he'd someday be able to wish her well. If not personally, then at least in his head.

Today wasn't that day, though. It was nowhere close.

But today *was* the day that he got his dad back.

"That'll work." He stuck out his hand, not knowing at first what else to do—nor what else to say—then grinned at both the absurdity of his actions and his words.

As his father hesitantly put his hand into Waylon's, Waylon shook his head and brought his dad in for an enveloping hug.

"I love you, Dad." He'd known he did, but he wasn't sure he'd ever said it to the man.

His dad's embrace surrounded Waylon. "And I love you, son."

If he'd seen it from an outsider's point of view, Waylon might have been embarrassed at the sight the two of them made on the very public street. But then again, maybe he wouldn't have cared at all.

He had his dad again. For the first time since he'd been seven years old, his world didn't feel as if it sat on ground waiting to crumble under his feet.

They finally separated, and as one, they turned for his truck. They'd gone about half the distance when Waylon looked over. He thought about the fact that Blu Johnson had made more than one appearance at his house recently. "If you're going to keep living with me, I say we set some ground rules. Namely, what you can and can't do with a woman in your bedroom."

His dad chortled. "I've already got that one covered. Loud music."

Waylon's jaw went slack as he recalled the music coming from his dad's room only two nights before, and Charlie Peterson nodded, as if impressed with his own ingenuity.

"That's right," his dad said. "You'll never hear a thing as long as I've—"

"Stop," Waylon interrupted. "I get it. And I'm incredibly sorry I brought it up." He felt as if he needed to wash his eyes out with peroxide—even though he'd seen nothing of what had gone on behind his dad's closed door. "*New* ground rules," he suggested as he thumbed the unlock button on his key fob. His truck chirped ten feet in front of them. "I buy you lunch today before we head home . . . and then you and I *never* speak of this again."

His dad laughed once more. "I can work with that deal. But I will go ahead and tell you," he continued, as he headed for the passenger's door, "that I *do* enjoy playing loud music."

Chapter Twenty-One

"When you tire of staring at the walls you've carefully erected, knock them down and create the future you want."

—Blu Johnson, life lesson #99

Waylon stood before the ten-foot-high wooden doors of the courthouse, his daughter on one side of him, and his father on the other. And relief filled every fiber of his being. He'd won. He had his daughter back.

The hearing had been short. The Jameses had originally been granted temporary custody due to Waylon's incapacitation, and though they'd come with depositions and statements from all manner of people willing to lie for them, Waylon's lawyer had a rebuttal for everything. And when he'd presented the money trail leading directly to Patrick, Marcus and Madelyn had picked up their things and left. They'd not only lost, but they'd left with shame. They might have originally had the best intentions for their granddaughter at heart—though Waylon could argue that point—but their intentions had gotten buried in their hubris.

Waylon looked down at his daughter, who'd insisted on wearing a very specific outfit today. A purple tutu, a green top, and her pink-and-black striped leggings. Then he recalled Madelyn's horrified expression when Waylon had escorted his daughter to the restroom, and she'd come back wearing this concoction. Her outrage alone had been enough to make the moment worthwhile. But the idea had been Rose's.

When they'd talked on the phone the night before, Rose had asked him to bring the clothes, and with that simple request, he'd seen so much of her mother in her. Rose might love her grandparents, but she wanted to be home with him. And she'd intrinsically understood the Jameses had been the ones who could prevent that. So she'd bucked the system. She'd *not* dressed the way Madelyn preferred. She'd been 100 percent herself.

And there'd been no way he would have said no to that.

"Are we going to open the door and go home, Daddy?"

He smiled at Rose. They'd been heard last today, so the court had emptied out. But he'd wanted to stand here for a moment and take in the power of the judicial system when done right.

He nodded. "We're going to open the door and go home, Rosebud. But first, I need to know where you want to eat dinner. Because we're celebrating big tonight, and we need to make sure we do it right."

She nodded solemnly, and he could see her thoughts start to churn. He shouldn't have said she had to decide *before* they walked through the doors. She could take days to reach a decision.

"Let's go to the truck," he suggested. "Grampa and I will get you strapped in, and you can keep thinking the whole time."

"That'll work." She nodded, and Waylon winked at his daughter as he took her hand. The two of them went ahead of his father, Waylon pushing on the outer door, and then he stopped in shock at the sight that awaited him.

"Look at all our friends, Daddy!" Rose squealed and ran out the door before him, and Waylon turned to his dad.

"Did you know about this?"

Charlie shook his head as the two of them followed Rose out. "No idea."

"What do you suppose they're all doing here?" Waylon spoke from the side of his mouth. There had to be at least seventy-five people standing on the steps to the courthouse, all from Red Oak Falls, and all having traveled over an hour on a workday to get there. Several of them had also come with signs.

"Congratulations."

"We Love You."

"Welcome Home, Rose."

"I'd say this here is called support," Charlie Peterson determined. "And it looks like you have it, son." His dad clapped him on the back. "You did good choosing Red Oak Falls to be your new home."

"I also did good when I invited you to follow me there."

He took another long pass over the faces crowded before him, and his chest overflowed with the fact that so many people cared. And not just because of Rose, either. He could see it when they looked at him. He could see their happiness that he had his family back.

A bubble of hurt poked at him from behind his ribcage, as if raising its hand not to be forgotten.

He didn't call on it to speak, though. He didn't want to hear what it had to say today. But neither could he forget. He hadn't seen Heather in a month, and if he let himself dwell on that fact, he'd be reminded that her leaving hurt as badly today as it had then.

He looked to his right and made eye contact with his dad, and his dad returned his contented smile. The family Waylon had envisioned only four short weeks before might be minus one person, but it wasn't all that long ago that he couldn't imagine any family larger than himself and Rose.

He'd take this.

~

Heather waited in the back of the crowd, taking in the joy on Rose's face as well as the pride on Waylon's. It seemed he'd found a family, even if he hadn't known he'd been searching for one.

Charlie stood next to him, a little closer in physical distance than Heather thought the two normally stood, and when the men suddenly hugged right there in front of everyone, her heart felt as if it might actually burst. Something had changed for them in the weeks she'd been gone. Not that they'd had a *bad* relationship before, but the love and support for each other was even more evident now.

Someone shouted out about having a church basement rented a couple of blocks over and a potluck dinner ready to set out, and the crowd began to disperse. Heather stood her ground. She'd wanted to call Waylon before now. To tell him what she'd been up to. But she had no idea how she'd be received. She couldn't *not* be here for this, though. Rumors had been circulating for the last two weeks that custody returning to Waylon had been a shoo-in, and Heather wouldn't have missed this party for the world.

The last of the people standing between her and Waylon moved down the sidewalk, and Waylon's gaze suddenly found hers. He said something to Charlie, and Rose—who'd returned to stand by the men's sides—gasped. Heather watched as Rose's gaze searched though the remaining onlookers until it landed on her, and then the four-year-old was sprinting in Heather's direction.

"Heather!" Rose shouted.

Heather scooped her up as Rose threw herself into Heather's arms, and she squeezed her tight. She'd missed this child so much. She might not get the chance she'd come here seeking, which would mean she'd likely continue missing this child in the coming days, but she intended to give it everything she had.

"Oh, Heather." Rose pulled back before planting a wet kiss on Heather's cheek. "I've missed you so much. And did you hear? I get to go home with my daddy again. *Every night.*"

Heather fought back tears. "I did hear. And I'm so super-happy for you."

Rose giggled, and the two of them put their heads together and talked for a few more minutes. But then Charlie was at her side, and he was suggesting to Rose that she go with him.

"How are you, Heather?" Charlie greeted her.

"I'm good, Charlie. And I hear you're treating Aunt Blu right?" Apparently the two were still dating.

"I'm treating her all kinds of right," he replied, face straight. Then he winked. "We might have to keep it down now, though, if this means you're back home."

She now knew where Waylon got his flirting skills, and as Rose climbed from her arms to Charlie's, she said, "You do know there's a good thousand feet between my house and hers."

"Is that all?" His brow furrowed. "Then I'll definitely tell her to take it down a notch."

"What are you talking about, Grampa?" Rose crinkled up her nose. "Who's taking it a notch?"

Charlie laughed out loud at the question, then he gave Heather a nod. "Nice to see you back. Rose and I will leave you two to talk, but I hope you'll come over and have some potluck after."

She hoped she would, too.

Charlie moved down the steps, in the direction everyone else had gone, and Heather noticed that Aunt Blu had stepped to the side to wait for him. Heather smiled faintly as Charlie reached out a hand to Blu, before the three of them followed along behind the disappearing crowd. And only then did Heather allow herself to turn back and face the man she'd already sensed now stood in front of her.

"Hello, Waylon."

He touched his hat in greeting. "How's the new job?"

She cringed. She'd hoped he wouldn't open with that. "Congratulations on the judge's decision. Rose is thrilled, and I know you are, too."

"Thank you." The tension in his shoulders eased slightly, and he nodded toward an empty bench. "Want to sit? It's in the shade."

It also wasn't dead center on the courthouse steps, she thought, but she only nodded in reply. She turned for the bench and Waylon followed, neither of them speaking on the short walk over. Once they reached their destination, Waylon did *not* sit. The bench was barely large enough for two people, and he apparently didn't want to get too close.

Twenty seconds of dead silence later, Heather sighed. She'd known he wouldn't make this easy on her. "I suppose I have to start," she muttered.

"Only if you have something to say."

He stood angled off to the side, his feet apart, his suit jacket hanging open, and his hands tucked purposefully into his pants pockets. Heather thought this was the look every Texan man should be going for. Black suit, white shirt, Sunday cowboy boots and hat.

And looking like Prince Harry, every day of the week.

"I'm sorry," she blurted. "I should have trusted you that night. I shouldn't have bolted because I was scared. I should have given you the chance to explain. I should have involved you in the decision about the job. And I shouldn't have done any of it in front of the entire crowd."

He angled his head in a slight dip. "That's a start."

"Waylon."

She stood to face him. "I'm sorry," she said again, pleading for him to give an inch. "It was horrifying for me, and I can only imagine how it must have been for you."

"I can handle a little embarrassment, Heather. That was the least of my concerns."

The lines in his body remained tight.

"Then can you handle taking me back?"

His chin jerked at her question. She hadn't meant to put it out there quite so bluntly, but she'd wanted a reaction from him. She didn't like this cold Waylon.

"You didn't answer my question," she pointed out.

"I haven't figured out my answer yet."

She threw her hands in the air. "You're not without fault here, you know?"

"And just how is that?"

"Because dammit, you made me love you too much. And it terrified me."

And honestly, that's about all he'd done wrong. The man had set out to woo her, and he'd done an excellent job of it.

His eyes had softened the tiniest amount at her declaration, but his hands remained firmly in his pockets.

"I'm sorry I didn't say it back when you told me you loved me," she said, her voice losing steam. She knew that had cut him deep. He'd never said those words to anyone, yet she'd not uttered one word in reply. "And to answer your earlier question," she added, "I don't know how the job is. I didn't take it."

His eyes shifted to hers.

"I went to Atlanta, but before the plane landed, I knew what I really wanted to do. So I contacted the guy I worked with over the summer. A consultant out of Nebraska who helped me lay out the plans for Jill and Cal's yard. And I flew out to learn more from him. That's where I've been the last three weeks. He started his business from the ground up, and I'm going to do the same thing. Only here. In Texas. In Red Oak Falls."

He pulled his fists from his pockets, but crossed his arms over his chest. "You're sure this is what you want to do?"

She nodded, the adrenaline that had been pumping since she'd first laid eyes on him now starting to drop. "I'm *positive*. I'll still take on the occasional project for the show. I don't want to give up being a part of what the three of us started. And there's a chance I'll sign on to do the same with other home improvement shows. I've been in talks about that, and if they want to pay me enough and the locale would make it worth a temporary stay, then I'll consider it. It would only help the business grow. But this is my thing, Waylon. I finally found my thing."

He hadn't changed his stance, but she thought the lines in his face might have softened. At least a little.

She took a deep breath and laid the rest of it out there. "I also forgave my father."

At her announcement, the tension seeped from his shoulders.

"He made a mistake," she told him. "As people do. But that didn't take away from his love for my mother or for me. *I* made a mistake when I left the reception that night."

Waylon studied her. "I've made plenty of mistakes throughout most of my life."

She nodded. "But the guy that night, he wasn't a mistake, was he? He's the one you told me about, who'd been upset that you won so much?"

"He was. He was also hired by Rose's grandparents to show up there."

That rumor she *hadn't* heard.

Waylon lowered his arms to his sides. "They didn't even fight when we revealed the money trail. And though I'm not opposed to them seeing Rose on occasion—because Rose *does* love her grandparents—"

"And family *is* special," she added.

He nodded. "Even so, it'll be a long while before I'm ready to let the Jameses make amends."

She risked taking a half step closer. "How about me? Will you let me make amends?"

He didn't answer, but she could see him thinking about it.

"I love you, Mr. Peterson. I love your daughter. I love your horses." She took his hand. "And I love the woman I am when I'm with you."

He closed his other hand over hers, and though his touch erased a chunk of the worry sitting heavy inside her, he didn't yet smile. He'd given her little more than the impersonal touch of one hand covering another.

"Waylon . . ."

"Two questions," he said, and she nodded immediately.

Her heart began to race.

He held up one finger. "What's the current state of your hips?"

"What?" She looked down at herself. "What are you talking about?"

"What is the state of your hips?" he repeated. Then he clarified. "Can you eat cake or not?"

"Oh." She nodded, her head moving in a fast jerk. She had no idea where this was going, but if he wanted her to eat cake then she'd eat cake. "Yes. I can eat cake."

"Good. Because Blu and Rose cut up the cake instead of eating it. Then they froze it in individual pieces. Rose won't let me throw any of it out."

"The orange chiffon cake?" He still had it? Because of Rose?

Hope took flight.

"There's one giant piece that is the entire section with your name on it," he told her sourly. "I want it gone."

Her budding enthusiasm waned. He hadn't warmed up at all since starting to talk, and she suddenly feared she'd not only find herself still alone after their confrontation, but also being force-fed half a cake.

That would take a heck of a lot of yoga to overcome.

He held up his second finger, and she held her breath. She silently begged his forgiveness.

"How do you feel about making redheaded babies? Rose is going to need siblings."

Her breath burst out of her. "Yes," she whispered. She nodded as she pressed her hands to her mouth, then she repeated the word again. "Yes. I feel *great* about making redheaded babies."

The smile she'd been waiting for finally appeared, and tears streamed down her cheeks.

"Waylon." She sniffed as she threw herself at him. She locked her arms around his neck. "Can we start on them today?"

His light chuckle eased the ache she'd been walking around with for a month, and his arms closing around her finished it off. "We can start on them whenever you want." He pressed his face into her hair and held her extra tight, and she wondered if she was the only one shedding tears.

Eventually he pulled back, but just enough to peer down at her. And that time when she met his gaze, she saw more than his smile.

He swiped at the tears on her cheeks, drying them with his fingers, but the love shining back at her only produced more. "I love you, Heather Lindsay." He gave up and cupped her face in his hands. "And I always will. No matter how scared you may be. No matter how much I sometimes want to strangle you for terrifying *me*." He slid his thumb over her bottom lip, and his voice dipped. "And no matter how big your hips may someday get."

She laughed on a sniffling hiccup.

"But there is one way I could love you more."

She swallowed and nodded. "What is it?" She'd do it, whatever it was.

He closed his mouth over hers before answering, the kiss lasting for far longer than was decent in public, and when they finally broke apart and stood staggering for breath, he captured her face once again. "I could love you just a little bit more, Heather Lindsay . . . if you would change your name to Heather *Peterson*."

Acknowledgments

I remain as in love with the women of this series as I was when I first dreamed up the story ideas last year, and I can't wait to have the opportunity to write Trenton's book. That being said, as always, I'm so completely grateful for my readers who not only pick up my books, but who are also more than willing to jump in and help me out with ideas and names and just generally anything that I toss out there. I adore adding bits and pieces to my books that have come directly from you, and I truly enjoy the conversations we have when I get the opportunity to chat online. Thank you for always being there.

I also want to say thanks to Lizzie Shane. You know what you did . . . Embassy Suites, just you and me . . . ;). Thank you for being such a *fabulous* brainstorming partner (and friend)!! This book owes tons to you.

About the Author

Photo © 2012 Amelia Moore

As a child, award-winning author Kim Law cultivated a love for chocolate, anything purple, and creative writing. She penned her debut work, "The Gigantic Talking Raisin," in the sixth grade and got hooked on the delights of creating stories. Before settling into the writing life, however, she earned a college degree in mathematics and worked as a computer programmer. Now she's pursuing her lifelong dream of writing romance novels. She has won the Romance Writers of America's Golden Heart Award, has been a finalist for the prestigious RWA RITA Award, and has served in varied positions for her local RWA chapter. A native of Kentucky, Kim lives with her husband and an assortment of animals in Middle Tennessee.

Visit her Facebook page at www.facebook.com/kimlawauthor, her website at www.kimlaw.com, or find her on Twitter @kim_law.